ALL IN GOOD TIME

CAROLYN ASTFALK

For my children: Michael, Felicity, Miriam, Jacob, and your sweet siblings in heaven.

You are the best things I've had the privilege of co-creating. You have each blessed me in ways too varied and numerous to count.

I love you.

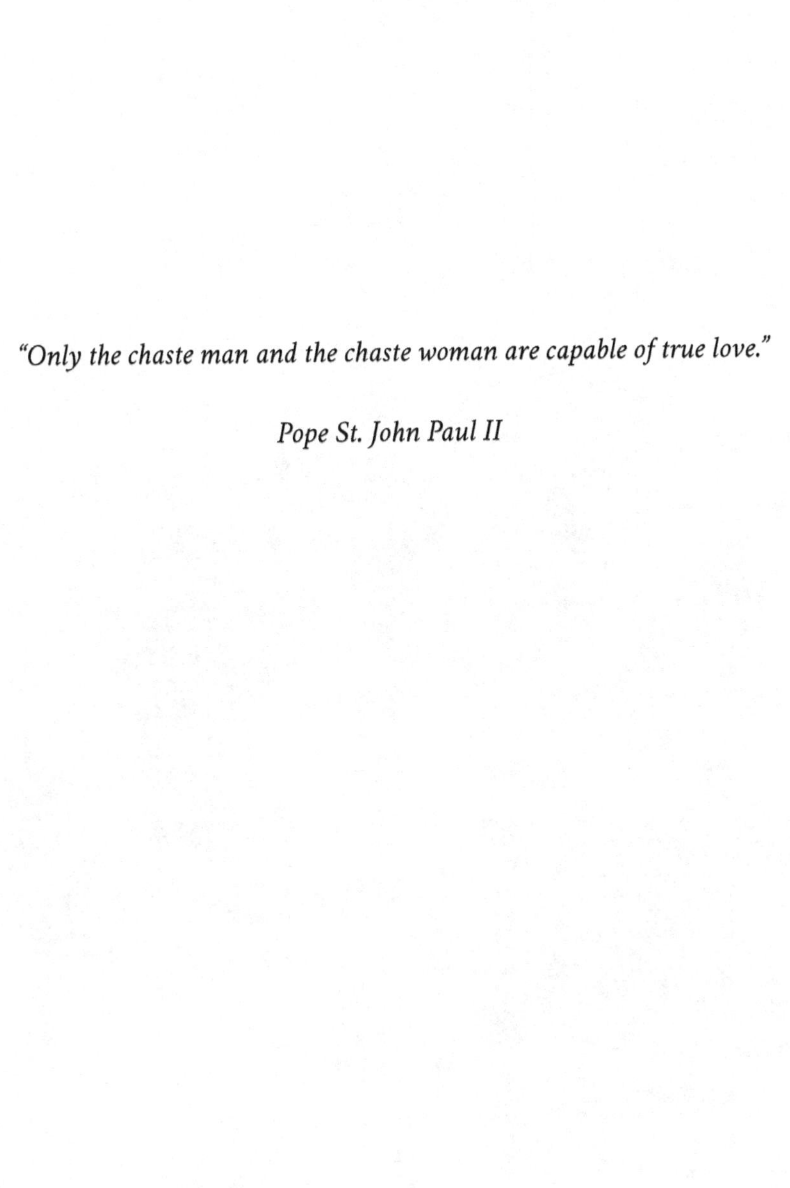

"Only the chaste man and the chaste woman are capable of true love."

Pope St. John Paul II

CHAPTER 1

Brian Perella peered through his fingers as he massaged the bridge of his nose, trying to make out the time on the stupidest motivational wall clock known to man. Bold, black letters stating "I don't stop when I'm tired" camouflaged the hour hand. Had to be coming up on five o'clock. He blinked, refocused, and narrowed his gaze on the minute hand, lodged over red letters. It read, "I stop when I'm done." *Or dead.* Best guess, it was about twenty-five minutes until quitting time.

The computer tower beneath the desk whirred to life, and Brian leaned back in the seat, waiting for the reboot to complete. His thoughts drifted to smooth pale skin, perfectly manicured peach-colored fingernails, and the tingling sensation of a single nail gliding gently along his skin, knuckle to wrist.

He tightened his hand into a fist then shook it out, wondering for the thousandth time what was wrong with him. Because there was definitely something. He pressed his fingers into his forehead, willing the thoughts away.

The monitor blinked to life, and he logged in and waited for the computer to complete its startup sequence. Had he made a huge mistake, breaking things off with Corinna? Long, wavy black hair, honey-colored eyes, she'd possibly been the sweetest girl he'd ever dated. And with the amount of dates he'd had, that was saying something.

If Brian had a superpower, his was letting women down easy. He'd honed the skill to perfection starting with disastrous high school breakups better left forgotten. By college, he'd acquired enough finesse that he'd been able to count his former girlfriends as friends. Over the last decade, as he delivered his personal twist on *it's me, not you*, they half thought they were the ones breaking up with him. What color tights did his kind of superhero wear? Pantywaist pink with a bedazzled cape?

"Hey, man, time to wrap it up." Jimmie Boguts, Jimbo for short, brushed by, jutting his bearded chin at the clock as he lumbered toward the exit.

With a squint of his eye and a tilt of his head, he peered again at the ridiculous clock. It appeared to indicate ten minutes until five o'clock. Without fail, this was the time things hit the fan—literal and otherwise. A burning sensation crept up his chest. He'd once seen a lady push back in her ergonomically-correct chair, jostling free her *Administrative Assistants' Day* balloon, which promptly whirled into the ceiling fan. It had taken Brian until five-twenty to release the daisy-covered Mylar and yellow curling ribbon from the five rotating paddles.

Not today.

His brother, John, had given Brian a standing invitation to Friday night pizza at his house, and with no plans to see Corinna tonight—or ever again—he was banking on a couple of beers with John and his sister-in-law, Kate. Hot pizza, cold beer, and company beat whatever he'd find at his house.

The computer beeped, and Brian scooted towards the desk, fingers tapping on the keyboard and hand maneuvering the mouse as he clicked through a series of folders. Something had been slowing this computer down, at least according to its user.

He glanced at the nameplate on the otherwise bare desktop. Raymond Boyle. A white push pin held a single photo on the beige cubicle wall. A heavyset, dark-skinned woman and two lighter-skinned kids—one boy, one girl—smiled at the camera. Wet hair plastered the sides of their heads, and balled-up towels sat alongside. Brightly colored wet chutes filled in the background. Looked like a water park attraction.

Brian called to mind Raymond, a stocky middle-aged guy. Average looks. Bad teeth. Or maybe too many for his mouth. Brian only knew him in passing. He did something for the Accounting Department. He thought . . . yeah, he'd gotten remarried last year. Brian had signed a congratulatory card. The people at the water park were probably his new wife and step-kids.

C'mon, c'mon. Brian clicked through a sequence of files and growled. What was the—

With a shove, he drifted backwards on his wheeled chair, eyes wide and all the blood draining from his face. The image file previews that had popped up . . . He glanced behind and to either side. Somehow, most everyone had slipped by, obviously eager to get the weekend underway. *Thank God.*

Brian breathed deeply, closing his eyes and steeling his resolve. He needed to document what he'd found for his supervisor, but he wouldn't allow his gaze to linger. He couldn't. He wouldn't even chance letting his vision drift to the focal points of the images. And yet, his eyes trailed the length of a ridiculously long, smooth leg. The inviting curves, blood-red lipstick, and seductive leather straps.

Eyes squeezed shut, he sent up a desperate prayer. *God, help me.* He'd discovered the source of the problem, and it violated company policy. "Your computer's running slow, huh, buddy? Well, Raymond Boyle, I discovered the source of your problem." He had an ethical duty to report it, but at what risk to himself?

How many months had he fought this particular demon?

How many times had he brought these same sins to his confessor? He'd fought and failed so many times until he finally regained—through grace alone—dominion of his mind and body. The temptation had been all but snuffed out these last few years.

Spine rigid, he scrolled though dozens of thumbnails, the knot in his stomach tightening and twisting as the pictures grew more lurid and perverse until his hand stilled over a single image. Dread pitted in his gut. *Lord, don't let this be what I think it is.*

He double-clicked.

With head half turned, he peered through squinted eyes.

His brow wrinkled and nostrils flared as he forced a dry swallow, disgust and sorrow rippling through him. He punched the monitor's on/off switch with an unsteady finger. Raymond Boyle wasn't just out of a job. He'd be looking at years in prison.

Forty minutes later, Brian braced himself over the old porcelain sink in the men's restroom. He stared blankly at his reflection and the milk-chocolate-colored stall behind him. Twisting the faucet on with one hand, he splashed cold water on his face with the other, his mind repeating in a loop the snippet of a verse he'd memorized long ago: *Create a clean heart in me, O God.*

He'd done what he needed to do. What he'd discovered, he'd diligently documented with log-in dates, server logs, and the internet cache intact. Then he'd sent multiple messages up the chain of command about not only what he'd found and how, but his recommendations for preserving company data when law enforcement inevitably confiscated or purged their system.

All second thoughts of Corinna scattered as he trudged through the cube farm, apparently the last person in the office. He glanced at the clock, wishing he could wind the hands back and take with them the vile images now burned into his brain.

While his appetite had waned, he longed for an evening of

normalcy with John and his family. So, he'd brave the commute east, longer and later on Fridays.

As he merged onto the interstate, he inched above the speed limit, hoping he could bypass the other commuters fleeing the city. Hoping he could outrun a past that had suddenly eclipsed the present and co-mingled with disgust so thick it nearly gagged him.

Traffic thinned as he exited the highway and completed a series of turns that took him deeper into suburbia and closer to family.

Brian rolled his white sedan into the driveway and killed the engine. The buff-colored brick ranch house was a mirror-image of the other post-war homes on the block. The bushes around the front remained bare, only the slightest hint of green tinting the branches.

He sat, staring through the windshield at the closed garage door while he tried to shift mental gears. He didn't want to let on what he'd spent the last hour of work doing and open himself to questions about it. He only wanted to forget.

A blast of warm, muggy air hit him as he opened the car door, making it unseasonably hot for an early spring day. He unbuttoned his shirt and tugged at the collar, fanning the undershirt beneath.

John sat in "his" chair at the corner of the wooden deck beneath an overgrown maple tree. Brian followed his gaze to the yard where his boys, seven-year-old Patrick and six-year-old Brady, threw a baseball back and forth.

John's head turned toward him as Brian's foot hit the first step to the deck.

"Late again." John glanced at his wristwatch, a hint of disapproval in his tone. His hand rested around a bottle of lager.

At twenty-nine, John was four years younger than Brian, but unlike Brian, who had a full head of chestnut brown hair, John's hair had receded and thinned to the point that he'd decided to shave it.

He had a few inches on Brian but more than a few pounds, so that the difference in height became barely noticeable. They shared the same color of blue eyes that were a perfect match for their dad's, but where Brian's were clear, John's had a few flecks of cobalt that made them seem more serious. Brian had thought them a direct contradiction to his personality growing up, but when John met and married the girl of his dreams, they seemed to fit his new maturity.

"Tunnel traffic," Brian mumbled as he crossed the deck. "Friday night. You know how it is." His gaze snagged on something new in the yard: a four-foot stack of stone pavers along the gray chain-link fence next to a smaller pile of firewood. Pavers. When would he be roped into *that* home improvement project? His back ached thinking about it.

Brian's butt had barely hit the Adirondack chair when John began his inquisition.

"How's things going with Corinna?"

Maybe inquisition was too strong a word, but from Brian's end, that's what it felt like. He didn't want to answer questions, not about work and not about Corinna. He needed to get hold of one of those beers and stay glued to the seat. He needed to chew the fat about Pirates baseball, and his nephews' latest feats.

"They're not going anywhere." Brian unbuttoned a sleeve and began rolling it up. Felt like summer out in the sun. Maybe he should move into the shade.

"Ha!" John's yelp, aimed toward the screen door, nearly knocked Brian out of his seat. "Kate, you owe me a foot massage."

Brian gritted his teeth, heat rising along his neck, and not from the sun. "You're betting on my dates now?"

John shrugged, the palm of his free hand lifting. "What? We

didn't put money on it. Kate was more optimistic about Corinna than me. So, what was her flaw?"

Refusing to engage John with even a look, Brian unbuttoned and rolled the opposite sleeve. "She doesn't have a *flaw*." He stood and spotted a cooler against the brick wall, next to the door. Lifting a bottle from inside, he glanced at the label before twisting the cap. "It just wasn't working." He flipped the cap in his hand and then lobbed it at John. It hit the deck with a tinny clink.

"Why not?" John tapped his fingers on the armrest, as if bored.

"I don't know. Different goals. She's way more into her career than she's into me."

John smirked. "Jealous much?"

Brian bit the inside of his cheek to keep from snapping. John didn't know the day he'd had and lashing out at him wouldn't be fair. Was he jealous of Corinna's job? Maybe a little. But it was more than that.

"I'm tired of dating. Sick of it, actually. I don't wanna mess around with someone who doesn't even have marriage on their radar."

"How many women is it gonna take? Cuz you've had a chance with more than your fair share, brother." He scratched at the label on his bottle before taking another swig. "You've got to loosen up a little bit. Your standards are too high."

"Which one, John?" No use trying to hide his irritation. They'd danced around this topic a half-dozen times before. It never ended well. "Because if I remember correctly, you didn't have to change *your* standards when you found Kate. In fact, she was the only girl you ever dated. So, you tell me, which of my so-called high standards should I drop so I can settle for someone I don't really want to spend the rest of my life with?"

It galled Brian to admit that John had succeeded where he'd

repeatedly failed. Without any apparent effort, John had found her, that elusive *her*.

Brian set his bottle on the floor, sat, and slapped his hands against the arm rests. "You know, I'm done. I've had it with dating." With uncharacteristic dramatic flair, Brian gestured with his arms wide open, raised to the sky. "If God has someone for me, He's going to have to drop her in my lap before I ask her out."

John chuckled. "Yeah, whatever. I won't be holding my breath until the Almighty lowers your princess from the heavens."

Seeing the conversation plummeting downhill faster than an elephant on a ten-speed, Brian searched for an emergency exit before it ended in an argument about God, religion, and a litany of all his persistent character flaws.

Brian stood and leaned on the deck rail, watching the boys hurl the baseball at one another. Patrick could hit Brady's glove without the ball bouncing in the grass. "They're getting better."

John cleared his throat. "That reminds me. I need some help."

Had to hand it to John. He didn't let his insults stand in the way of trying to squeeze out another favor. What now? The pavers?

"I'm coaching Patrick's Little League team this year. I've got two dads willing to help, but it's a big group of boys, and I could use another hand."

Brian ran a hand through his hair. Not back-breaking work like the pavers, but it would be a big time commitment.

"Practices are early," John said, as if reading his mind and wanting to minimize the job. "I wouldn't expect you to make those with work and all, but if you could at least be at the games. Might need a third base coach."

Brian sighed, pretty certain John had already counted on him saying yes.

Patrick tossed the ball in the air and swung at it with his bat. *Whiff.*

"How long does the season run?" Probably amounted to a matter of weeks. He'd want to see Patrick play anyway. He loved hanging with his nephews, being the fun uncle.

"April to mid-June. You in?"

"I don't know." Brian grinned as Brady tried to wrestle the bat from Patrick, yanking on it until his brother suddenly let go, laughing. "You sure no other dads can help?"

"No one's responded to my email except the two guys I've got." No mention of Corinna or Brian's too-high standards now. Just a pathetic please-help-me smile.

Part of Brian wanted to say no, if only to let John know he couldn't continually take advantage. Just because he was single didn't mean he didn't have a life and responsibilities of his own. Then he glanced at the boys, both laughing now even as they rolled in the grass, each holding tight to the other's shirt. This favor was as much for Patrick as for John. "I guess I can do it."

"Awesome." John grinned and raised his beer.

Patrick and Brady scrambled up, raced across the yard, and bounded up the steps onto the deck.

"Hey, Uncle Brian." Patrick high-fived him as he headed for the cooler, Brady on his heels.

"Will you pitch to me?" Brady grabbed Brian's wrist, yanking him toward the steps.

"Sure. Let me—" Brian set his beer on the rail. "I want to see you hit it over the fence and right into the Kings' pool." He pointed to the yard opposite theirs, where a mottled terrier paced with its nose to the ground.

"He can't hit that far," Patrick said before sucking the juice from his drink pouch.

The image Brian had tried to expunge came back to him, the sick visual he feared he'd never rid his mind of, thanks to Raymond Boyle. The kids in that picture couldn't have been much older than his nephews. He forced his attention back to Patrick, pasting on a fake smile.

"We'll see about that." Brian took the baseball from Brady and headed to the yard, wishing he could wipe his memory the way he could wipe a computer's. *Create a clean heart in me, O God. And a clean mind.*

CHAPTER 2

An American flag flapped in the breeze, and something metal clanked against the pole. Three toddlers circled the concrete base while clutching the pole with one arm and holding a doll or stuffed animal in the other.

From behind the chain link fence, Melanie Lombardi squinted across the baseball field into the setting sun, trying to make out the runner on third base. If he turned just a little, maybe she could decipher the number on his back.

She should be grateful for the weather, the park, and the opportunities her healthy, active kids had to play and learn. Grateful she got to hang around a baseball field and not a frigid ice rink or an oppressive natatorium. Yet her attention remained scattered amongst the to-dos looming over her when they returned home: baths, bedtime, dishes, laundry, bills. Pushing the distractions to the side, she focused again on the field.

The pint-sized third base runner was uncooperative—in more ways than one. No visible number, and now he was jumping up and down on the bag. *Futile.* They all looked the same in their uniforms. She turned her back to the sun and scoured the bustling playground for her middle child.

"Kevin!"

A lean five-year-old extracted himself from the monkey bars and ran towards her. His sweat-dampened hair stuck to his forehead and the back of his neck. "What, Mom?"

"Is that Matthew on third base?"

He glanced at the field. "I don't know. Sun's in my eyes." He peered through the fence, moving from side to side to see around the first baseman and first base runner. "Lemme go see."

Kevin took off in a sprint into the sun, rounding the benches, bleachers, and backstop, and then catapulted himself onto the fence, yelling at the base runner. The boy turned and, based on his wild gestures alone, she knew it wasn't Matthew. He must've been waiting to bat.

Melanie glanced at the playground behind her, ensuring Penny hadn't strayed. The two-year-old clutched two fistfuls of mulch, lifted them high, then opened her hands, letting the bark and dirt fall into her thin golden hair and onto her face. She squatted and scooped more from the ground, then let it trickle onto the yellow slide beside her.

A tween girl—too big for the little kids' equipment—screeched and crammed her body onto a slide near Penny, squeezing herself down ahead of a younger boy. They nearly trampled poor little Penny as they raced toward the tire swing.

With a hand to her chest, Melanie sighed, relieved her little girl hadn't become a playground casualty. They'd managed to stay out of the hospital emergency room thus far, and she wasn't eager to break their string of good luck.

Kevin still perched on the fence next to third base, having a protracted, animated discussion with the third base coach, who was *supposed* to be watching the runners.

Melanie waved her hands in the air, hoping to catch Kevin's attention to motion him back to the first base side of the field, but his gaze never moved beyond the man he was talking to. More like distracting, if she knew her son.

With a sigh, she scooped a filthy Penny from the ground and plopped her on her hip. "C'mon, Penny. Let's see what your brother's up to."

By the time she'd reached Kevin, her hip ached and the late May sun burned her bare arms, reminding her she should've coated the kids with sunscreen.

"Down you go," Melanie said, grabbing Penny under the arms.

"No!" Penny gripped Melanie's neck and squeezed.

"Mommy can't carry you right now, punkin." She pried Penny loose and set her on her feet.

With the toes of his tennis shoes wedged between the aluminum chain-link fence, Kevin leaned over the metal rail, his arms lifted in a ready stance as if he were behind home plate, waiting on a pitch.

"Kevin!" Melanie grabbed Kevin around the waist, wringing him from the fence. "Hey, you're done distracting the coach. Go play."

"Sorry," she said to the third base coach as she dusted mulch from her khaki shorts. "He's a talker." She caught sight of the coach, and her polite smile snagged. Clear blue eyes brightened his whole face. His short blond-brown hair held a hint of wave that would probably grow into full-blown curls if he let it get any longer. Nothing in particular distinguished his features, but taken all together, she couldn't deny his all-American good looks.

Kevin's nonstop blathering hadn't bothered him, so he was either easygoing by nature or a good actor. His gaze flicked between her and the playing field, his smile saying it was the former. "No problem." He paused as the batter hit a grounder toward the pitcher's mound. The pitcher bobbled it three times before overthrowing the ball to first base. "He said his dad played in the minors."

As always, mention of David generated a fresh stab of pain in her heart, and she dropped her gaze to her feet. "Oh gosh, for a short time many years ago. I'm surprised he even remembered that." She recalled the pictures of David stashed in a plastic container at the top of her closet. So young and handsome in his Williamsport Crosscutters uniform, he'd barely looked old enough to drive. A second stab pierced her heart. She had no business noticing another man's good looks, not when she couldn't get through a half day without some reminder of the gaping hole David's absence left.

The next batter hit a grounder toward the shortstop. "Hustle, Cameron!" the third base coach called as he urged a boy toward third. Cameron, apparently impervious to his coach's instructions, trotted to third at his own pace. The third baseman touched the bag, ball in hand, and Cameron slowed to an amble.

Squinting into the sun, the coach shot Melanie a grin as he motioned the runner toward the bench.

A sudden rush of tears formed behind her eyes, and she blinked them back. Random onslaughts of mixed-up emotions had plagued her for months with no end in sight. Not wanting to seem rude, she forced a smile, but her lips had only half-curved when a familiar shriek pierced the air.

Melanie spun in the opposite direction. Penny! She stood alongside the bleachers mere yards behind Melanie, a long, pointed stick in her hand. Tears rolled down her dirt-smeared cheeks.

Melanie started toward her, arms extended. "What happened, honey?"

"Ken-in," she said.

As if on cue, Kevin appeared from behind the bleachers, moving at a half gallop, blood trickling down his left shin.

The blood from his wound barely concealed the pre-existing

scrapes and bruises in various stages of healing. "What happened to—"

"Penny jabbed me with that stick." He flung an accusatory arm in Penny's general direction, but his little sister ignored him, using the stick to draw a line in the dirt.

Melanie narrowed her eyes and gave him a look. "And what did you do to cause her to shriek and retaliate?" She fished in her pocket for a napkin or tissue to mop up the blood.

"Nothing."

Standard answer. *Nothing.* Irritation crept up Melanie's spine as she took both children by the hand and headed toward the concession stand, where she hoped she'd find clean paper towels.

Kevin hopped on one leg, yelling "ow" as he went, while Penny pulled in the opposite direction. They passed behind little girls on a blanket dressing their dolls, a baby sitting idly in his mother's lap, and three boys lining up Hot Wheels cars on an old tree stump. All quiet, contented, orderly children.

Penny chose that moment to go boneless, forcing Melanie to half drag her. With a howl of pain, Kevin caught his good foot on a rock, causing him to stumble.

Heat blazed Melanie's cheeks as all eyes turned their direction. Tears threatened again, but she swallowed the lump in her throat and pretended this was normal. Not too difficult to do, considering the regularity with which these things happened. She glanced at the field, mortified to think the third-base coach had witnessed her multi-child meltdown.

But, oh, he had. His gaze remained fixed on her despite the fact that a boy raced toward him from second base.

"Should I go home? Home?" the boy yelled. A fly ball miraculously dropped into the pitcher's glove.

"Go back! Back to second!" the coach shouted, waving him in the right direction.

Melanie slunk the remainder of the way to the concession

stand, sorry the coach had muffed a play but grateful it had taken the focus off her parenting-fail sideshow.

Within minutes, Penny sucked happily on a blue raspberry Ring Pop as she spun in increasingly dizzy circles in the grass while Kevin held a gauze pad to his leg wound. Melanie breathed deeply, relieved the crisis and embarrassment had passed.

The field went quiet as the teams traded places at the start of the inning, and the conversation from the nearby bleachers caught her attention. "So glad I'm not on snack duty tonight. We're clean out of fresh fruit until I can get to the farmer's market."

Melanie's chest tightened. Snack. Who was on snack duty tonight? She slid her phone from her pocket and glanced at the calendar. *Please Lord, let it be someone else.* Sadly, her prayer was ignored, because right beside the game time and field location it read: Snack – Matthew L.

She glanced at the time. Could she get home and back before the game ended? There had to be something at home that would suffice for a snack. But what? No time to bag cheddar fish crackers or pretzels. *Wait! A box of grape Popsicles.* No one would know they'd melted and refrozen after Matthew had left the freezer door ajar overnight.

In fifteen minutes' time, hungry boys had left their gear with their parents and gathered around her collapsible cooler behind the bleachers. Penny's hands grew a deeper shade of purple with each frozen treat that passed through her warm hands to a hungry boy's.

"Any left for me?"

That voice sounded about two octaves too low to be a Little Leaguer.

"Yup," Penny said, her smile spreading to show all her beautiful white baby teeth. She grabbed a Popsicle from the bottom of the bag and handed it to the third-base coach, who rested on one knee in front of her.

Melanie's heart pounded as the embarrassment swept over her. It had to be embarrassment, not the five o'clock shadow she hadn't noticed earlier.

"Thank you," he said, his gaze shifting from Penny to Melanie. He stood, extending his right hand. "I'm Brian Perella, by the way. You're Matthew's mom, right?"

Melanie's cold, wet hand almost met his before she retracted it and wiped it on her shorts. How did he know she was Matthew's mom? What had he done? "Yes, Matthew's mine." She offered him her dry, still chilled hand. "I'm Melanie Lombardi, and this is Penny." She brushed her hand lightly over Penny's sweaty, dirty head. "And I've got another around here somewhere." She spotted him rolling down a small grassy hill with Matthew and his teammates. "Kevin. He's with his brother," she said, gesturing to the hillside.

"Are any of these yours?" she asked, nodding to the boys milling around, finishing their Popsicles.

"These Popsicles are gross," one kid mumbled, kicking at the grass with his cleats.

Melanie shot a glare in his general direction. Probably the kid whose mom only offered locally-grown organic produce for snacks.

Brian grinned at Penny, who licked the sticky purple goo from her hands, and shrugged. "I like 'em. Looks like Penny does too." He raised his gaze to Melanie. "I don't have kids. My brother, John, is the head coach. He asked me to help out." Unsuccessful at tearing the Popsicle open by hand, he tore at the wrapper with his teeth.

"Oh." Melanie twisted her wedding band while casting a furtive glance at his ring finger. Bare. Didn't mean anything. Lots of married men didn't wear them, and why did she care anyway? Romance had no place in her life. Not anymore. And in truth, it hadn't for quite a while. "It's good of you to help out."

An excuse about why she couldn't help more died on her lips. She didn't owe him an explanation for her hot mess of an existence. She'd cried so many tears over the past year that she half expected to look in the mirror one morning and discover she'd become no more than a shriveled mass of skin and bones. And some pockets of cellulite.

While the volume of tears, which had become less about David and more about herself, had diminished somewhat over the past couple of months, the mood swings hadn't. One day she'd been so beset by her inadequacies, she'd mentally mapped an escape plan with a Caribbean destination. Lately, she could see her life with something like hope, only to have guilt rise in its wake.

David was a reasonable man. He'd want her to live, to fall in love again, maybe even marry and give their children a father. Then why the guilt for merely noticing an attractive man? Did the dearth of masculinity in her life cause her to hyper-focus on things like strong forearms, a deep voice, or some beard stubble? Because noticing was pointless. Even if a guy looked once, he wouldn't look twice, not with three young children trailing her.

"Well, I've gotta round up the lost gloves and gear and see that the sunflower seeds and wads of bubble gum are cleared from the bench." He wrinkled his nose but grinned. "See you next game."

"Bye." Oh, she'd see him. And he'd see her. But she'd bet a gross of her beloved Mr. Clean erasers that it would be the last time they'd speak. Once he learned of her circumstances, he'd get his refrozen store brand Popsicles somewhere else. People acted as if widowhood were contagious and she were the carrier, mumbling an "I'm so sorry" then slipping away to more comfortable conversations. Brian would be no different.

CHAPTER 3

Fat raindrops spattered the walkway running between the pool and pavilion. The breeze carried the faint scent of chlorine as it pushed threatening clouds east. The baseball team's season-ending picnic and pool party would go on as planned once the looming gray cloud overhead passed.

Brian stuffed his hands in his pockets. The overhang on the picnic shelter provided cover while he waited for the rest of the kids and their families to arrive. He'd helped John and Kate, who chatted at a wooden table with the first family to arrive, by setting up the plates, utensils, and fixings for hamburgers and hot dogs. Now, with nothing to do, he wished he'd skipped the shindig all together.

Families strolled through the open gates, toting swim bags, beach towels, and casserole dishes covered in aluminum foil. Raindrops gave way to a glimmer of sunlight, and the kids took off at a run toward the pool while the parents, yelling for the kids to wait up, headed for the pavilion.

No wife, no kids, no way to relate to these people other than small talk about their 2-10 season. Technically, not 2-10 since the coaches didn't keep score, but the kids did.

An angry shout drew Brian's attention to a dad reaming out his kids—pretty loudly—for some transgression. Melanie slipped in behind them. She wore her wavy chestnut-brown hair swept off her neck in a loose knot and a red-and-white checkered blouse with denim shorts that screamed summer.

His gaze drifted to her little entourage and one side of his mouth lifted in a grin. The little girl dragged a Minnie Mouse beach towel, stopping to adjust her pink flip-flops every three steps. The boy who had hung over the fence to talk to him followed, snapping his frog-green goggles into place. Matthew jogged around them toward the edge of the giant sandbox where his teammates had gathered.

No husband? Only Melanie and the kids had come to the games, but maybe he worked evenings, which was a shame, because it seemed she could use a hand juggling all their needs. The younger two kids seemed incapable of remaining still for more than five seconds at a time, making it difficult for her to watch the games.

His heart did a funny flip. Ever since he'd spoken to her over the fence at third base, he'd unconsciously sought her out at every game. Looking was harmless, right? He'd allowed himself a few seconds here and there but didn't allow his gaze or his thoughts to linger.

What if she didn't have a husband?

Of course she had a husband; he'd seen her wedding band, which she had a habit of twisting during conversations.

Even when in idle moments, his brain conjured random conversation starters, he'd resolved to avoid her for the remainder of the season. No good could come from developing a crush on a married woman even if he had no intention of pursuing anything.

She headed in his direction, a container of fruit salad or whatever she had in the large bowl under her arm, her eyes scanning the pool.

Brian glanced to either side and behind him, looking for a quick escape—one that didn't signal his obvious avoidance. Nothing behind him but a mound of sand. Clusters of parents stood on either side. He didn't know any of them. *Shoot.*

Melanie stopped and bent to help Penny as she hopped—sort of—on one foot. After fitting the flip-flop thong between her tiny toes, Melanie stood. She'd spotted him, but would she remember him? Maybe she'd pass by with her container.

She stopped in front of him, her smile brightening emerald-green eyes with long lashes and cheeks flushed from the heat. Damp curlicues of soft hair clung to the nape of her neck. "Brian, right?"

"Yup. And you're Melanie."

She clutched the bowl tighter with one arm while she pushed the strap of her bag back up her shoulder with the other. "You have a good memory." As if he needed a reminder, her wedding band glinted in the sunlight emerging from behind the clouds.

"Not typically, but your name stuck for some reason." What a goof. It stuck all right, like a splinter lodged beneath his skin, drawing his attention at every touch when he knew he'd be better off with it gone.

"So, season's done. What did you think of coaching?" She retrieved sunglasses from her bag pocket and slid them on.

"Well, mostly I waved kids around the bases and collected lost caps and gear, but it was fun." He hesitated to ask the question on his tongue, but it would be best to hear it from her lips and nip his ridiculous attraction to her in the bud. Besides, he was genuinely curious where the man with a matching gold band was. "I'd, uh, have thought, with your husband being a former ball player, he might want to help coach."

With sunglasses covering her eyes, her expression remained unreadable, but she turned her head away from him. Her kids had drifted to a grassy area during the minute-long conversation.

"He would've enjoyed that," she said, facing him again, her teeth biting into her lower lip for a fraction of a second. "But my husband passed away last year."

Brian's eyes widened. He hadn't considered the possibility that she was widowed. Not at her age. "I'm so sorry. I, uh, I didn't know. I saw your ring, and I assumed—"

She used the thumb on her free hand to twist the band around her ring finger.

He lost his train of thought. "Was it, uh, was it sudden?"

"His car hit a tractor trailer head on."

He didn't need to see her eyes to know he'd just pounded a nail in the conversational coffin. *Bad analogy.*

"I shouldn't have asked—"

She shushed him with a wave of her hand. "It's okay. It's good to talk about it. About him."

Penny ambled back and grabbed her mom's arm, causing the bag to drop to Melanie's elbow. "Mama, Mama, Mama. Swim!"

Melanie hoisted the bag up. "In a minute, honey," she whispered.

"I'm sure it's been tough handling the three of them on your own." Probably a gross understatement. He recalled her dragging Penny and Kevin toward the concession stand, one or both bawling.

She chuckled. "Well, it's humbling. I depend on others more than ever. People probably run and hide when they see my name on their caller ID."

Not sure what to say, Brian fiddled with his baseball cap, taking it off and running a hand through his hair before settling it back on his head.

A few seconds of uncomfortable silence ticked by.

"Well, the kids are anxious to swim." Her chest rose and fell and her features settled into a resigned, tight smile. "Nice seeing you again."

"Yeah. Bye," he mumbled as she pushed past him in the direction of the pavilion. The smell of grilling hamburgers drifted toward him in her wake.

Did he detect an iciness to her tone? What had he done wrong?

"Brian!" John called from his position behind the grill. He waved away the smoke in front of his face. "Give me a hand with these wieners?"

Brian bit the inside of his cheek, sure that his brother's choice of hot dog monikers wasn't an accident. "Yeah. Be right there." He glanced in the direction Melanie had headed but couldn't spot her amidst the adults crowding the picnic tables.

Moving burgers and dogs around the grill with a pair of tongs proved a mindless, innocuous way to pass the afternoon. Occasionally, Brian looked up from his station to see the kids doing cannonballs into the water or playing a pick-up game of Wiffle Ball. When his thoughts or gaze drifted to Melanie, he redirected them to the sizzling patties before him.

Of course, now that he knew she wasn't married, entertaining the idea—No! Hadn't he told John he was done dating? And didn't she brush him off after their brief conversation?

Three hours later, when the last of the families trudged toward the exit with tired kids and wet towels draped over their shoulders, he helped Kate and John scoop up the trash, wipe clean the tables, and gather whatever needed to be carted home.

Brian accepted a tower of dirty plates and napkins from Kate and dropped them into the trash can nearest John.

John stood up from a cooler and pushed a brown bottle in a red koozie toward him. "From my private stash. Kids are gone. Little League rules no longer apply."

"Thanks." Probably one of John's weird, exotic brews. He sniffed it. *Grapefruit?*

"Seemed like the kids had fun, huh?"

"Hmm?" Brian pitched half-drunk water bottles and empty but puffed-out juice pouches into the garbage can. "Yeah. They had fun."

"What about the parents? Think they enjoyed it?"

Between smearing kids with sunscreen, shoveling food onto their plates, and toting all the stuff, yeah, they probably did. "Sure."

"The moms?" John pulled a white plastic cover from a table and rolled it into a ball. "Were they able to relax?"

Brian crushed an empty aluminum can under his shoe. From what he saw, moms didn't generally get a lot of relaxation. At least not at something like this. "I don't know. I guess."

Seconds passed as they stripped the plastic cover from another table. "Matthew's mom, what's her name? She seemed to have a good time, huh?"

It dawned on Brian then, the point of this conversation. With clenched fists, he twisted the balled-up plastic cover, shoved it into the trash can, and then spun around.

Kate shoved a stack of napkins into a cardboard box. She wore her blond hair in a bob, a style he hadn't seen on her before. But then she changed her look as often as other people changed the page on their calendars. A decade ago, when John had first introduced them, she reminded him of a fair, blonde, blue-eyed sylph, an imaginary air spirit. Age and motherhood had added a few pounds to her frame, which only made her more attractive.

"Kate, can you come here for a sec?" Brian said between gritted teeth.

"Sure." She grabbed a couple of Styrofoam bowls and plastic forks, spooned something into them, and brought them to where he stood with John. The sweet smell of ripe cantaloupe made his mouth water as she handed him a bowl.

"What's up?" she said, reaching into his bowl with a fork and popping a piece of his melon into her mouth.

"John's curious about whether Melanie Lombardi had a good time today."

"Oh." She reached across the table and handed John a bowl and fork. "Yeah. I feel bad for her. She doesn't seem to hang with the other moms, and I couldn't get away from this stuff." She gestured to the bags of buns and containers of leftovers waiting to be packed.

"And?" Brian stabbed at the melon and slid a piece over his tongue. So sweet it nearly melted.

"And what?" Kate gave him that doe-eyed look that typically reduced John to a sniveling puddle. Didn't work on Brian.

He batted his lashes right back at her, mimicking her expression. "Didn't John tell you I'm done dating?"

She shrugged and returned to condensing the empty containers and stacking them in the box. "You want to get married. And short of a mail-order bride, the best way to accomplish that is to date."

Huh. Mail-order bride. Was that still a thing? Probably an email-order bride these days. Maybe there was an app for that.

"Listen," she said, letting her head loll to the side. "I'm too beat to argue. I saw you talking to her. She seems like a nice person, she's pretty, and you like kids. I thought if John encouraged you . . ." She shook her head. "Never mind."

Brian pitched his fork and bowl then cinched the trash bag and yanked it from the metal container. A few bees buzzed as they followed the bag to its new location in the dumpster behind the pavilion. With a forearm over his nose, Brian tried to block the stench of heat-soaked garbage as he rushed away from the refuse and back toward John.

"You like her, don't you?" John gave him a goofy grin.

Brian flashed back to his brother's discovery of every grade school crush he'd had. He could almost hear the childish, sing-song voice: Brian loves Mel-a-nie.

Deny, deny, deny or 'fess up? He wasn't ten years old anymore. "Maybe. I wasn't flirting though. Until this afternoon, I thought she was married."

"Did you ask her out?" Kate gathered her purse and set it alongside their box, then sat on a picnic table. Her gaze rested on Patrick and Brady in the grass taking turns snapping each other with towels.

Instant panic seized his chest. "What? No. No. Is that even appropriate?"

Kate tilted her head. "It's been a couple of years since she lost her husband, hasn't it?"

"She said he died last year."

"Oh. Well, it can't hurt to ask." She pushed off the table, slung her purse over her shoulder, and scooped up the box. "If she's not ready, she'll tell you."

"Honestly, Kate, I hadn't thought about it." But he had. The idea had been lurking at the edge of his mind since he found out she was widowed. He hadn't meant to lie to Kate; it just came out. A defense mechanism against her matchmaking.

"Besides," John said, smacking him across the back. "Brian's sworn off dating until God plants a beautiful, marriage-worthy virgin in his lap."

Brian scowled but clamped his mouth shut. He knew from experience any retort would only egg his brother on.

"I'll say one thing, and then I won't mention it again." Kate bumped John with her hip, urging him to grab the remainder of their things. "You have to make the first move. You can't expect a woman widowed a year with a passel of kids to come on to a never-been-married, slightly younger man. Ain't gonna happen. It's on you."

"Point taken." Brian reminded himself that Kate meant to help. John too. Maybe. Still felt like meddling though.

Kate strode through the grass, calling to the boys that it was time to go and then turning back to where he and John scooped up the remaining items. "We just want you to find the right woman, Brian, and be happy."

"Yeah, fat chance of that," John mumbled as he pushed past Brian.

Brian fished his car keys from his pocket and followed. He couldn't disagree.

CHAPTER 4

A pair of altar servers, a boy with shaggy brown hair and a girl with a long, blond ponytail, crossed the sanctuary in their red cassocks, lighting the candles on either side of the altar and then the tabernacle. Baskets of lavender miniature lilies and white roses sat in front of the altar, their sweet fragrance drifting along with the faint, lingering scent of incense.

Brian genuflected, slid into the second pew, knelt, and prayed. He liked sitting up front. Fewer distractions, and God knew his mind tended to wander far, wide, and a gazillion miles away during Mass. If he sat farther back, his gaze drifted to wriggly kids slumped and fidgeting in their seats. Their activity alone would be a distraction, but they also tempted him to envy. Would he ever have his own brood of wriggly children? He wanted a whole pew full of them. Maybe one of those short pews cut off by a giant pillar, but a pew.

His back to the commotion of families filing in behind him, he silently uttered his standard prayer, the same one he uttered as he knelt each Sunday before Mass. *Lord, if it's Your will, lead me to the woman who will be my wife.* Apparently, it wasn't God's will. At least not yet.

A young family with a gaggle of little girls in frilly dresses and sparkly shoes slipped into the pew beside him. He thought of Keith, who used to work with him. They were roughly the same age, which at the time was about 27. Keith, with four young girls, didn't last long at the company, probably due to the fact that he didn't want to put in the eighty plus hours his manager wanted. On casual Fridays, he wore a t-shirt that read, "Got a quiver full?"

Not getting the reference, Brian had asked what it meant.

Keith's face lit, and he launched into a long spiel about Psalm 127 before spending the next forty minutes trying to ferret out whether Brian was saved or not and then trying to convince him the Catholic Church was the Whore of Babylon mentioned in Revelation. Come to think of it, maybe *that* relentless campaign was why he'd been fired.

At any rate, Brian had looked up Psalm 127. "Certainly sons are a gift from the Lord, the fruit of the womb, a reward. Like arrows in the hand of a warrior are the sons of one's youth. Blessed is the man who has filled his quiver with them."

That was what he wanted: a quiver full. A bunch of little ones to love and raise up and, of course, a woman to cherish them with. Preferably one that could withstand his faithful membership in the Whore of Babylon.

* * *

THE QUIET SANCTUARY soothed Melanie's frayed nerves for all of three seconds. She'd situated the kids and dropped to her knees, ready to pour out her overflowing heart, leaving all her unmet needs, grief, inadequacies, and desperate pleas for help at the foot of the cross. She hadn't gotten beyond, *"Lord,"* before Penny pawed at her elbow.

"Mama . . . Mama . . . Mama." She pointed at her white sandal. The golden buckle had come undone.

As Melanie bent to adjust it, Matthew smacked her back. His attempted whisper came out in a too-loud croak as he leaned across his little brother and sister, knocking Penny's sippy cup onto the floor with a thunk. "Is that Coach Brian?" Matthew leaned closer, trying to get a better look.

Her heart skipping and a knot tightening in her belly, Melanie angled to the side, trying to see around the family in front of her, the one that obviously shopped at the Big & Tall store. The smallest of the big ones ducked for a moment, improving her view. A man about average height, tawny hair and a light blue shirt stood in the second row. Sure looked like Brian.

With every ounce of will she could muster, Melanie tried to concentrate on the Mass. Bad enough her kids didn't allow for more than an uninterrupted moment or two, but now, with laser-beam focus, her gaze moved to that second pew.

As the Communion line formed, she slid the hymnal into the pew rack and looked up just as he turned to get in line. Her heart leaped. It was him. Not that her gaze could linger.

She caught a tug-of-war going on in her peripheral vision, but by the time she recognized the red blur and the impending disaster, Kevin had wrenched an open package of Skittles from Penny's sweaty hand.

An angry shriek pierced the quiet church followed by the plinks of dozens of tiny coated candies scattering over the tile floor. *Oh no!* Penny must have rooted through her bag when she wasn't looking.

Melanie's cheeks flamed, and she fought to retain her composure. Grabbing Kevin by the arms, she pulled him close and spoke into his ear. "Pick up every one of those—right now!" she commanded between gritted teeth.

"But, Mom—"

With a shaking index finger to Kevin's lips, she silenced him, glaring at the rainbow of candies littering the area, still trickling, down, down the sloped floor. The temptation to get down on the floor herself was great—if not to help, at least to hide.

Too late for that. Most of the people in front of her—please no, God, not Brian—had turned to see the source of the interruption.

Many a Sunday had passed when the priest's sweet words, "The Mass is ended," brought a swell of relief so great Melanie thought she'd cry. Today, the humiliation of the candy catastrophe tempered that relief.

Matthew leaned across the padded pew, tapping her arm. "Mom, can I go say 'hi' to Coach Brian?"

"Sure," she said on a sigh. There would be no escaping the embarrassment now.

Matthew genuflected, scooted out of the row, and racewalked toward Brian as he exited his pew. Kevin tagged behind, his attempt at genuflection landing him on the floor for a few seconds.

"I wanna go wit' dem," Penny whined, apparently not caring that both of her shoes now hung open, unbuckled. She plopped on the kneeler, stomping her feet.

"Hang on, sweetie," Melanie said as she gathered the children's bulletins, Penny's cup, and other debris. With a gentle nudge, she prodded Penny toward the aisle while stuffing items in her purse.

"Hey, there."

At the sound of Brian's voice, Melanie's eyes shot up and her heart faltered. She might as well have been twenty-two again, scoping out all the eligible-looking young men at Mass, hoping to catch one's eye.

"Hi." She grabbed Penny's hand to keep her from straying up or down the aisle. "Matthew spotted you and wanted to say hello." Duh. He'd probably figured that much out already.

With his neat shirt, pressed pants, clean shave, and every hair in place, Brian looked so put-together.

Melanie pressed a hand to the side of her head, smoothing back the locks that hadn't stayed in place this morning. Why hadn't she spent five minutes applying makeup instead of washing the breakfast dishes?

"I was making my way back." Brian jutted his chin toward the rear exit. "We can talk better out there."

Before she could answer, Matthew launched into an update on his backyard batting practice, keeping pace with Brian as they moved toward the back of the church.

When they reached the glass doors, Penny pushed her way in front of them, reaching greedily for the holy water font. Brian scooped Penny up, her sandals dangling as she thrust her hand into the damp green sponge.

"Other hand." Brian folded his hand over hers, helping her dip her fingers and then make a sloppy gesture that resembled the sign of the cross.

Melanie stared in disbelief. Penny, who had a habit of hiding behind Melanie's legs when confronted by an adult, had allowed a virtual stranger to pick her up. Everything about this picture felt wrong. Or right. Or maybe just off. Yes, off. Everything lately had been a distorted reflection of her old life, as if she were trapped in a fun house hall of mirrors.

The door behind her hissed shut, bringing Melanie into the vestibule and out of her reverie. Matthew's chatter had ceased for a moment as Brian reached for a bulletin from the stack on the window ledge. "Do you go here? To St. Michael's?" They hadn't run into him before, but it was a big parish with several weekend Masses.

"No. I, uh, slept in this morning." He gave her a sheepish look. "Missed Mass at my parish."

Melanie's thoughts tangled. Her small talk skills had suffered lately, probably due to neglect. As they stepped out of the church and into the parking lot, her hand tightened around Penny's and her gaze darted to Matthew, Kevin, and various cars pulling out of parking spaces and moving through the lot. To make matters worse, a glance to her left snagged on Brian's nicely shaped bicep. It poked out from beneath his short-sleeved shirt as he raised an arm to fist-bump Kevin. He probably didn't even lift weights or anything, but his mere presence had somehow driven her body into high alert. *I'm a pathetic mess. Get a grip, Melanie!*

Brian caught her gaze over top of the kids' heads. "Are you going for D-O-U-G-H-N-U-T-S in the gym?"

He spelled "doughnuts" the traditional way. This might be love!

Before she could eke out a response, Matthew bounded between them.

"Doughnuts! Can we, Mom?" Matthew walked backwards along the crosswalk, nearly tripping on the curb surrounding an island of wildflowers.

Brian winced. "Sorry, I didn't know how well he could spell or that he was in hearing range."

"I've got one literate child now. It complicates some things." Melanie maneuvered around Kevin, who blocked her path, his hands folded and raised toward her in a desperate plea. A grin slipped out despite her minor frustration. "Yes, we can get doughnuts."

A small chorus of cheers erupted, and the kids' pace increased as they neared the entrance to the parish center.

"No boring Rosary after Mass *and* we get doughnuts. This day is awesome!" Matthew pumped a fist in the air.

Melanie ignored her little heathen, praying no one heard his cheer but her. She felt Brian's gaze on her and chanced a quick glance in return.

He stared straight ahead and planted his hands in his front pockets. "Your dress . . . it's nice." He smiled and finally made eye contact.

Glad she had chosen her turquoise maxi dress and sandals this morning instead of the less feminine black pants and nondescript white blouse she had first pulled out of the closet, she smiled her thanks. "I only wish I'd picked something that'll hide the jelly stains and powdered sugar."

A more self-assured woman wouldn't care about her wardrobe or the stains. Melanie was not that woman. Besides, her unease kept her from dwelling on the fact that Brian recognized her as a frazzled widow with three, uh, "spirited" children yet hadn't skedaddled.

CHAPTER 5

Despite the bright sunshine outdoors, darkness shrouded the hall linen closet as Melanie riffled through a variety of soaps, over-the-counter medicines, and hair accessories. She'd dashed into the house on a mission, the van running in the driveway. Desperately seeking sunscreen, she nudged aside a bag of cotton balls and chastised herself for neither making a list of things to take to the ballpark nor going to an earlier Mass.

She'd prodded the children to hurry, rushed home, and urged them to change their clothes. Her voice may have risen to a harried harpy pitch while they fussed and dawdled. She'd nuked some leftover macaroni and cheese and a few green beans, feeding it to them in the hope that they wouldn't load up on pricey ballpark junk food. They'd all crowded into the van when she'd remembered the sunscreen, delaying their departure even longer.

The combined fragrances of jarred candles, body lotion, and baby powder mingled into a semi-noxious perfume-like smell that tickled her throat. Frustrated, she jammed a package of light bulbs onto the upper shelf. A half-used, expired bottle of off-brand sunscreen must be hiding in there somewhere. *St. Anthony, help!*

As Melanie shoved aside an extra tube of toothpaste, the hot water bottle, and spare linens, her wedding band shone in the light trickling across the hall from Penny's bedroom window. Spinning the ring with her thumb, she drew her hand back carefully, studying the plain gold band that David had placed on her finger almost ten years ago.

"It's time," she whispered to no one, tugging the ring from her finger and slipping it into her front pocket. Glancing up, she spotted the sunscreen, front and center. How could she possibly have missed it?

* * *

AFTERNOON SUNLIGHT BEAT against the aluminum seats as a warm breeze drifted through the ballpark, fluttering a trio of flags alongside the jumbotron scoreboard. A vendor hoisted a crate of pink and blue cotton candy on his shoulder as he climbed the stadium steps, veering around a giant costumed mascot playing peek-a-boo with a baby bouncing on his dad's knee.

Brian glanced at his ticket stub and then located the section reserved for Little League kids and their families. Not a bad view from behind home plate. He sat in the aisle seat assigned to him and took in the empty rows above and below. John sat two rows down, closer to center with his boys on either side of him. A couple of other families dotted the section, but Melanie and her kids weren't among them.

"Am I in exile?" he called down to John.

John rested his arm on the back of Brady's seat and turned. "Those seats'll fill up. People are late."

By the time a small but perky ten-year-old girl belted out the national anthem to a large round of whistles and cheers, all the seats except the four next to Brian had filled. At least until the bottom of the first inning when Matthew, glove in hand, sprinted up the metal stairs.

He stopped in front of Brian, out of breath. "This row H?"

"Yessiree," Brian said, standing to let Matthew in. He'd just sunk into his seat when he noticed Kevin coming toward him.

The stadium noise level waned as a batter stepped to the plate, and audible thuds followed Kevin's every footfall as he climbed the steps, courtesy of a souvenir bat. Melanie trailed Kevin, balancing Penny on her hip.

Brian imagined Kate carefully arranging the seating to ensure his proximity to Melanie and her children. He'd thank her later.

Kevin reached their row, and Brian stood again to let him in. Melanie followed, sweat beading at her temple as she lowered Penny to the floor.

"Thank you," she said, her breath labored, probably from hauling thirty-plus pounds of toddler up umpteen steps. She wiped the perspiration from her forehead. "Sorry to interrupt the game."

"No problem." Brian stepped into the aisle, wondering— hoping she'd take the seat next to him.

To his disappointment, Melanie pushed on the seat next to Brian and encouraged Penny to hop up. Did she not want to be close to him or was she merely trying to keep the boys within reach?

"Any score?" Melanie settled in her seat, encouraging Penny to sit rather than stand on hers. She wore a navy tunic-style tee and denim shorts cuffed above her knees with a pair of sturdy sandals.

He glanced at her feet. No polish. Did she not have the time or money for the fancy pedicures Kate got or did she simply not care about something so frivolous? "Uh, no score. Three up, three down in the top of the inning."

About five batters later, the kids launched a relentless campaign for hot dogs and soft pretzels. "Please, Mom," Matthew begged, his hands folded and a ridiculous toothy grin on his face.

Melanie sighed. "Okay." She shooed them out of their seats and Brian stood again, letting them pass.

At the end of the aisle, she turned, a sweet smile lighting tired eyes. "Would you like anything?" she asked.

"No, I'm good." But wait, how could she . . . "With what third arm would you carry anything else?"

Melanie shrugged and started down the steps." I don't know," she said over her shoulder, smiling. "It didn't seem polite not to ask."

Once the rambunctious group had rumbled down the stairs and turned the corner toward the concession area, John's head turned toward Brian. He waved, a sly grin making his thoughts known. Amazing that a simple look conveyed all the teasing remarks Brian knew waited on the tip of John's tongue.

Brian scowled, but it only lasted a second before twisting into a grin. So he liked Melanie. They were grown-ups. Nothing to be embarrassed about.

Half an inning later, the kids traipsed up the steps with their munchies. Again, Brian stood to allow them to pass. Kevin held tight to his mother's hand—or maybe she held tight to his. Either way, Brian noticed that her hand was bare. No wedding band. He wondered if it had anything to do with him and quickly dismissed the thought. *You're not all* that, *Brian Perella.*

The kids spent the next half inning alternately eating and spilling or dropping their food. The concrete floor beneath them looked like a raccoon had ripped through a trash bag. Hunks of pretzel, a smattering of salt, globs of ketchup, and a puddle of mystery liquid would make cleanup a challenge for someone.

Between the spills and constant stream of questions from

the kids ("Is a foul a strike?"), small talk was tough. Still, it was obvious that while Melanie didn't know the team well, she knew baseball, inside and out. Made sense if her husband had played.

Taking a baby wipe from her bag, she cleaned the ketchup from Penny's hand. "I was a baseball fan long before I met David." She proceeded to wipe the red smears on the girl's face too. "My brothers played in high school and college. I more than put my time in on the bleachers. Not that I'm complaining." Melanie shrugged. "Lots of cute guys and all." She smothered a saucy grin as she tucked the wipe in an empty cup and turned her attention toward the field. "Did you play? When you were a kid?"

"If you wanna call it that. They put me deep in right field where I couldn't do much damage." His gaze lingered on her, wanting—but not getting—another peek at that grin.

By the bottom of the fifth, the home team had made it a tie game, but the kids were oblivious, more intent on doing the wave than watching the action on the field. "Mom, slushies?" Matthew asked, his eyes glimmering with anticipation.

Melanie let out about the fifth weary sigh in the past hour. "In a moment of desperation, I promised them slushies." The apologetic look in her eyes and tilt to her head were comical. "We'll need to, uh, get out. Again."

Brian pressed his hands to the armrests, ready to stand when Melanie waved him off.

"Stay put. We'll scoot by."

Penny slid easily out to the aisle, and the crack of a wooden bat and a round of cheers indicated a base hit Brian couldn't see. The batter had advanced to third by the time Melanie returned with the kids. They each sucked intently from long straws, gulping icy drinks in vibrant colors not found in nature.

The game remained tied through the bottom of the ninth inning. Runners led off of first and second bases with only one out. The stadium noise dulled as fans concentrated on the game, and Melanie's kids occupied themselves throwing straws back and forth with the boys seated in front of them.

Brian's heart pattered. He'd test the waters. See if Melanie had any interest in seeing him outside of baseball. "So, uh, after the game—"

A burst of cheers smothered his question as a runner stole third base.

Kevin squeezed in front of his mom, alternately wiggling and squeezing his legs together. "I've really gotta go," he said, his expression earnest.

"You can't wait?" Melanie gestured toward the field. "It's kind of a critical point in the game."

Kevin shook his head and grabbed his crotch for good measure. Matthew had joined him because, of course, now he had to go too.

The pitcher gave up a walk while Melanie attempted to discern just how long her boys could wait and whether they were merely bored or an accident was imminent. "Just a few minutes?" she pleaded.

Negative.

"Excuse us. Yet again," Melanie said. "I'm so sorry. We should've switched seats with you from the get go. Too much slushie, I guess." She glanced at Penny, who stood tapping the shoulder of the boy in front of her with her chewed-up straw. "Can Penny stay here with you?"

"Sure." He smiled at the little girl whose formerly-white t-shirt featured a ketchup/slushie rainbow only bleach could fade.

Melanie took one step in front of him, Kevin on her heels and—

"Oh!" Melanie lurched forward, her foot landing on Brian's before she fell into his lap.

Brian bit his lips together and swallowed the pain throbbing in his little toe.

"Stop pushing," Kevin yelled, shoving Matthew back a half step.

"Oh my gosh." Melanie's face reddened as she scrambled off of Brian. Her hands flailed as she searched for a safe place to put them while righting herself. Settling on the armrest and Brian's shoulder, she stumbled toward the aisle. "I'm so sorry."

With a hand to her elbow, Brian guided her around his feet, curling and uncurling his little toe a few times to make sure it still bent. "I should've gotten up to let you out. My big feet got in the way."

"Nice try," Melanie said, brushing nothing but embarrassment from the front of her shorts, "but that was all us." Then turning to Kevin and Matthew, she said, "Let's go, boys."

Penny materialized amidst the fray. "I have to pee, too, Mama." She crossed one leg in front of the other, making a convincing case.

"Okay, sweetie." Melanie beckoned to Penny with her hand. "Come on." Did he detect a crack in Melanie's voice? Surely this kind of thing didn't make a woman cry, did it?

Admittedly, operation potty had quickly gotten out of hand. How did Melanie handle getting them to two separate restrooms? He hadn't noticed any family restrooms, though he hadn't looked. "I can take the boys," he said, wanting to help. "I should go anyway."

Melanie smiled but lifted her brows in an *are you serious?* look. "It's the bottom of the ninth. Bases loaded. Are you sure?"

"I'm sure." This had been a long afternoon for Melanie, hardly a relaxing day at the ballpark. Probably one of many long days she'd had over the past year trying to be both mother and father to her children.

Brian got the boys in and out of the restroom with minimal hassle, the huge swath of paper towels Kevin had tugged from the dispenser notwithstanding. The announcer noted two outs now and a pitching change while they waited for Melanie and Penny to emerge from the ladies room.

Kevin gazed up at Brian, his head titled so far back his cap slid back on his head. "How tall are you?"

Brian slapped the bill of Kevin's cap. He stooped to his level. "Taller than you."

Kevin jumped, slapping the bill of Brian's cap. Not to be left out, Matthew got in a swing, knocking Brian's cap to the floor.

Brian bent to retrieve it, slapping both the boys' caps on his way up. They erupted in laughter as Penny and Melanie approached, both wiping their hands on the front of their shorts.

Melanie grinned. "You're good with kids. Very tolerant for someone who's not a parent."

Brian adjusted his cap, settling it evenly on his head. "I can thank my nephews for that, I guess. They broke me in."

A grand slam ended the game the minute they'd returned to their seats, and the stadium echoed with the booming stomp of thousands of feet nearly drowning out the cheers and claps.

The slow march to the exits commenced. Seeing the crush of people and Melanie's repeated anxious glances to make sure her kids were all in tow, Brian swung Penny onto his shoulders. "Where are you parked?"

"Oh, we were late. As usual. So, we're at the far end of the lot." Melanie shifted her purse and grabbed Kevin's hand.

Kevin seemed to be the wildcard of the bunch. Not a bad kid by any means, but the one most likely to wander.

They meandered across the parking lot, weaving in and out between the cars, the sun so hot Brian caught a whiff of tar in the air as it melted beneath their feet. Walking single file in places as they squeezed through narrow spaces, Brian still couldn't manage a conversation with Melanie. Even so, he'd enjoyed the afternoon. Enjoyed this little family. This strong woman who held them all together. Too bad he'd sworn off dating. Probably a good thing that his stupid question as to what she was doing after the game had gone unfinished and unnoticed.

He held tight to Penny's ankles as she shifted on his shoulders. So light, compared to his nephews. Of course, none of them were light when they threw themselves on top of him as they were wont to do. Melanie's less-than-graceful plunge into his lap came to mind. Her pink cheeks and her flustered attempts to get off of his lap. *Off of my lap.*

God wouldn't take him literally. Would He? Dropping her into his lap?

No, God didn't really mean for him to ask her out. Did He? Brian's off-the-cuff remark was meant only to emphasize how done he was with dating.

Finally at their destination, Melanie opened the rear of the van and piled in the gloves, souvenir handbooks, and plastic helmet-shaped cups still stained with a blue Slushie color that Brian deemed to be permanent. Kevin ran small circles around the souvenir bat that his mom had returned to him.

Melanie started the engine, cranked up the air conditioning, then returned to close up the rear.

Brian took a step toward her, heart pounding as he considered what he should say. Should he simply say "goodbye" or suggest the possibility of seeing each other again, outside of baseball? "You got everything—"

A sudden surge of pain came from his groin, doubling him over, leaving him struggling to breathe. He cussed under what little breath he had left, confident he knew the culprit but caring little. *I might die right here, in a fetal ball, at the foot of the woman God may have hand-picked for me.* Was that groan from him? Had to be. When he recovered—*if* he recovered—he was going to track down the marketing whiz whose bright idea it was to hand out bats and shove one up—

"Oh my gosh, Brian, are you okay?" Melanie's words were muffled behind her hands, her eyes wide.

"No." The pain relented enough for embarrassment to flood whatever senses weren't still reeling from the death blow to his genitals. He turned away, propping his hands on his knees and gulping in air.

"Hand me the bat! Now, Kevin." Melanie's stern voice left no room for protest, and Kevin didn't offer any. "You will apologize."

From behind Brian came a contrite, "Sorry, Coach."

Brian waved him off, turning and collecting himself enough to mutter, "Apology accepted" as Kevin ducked into the van.

Seemingly unable to meet Brian's gaze, Melanie stowed the bludgeon that may have ended Brian's dreams of fatherhood into the van, and then buckled Penny into her seat. She slid the side door closed and finally turned to Brian.

"I am *so* sorry. Are you okay?"

"I think I'll live. He has a pretty good swing though."

"You're sure?" Melanie pressed. Her voice had that crackly edge again, like in seconds she might burst into tears.

Brian nodded. "I'm sure."

She cleared her throat. "Well, thanks so much for your help today. I really do appreciate it." She smiled weakly and then bolted toward the driver's side door.

"Wait!" A sudden anxiety more intense than the diminishing pain in his groin gripped Brian. He may not see Melanie again—not with any regularity anyway. Maybe God *had* taken him literally. *Now or never.*

She turned, one hand on the door handle.

"I wondered if we could see each other again sometime. You know, before next baseball season."

She stared for a moment, blinking, and then burst into laughter. Not a chuckle, but a full laugh that bubbled up from her chest, resulting in an unladylike snort. She clamped a hand over her mouth.

Unsure what had made her laugh so hard, Brian's confidence flagged. "I've been turned down before, but no one's actually laughed at me."

"I'm flabbergasted," she managed between laughs. "Kevin whacked you in the . . ." She gestured toward his midsection. "My kid hit you with a baseball bat, and you want to see me again?"

He shrugged. Kids were kids; accidents happened. Not like he'd never whacked anyone with a bat on accident. The image of his sister, her eye a gruesome purplish-blue, came to mind. "I guess I'm a glutton for punishment."

Melanie shook her head. "You're either brave or crazy. I'm not sure which. Either way, yes, it would be nice to see you again before next season."

Matthew pounded on the van window, bellowing, "Mo-om!"

Melanie smiled and tapped the car window with her fist. "My fan club is calling me. You have my number from the team roster, right?" She opened the door, ready to hop in.

She'd said yes. His disavowal of dating had lasted, what, a couple of months? "I can get it from John."

"Good." She slipped into the driver's seat, then turned. "Thanks again." She waved and shut the door.

Brian watched her pull away, wondering if he'd recovered enough to walk to his car, but happy nonetheless.

CHAPTER 6

$\mathcal{B}$rian shifted the car into park beneath a large cottonwood tree that he hoped would shade his car from the brutal late-afternoon sun. A blast of hot but, thankfully, dry air hit him as he exited the car.

Settlers Park, situated at the edge of a couple of 1970s housing developments, remained mostly wooded. Picnic tables and benches dotted the grassy area beyond the parking lot. His gaze snagged on a patch of brown earth where he remembered a playground years back. A smile playing on his lips, he recalled rubbing the metal slide with waxed paper, landing hard on the seesaw when John had jumped off, and hanging—suspended by his feet—from the old-school merry-go-round. He'd lain on his back, his neck hyperextended and hair nearly dragging in the dirt while John spun the wobbly, rusted equipment faster and faster.

He slammed the car door and rounded the car, pulling John and Kate's wicker picnic basket from the trunk. Funny the playground hadn't been replaced with the modern equipment and bed of mulch standard to virtually every open area kids congregated in these days. Less dangerous than what he'd enjoyed as a kid. Less fun, too? He thought so.

Prying open the latch and lifting the lid, Brian checked the picnic basket to be sure he hadn't forgotten anything. Tablecloth, blanket, chicken, macaroni salad, fruit, and lemonade. Wait a second—he shoved aside a plastic grocery bag. There! Marshmallows for roasting on the—

A quick glance to the former playground area confirmed his fear. They'd removed the grill and fire pit too. Dipping his hand in his pocket, he fingered the utility knife he'd brought to carve roasting sticks and sighed, disappointed Melanie's kids would have to eat the sugary treats cold, not melted and gooey, the way God intended.

Minutes after he'd stretched the checkerboard-style cloth over the splintering edges of the table, securing the edges with rocks he'd found nearby, Melanie's van pulled into the lot.

The sliding side door of the van ground open then slid partway back. Kevin darted out, leaving Matthew half-trapped and throwing his weight against the closing door. Before Kevin reached the grass, they'd all exited the van, Penny and Melanie trailing behind the boys. Close-up, Penny's red cheeks and damp forehead indicated the heat better than any thermometer.

"You made it." Brian stopped fiddling with the plastic cups he'd pulled from the basket, his attention drawn by a scraping sound. Penny dragged a plastic lawnmower behind herself, bumping it over a concrete slab. Probably a remnant of the defunct playground.

"You doubted me?" Melanie's voice carried the same happy— was it flirty?—tone he'd heard on the phone when he'd called to arrange the date. *Was* it a date?

She'd pulled her hair up in a short ponytail and wore a pink scoop-necked t-shirt with khaki shorts and tennis shoes. Nothing special, but it suited her. Practical but a little feminine, as evidenced by the little lacy stuff on the shirt trim.

Penny stood alongside an evergreen tree of some type, dragging a stick through drippy sap while her brothers chased an errant Frisbee rolling on its edge in a wide, grassy circle. This was not like any date he'd been on before, that was for sure.

"Can I help?" Melanie's gaze dropped to the basket and containers he'd laid on the table.

"Uh, sure." He shoved the plastic dishes and cutlery to the center of the table and nudged the food in Melanie's direction, suddenly nervous. What if the kids didn't like what he brought? Every kid liked fried chicken, right?

Brian glanced up at the sound of another vehicle rolling over twigs and gravel in the parking lot. He'd hoped they'd have the area to themselves for an hour or so. A gray sedan came to a stop, idling in a parking spot.

Once they'd set the table, Melanie called the kids over to eat.

Kevin swung a leg over the bench and sat, legs swinging as he eyed the meal. "Is this all you got?"

"Kevin," Melanie scolded. "There's plenty of food here that you like." She set a chicken leg on his plate with a scoop of macaroni and a few strawberries.

His freckled nose wrinkled as he shoved himself back on the bench, as far as possible from the offensive food.

"Picky eater?" Brian caught Melanie's gaze and tilted his head in Kevin's direction.

Matthew, obviously *not* a picky eater, scooped more macaroni onto his plate, creating a mound to rival the mashed potato heaps in *Close Encounters of the Third Kind*.

Disappointment crept in as the meal concluded. Brian had only managed to get a few complete sentences out of Melanie, who was preoccupied by Kevin's picking, Matthew's begging for seconds and thirds, and Penny's difficulty in getting food from her plate to her mouth while seated on a bench farther from the table than she was accustomed to.

"Maybe we could all take a walk." Melanie smiled, hope shining in her eyes.

His disappointment dissolved, replaced with shame. What did he expect? Her undivided attention while she tended to three children? And it wasn't as if he didn't like the kids' company.

"A walk sounds perfect. A trail runs down that hill . . ." As he turned in that direction, gesturing toward the woods, he spied the gray car, still there. Still idling. No one getting in or out.

Something about it raised his hackles. He shook off the feeling. *Ridiculous.* People sat in their cars for all sorts of reasons. His sister-in-law had admitted to driving the boys around when they were little just so they'd sleep while she read a novel without interruption.

Twigs snapped beneath Brian's feet as he clomped down a well-worn trail that started along the edge of the grassy area and proceeded deeper into the woods. The boys ran ahead, darting past him where the trail widened.

"Oh, man!" Matthew cried. "Look at this!"

Brian glanced behind him to where Melanie poked along with Penny, who stopped to pick up random leaves, rocks, or flowers.

"Go ahead," Melanie said, motioning him forward. "We'll catch up."

Standing on the far side of a deteriorating log, Matthew held up a garter snake, maybe ten inches long. "Check him out."

Grasping at the snake, Kevin badgered Matthew, "Lemme hold it!"

Matthew twisted away then lowered the snake for Penny to see as she ambled in his direction.

"Matthew," Melanie said, eyeing the reptile with a wary look, "take a look and then put him back where you found him."

The trail took a turn followed by a steep descent.

"Mama!" Penny slipped, her dirty little Crocs offering little traction. A skinned knee resulted in a few minutes of tears and whining, but she perked up when Kevin called from beyond the next switchback.

"There's a crick down here!"

Brian grinned. "Crick" was Pittsburghese for a creek, the focal point of many a local childhood.

The boys scampered ahead and as the water came into view, Melanie grabbed hold of Penny's hand, keeping her at her side. "Boys," she called, "keep a safe distance from the water."

Brian stopped as the ground leveled out and flexed his knees, which had borne the brunt of the last, steepest stretch of trail.

The scent of wildflowers carried on the breeze. Along the creek bank and in shaded spots, purple flowers grew in large clusters. Smaller white flowers poked up between them here and there. "I forgot how pretty it was down here."

Melanie came up behind him. "So, you've been here before?"

Brian nodded. "Rocco and I—he was my beagle—we used to hang out here skipping stones, hunting crayfish, dragging sticks along the water." The blue-brown creek water made gentle riffles in the center where it flowed over a large rock. "One of my favorite places."

Melanie pushed some stray hairs into her ponytail. "I miss those carefree days." She glanced at Penny, who examined a rock at her feet, and the boys standing alongside a large tree trunk near the creek's edge. "I wish my kids could do that. Roam free, like we used to."

Couldn't they? Was the world so different? Or had the culture just exchanged one set of dangers for another, maybe *more* damaging set?

Melanie stood, taking in the scenery, unguarded and relaxed. Her green eyes shone, sharp and pretty, but tired. Maybe not sleepy, but worn. What had the last year of her life been like? Loss, grief, increased responsibilities.

The boys discovered a thick vine hanging from the tree they'd been circling. They tugged on it, testing their weight. It held. "They seem right at home out here. You must spend a lot of time outside."

She turned toward him, smiling. "We try. When David was alive, he took them on short hikes. We used to—"

A splash, then Matthew calling, "Mom! Mom!" drew their attention.

Melanie, her eyes wide, jogged toward the water, pressing Penny behind her as she slipped between brambles and weeds.

Matthew stood at the water's edge, his shoes covered in mud, gesturing at his brother.

Kevin flailed around in the slow-moving current, his chin barely above the water, fear in his eyes. "Help!" His chin slipped beneath the surface as he thrashed the water with wild and frantic movements.

Brian knew this spot. Knew the large protrusion halfway up the southern side of that fat trunk. Knew where a fat muskrat made its home amidst its roots in the water. Knew the approximate depth of the creek. "Kevin, stand up!"

Kevin stared back, his palms slapping the water.

Melanie gripped Brian's forearm. "Brian—"

"Kevin," he called again. "Stand up!"

This time Kevin obeyed. As his shoulders rose above the water, his fearful expression disappeared, replaced by a sheepish smile. He stood, the water barely reaching his waist.

Matthew howled with laughter, pointing at the mud caked to his brother's legs as he trudged toward the shore. Brian bit his lips to keep from laughing, but when Kevin himself chuckled, he lost it.

Melanie's lips twisted, her eyes narrowed and stern. "Out of the water, Kevin Peter." But even her angry-mom look collapsed when Kevin barreled toward her, arms outstretched for a hug.

With a yelp, she backed up, moving Penny in front of her as a shield. "Don't you dare!"

"What do you say we head back up the trail?" Maybe Brian could divert their attention, avoiding the awkward scolding sure to come for Kevin's adventure in the water. He glanced at Melanie. "You ready?"

Melanie's gaze lingered on Kevin another second, and she shook her head and sighed. "Sure. Just thinking of whether I have anything dry for him to sit on in the car."

Brian shrugged. "It's hot. He'll probably dry off on the way back."

"Probably." She seemed to force a smile. "I'm too uptight, aren't I? It's just a little water."

He turned, extending a hand to Penny, who clutched a fistful of wildflowers, and motioned to the boys with the other. "What do I know about kids?"

She pinned him with a look until he buckled.

"Maybe. Just a little?" But his own question reverberated in his brain. What *did* he know about kids? Did he have any business pursuing something with a mother of three young children?

They trudged uphill at a much slower pace than they'd descended. The boys argued as they went.

"The cobra is the most poisonous snake in the world," Matthew insisted. "My friend Mason told me about this video where a cobra kills a mongoose."

"Nuh-uh," Kevin countered, grabbing a tree root to pull himself up a particularly steep stretch. "Black Mamba'll kill ya faster."

Brian panted so hard, he couldn't contribute to the conversation. A glance at Melanie told him she wasn't faring any better. His mind wandered back down the trail to the creek, to Kevin's plunge, and to his own days meandering these woods. To a magazine he found jammed in a tree hollow, crumpled, dirty, and obviously suffering from exposure to the elements. But it didn't stop him from flipping through the pages, transfixed by the images of women. Some semi-clothed. Some not. In retrospect, tame stuff. But at twelve years old, it had been more than enough to fan the flame of what he'd already discovered at home. Decades later, he still wasn't free. Not entirely.

He thought he'd finally killed the impulse that for years hadn't proven a temptation. Apparently, it was merely lying dormant, because lately it had been rearing its ugly head. Ever since he'd stumbled on that vile cache of images at work.

Week by week, he'd been plagued by lurid thoughts more often. First, revulsion at the kiddie porn. Then flashes of the other stuff, the "normal" porn he'd seen. And lately, the urge to seek it out when bored or distracted.

The kids seemed to regain their energy when they crested the hill and went running toward the open area where they'd picnicked. Only their two vehicles remained in the parking lot; the gray sedan had left.

Now what? He'd help her load up the kids and . . . and what? He'd enjoyed the picnic and the hike even though they hadn't managed much conversation. But you didn't have to talk about deep stuff all the time to learn about a person, did you? He learned all sorts of things about Melanie just by watching her care for her children, seeing her gaze at the wildflowers, and hearing that little lilt in her voice that made him think maybe she liked him. At least a little.

Should he mention getting together again or let her take the lead? Give her an easy way out if she wasn't ready.

They'd reached the van, and already she had all the doors open and the air conditioning running. He opened his mouth to speak when she spoke first.

"Would you like to come back to our house for a little while?" She glanced up as the sun continued its westward journey, leaving the sky a dusky purple. "We saw a couple of lightning bugs last night, and I promised the kids could stay up." She shoved more stray hairs into the ponytail. "And you've done such a good job tiring them out, the least I can do is offer you an iced tea or an adult beverage."

Something sparked in his chest. She'd enjoyed the day too. At least enough that she was willing to extend it. The spark died and new questions shot to the surface. Was this good for her? What *did* he know about kids? And this whole porn thing. What if he slipped?

Another glance at her—her hair, her eyes, her courage, the way she loved these kids, and he shoved aside his concerns, burying them beneath his growing attraction to her. "Sure. Lead the way."

CHAPTER 7

The minivan rolled to a stop in front of the house, and Melanie shifted into park, trying to imagine how Brian would view it. Under close examination, would her home —her life!—look more like a cozy refuge spilling over with love and laughter or more a chaotic mishmash of flawed humans held together with a little spit, Elmer's glue, and desperate prayer? Most days, it felt more like the latter.

Modest houses lined either side of their tree-lined street. What light remained slanted across the sky, casting shadows from mature maple trees onto Melanie's brick Cape Cod. In front of the house, dim light crept through the tree cover, mottling the red petunias and yellow marigolds Melanie had planted this past spring. Visible around the side of the garage, decorative aluminum fence marked the perimeter of the back-yard. And, of course, the kids' toys lay scattered in the grass: several large balls, a scooter, and two pool noodles—though they had no pool.

To Melanie, it appeared comfortable and homey, a happy little oasis in a sometimes harsh world. At least that's how it seemed when they were a family of five.

55

The side doors of the van slid open, and Matthew bolted toward the backyard followed by Kevin. Melanie unbuckled Penny and set her on the ground, where she scampered toward the boys. Purse in hand, Melanie stooped and snatched a crumpled fast food bag from the van's floor.

"Need any help?" Brian came up alongside her, hands in his pockets, his face and neck not as red as they'd been in the park, probably thanks to the car's air conditioning.

"I got it." She closed the doors and motioned to where the kids were headed. "There's a couple of chairs beneath the awning in the back. I'll get us something to drink. Wine, beer, iced tea?"

He started toward the backyard, where one of the kids was shout-singing the ABCs. "Whatever you're having."

From the darkened kitchen, Melanie observed the kids climbing up and over a small plastic slide while she retrieved a couple of wine goblets from the back of the cupboard. She poured two glasses, smiling as she recalled Kevin's dip in the creek. Then her smile faded. Was Brian amused by the kids' shenanigans or was he sitting outside trying to formulate a polite way to end their nascent relationship?

Another glance out the window revealed the kids engaged in a game of monkey-in-the-middle sure to leave poor Penny frustrated and angry. Melanie stepped through the backdoor, a blast of heat warming the cool sweat on the back of her neck. She crossed the concrete slab they called "the patio" and handed a glass of red wine to Brian.

"Thank you." He accepted the glass, smiling, his gaze following her as she collapsed into the wrought iron chair. Feet crossed at the ankles, he sat comfortably in the matching chair.

Melanie brought her glass to her lips.

"Ma-ma!" Penny shrieked and ran to her. She must've hit her limit with her brothers' taunts and came crying. Hiccupping between sobs, she pressed her sweaty head into Melanie's lap.

Kevin and Matthew raced over, each tugging at the other's arms as they clambered to reach their mother first. "Mom, we were just playing," Kevin insisted. "We didn't do nothin' to her."

"She's a crybaby," Matthew added, hooking his foot around Kevin's ankle in an attempt to trip him.

Working hard to keep her exasperation in check, Melanie soothed Penny, admonished the boys, and shooed them back into the yard. "Look," she said, trying to infuse her voice with excitement. "The lightning bugs are coming out!" She pointed to the corner of the yard where little yellow bursts illuminated the heavy shadows.

She sighed, leaned back in her chair, and savored a sip of the dry wine.

Brian offered her a sympathetic smile and took a drink from his glass.

"You sure you're up for this?" Then to clarify, she added, "Not just this," motioning toward the yard and the tear-inducing monkey-in-the-middle dust-up, "or even today. Just . . ." She'd started down this road, wanting to give him an easy out and now what? "It's just, you're probably used to being able to complete a thought or a sentence. You live in peace and quiet."

"Yeah." He stared into the yard, a grin playing at the corner of his mouth as Penny's pale limbs shone in the near dark, jumping to capture a lightning bug just out of her reach. "Too much of it." He turned then, his gaze softening. "Hey, I'm still here, aren't I?"

Her heart swelled, grateful for his presence, no matter for how short a time. She'd missed the simple company of another adult. "Yes. Yes, you are." She felt more than saw his gaze still on her.

"You're exhausted."

Laughter bubbled with the wine, so she pressed the back of her hand to her mouth. "Thanks for noticing." She couldn't keep the hint of sarcasm out of her voice. She smoothed the stray hairs matted to her sticky neck, her cheeks still burning from her hike in the heat. She must look a wreck. The evening had worn her out more than it should—an indication that she was sorely out of shape.

"Cute," Brian said, a cheeky grin on his face, "but exhausted."

The compliment—there was one in there, right?—warmed her. "That's my signature look."

Brian uncrossed and crossed his feet as he turned the wine glass in his hands. "Did David help out a lot at bedtime?"

How *good* it was that Brian wasn't afraid to speak his name. Most people wanted to pretend that David never existed. As if there wasn't a giant void in her and her children's lives.

"Honestly? No." She closed her eyes, recalling so many evenings when, worn and tired, she juggled getting the kids settled on her own, resentment escalating with each passing minute. "Not much has changed in that respect. He'd be asleep in the armchair by the time I started wrangling them into bed." She glanced at Brian, mildly uncomfortable with saying anything ill about her deceased husband. To another man of all people. But it was *so good* to talk. "It was a bone of contention between us, but it seems so insignificant now."

Brian nodded, not defending or attacking. Just listening.

The sun had set, the shades of gray fading to near black. Lightning bugs flashed in the dark fringes of the yard along the fence line and beneath the towering oak tree. The kids darted about, laughing and talking excitedly, chasing.

She snuck a peek at Brian and a tingling sensation shot through her core. *Nerves.* She'd barely dated a man besides David, and that was so many long years ago. Yet here she sat, sipping wine with a man, unsure what happened next.

Not brave enough to look him in the eye, she stared into the yard as she spoke. "I feel like a teenager on my first date. Uh, not that I actually dated when I was a teenager, but if I had, this is what I imagine it would've felt like." She felt his gaze on her but kept her attention fixed straight ahead, a bundle of both nerves and embarrassment.

He laughed. "Nervous?"

"A little." She chanced a glance from the corner of her eye.

His posture and his voice both reflected his relaxed state. He must think her crazy. "Well, I probably have enough dating experience for the both of us."

She glanced again, long enough to catch his smile.

His voice softened to a near-whisper. "And you can rest easy. I'm not going to try to kiss you tonight."

Her cheeks heated and her pulse hammered. *Worse* than a teenager!

Brian grinned, seeming to take pleasure in her discomfort. With a twinkle in his blue eyes, he leaned in, "No matter if I want to or not."

Uncertain if he was serious or messing with her, "Oh," was all she knew to say.

He laughed. Yep. Messing with her. "I can't tell if you're relieved or disappointed."

She ran a hand along her hair, stuffing some stray pieces into the ponytail. "I don't know what I am."

Serious now, Brian said, "You're a busy woman with a lot of responsibility. One who's long overdue for a little fun and relaxation."

"No argument there." She sipped her wine, wishing the alcohol would settle her jitters.

"Maybe I can help a little with that." He glanced at the dark sky and then her kids, still intent on catching as many lightning bugs as possible. "I'd better go." He handed her the wine glass and stood. "How does miniature golf sound?"

Despite her love of miniature golf, Melanie's thoughts went immediately to the kids swinging metal clubs at weeds, pint-sized windmills, and one another. And still she heard herself say, "It sounds good."

And then he left her to corral her children, clean them up, and tuck them in. Most nights, fatigue and drudgery weighed her down, making the task burdensome. But tonight her steps and her mood felt feather light. Hope flickered in time with the lightning bugs now scaling the inside of an old jelly jar. Her date had that effect on her.

$\mathcal{M}$atthew skipped backwards, facing Brian, rambling about his latest video game conquest and tripping over the brick edging into the eighteenth green. Behind them, Kevin frog-hopped over Penny, who lay prostrate on the artificial grass, peering into the hole to see where her golf ball had gone.

Melanie collected their putters and laid them on the golf shack's counter in a rainbow array: red, orange, yellow, green, and blue. Why did it feel so good to control the little things? Maybe because the big things were beyond her control and wildly out of whack.

She turned, her gaze flickering over the mini-golf course. Colorful flowers lined the putting greens, water trickled from a miniature waterfall, and birds sung from the trees shading the course. A surprisingly beautiful scene in the evening light.

Brian held the paper scorecard in hand, totaling their scores with a miniature pencil. "Uh, let's just call it a win, shall we?" He shot Melanie a look, humor dancing in his eyes.

"What's wrong, Coach? Your mental math skills rusty?" Had

anyone even counted Penny's strokes as she whapped the ball out of the water, sand, or beds of pebbles?

"Something like that," Brian muttered, doing a double-take at the teen who just appeared in the golf shack to collect the clubs and pencils.

Curious, Melanie glanced in the shack. A girl, maybe fifteen years old, snapped her bubble gum and re-aligned the returned clubs according to height. Her snug pink t-shirt with shimmery gold lettering caught Melanie's eye. "Porn Star," it read, the *A* replaced with a star.

A pang of sadness sobered Melanie as she turned and guided her children to the parking lot. Who let their daughter out of the house wearing *that*? Did she have any idea what kind of attention she was inviting?

Melanie turned her own attention to the parking lot, where her kids shuffled through the gravel toward their van. The golf game could be considered a success. The kids had fun, no property was destroyed, only two balls were lost, and—praise Jesus—Kevin hadn't aimed his club at Brian's crotch.

They slipped single file between the cars, Melanie's hand around Penny's and her gaze glued to Kevin. Passing through the first row of cars, Brian came up alongside her.

"Is it okay if I buy them ice cream?" His hand grazed her back as it had earlier when he'd ushered her ahead of him. Like before, a small jolt of pleasure accompanied his touch.

"Only if you're buying for me too." She hoped he took it with the humor she intended, not like she was trying to bleed the guy dry after he'd already sprung for a round of golf.

The boys, who were out front, were within a couple yards of the van when a car, seemingly out of nowhere, barreled toward them—too fast for a small parking lot.

Her heart hammered in her chest. "Boys! Move!" Melanie yelled. Where had the car come from?

Matthew grabbed Kevin's hand, pulling him to safety.

Rather than stopping, the gray sedan sped up, pebbles flying from beneath its tires. An elderly gentleman crossing the lot with a couple of school-age children in tow waved his fist as the car rolled by.

Brian jogged ahead, meeting the boys at the back of the van. "You okay?" he asked, guiding them toward the side door.

Kevin, oblivious to his brush with danger, examined a handful of pebbles then pitched them into the grass.

"Yeah. That guy was goin' too fast, don't ya think?" Matthew said.

"Yeah, he was." Brian scanned the parking lot, as if searching for the gray car.

"Way too fast." Melanie's hand shook as she used her key fob to open the van's doors. "Please don't get so far ahead, okay, boys? You're short, and drivers can't see you."

Matthew nodded, but Kevin stooped for more pebbles.

Brian set a hand on each of Kevin's shoulders. "Got that, buddy? Stick close to me or your mom, okay?"

The sun slipped behind the treetops as they rolled down Melanie's street forty minutes later, well sated by chocolate soft serve ice cream. Brian's car sat alongside the curb in front of her house, where they'd left it.

Melanie turned to Brian as she shut off the vehicle, a grin slipping at how his legs were crammed against the dashboard due to the positioning of Penny's car seat behind him.

"I'll help get them in," Brian said, "if that's okay." He carefully unfolded his long legs, stepped onto the sidewalk, and released the kids from the rear of the van.

"Mama, Mama, Mama," Penny whined. "I'm thirsty." She sounded as if she'd returned from an expedition in the Sahara, not a treat at the local ice cream shop, but ice cream always did make her thirsty.

They piled into the kitchen, and before Melanie could set her purse down, Penny pulled on her Capri pants pleading,

"Can I have cold water?" Short on patience, it seemed the kids could never allow her a second to get in the door before they asked for something.

"I'll get it." Brian grabbed a sturdy pink princess cup and lid from the dish rack. He turned on the tap and ran his fingers under the water, checking the temperature. After a few seconds, he filled the cup, turned off the water and screwed on the spouted lid. A steady drip continued to trickle from the spigot even after he'd pushed the handle firmly down. "Here, Penny." He squatted at her level and smiled, handing her the cup.

"T'ank you." Penny snatched it from his hand and galloped toward the living room, where one of the boys had started a videogame. *Without permission.*

Melanie glanced at the wall clock, considering how long she should allow them to play and how long Brian intended to stay. He'd said he'd help her in—

"Your faucet's leaky." Brian's voice came from behind her, near the sink, his tone matter-of-fact.

With seldom enough quiet to hear a perpetual drip, Melanie hadn't given the leak much thought. "Oh, yeah. It's one of many little chores on a very long but growing list. There's also an intermittent leak under the sink, the toilet runs on humid days, the fluorescent light in the basement takes a minute to come on . . ." She ticked off the jobs on her fingers, sure she'd need as many hands as an octopus had tentacles to count them all. "I need to knuckle down and learn some new skills or pay a handyman to do it."

Ambling to the sink, she moved a few stray dishes from the countertop to the sink basin, suddenly hyperconscious of her home's appearance.

Brian surveyed the room, hands on his hips, as if searching for other obvious malfunctions. He wouldn't be able to spot the cabinet with the loose hinge, the dirty coils in the rear of the refrigerator, or the hole in the window screen above the kitchen sink.

"I'm fairly handy with tools, thanks to working on the stage crew for spring musicals in high school." She heard herself prattling on but couldn't seem to stop herself. "My mechanical ability is lacking though. And forget about plumbing and electricity." She really should call a handyman. Grieving or not, she shouldn't have let the house deteriorate the way she had.

"How 'bout you get your list together," Brian said, "and I'll come over Saturday with my tools and see what I can get done." He scanned the ceiling—as if he expected it to cave in on them?

"Oh. I wasn't trying to con free work out of you." Melanie turned her back to the sink, her fingers itching to twist the ring that was no longer there.

Brian's gaze dropped to her face. "I know." He turned in a slow circle, looking over the rest of the kitchen.

She felt naked, her culinary unmentionables exposed for his perusal.

He smiled, oblivious to her discomfort. "I'm volunteering."

"Well . . ." It wouldn't be taking advantage if he offered, would it? She'd been putting these things off. And, it would save money. "Okay. If you're sure."

"I'm sure." He stuffed his hands in the front pockets of his khaki shorts. "I oughta go so you can put them to bed, huh?" He sauntered toward the door, seeming reluctant to leave.

If he was reluctant, she was doubly so. They'd hardly had a chance to talk over wayward golf balls and dribbling ice cream cones. "I guess so."

He stopped at the threshold and faced her. After a moment's hesitation, he rubbed her bare arm, and his gaze drifted to her lips.

Melanie's heart sailed up into her throat. *Kiss me . . . No, don't kiss me.*

With a final pat to her arm, he turned and let himself out onto the porch. "Goodnight."

She flicked the porch light switch absently—futile, since it no longer worked—then stepped out behind him into the warm night air, the lightning bugs flashing again beneath the trees now that the sun had set. "Thank you. We had fun."

"Me too." He trotted down the steps then turned back again. "See ya' Saturday morning, okay?"

She nodded and stood, watching him get into his car. As the white sedan rolled down the street, she closed her eyes and tilted her head up. The warm breeze whisked a few stray hairs across her face. She inhaled deeply, catching a whiff of someone's late evening barbeque.

Maybe if she could string together a few of these quiet moments, she could make sense of the wild turns her life had taken. Brian was an unexpected delight. Gentlemanly, good with her kids, handsome. But something kept her from relaxing in his company. Was it jitters or something deeper? Could she welcome him into her life, and her kids' lives? David's death had shattered her trust on so many levels.

She let herself back into the house, the storm door smacking loudly behind her. Had he noticed the pneumatic pump was broken?

Her heart rate settled as she considered her next tasks: wrestling the kids into their pajamas and tucking them into bed. And that "honey do" list that had been languishing for lack of a honey.

CHAPTER 9

Melanie's eyes flew open. Faint light crept in at the edge of the window shade, casting a dull glow on the foot of her bed. A pink cowgirl hat, Nerf gun, and several Hot Wheels cars lay scattered on her covers. She closed her eyes and soaked in the glorious silence. For all of three seconds. This mama had been conditioned for nonstop noise. She pushed back the covers and crawled to the end of the bed, shoving the hat and odd assortment of toys onto the floor as she reached beneath the shade. She unfastened the window lock and slid the pane up, making sure the screen stayed in place. The sun inched above the horizon, coloring the sky a dusky purplish orange.

Birdsong drifted in with fresh morning air. Melanie breathed deeply, let the shade flap over the open window and crawled back into bed. What had roused her so early on a Saturday morning? Her disappointment at lost sleep faded as she considered what she'd gained: a few private moments to rest, pray, and think.

With her head propped comfortably on her pillow, she made the sign of the cross. Attempting to center herself, she breathed deeply. What had her life become? She scanned the master bedroom, trying to look at it as if she hadn't seen it nearly every day for the past decade. The eggshell paint had grown dingy and dirty where the kids lay on the bed and pressed their feet against the wall. The mismatched furniture sported varying colors of stain and hardware. A children's dresser, David's from his childhood home, sat alongside the closet, nearly empty save for a drawer of old photos and mementos she didn't know where to store. Her larger dresser sat next to it, several strips of veneer missing and the round mirror above it cloudy in places. A large wedding portrait, she and David beneath a white gazebo, hung on the wall.

Her stomach clenched and her chest tightened. She patted the empty side of the bed then grabbed the pillow and squeezed it to her face. All traces of him, even his scent, gone. For months after his death, she washed her hair using his shampoo, soaking in its masculine scent at night as tears mingled with her wet hair on his pillow.

The bed remained the only furniture in the room they'd purchased together. Sturdy, comfortable. The bed where Matthew, Kevin, and Penny had all been conceived.

A warm, secure feeling enveloped her and Brian came to her mind. He'd sat beside her outside the ice cream shop, looking summery and sporty and oh-so handsome in shorts and a blue polo shirt that matched his eyes. He'd pretended to devour Penny's cone, spurring a fit of giggles. With a huge smile, he'd caught Melanie's gaze and winked. She shook her head to stop that train of thoughts. What subconscious associations had her mind made to bring her so quickly from conceiving babies to him?

She'd grown to care for Brian. A lot. How long had it been since she felt this way about a man? Had she *ever* felt this way at all?

At this stage in her life, she'd never expected to feel the giddy pleasure his presence induced. Of course, she'd never expected to be single again at thirty-four with three small children. Melanie rolled onto her side and sighed. Whether it was "too soon" or not, Brian made her feel more alive than she had felt in a long, long time.

Death had ended her marriage to David, and sooner or later, she had to move on. For her sake and her children's. Her gaze drifted back to the wedding portrait. So why did her attraction to Brian, despite its sweetness, smack of betrayal? The tension had played out at her door the other night as her desires ping-ponged between "kiss me" and "don't kiss me."

She set the pillow aside and glanced up at the crucifix hanging above the bed. With what felt like heroic effort, she slid from the bed onto her knees and closing her eyes, recalled her favorite morning prayer.

A bed creaked on the other side of the wall in the boys' room. In seconds, one or both boys would be in her bed, either bouncing or snuggling close for a cuddle. She considered the rest of the day and her pulse quickened at the thought of Brian's arrival later in the morning. He might only be there to make some minor repairs, impelled by a sense of pity.

But maybe not.

* * *

BRIAN LIFTED HIS HAND, ready to depress the doorbell button, then hesitated. Somewhere on the other side of Melanie's front door, a child screeched, "I hate you!" A series of whacks or stomps followed, and Brian counted to ten, allowing the vitriol to dissipate before making his grand entrance. The morning sun warmed his back as he pressed the doorbell and stepped back, glancing at the potted red geraniums on either side of the door. A glance upward revealed no bulb in the outdoor light fixture, only cobwebs. Broken or just neglected?

He shifted his tool bag to the opposite hand. Should he ring the bell again or give her another minute? There hadn't been a second blood-curdling scream, so either the offender had been silenced or the issue resolved.

As he raised his hand to the bell again, the door swung open. Melanie pushed open the storm door with one hand and rubbed a knuckle beneath her eye with the other. Had she been crying?

"Uh, good morning?" He stepped across the threshold, inhaling what smelled like pancakes or waffles with syrup.

"You heard that, huh?" Melanie closed the door behind him. "Kid's got a set a lungs, I'll give him that."

She walked ahead of him, toward the kitchen, her white anklet socks gliding over the hardwood floor. Beneath a long, white tunic-style t-shirt, she wore those stretchy, clingy black pants women liked so much. He wasn't opposed to them himself.

Inside the kitchen, he set his tool bag on the floor. As he stooped, he caught a glimpse of Penny under the table. She peered out between the chair legs, a ratty brown stuffed bear hugged to her chest.

"Hey, Miss Penny. How's it goin'?"

She stretched her legs in front of her, the hole in the toe of her purple-and-orange-striped tights showing. "Okay."

Seated at the table, Kevin swirled syrup around his empty plate with a fork then lowered his head to lick it.

Melanie whisked the dish out from under his nose. "You're done, buddy."

Based on his conspicuous absence and the loud stomping coming from overhead, Brian guessed Matthew to be the hater. Melanie was used to those kinds of outbursts, wasn't she? He hadn't glimpsed a smile from her yet though.

She stood with her arms folded, her back to the sink. A batter-splattered mixing bowl and wooden spoon sat behind her on the counter.

"Hey." He touched her elbow, speaking softly. "You okay?"

Her lips turned up, but the happiness didn't reach her eyes. "Yeah. Sure. Let me get my list for you. There's coffee on the counter if you'd like some." She pushed off the sink and disappeared into the dining room.

Kevin slid from his chair and shuffled to a brightly-colored plastic tool box Brian hadn't noticed before. "Okay if I help?"

Brian grinned. "Sure. I could use an assistant."

Melanie returned and handed him a narrow, lined piece of paper. Her neat, precise writing filled most of the page with the odd jobs she was either unable or unwilling to tackle.

Brian knocked off the simplest tasks first: loose hinge, childproof latches, busted switch plate cover, running toilet, leaky faucet. He saved the kitchen drain trap for last. Melanie had piled the pans, bowls, and cleaning supplies normally stored under the sink in a cardboard box. Lying on his back, he scooted beneath the sink basin.

"Okay, Kevin. I need you to shine that flashlight right here." He tapped the metal trap that he guessed to be the culprit.

Squirming into the other side of the kitchen cabinet, Kevin waved the heavy flashlight wildly, blinding Brian twice before aiming the light in the right spot.

"Perfect." Brian checked for signs of a leak then slid his fingers over the trap. Some corrosion around the back confirmed his suspicions.

Kevin sneezed—probably from the cleanser odor that permeated the cabinet—and the light swung wildly, blinding Brian a third time. "I deed a tissue."

The flashlight clunked to the cabinet base and Kevin scurried away. Brian waited a minute for his return. The high-pitched sounds of a cartoon beckoned from the next room, where Penny watched TV. And, he suspected, now Kevin. Plumbing repairs couldn't compete with Netflix.

Brian flicked the flashlight off. Just as well, considering Brian's eyes still hadn't refocused.

Black shimmery pants came into view, and Brian grinned. *New assistant!* Much prettier than the last.

Melanie set a pile of syrup-coated dishes in the sink and tapped his shin with her foot. "So, you keep coming back. Makes me wonder."

"Wonder what?" He shifted his position. Maybe he didn't need the flashlight after all.

"Do you pity us, or is it something else?"

Brian tried loosening the slip nuts by hand. "Definitely something else."

Melanie shuffled to the table and back, probably carting more dishes or silverware. "So, you sure you're not just doing a good deed here, helping a poor widow and her children?"

Is that what she thought? He slid out of the cabinet, careful not to whap his head.

Melanie stood twisting the nonexistent ring on her left hand. Her eyes—a little glassy—and her meek tone . . . How had he missed this vulnerability? He'd noticed her strength, how she kept it all together despite the ups and downs of daily life, but he'd overlooked the insecurity and fear lurking beneath the surface.

"I'm here because I want to be. It'd be nice to say I'm here to help and that's it, but . . . that wouldn't be true." He reached for a pair of pliers. "I like you. I like your kids. You're not a charity case, and I'm not here to earn my do-gooder badge." He slid back under the sink and loosened the slip nuts.

A few beats of silence passed as he removed the washers.

"Thank you." Soft and sincere.

His heart swelled with emotion that he swallowed, refocusing on his task. "Hand me the bucket?"

She pushed a small red bucket into the space Kevin had occupied.

He dropped the leaky trap in the bucket. A blob of dirty sludge dripped from the drain onto the shoulder of his white t-shirt. Using a rag Melanie had given him, he tried to wipe it away, merely smearing it in the process.

Brian grabbed the new trap and fit it into place. "Besides, I don't like the idea of some brawny handyman comin' in here, checkin' you out."

Laughter bubbled above him. *Finally. Made her smile.*

"You've not met Mr. Palmer. Mid-sixties, greasy comb-over, serious case of plumber's crack."

Smiling with satisfaction, he bent his knees and twisted to tighten the washers on the new trap. His t-shirt crept above his waist, the cool air brisk against his warm skin.

Melanie cleared her throat. "Uh, do you need me here? 'Cause I can—"

"Yeah. Run the water for a minute, will you?"

Water flowed down the drainpipe and not onto Brian's head. *Good. Got it right.*

"You can turn it off. I wanna show you something here though." He grabbed the bucket and set it on the kitchen floor, shoving it out of the way with the tip of his boot.

Melanie sat on the floor beside him then ducked her head and lay back, brushing something from her eye. "Cozy under here." She gave him a shy smile.

He was pretty confident he'd solved her problem, but if it leaked again, he wanted her to know what might be causing it. He handed her the flashlight, and without being told, she switched it on and aimed it in the right direction, sparing his vision.

"Your trap had a leak, so I replaced it. But see this?" He pointed to the old copper water lines behind the sink basin. "See the green? Corrosion. Looks like there's been a leak, but feel this." He took her hand, so soft and small in his, directed it to the pipe, and slid her hand along the cool, relatively smooth surface. "Bone dry."

Did his voice just crack? Without turning his head, he glanced sideways.

She stared straight up, eyes on the basin above her, not the pipe. Her chest rose and fell a beat or so faster than he would've expected. His gaze lingered a half-second, his whole body heating. She lay in a perfect position for him to ogle her curves. Not his intention, but . . .

He forced his gaze back to the copper pipe, suddenly aware of how he still gripped her hand. What was his problem, anyway? Somehow he'd managed to turn a simple household repair into a near-sexual encounter. *Pathetic, Perella.*

He released her hand and slid out of the cabinet. "So, if it starts to leak again—"

His head smacked the cabinet frame, pain shot through his forehead, and he cursed.

Ducking his head out, he sat up and rubbed his temple. "Sorry." At least the kids weren't in earshot.

She emerged from the other side and folded her legs beneath her, her hand hovering over his forehead, seemingly afraid to touch it. "Ouch. You okay?"

"Yeah. Uh, so, if you see evidence of a leak, you may need a real plumber—your comb-over guy—to replace that line."

He didn't know if his collision with the cabinetry left a red mark, but he was fairly certain his cheeks flushed red. Probably best that he gather his tools and get out. What the heck was he doing, guiding her hand along that pipe? In an instant, a scene flashed in his mind. Some stupid porn movie he'd watched in his college dorm room about a lonely woman and a handyman. Shame burned in his chest and he cringed, generating a string of excuses to leave. Pronto.

Melanie stood, dusting dirt from her shirt and pants. "You want to stay for dinner?" She reached for her ring finger, then dropped her hands. "It's spaghetti with jarred sauce, nothing special, but it's the least I can do to thank you."

If she was as embarrassed as he was, she didn't let on. Maybe her brain wasn't as twisted as his, and she hadn't made the connection he had. Or she'd pretend it hadn't happened. Besides, he wasn't looking forward to spending the evening at home alone. Not when the privacy and boredom might tempt him to indulge in old, bad habits.

The temptation seemed to multiply, day by day over the past several months. *Just a few videos. Just to get it out of your system.* That voice. The one he thought he'd permanently silenced. It nagged him.

"Well, if you're sure? I mean, I don't want to intrude on your family time."

She shook her head, her smile saying his decision pleased her. "Not at all. Let me repay you."

Brian breathed a sigh of relief. Maybe he'd overreacted. With God's help, he'd conquered this demon. He'd been absolved of his sins. And temptation wasn't a sin. God had brought Melanie into his life. His attraction to her was good, innocent.

So why did he feel like the sludge that'd poured out of that drain?

CHAPTER 10

*B*rian hid his grin behind a paper napkin. Kevin, the proclaimed picky eater of the bunch, shoved spaghetti into his mouth by the forkful, slurping up noodles dangling from his mouth. "Picky eater, huh?"

Melanie glanced up from wiping Penny's face and rolled her eyes. "One of his favorites. He could eat it every night."

The kids proved to be an effective distraction from Brian's discomfort and embarrassment. That and Melanie's careful avoidance or ignorance of whatever had happened under the sink. Her sincere gratitude for his repairs left him satisfied that he'd done something good and worthwhile. He'd made a difference by lightening her load.

Once the last dinner dish had been cleared from the table and every errant meatball cleaned from the floor, Brian figured he'd head out. But Melanie dangled an enticing carrot in front of her little brood.

She glanced at her watch. "If the living room is clean in ten minutes—that means no toys on the floor, everything in its place—you can watch a movie."

The ensuing whorl of activity reminded Brian of the

animated Tasmanian devil, whirring through the room and depositing stray LEGOs in bins, blocks in a basket, and crayons in a plastic container.

Closer inspection would reveal some papers shoved beneath the couch, a superhero cape between the couch cushions, and what looked like a miniature shrunken head dangling from the ceiling fan. Apparently, it satisfied Melanie, because she hit play on last summer's animated blockbuster.

For the first time since he'd met them, the kids sat perfectly still, their small bodies pressed together in the center of the couch. Their faces, while wiped clean, still held a tinge of orange around their mouths. Penny burrowed into Matthew's side, and he absentmindedly swung an arm around her.

Brian leaned against the living room entryway, a deep sense of longing striking him square in the chest. He didn't tolerate these kids, he *cared* about them. Their exaggerated injuries, their crocodile tears, their hard-won accomplishments. Even their stupid knock-knock jokes.

"I'll be on the front porch if you need me, guys." Melanie stepped in front of the screen, demanding a response.

"Okay, Mom." Matthew removed his arm from Penny, shoving her off his side.

Seeming satisfied that at least one child would know her whereabouts, Melanie returned to the kitchen. "I thought we could sit outside. I've got ninety-six minutes of electronic babysitting, so we might as well take advantage of it." She removed a large glass pitcher with flowers painted on it from the refrigerator. "How about a glass of lemonade?"

"Sure." While she poured two glasses, he glanced at his still-dirty clothes. Dirt and an unidentifiable stain smeared the hem. He hadn't planned on staying and wished he at least had a clean shirt.

He followed Melanie to the porch and the wooden glider that sat at the far end. Sunlight slanted through the trees, the huge, orange ball making its descent to the western horizon. Temperatures had cooled following an afternoon rain shower, but the air remained heavy with humidity. A dog barked and children shouted from a yard on the opposite side of the street.

Brian sat and held the glider steady for Melanie. She'd changed into a blue and white peasant blouse before dinner, still with the clingy pants. Light makeup and some jewelry made him even more self-conscious about his current state. He flicked away crusty, rusty debris caked to his jeans.

Inching the glider back and forth, Brian sipped the tart lemonade and gazed beyond the front yard to the street. Car doors slammed, and three teenage girls stepped onto the side-walk, hunched over their phones and giggling as they ambled toward a split-level house. He stretched his arm across the back of the glider, careful to keep the condensation on his glass from dripping on Melanie's back.

"I can't seem to scare you off." Something about Melanie's statement seemed somber, resigned. Maybe disappointed.

He stopped moving his feet and the glider slowed. "Do you want to?"

She shook her head and set her glass on the porch rail. "No." With her stocking feet, she gave a little shove, sending the glider into motion again. "This is just unexpected . . . and confusing . . . and complicated."

Yes to all three. And yet, to Brian anyway, it seemed worth exploring. Despite her grief, the children, and his personal struggles, he couldn't help thinking this relationship was a God-ordained thing. He felt it in his gut.

"What can I do to make it easier?"

She rested her hand on his knee, despite the filth. "You're doing it." She caught his gaze and held it. "You're patient. With me. With the kids."

Happily, patience was a virtue that came naturally to him. Chastity on the other hand . . .

"There is one thing though." Melanie fiddled nervously with the silver bangles on her wrist. A substitute for the wedding band maybe?

"Let's hear it."

"I don't want you to misunderstand. My children like you. A lot. And I don't have any reservations about your influence on them. Not one."

But you might. If you knew my history. He stifled that fruitless line of thinking. "I sense a 'but.'"

"But . . ." She smiled up at him. "I don't want them to be hurt if it doesn't work out between us."

He nodded, understanding her concern. "So, you don't want them to get attached to me."

Her brow wrinkled. "It sounds harsh when you say it, but, no I don't want them to get attached. Not yet, anyway."

For his part, that ship had sailed. He'd already committed to heart Penny's chubby cheeks and hands, Kevin's adventurous bent, and Matthew's thoughtful manner. But the wisdom in Melanie's desire was obvious.

"So, where does that leave us?"

"Late evening dates? Once they're asleep?" She peered up at him. "I'm not opposed to the occasional babysitter. It just gets expensive. And it's not like you can't *ever* see them. I'd just like to see you—" She clapped a hand over her mouth.

Brian grinned. "See me what?"

Her cheeks red, she pushed the ground harder, making the glider move faster. "I'm being presumptuous." She jangled her bracelets again.

"About?" She was going to make him pull it out of her. And he would.

She shrugged, her eyes downcast. "I'd like to see you often. I'd like to have adult conversations, like this one, without the constant interruptions." She shifted, turning toward him. "I want to *know* you."

He chewed the inside of his lip, struck by her simple admission. "I want to know you too." He tempered the growing emotion in his chest with a last gulp of lemonade. "I guess that's kind of tough when the conversation revolves around potty reports, disciplinary action, and video games."

Melanie chuckled. "Yep. And, I-I've been hiding behind the kids. A little. Maybe."

Wanting to curl his arm around her shoulder, he transferred his empty glass to the floor and moved his arm from the back of the glider.

"I've had a hard time believing that you want to spend time with a boring, suburban mom of three. It's a bit scary."

"Believe it, Melanie," he said, squeezing her shoulder.

"I'm trying. Living alone with small children hasn't done much to refine my social skills." She smirked. "But I promise not to tell any fart jokes."

He laughed. "I'll hold you to that."

"Are you *sure* you're up for this?"

With a boot firmly planted to the porch floor, he stopped the glider's motion. Turning toward her, he placed a hand on each of Melanie's shoulders and looked her square in the eyes. There would be no doubt. "I'm sure. And if I change my mind, you'll be the first to know."

She smiled, delight brightening her green eyes. "Good enough." She glanced at her wristwatch. "We still have some time. So . . ." She crossed her legs beneath her as if settling in for a long conversation. Her tone shifted to sassy. "I'm curious how a gentleman such as yourself, who likes kids so much, has never been married."

"Short answer? Haven't found the right woman." Haven't or hadn't? He may have botched the tense.

"But you've done a lot of looking. You said you've dated a lot."

Brian ran a hand through his hair, dismayed that bits of

something fell from it. "Too much but not enough, I guess." He shrugged. "Lots of first dates. A couple relationships that lasted longer."

"Tell me about those."

He glanced sidelong at Melanie, who apparently meant it when she said she wanted to know him. "Okay. So, there was Becky. That lasted six months or so. Don't know how. The only thing on her mind was marriage. I met the requirements: single, heterosexual, and nonviolent. You know what obsequious means?"

"Not sure. Like, fawning all over you?"

He tapped his nose. "Yup. I was a means to an end. So I ended it."

Melanie giggled. "And the other relationship?"

"Abby." He rubbed his chin. "Not obsequious." He'd loved Abby. Or thought he did. "We wanted different things. She didn't foresee marriage—as in ever. So, we parted ways."

"I'm sorry."

He shook his head. "Don't be. She married some other dude within eight months of our breakup."

Her eyes widened. "Ouch." The bangles jangled again. "All the other dates?"

"Nothing to tell." Was she fishing for something in particular? Did she think he'd done more than just *date* them? "First dates that became last dates, mostly."

That seemed to satisfy her. If she wanted to know more, she'd ask. Or so he guessed. He might be the only guy his age left who was still technically a virgin. Though he and Abby had tested those limits. And then there were all the *other* women, the digitized ones who remained readily available, uncomplicated, and didn't require anything of him. Shame pooled in his gut. Time to change the subject.

"What about you?"

"Me?" She waved her hand dismissively. "Only David."

He waited, not willing to prod her but hoping she'd say more.

"Only guy I dated. I chose to love him." Curious choice of words. And funny that she stared straight ahead. Almost disconnected from the subject.

"You *chose* to?"

She nodded. "Yeah. He embodied all the qualities I was looking for. The big important stuff: good character, faithful, devout. All of it. I did love him. I miss him." She swiped a hand across her face. Crying?

Brian slowed the glider. "Hey. You okay?"

She nodded and rested a hand on his knee. "I feel . . . I-It's hard to talk about now that he's gone. But it's all here." She tapped her heart with her free hand. "Trapped."

He slid his hand atop hers, stroking her bare ring finger, the skin a little paler where her wedding band had been.

"I never let on . . . to anybody." She laughed, not a humorous laugh but more a laugh of disbelief. "Maybe not to myself even. Love is a decision, right? Times get tough and you choose. Because it's the right thing to do, but I think, too, because once upon a time, your heart chose for you. Y'know?"

"I think so." He squeezed her hand, certain now that he'd seen a tear or two. Beyond the porch, the sun had almost sunk beneath the horizon, casting long shadows over the front yard.

"I skipped that part with the heart. I didn't think there would be anyone else. That if I let David go, I'd never find anyone else that had all those qualities. So, I held on. I loved him." She slid her hand from his and wiped her cheek, giving him a sad smile, maybe to let him know she was okay with it. "I never felt gooey about him."

He couldn't stop the chuckle. "Gooey? Like fudge brownie filling?"

She laughed. "Yep. I thought I could forego gooey. And I did. I led with my head and not my heart."

Brian considered the analogy. "Well, you can make brownies without the fudge."

"You can. And they're pretty darn delicious."

The glider came to a stop, each of them apparently too distracted to push.

Melanie stood and walked toward the steps, hugging her arms to her chest. "But I missed the gooeyness. Isn't that ridiculous?"

Nah. Not at all The gooeyness was the best part. But it sounded like she knew that already.

She turned to him. "Thanks for letting me get that out. I'm a little short on friends. Everyone's so busy with their own family." One more wipe, and the tears disappeared.

Brian met her at the steps, unsure how to comfort her. His gaze dropped to her lips and a surge of heat rose in him. But her eyes. Something there reminded him of a frightened rabbit. No kisses tonight.

Slow and with great care, he pulled her to him, encircling her in his arms and pressing her head to his shoulder. On the side *without* the sludge, because that wasn't the kind of goo she needed.

She relaxed into him, her arms wrapping around his back. "Thank you," she murmured.

For what, he wasn't sure, but no more needed to be said. This moment, together, was enough.

Tires squealed from the street, and she broke his hold on her, searching the street for the source.

A gray sedan sped from in front of her neighbor's house toward the main road.

"Wow. Must be in a hurry," Melanie said.

Something about the car struck him as familiar. Where had he seen it? "Neighbors of yours?"

"No." She shook her head. "I don't think so. An older man lives there, alone. He drives a big blue car."

Where had he seen that car before? Moving fast, just like that. He didn't want to worry Melanie unnecessarily, but a memory nagged at him. That car . . .

On her tiptoes, Melanie peered through the porch window into the living room. "Credits are gonna roll in a minute. I've got to go." She slid the bangles up her arm and let them fall. "Thanks for everything. For all the work you did and for tonight. For listening."

"No thanks necessary. You paid me in food." He smiled. "And I'm happy to listen. Always."

He'd pulled out and rolled toward the stop sign before he remembered. The gray car. It looked like the one in the mini-golf lot. The one that had nearly clipped Kevin.

CHAPTER 11

Hand gliding along the banister, Melanie hurried down the stairs and rounded the newel post on her way to the kitchen. A reflection outside caught her attention and she stopped and peered out the window. Her heart pattered either from nervousness or the mad rush to get ready. Probably both.

Brian's car sat in the driveway, a dull white in the evening light. He sat in the driver's seat, running a hand through his hair, primping in the visor mirror. He tightened the knot on his necktie, all spiffed up—for her!

A strange tingling sensation started in her stomach.

Brian flipped the visor up.

Melanie jumped. "I'm late, I'm late, I'm late," she murmured.

She raced into the kitchen, skidding in her stockings. Shoes, purse—oh, she needed to get something going for dinner!

Hannah, the babysitter, leaned against the kitchen counter, staring at her phone. Seeing Melanie, she slipped it into the rear pocket of her jeans. "Wow. You look great, Mrs. Lombardi."

Melanie yanked open the cabinet under the sink and snatched a saucepan. She glanced at Hannah as she straightened. "Huh? Oh. Thank you." She ran a hand over the silver pendant resting on her chest and smoothed the front of her black dress. Cinched at the waist with a full skirt, it remained a favorite. One she hadn't worn since—Oh, no. She'd last worn it at the funeral, hadn't she? Well, she'd put that out of her mind.

Brian had asked her on a real date—outside of her house and with no children tagging along. She planned to enjoy every second of it, regardless of what she wore.

"Hannah, how old are you?" She pulled a half-cup measure from a drawer.

The girl stepped away from the counter, hands at her sides, as if she wanted to help but didn't know what to do. "I turned twenty last month."

"Call me Melanie, please." She'd grown increasingly uncomfortable with "missus" over the last several months, but with three children, "miss" didn't feel right either. "And would you boil a half cup of water in this pan?"

Hannah poured water into the saucepan and set it on the stovetop. "I can make dinner. Just tell me what you've got."

"That would be great." The wall clock read five o'clock. Brian would be done killing time in his car and come to the door any second. "Just heat the bag of green beans that are in the freezer and warm up the leftover macaroni and cheese." She opened the freezer, pulled out a plastic container with a red lid, set it next to the stove, then flicked on the oven to preheat.

Penny moped into the kitchen, still sulking after she'd been refused chocolate candy earlier. "Mama, Mama, Mama."

"Hey, peanut. Hannah's going to have dinner ready in a little bit. You hungry?"

The doorbell rang, cutting off Penny's answer.

"I got it!" Matthew yelled from the living room.

Melanie's stomach buzzed with nervous energy as she struggled to remember what else needed to be done. "Hannah, no baths tonight. Pajamas are on their beds. Lights out around 8:30."

Hannah lifted her head to nod, but her attention shifted midway to the opposite side of the kitchen.

Brian sauntered toward them, Matthew on his heels. "Hey. Am I early?"

Melanie's breath caught. Up to this point, she'd only seen Brian in jeans, shorts, or casual clothes. He'd always looked good to her, but *this*—in a suit and tie? He wore a pale blue button-down shirt with a gray and blue diagonal-stripe tie beneath a charcoal-colored suit jacket. Clean shaven and with possibly a bit of gel in his closely-cropped blond-brown hair. *Wow.*

If Hannah's wide eyes and vacuous grin were any indication, she'd been disarmed by how well he cleaned up too.

Melanie stilled her hand midway to reaching for the wedding ring that wasn't there. She toyed with her twisted silver bracelet and gathered her thoughts, which had scattered to the recesses of her brain upon Brian's arrival.

"Uh, no. You're right on time. It's me. I'm, uh, almost ready." She stepped into the mudroom and pulled her open-toed black heels with the ankle straps from the top of the shoe rack and returned to the kitchen.

As she slid on one shoe and then the other, Penny latched onto her leg. With Penny still attached, she grabbed her purse from the counter and stuffed her phone and keys inside.

Kevin ambled in from the living room, his gaze darting back and forth between Brian and his mom. "You look beautiful, Mom."

"Thanks, honey." She ruffled Kevin's hair as she opened the junk drawer, grabbed a pen, and scribbled Brian's cell phone number on a notepad. Penny slid along with her every movement.

"You have my number. This is Brian's in case—oh! I'm sorry.

Hannah, this is my friend Brian." *Friend?* Whatever. She didn't know what he was to her yet. "Brian, this is Hannah. She's been babysitting for me since Matthew was a year old."

Brian extended a hand to Hannah. "Nice to meet you, Hannah."

Hannah twirled a lock of long, golden hair around her finger as she accepted his handshake—giggling? *Oh my word.* She had to get out of here.

Penny squeezed tighter. "I don't want you to go, Mama."

Brian's expression sagged as he gazed at Penny, whose hands slip-slid along Melanie's silky pantyhose. "Maybe this wasn't a good idea. I remember when my nephew Brady was her age, and John and Kate would try to leave . . ."

Oh no. Separation anxiety would *not* ruin this date. Penny had always loved being babysat. Of course, it had been a while since Melanie left them with anyone.

Penny's hands inched higher up Melanie's leg until she had to bat her little hands away. "Honey, we've got to go. Dinner will be ready soon, and Hannah's gonna play with you."

"But your legs are so sofffft." She dropped onto her bottom, gliding her hands over Melanie's calf down to the strap of her shoe.

Melanie laughed and met Brian's worried gaze. "It's not about me leaving. It's about the pantyhose." Penny wouldn't pose a problem.

The little girl rubbed gently. "Feel 'dem," she said, her gaze locked on Brian. "They soft."

Brian smiled and tucked his hands into his pants pockets. "Uh, that's okay, Penny. Maybe later." He shot Melanie a grin.

Hannah sighed, a dreamy look on her face.

Melanie slung her purse strap over her shoulder. *Good grief.* They needed to leave before the girl melted into a puddle at Brian's feet. Melanie kissed each child's head and traced a cross on their foreheads. "Behave, listen to Hannah, and I'll be back after you go to sleep."

Brian held the door for her as she stepped onto the porch. Late afternoon sun still heated the covered porch, rays beating on the wilted geraniums outside the door. She made a mental note to water them in the morning.

"Kevin's right. You look beautiful." Brian waited at the top of the steps with an appreciative glance and his hand extended to her.

She grasped his hand and teetered on the top step, her left ankle wobbling. "Thank you. Not sure if I remember how to walk in heels, but I'm going to give it a shot."

Safely tucked in the passenger seat of Brian's car, Melanie noted the few vehicles parked along the street. All quiet on a late Saturday afternoon. "So, care to tell me where we're going?"

"You don't want to guess?" Brian slanted a grin at her.

"About eighty-five percent of Kevin's sentences start with 'guess what,' so, no, I'm gonna pass." She smoothed her skirt over her knees, reminded of the funeral and how she'd sat numbly in the passenger seat of their van while her brother Scott chauffeured them from the church to the cemetery.

"Fair enough." Brian turned the car, heading in the direction of the city. "Dinner at PJ's Brasserie, symphony concert, and, if we're up for it, maybe a drink on the way home."

"So, let me get this straight. I'm going to eat without having to cut up anyone's food or take anyone to the potty. Then I'm going to listen to live music performed by people not dressed as undersea creatures or other costumed characters, and then, possibly, an adult beverage?"

Brian's voice held the hint of a laugh. "Not gonna guarantee I won't need you to tie a bib on me or supply me with bendy straws, but that sounds about right."

Melanie clapped her hands. "And the symphony. It feels like

a lifetime since I've been to the symphony. What kind of music?"

He shot her another glance. "Tchaikovsky."

Her eyes widened. "Get out. How did you know?"

The car slowed to a stop at the traffic light. "So, when you sent me up to the attic to hang that smoke detector, there was an open box of stuff at the base of the steps. I might've seen a pile of classical music CDs there. Which, I might add, you should probably move. Too hot up there."

"Duly noted." *The symphony!* A thrill shot through her. This date would be like reliving a past life. Only better.

Plenty of moms fretted about leaving the kids with a babysitter. Melanie knew because she'd overheard them. She'd seen them checking in with sitters and grandparents. *Are they being good? Don't forget his allergy medicine. Call so I can tell them goodnight.*

If enjoying an evening free of those worries and distractions made her a bad mom, so be it. She'd placed a proven, responsible sitter in charge. Her kids would survive the evening without her just fine.

She didn't give the kids another thought over dinner, during which she and Brian leisurely savored a scrumptious meal at a rustic eatery outside the city limits. They lingered over pistachio gelato, killing time until they had to leave for the concert.

"I'm totally on board with this private date night thing, just so you know." Brian scraped his spoon along the bottom of the dessert dish, but no clinking glasses or silverware could be heard above the murmur of conversation and the soft instrumental music coming from the overhead speakers. "But, can I ask how the kids are doing?"

A spoonful of rich, flavorful gelato melted in Melanie's mouth. "Of course." She appreciated that he took an interest in the kids. She wouldn't look to Brian to parent them, but she'd missed David's input on a myriad of decisions over the past year. How to handle this or that. Was she being too strict? Too lax? Aside from consulting her brother or sister-in-law on rare occasions, she'd been left to muddle through parenting on her own.

"They're great. Kevin lost a tooth." She wiped her mouth with the napkin and set it aside. "That slacker the tooth fairy didn't show up though. Not until two nights later." The tooth fairy and the Elf on the Shelf: the Achilles' heel of modern parenting.

Brian shook his head as if dismayed. "Someone ought to dock her pay."

She laughed. "Maybe I will. And Penny's, well, Penny. I got this crazy idea we were good without the nighttime training pants, and I had to change the bedsheets in the middle of the night three times this week." A waitress passed with a steaming platter of chicken and waffles, its aroma heavenly. "But it's all good. She's been dressing herself, and she actually does a pretty good job matching colors and stuff."

"Must be a girl gene." Brian slid his dish forward and glanced at his watch. "We should probably go in about ten minutes."

"Okay." Melanie considered what kind of update she could give on Matthew. There was *one* thing. Maybe Brian could offer her some perspective.

"I've been trying to figure out how to handle a situation with Matthew's friend." She twisted her bracelet a couple of times, gathering her thoughts. "It's a boy from his scout pack. Mason's had a tough go of it. Far as I know, his dad's in jail, and he spends most of his time with his great-grandmother, who seems like a nice enough lady, but she's not very vigilant, I guess."

Brian leaned back, resting his hands in his lap. "How so?"

"No one supervises who he's with or what he watches or what kinds of games he plays. He's got his own phone and no restrictions."

Brian leaned forward, brows raised. "Second graders have their own phones?"

Melanie laughed. "Oh yeah. Where've you been?"

He tapped a butter knife on the table, his gaze unfocused and thoughtful. "I can see why that'd concern you. That kid's about two clicks away from all kinds of danger." He met her eyes then, serious. "You should assume he's found it."

He was right. That's why, despite her attempts to reassure herself that Matthew wouldn't be exposed to whatever poison Mason might be viewing, she'd been wary and unable to dismiss that uneasy feeling in her gut. "But they're so young. Surely, he wouldn't go looking—"

"It's not about going looking, Melanie." He shifted in his seat, his hands folded on the table, his jaw tense. "Do you think the multibillion-dollar pornography industry sits backs and *waits* for people to find them?"

"No. I guess—"

"Click on a link, look at a profile, an ad, a hashtag, a message. It could seem completely innocent and then BOOM!" He shook his head, a defeated frown marring his handsome features. "And you can't unsee that stuff."

She'd never seen that kind of passion from Brian. He cared about this issue. A lot. But why?

"It's easy now. So accessible. But this has been going on for decades." He rubbed his jaw. "John and I stumbled on it when I was about Matthew's age. Maybe a little older. And we didn't need the internet or a cell phone to do it."

"What happened?"

Several seconds ticked by while he stared somewhere beyond her. The exposed brick on the far wall complemented the richly-colored wide-plank floors.

"It was a rainy summer day, so we couldn't play outside. My sisters were having this girls' visit with our Aunt Lynn. Dad was at work. Mom was holed up in her room with a migraine. For a while there, she had them maybe a couple times a month. All she could do was pull the drapes closed and lie in bed."

She nodded, eager for him to continue.

"My dad had a lot of movies stored in the closet. VHS movies. We'd seen most of them already, but we found some in the back we hadn't seen. One was an Indiana Jones movie—the second one, the one that led to the PG-13 rating. We weren't allowed to watch it. But, no one was there to stop us." He gave her a mischievous grin.

"Okay. Too much for little kids with the scene where the heart is ripped out, but hardly a porn movie."

"Right. If that had been the movie in the case, I might've had trouble going to sleep for a couple nights." He took a long drink of water, the suspense building.

"Problem was, the movie in that case—and a bunch of others at the back of the closet, as we discovered—wasn't what was on the cover. They were porn films that I guess my dad had hidden thinking no one would find them.

"And you and John . . .?"

He tugged at his collar. "Got a quick and unwelcome introduction to the wonderful world of sexual depravity."

Melanie stretched her arm across the table, resting her hand on his. "I'm sorry. And that's exactly what I'm worried about."

"You should be. And I know I'm not a dad, and you didn't ask for my opinion, but I wouldn't let Matthew out of your sight with that kid unless they're in your own house."

"Well, that's what I was thinking. The boys get along really well, and Mason could use a good influence. Not that Matthew is perfect or our lives are problem-free, but even without a dad, Matthew's life is way more stable."

Brian nodded. "So, maybe they only play at your house or out somewhere together—*without* his phone." He glanced at his watch. "Sorry if I got carried away. We should go."

"I'm ready." She squeezed his hand and let go. "Thanks for

sharing that. And helping me work through it. I feel better now about my decision." She pulled her purse from behind the chair, readying herself to leave.

Brian gave her a tight smile. "You're welcome."

"And hey, despite that, you didn't get sucked into all that trash, so there's hope for Mason too if he's been exposed to it." She stood while Brian pocketed their receipt and grabbed his suit coat. Smiling, she waited for him to look her way.

He didn't.

CHAPTER 12

Raindrops pelted the pavement as Brian ushered Melanie into Allegheny Alehouse. Dark splotches marked where water soaked his shirt. Outside, what started as distant flashes of heat lightning had turned into a summer storm. Thankfully, the torrential downpour had been brief.

Inside, he scanned the bar area. Couples and singles filled the barstools, but several high tables for two remained empty. He nudged Melanie in the direction of one in the far corner, away from the television screens and the jukebox.

She ran a hand over her hair as she walked, probably assessing the wind and rain damage. Bracing a hand on the back of the chair, she boosted herself into the seat.

"What can I get you?" Brian surveyed the beers on tap and drink specials written in brightly-colored chalk above the bar.

Melanie glanced at the bar then the drink menu on the table. "I've never had a martini." She flipped the menu over and scanned the selections. "Ooh. A chocolate martini. I'll have that."

"Be right back." Brian meandered to the bar, mulling over the choices. He'd lost focus on their date precisely when Melanie had shared her concerns about Matthew's friend, and he'd spilled a secret only he and John knew about finding Dad's porno flicks. It hardly seemed like a relaxing date-night topic, and yet he'd felt compelled to share it, both in hope of safeguarding Matthew and in unburdening his conscience.

"For you, sir?" The bartender slid a couple of coasters in Brian's direction. He ordered Melanie's martini and a Scotch whiskey for himself.

Melanie sat gazing out the window. He hoped she'd enjoyed the evening. She'd sat entranced during the concert, engrossed in the music.

He squared things away with the bartender and headed back to the table with their drinks.

Melanie smiled, and the look she gave him—like he was the only man in the world—about did him in.

"Chocolate martini for the lady." He placed the glass in front of her, grinning at the wide-eyed, wondrous look on her face. "I'm guessin' you and David didn't get out much."

"Gosh no. We were stupid." She sipped the drink. "Mmm. Smooth, sweet, and decadent."

She repositioned the glass, examining the drink and the chocolate shavings stuck to the rim. "I guess we took each other for granted. After three kids, we seldom had room in the budget to do anything more than a matinee and a cup of coffee. If that." She shifted, crossing her legs and giving him a view of her strappy, sexy shoes. "And Hannah's great, but she doesn't work for free—not that she should."

He nodded, making a mental note to never, ever take this woman for granted should he be blessed to call her his own. Classic rock music blared from the jukebox, momentarily distracting him before someone adjusted the volume.

She leaned toward him and whispered in a conspiratorial tone. "I feel like such a grown-up. Out after dark. With a man. In a bar. Having a martini." She gestured toward her mixed drink like a game show hostess and giggled, looking half her age. Her eyes sparkled with excitement and glee.

They passed a quarter-hour or more brainstorming more "grown-up" date nights, since both hoped this would be the first of many such evenings out, even if they only happened once a month or so.

"I gave you the update on the Lombardi family. Tell me about your week." She sipped again, probably anticipating a droll retelling of some office mishap. But when he thought of the work week, only one thing came to mind—being summoned to human resources.

A flash in his peripheral vision caught his attention, drawing his gaze to the three screens mounted perpendicular to the bar. On each, a montage of scantily clad swimsuit models flashed. The montage disappeared, replaced by a single model—tan, long-legged and gorgeous, in a succession of seductive surfside poses. The swimsuit issue cover girl, he guessed.

A pang of guilt stung him in the chest. Here he sat across from a flesh and blood beautiful woman, attractive to him in so many ways, ogling other women.

Weak. He'd become so weak, lured by a flash of female skin on a stupid sports entertainment segment.

"C'mon. You had to have done *something* this week." She peered up at him beneath long, dark lashes, coy and sweet. As if he had something highly interesting to share.

"Well . . ." Ought he tell her? Did their entire date night conversation have to revolve around the topic he reviled most? Still, it might be good to share it with someone. At some point soon, it would be front and center in a court of law, requiring him to deal with it outright.

"Back in the spring, before we met—right before, actually, there was an, uh, incident at work."

Her brow wrinkled. "What kind of incident?"

"Someone got let go in a pretty dramatic fashion. Because of something I discovered." He tilted his drink and the ice cubes clinked. "I'd been doing maintenance on a department's computers. There had been complaints about missing data and things running slow. In the process of trying to fix that, I discovered this one guy, Raymond, who'd complained the loudest, had a giant cache of pornographic pictures stored on his computer."

"Oh my gosh." She sat straight in her chair. "Who would put that on their work computer of all places?"

"Happens more than you'd think. But this wasn't just *normal* porn, if there is such a thing." He drained the last drops of Scotch from the glass, pursing his lips as he swallowed. "He was storing and transmitting child pornography."

She shook her head, her eyes downcast. "Sick. How can people *do* that?"

He wondered the same thing. The idea disgusted him. And yet saying as much left him feeling hypocritical since he'd once had a secret electronic stash of pornographic images. Not the most vile kind. Not on his work computer. And none of children. Ever. But still, the root of his sin and Raymond Boyle's were the same.

"The guy was fired, of course, but there are federal charges pending against him. HR informed me this week that I'll be called to testify at some point." An invisible weight pressed on his chest every time he thought of it.

"That's awful. All of it." She uncrossed her legs and sat forward. "Can you imagine having a job where all you did was wade through that filth and block it on social media sites? Or prosecute it?" She shuddered.

The weight pressed harder against his chest, sucking any traces of joy from his soul. He needed to redirect the conversation. He'd meant for tonight to be light and fun, and yet here they sat talking about kiddie porn.

He glanced at his watch. "What time does Hannah expect us?"

"Oh. I didn't give her an exact time. Only before midnight."

He nodded. Maybe a change of scenery would restore a little levity. Only a few drops remained in her glass. "You ready to head back?"

For a half second, her eyes drooped in disappointment, but then she smiled. "Sure. Anytime you are."

He'd take her home and say a proper goodnight. Maybe with a little coaxing, he could restore that giddy mood he'd glimpsed earlier.

* * *

MELANIE CLIMBED THE STILL-WET STEPS, her hand tucked in Brian's arm, reluctant for the night to end. They reached the dark porch, and she dug for her house key from the bottom of her purse. With only the dim glow from the streetlight, it took her a minute to find. While Brian held the storm door open, she turned the key in the lock and then hesitated.

With the realization that their date would soon end, disappointment pressed heavy on her heart. "Just a second." She ducked beneath Brian's outstretched arm and peeked through the living room window.

Hannah sat in the blue glow of the television, staring at her phone.

"Looks quiet." She leaned over the porch rail, examining the side windows. Lights out.

"Everything okay?" Brian let the storm door close and glanced at his wristwatch. "It's almost eleven o'clock. I'd hope they're all asleep."

"Looks like it. But they have this sixth sense. I walk in the door, and one of them wakes up." And she wasn't eager to deal with her kids. Not yet. "Can we stay out here? Just for a minute."

"Uh . . ." He blinked a few times then smiled, a playful glint in his eye. "Sure."

"When I open that door, it'll kill the mood." They'd laughed half the way home after leaving the bar, swapping stories about nights out gone horribly awry, spoiled by everything from a flash flood to vomiting kids. With all her heart, she wanted to prolong this date. "I've got to find out how it went, pay Hannah, and then if one of them wakes up . . ."

He stepped closer, giving her arm a reassuring caress.

She inched closer, into his space, lifted her face to his, and swallowed. "Thank you for tonight. I had the best time. I haven't had a night like this in a very, very long time." Unsure what came next, she lay her hands on the front of his suit coat, his chest so firm and solid beneath.

"Good." He leaned close, his voice low. "I really enjoyed it too." Like the last time they'd said goodnight, his gaze drifted to her lips.

Anticipation caused warmth to purl in her tummy, and she squeezed the fabric of his suit coat.

He shuffled back a half step, his gaze bouncing back to her eyes. "I don't want to rush you. David was the last man you expected to kiss, and I . . . I can wait."

Sweet, sweet man. So thoughtful, yet unnecessary. "I can't."

It took a half second for her meaning to register, but with a gentle tug to his suit coat, he moved closer, his eyes a smoky blue in the dark, his lips quirked on one side in a sort of half-smile.

She let her eyes drift closed, and a couple of seconds later, while her heart thumped in time with the first summer calls of the cicadas, his lips brushed hers.

A barely-there kiss and a retreat. A second kiss, lingering a smidgen longer. Then a third, tender and sweet, laying bare the growing affection between them.

Feeling a flush of bewilderment, equal parts euphoria and

bashfulness, she dipped her head and released him, turning to the door with a giddy smile. The warmth of his presence followed her into the kitchen, where she dropped her purse and slipped off her shoes.

Hannah punched furiously at the television remote until the ridiculous-looking reality show she'd been watching (little people driving trucks across ice?) went dark, then she strolled toward them, tapping on her phone.

"How'd it go?" Melanie braced herself for whatever shenanigans may have gone on. The house appeared orderly and Hannah still well put together, so maybe it had been an easy night for her.

Brian sauntered into the living room and switched the table lamp on.

"Mrs. Lombardi—"

"Melanie, remember?" She pulled a few bills from her purse, grateful they'd stopped at an ATM machine on the way home.

"OMG. He is soooo hot." Hannah's breathy tone reeked of watermelon lip gloss and infatuation.

Melanie's cheeks warmed, recalling their kiss. She glanced at Brian, who had draped his suit coat over the end of the couch and stood loosening his tie. A swell of attraction ballooned inside her. Yes, very handsome.

But Hannah! What happened to the shy, awkward teen who could barely meet David's eyes and said little more than "yes" or "no"? Even now, she had her phone out—was she trying to get his picture?

"Hannah!" Melanie didn't need a picture of her date out on Snapchat, where a gaggle of Hannah's friends would be affixing lip smack stickers to his cheek.

She lowered the phone and tucked it in her back pocket. "Oh. Uh, the kids were real good. Kevin has a little goose egg on his head where he ran into the chair outside, but that's it."

"Is Penny wearing training pants?"

"Yep. Oh, there was this one thing." Hannah gestured, setting up her story

"What?" Melanie's attention drifted to where Brian sat on the couch. They'd kissed. Now what?

"So, we just walked two blocks down, two blocks back, but there was this creepy guy."

Melanie's attention snapped back to the conversation. "A creepy guy?"

"Yeah. He didn't do anything. Just sat in his car in front of your neighbor's house."

"So, he didn't leave the car?"

"No. So I couldn't really make out what he looked like." She shrugged. "Maybe I'm paranoid."

"No, I'm glad you're aware of your surroundings. Did you get a look at the car?"

She wrinkled her nose. "Gray maybe? Four doors, I think."

Melanie didn't know what to do with the information. The guy could've been waiting for somebody. Might've been the same gray car that had been at her neighbor's last weekend.

Hannah had already shifted mental gears and went on about how her parents should upgrade her phone and her brother always got the upgrade, which wasn't fair because he had a job, and he could pay for his own stuff.

Ready to hustle her out the door, Melanie tuned her out and pressed the cash into her hand so she could join Brian on the couch.

"Thank you, Hannah. Tell your mom I said hello." She shut the door on Hannah's wave but watched out the window to see that she got safely in her car and on her way.

Melanie breathed deeply to keep her pulse from racing as she approached the living room.

Brian's arm rested on the back of the couch, and he'd leaned his head back, eyes closed.

She sat close beside him, propping her stocking feet on the coffee table and turning to sling her arm across his waist.

"Hannah gone?" he murmured.

"Uh-huh. She's a fan. I think she was trying to sneak a picture of you."

He chuckled. "She shoulda' asked. Always happy to do a selfie with a young lady."

Melanie thumped his belly with her fist, a grin splitting her face.

"Oof." He sat upright. "Joking, joking." He tightened his arm around her shoulder. "I should go too."

"Yes, you should." She curled her legs behind her and nestled her head on his shoulder.

Neither moved for several minutes, and Melanie soaked up the comfort and peace of being tucked comfortably against his side.

Finally, he shifted them to face one another. He pushed a lock of stray hair behind her ear, rubbed a thumb down her cheek, then grazed his knuckles along her jaw. Using his index finger, he tilted her chin up, staring with blue eyes that penetrated her soul. Then he lowered his lips to hers.

This kiss varied one-hundred eighty degrees from the first. If the first kiss was sweet as spun sugar and light as a wispy vapor, this one was as rich as warm ganache and as unsettled as a voluminous storm cloud. Deep in the recesses of her heart, something sprung to life. Something boundless and beautiful. Something both fragile and powerful that left her heart thudding and her brain muddled.

Brian's voice came rough and raspy above her ear, his breath warm. "I'm sorry. I shouldn't—"

Melanie pressed him back, intent on squelching that half-spoken thought. "Please, don't. Please don't try to take it back."

"But that wasn't how a second kiss should—"

"Just stop. For a long time, I've been 'Mama.' Matthew's

mom. Kevin's mom. Penny's mom. David even called me 'Mom,' most of the time. This night—*that* kiss—made me feel like a woman again. Like maybe there's something more to me than the nose-wiping, diaper-changing, and dispute-settling."

Brian stared, probably taken aback at her mini-rant. Poor guy, trying to be a gentleman.

"Your motherhood is one of the most beautiful things about you, Melanie. The way you love and care for your children is . . . captivating. But I have not forgotten for one second that there's more to you than that."

They sat in silence for several seconds, her heart rate slowing as she absorbed what he'd said—both with that kiss and in words.

He stood, his hand grazing her leg as he pushed off the couch. He extended a hand and pulled her to her feet. "I'm gonna go."

At the door, he swung his suit coat over his shoulder and kissed her cheek. "And Penny's right. Your legs are like satin." He grinned and headed down the steps to his car.

She waited until he got into his car and drove away, grinning like the village idiot the entire time.

"Mama?" A groggy voice came from upstairs, and Melanie instantly reverted to mom mode.

"Coming, Penny." She flew up the stairs, her burdens and her spirit equally light.

Using his fist, Brian wiped condensation from the bathroom mirror then removed his five o'clock shadow with a clean razor and checked his appearance. Freshly-shaven and showered, the dark circles under his eyes could be easily overlooked. He ran a comb through his hair, splashed on a bit of sandalwood-scented aftershave, and yawned. Oh, that he could climb into bed now.

For a couple of months, his long, late-night dates with Melanie had been the highlight of his day. He'd arrived at her house eager and full of energy. The last couple of weeks, despite adding a late-afternoon cup of coffee, he struggled to muster the stamina. He didn't enjoy Melanie's company any less. In fact, day by day, he'd grown to care more and more about her, wishing he could spend all his time with her. He'd probably amassed a sleep deficit so big he couldn't make it up by sleeping in on Saturday mornings anymore.

On his way out of the bathroom, he checked the calendar app on his phone. Two more days until his Friday court appearance. When he'd first told Melanie about the case over summer, he thought he'd be called any day. And now, finally, in November, he'd gotten the summons.

Brian stopped at a convenience store halfway through the fifteen-minute drive to Melanie's house. The garishly-lit red store and gas station seemed to be doing a brisk business for nine o'clock on a Wednesday night.

He scoured the rack of impulse buys at the checkout, finally selecting an energy-booster. He examined the label on the bright orange and purple bottle. *Instant boost! All natural!* These were safe, right? Otherwise they wouldn't sell them, would they? If anyone could use an all-natural instant boost, it was him.

Back in the car, he guzzled the neon orange liquid, trying to ignore the taste he identified with low-dose aspirins. He shuddered, wishing he had bought some bottled water to chase the nasty elixir.

He'd hoped by the time he arrived at Melanie's the "instant boost" would have him jogging up her steps like Rocky Balboa. Instead, he felt like Droopy Dog.

He knocked lightly, wanting to get Melanie's attention but not wake the whole house with the doorbell. Two gooseneck gourds and a pumpkin replaced the frost-blackened geraniums he'd seen by the door last week. A cold breeze rustled the dry leaves clinging to the trees, and he zipped his jacket up to his chin.

The door swung open, and Melanie motioned him in. "It's getting cold!" She rubbed the long sleeves of her green Henley shirt, which she'd paired with faded jeans. A blast of air fanned the storm door out before she tugged it shut.

A glance toward the dark stairs and second floor confirmed the kids were all abed for the night.

Catching his gaze, Melanie smiled. "I wore them out so bedtime wouldn't take forever tonight." She kissed his cheek, took his jacket, and then hung it on the coat rack. "After-dinner calisthenics for everyone." She flexed her bicep and giggled.

"For someone consistently outnumbered by her little charges, you keep them in line." He flopped onto the couch, hoping he'd be able to muster the will to leave in a couple of hours. Sleeping on her sofa looked better every visit. Maybe he ought to consider making himself a permanent fixture in the household instead. *A permanent fixture . . .* He rubbed his smooth jaw. *Hmmm.*

"Truth is, despite the fact they're gonna make me gray, I don't mind being outnumbered. I can't imagine my life without them." She took a seat alongside him, her back to the corner of the couch, and faced him.

But life threw curves that no one could imagine until they sailed straight over home plate. Melanie probably knew that better than most. How would her life have been different had David lived? "So, how many kids did you hope to have?"

She sighed. "I never had a set number. We took them one at a time." She picked at a thread on the hem of her shirt. "I thought for sure there would be a fourth."

"What do you mean?" She'd never mentioned a miscarriage or any infertility issues.

Her hand moved from her finger to her wrist, and then she laid her hands in her lap. No jewelry to twirl. "After David died, after the funeral . . . I felt tired, sick. I felt like I did when I was pregnant. David had been in the ground a week when I shut myself behind that door . . ." Her eyes filled with tears as she gestured to the bathroom. "I locked myself in there and took a pregnancy test, sobbing the entire time."

Brian moved closer, wrapping his arm around her shoulders so she could lean against him. "I'm sorry." He hated that she'd gone through so much alone, except for the kids, who needed her to keep it together most of the time.

She wiped the tears from her eyes with her sleeve. "I was scared to death. How could I do it alone—three little kids *and* a new baby? Penny hadn't even been weaned." She sniffed and wiped her eyes again. "So, you'd think I was relieved when the test was negative, but I cried even harder."

He pictured her huddled on the bathroom floor sobbing, and his heart ached. How much had she kept bottled in? "I think conflicting emotions at a time like that are understandable."

She snuggled close to him, laying her head on his chest.

"Tell me about when David died." He wanted to know it all, to somehow absorb a fraction of her pain.

She sighed against him. "It was a day like any other. The boys were at school, and I was fixing lunch for me and Penny when David's manager called and said there'd been an accident. He'd been late for an appointment about forty-five minutes north of here. When he didn't show, they tracked the GPS on his work equipment—the laptop or something."

"How'd it happen?"

"Black ice." She hiccupped against his chest. "He hit a patch of black ice, spun out of control and collided with a tractor-trailer head-on."

He rubbed her shoulder, trying to sooth the wounds he'd reopened.

"They said it was instant." Her voice caught. "I'm glad he didn't suffer, but I wish he'd had time—even a few minutes—to prepare."

Now that he'd encouraged her to open up, she seemed to want to continue. "The worst part, worse than the shock, was telling the kids. I'd rather die myself than to have to do it again."

Brian grabbed a box of tissues from the end table and handed one to Melanie.

"Thank you." She sat straight and wiped her eyes and nose. "Penny was so little. She didn't understand at all. She'd ask for

'Da' again and again. Matthew and Kevin seemed to get it, but their emotions were so random. Sad or inappropriately happy. They pingponged all over the place." Staring blankly at the coffee table rather than face him, she continued. "And Kevin still sat by the window every afternoon. Waiting for his dad's car to pull into the driveway."

She balled the tissue and walked it to the kitchen trash can then ambled back to the couch, putting some distance between them. "And that's it." She raised her hands and dropped them on her thighs, as if there were nothing more to say. "Everyone's life went back to normal. Everyone's but ours. Within weeks, the cards and calls and meals stopped coming, and we learned to fend for ourselves."

He leaned forward, elbows on his knees, his gut urging him to fix something he knew to be unfixable. He couldn't bring back her husband. In truth, he was glad he couldn't. He'd come to care deeply for Melanie, and while he could only will the best for her, he wanted that best to include him. He turned his head, assessing her, wanting reassurance that she'd be okay. "You've been carrying this around for too long."

She waved a hand, dismissing his comment. "You make it sound like I haven't grieved."

"How did you get through it?"

"I did what I had to, for the kids' sake. And I prayed. I prayed like I've never prayed in my life." She breathed deeply then massaged his shoulder, smiling despite the forlorn look in her eyes. "This feels so one-sided."

His brow wrinkled, and he sat back, taking her hand in his. "What do you mean?"

"You and me. I'm so needy. Emotionally, socially . . . even physically. All I do is take. And you're so patient. You listen . . . without judgment."

He turned fully, cupping her face in his hands, drowning in

those emerald eyes. "You give me everything, Melanie. A reason to get up in the morning. A reason to leave work at a decent hour. A reason to hope."

Chin dipped, she bit her lower lip. "Hope for what?"

"Hope for a future with you."

CHAPTER 14

Outside the courtroom, Brian breathed deeply of the crisp air. He leaned against the cold, beige stones of the historic building and glanced at the turrets of the courthouse high above him. Thick, gray clouds blanketed the sky. Pigeons flew back and forth, moving from one urban roost to another, oblivious to the blaring of car horns, the rumble of diesel engines, and the wail of a distant siren.

His part in the Raymond Boyle case was over.

In response to the questions from both the prosecution and defense, Brian had explained what he'd discovered and how, and he'd provided various details of the company's systems and procedures.

The day had failed to meet his dismal expectations—thank God. He hadn't been beset by reminders of the depravity of porn purveyors or his own past with images that exploited and objectified women. To his surprise, he felt a sense of closure. More than that—relief, gratitude, and hope.

Despite the emotional exhaustion related to the court case and the physical exhaustion that had been his constant companion lately, his weary yet thankful soul urged him to take a detour on his way home. He pushed off of the wall, heading on foot to the only Catholic church in downtown. A glance at his watch told him if he didn't make it in time for midday Mass, he'd at least be able to make it to confession. A prayer of thanksgiving was in order and then, once he got home, a solid nap.

ONLY A SMATTERING OF PENITENTS REMAINED, an odd combination of vagrants and business professionals genuflecting before the bronze tabernacle before scuttling up the marble-tiled aisle. Most visitors had likely returned to work after their lunch breaks, leaving behind the transcendent mosaics and statuary for ordinary cube farms with metal desks.

On his knees, with his head bowed, he gave thanks for the morning's proceedings. An overwhelming sense of peace filled him, making him feel utterly free. His chest light, he felt no attachment to the temptations that had been plaguing him for months.

With satisfaction, he recognized that despite more than a half-year's worth of persistent temptation, he hadn't had a single setback. Through God's grace, not one.

Then with disappointment, he realized how little he'd relied on that grace. Or on any of the other things he'd done to resist pornography the first time around.

Melanie's reliance on faith when everything in her life had imploded inspired him. All these months, he should've been doubling down, praying more often, fasting, and finding an accountability partner. Sure, he'd mumbled a lot of desperate prayers and blessed himself a whole bunch of extra times, but he'd been foolish to ignore what had worked in the past, not only in avoiding porn but in strengthening his faith, like sacramental confession. He couldn't deny that no matter how humbling his frequent admissions of "impure things" were, he always left that dark, little room in the back of church floored by God's mercy and jacked up on grace.

He'd rectify that. Even though he presently felt not a whit of temptation and he'd not had an accountability partner since college, he'd find someone. He'd block off time for prayer. And fasting . . . he hadn't had much of an appetite lately, but there were other kinds of fasting. Starting with the phone in his back pocket.

FIVE HOURS LATER, he awoke to a buzzing sound and groped for the phone, which lay facedown on his nightstand. He flipped it over, alarmed when he read the time. How had he slept so long? After church, he'd come straight home and fallen asleep, still dressed in his shirt and pants from this morning's court appearance. At least he'd removed his tie. He hadn't eaten lunch but still didn't feel hungry.

He tapped on the text that had triggered the buzz. A message from Melanie:

So glad it went well today. Still on for tonight?

He grinned at the little heart-eyed emoji she'd used at the end and tapped out his reply.

Leaving now. Want me to pick up pizza?

He grabbed his tie, hung it in the closet, and searched for something to throw on.

A couple of times a month, they had a family date, like tonight. He'd picked up some candy from the store in town, a little treat for each of them.

Even when a half-hour later the robust aroma of tomato sauce, oregano, and mozzarella filled his car, his hunger remained minimal. At least they wouldn't run out of pizza, which happened last time. He smiled, picturing Kevin lowering a piece of pizza, cheese dangling from its tip, into his mouth.

The kid didn't like a lot of foods, but the ones he liked, he loved. Pizza was one of them.

He pulled into Melanie's driveway, pocketed his keys, and balanced the pizza on his open palm while holding the candy bag in the other hand. Mounting the steps in the dim light characteristic of November evenings, he kicked himself for the umpteenth time for not seeing about that porch light. He raised the hand holding the candy bag to press the doorbell when the door swung open.

Matthew stood in the entrance, a greedy grin on his face and rubbing his hands together as if ready to devour the pizza on the spot. He pushed open the storm door for Brian. "Hey, Coach. What's in the bag?"

Darn. He should've hidden the candy or left it in the car until later. Now they'd want it before pizza. "Uh, a treat for each of you once you've finished your dinner." He strolled to the kitchen and placed the pizza box on the counter and the candy bag on top of the refrigerator, out of the kids' reach.

"What is it?" Matthew lifted the lid of the pizza box and fanned the savory smell toward his face.

"Hey. You made it." Melanie entered from the dining room, where she'd set out plates, napkins, cups, and a few forks. She wore a loose yellow sweater dress over black leggings. She'd done something different with her hair too. Gotten it cut shorter maybe.

"Yeah." He stared, his deepening feelings stirring in his chest. "You look great." He closed the pizza box, nearly scraping Matthew's nose. "Your hair too."

She smiled, her eyes aglow. "Thanks. Got it trimmed." She ran a hand over her shorter locks, which almost reached her shoulders. "Let's eat."

He kissed Melanie's cheek, then removed his jacket and hung it on the rack in the entryway. When he returned to the dining room, Kevin and Penny had materialized out of nowhere, probably drawn by the scent of food, and sat with Matthew waiting for their pizza.

Melanie placed a slice on each of their plates, and they said grace, Penny a full syllable or two behind everyone else. An easy silence descended on them as everyone gobbled the pizza.

Matthew finished his second piece, wiped his mouth, and turned to his mom. "It's not even seven yet. You could still run me over to Mason's."

Melanie shot Brian a wary glance.

He squinted, thinking. It took a few seconds to place the name. Mason was the friend from scouts, the one who lacked parental supervision. Melanie had obviously discouraged Matthew from going to his house this evening.

"We already discussed this, Matthew. I'm not comfortable with you going over there. If you want to invite Mason here—"

"It's boring here. And *they're* here." He glared at Kevin and then Penny, who paid him no mind as she scraped cheese from her pizza. "Why can't I spend time with my friend? Just *me*." His voice grew whinier with every word.

Melanie heaved a sigh. "You know why. End of discussion."

With a huff, Matthew shoved his chair away from the table and stomped into the living room.

Not interested in the remainder of his second slice of pizza, Brian patted Melanie's hand. Would it bother her if he stepped in? "Mind if I talk to him?"

She sighed again. "Why not? It's not like I'm getting through to him. Mason wants him to sleep over, and I couldn't even get a straight answer on who would be in the house. It's not gonna happen."

Brian nodded and left the table, giving Kevin's back a passing pat as Kevin lifted a huge glob of cheese to his mouth. He grabbed the bag of candy from the top of the fridge, hoping to persuade Matthew home wasn't so bad.

Matthew sat slumped on the couch, his arms folded over his chest, his expression sullen.

Maybe Brain could be the buffer between mother and son. He dragged the ottoman closer to the couch and sat across from Matthew. "Hey. Your mom's just looking out for you."

Matthew glared at Brian, not moving. "You would take *her* side."

"*Her* side is your side, buddy. She's not trying to punish you; she's trying to protect you." Though he doubted Matthew was grateful for such protection. He'd understand, someday.

"Listen, why don't we play a game or something, just me and you? And, I've got something for you." He reached into his bag and pulled out a couple of Cow Tales.

Leaning forward, Matthew reached for them. "Aw, thanks, Coach. I love these."

Brian chuckled. "I know you do."

Penny ambled in, patting her tummy and studying the open bag. Kevin trailed her, peering as if to see what he'd missed.

"Hey, where's mine?" Kevin asked.

"Kevin!" Melanie's voice traveled from the dining room. "You either ask politely or you get nothing."

"Sorry," Kevin mumbled. "May I have some candy?"

Brian reached into the bag. "For you I have . . . Atomic Fireballs."

Kevin's eyes widened as he scooped them from Brian's hand. "Thanks."

Penny stood, waiting more patiently than Brian would've guessed her capable of. "So, Miss Penny. What's your favorite?"

"Choc-lit," she answered.

Just like her mama. Brian handed her candy in a yellow wrapper and tapped its top. "These are chocolate with marshmallow. Mallo Cups." He leaned closer and whispered, "They're *my* favorite."

He unwrapped it and handed her one of the cups.

"T'ank you." She bit off a large piece, smearing some marshmallow on her lips. "Yum."

Melanie came up behind him and laid her hands on his shoulders, massaging them gently. "Nothing for me?"

He turned in time to spot her pouty lip. Grinning, he handed her a slim blue box with a bow.

Her eyes widened. "I was joking. You didn't need to bring me anything."

"But I did." He broke the seal and lifted the lid.

"Ooh, chocolate truffles. Thank you." She popped one in her mouth and moaned. "Mmm. These are perfection."

Brian crumpled the now-empty bag and sauntered to the kitchen to dispose of it. He returned a minute later to find Matthew had set up his Clue! board game. The game board looked different than Brian remembered, but he supposed the game play was the same.

Kevin grabbed Candyland from the bottom shelf in the corner. "Hey, Mom. Can we play this?"

"Sure," Melanie said, taking a seat on the floor. Penny dropped immediately into her lap, chocolaty fingers, face, and all.

Brian squatted and then sat with his back to the couch, facing Kevin. A guy could get used to this. Nothing about the place was perfect, from the faulty porch light to the leaky plumbing to the people within it—a grieving mom, a boy who thought he knew best, a sometimes reckless younger brother, and, well, Penny may just be perfect, even coated in chocolate. But they loved one another, come what may. They stuck it out. *She* stuck it out. And more and more, he wanted to stick it out with them.

CHAPTER 15

A knock sounded on Brian's front door, pulling him from the verge of sleep: rap—rap, tap, tap—rap, tap. The Perella boys' super-secret knock circa 2006.

Must be game time. "Come in!" Brian yelled from the couch, his feet propped on the coffee table next to a ceramic bowl filled with corn chips.

The door clicked shut, and John darted for the opposite end of the couch, bumping the table and nearly knocking the chips to the floor. "What up?" He rolled up the sleeves of his Steelers sweatshirt as if he were ready for action.

Wanting to shake the sleepiness, Brian grabbed the remote from the arm of the couch and boosted the volume. "Barely made kick off." He shook his head. "Trouble putting the boys to bed?"

John swiped a handful of chips and leaned back, dropping them into his mouth. "Nah," he said around a mouthful of chips. "Just the usual. Had about ten thousand questions I had to answer before they went to sleep."

The Steelers and Bengals trotted onto the field for a Thursday-night football game.

"What's to drink?" John twisted in his seat, gaze on the refrigerator.

"Coke, beer. Might be an iced coffee thing in there." Brian leaned his head back, closing his eyes to steal a moment's rest, even though he knew it would do no good. *And a six-pack of energy drinks you'd better not touch.* Those would get him through the weekend. He hoped.

Brian soaked in the sounds from the kitchen, as harmonious as a well-tuned orchestra: the whoosh of the refrigerator door, clinking metal in the utensil drawer, the pop of a bottle, and the opener smacking the counter.

The cushions next to him shifted as John plopped onto the couch. With great effort, Brian opened his eyes. "How's Kate and the kids?" Did John even realize how lucky he was to have them?

John kicked off his tennis shoes and shoved them under the coffee table. "Good." He took a swig of beer and then gestured toward the TV with the bottle. "You need a big screen. You could mount it right on the wall."

Brian turned, staring at John. "You gonna pay for it?"

"This set's fine." He brushed crumbs from his lap and smothered a grin behind his beer bottle. "How's Melanie?"

Perfect. Best thing that ever happened to me. Pretty sure I don't deserve her. "She's good." He stood, stretched, and sauntered to the kitchen for a Coke. Caffeine might give him a boost.

"How many dates has it been?"

Not enough. Never enough. "Not counting." He snapped open the can of Coke, waited for it to stop fizzing, and took a swig.

"Really?" John's attention remained fixed on the not-so-big screen, where players' pictures and stats flashed every few seconds.

"Yes, really." Brian, leaning a hip against the kitchen counter, tried not to be insulted, but John's incredulous tone implied that

Brian would never—*could* never—find a woman who met his supposed standards.

"Is your holy roller morality still keeping you from getting laid?"

Brian coughed and, with a hand to his mouth, narrowly avoided spewing cola across the kitchen. *What the heck?* He despised that expression. Decade-old scenarios replayed in his mind. His best friend from high school: "You're too uptight; you need to get laid." His college roommate: "You study too hard. You need to get drunk and get laid."

His Coke can hit the counter hard, splashing sugary brown liquid onto his hand. Great. Now he'd be sticky. What he needed was for people to mind their own darn business. "Do I ask you about your sex life with Kate?"

John snorted. "No, but if you wanna know—"

"I don't." Gritting his teeth, Brian returned to the couch and sat ramrod straight and as far from John as possible.

Hands raised in surrender, John's tone was almost, *almost* conciliatory. "Guess I hit a nerve. Just sayin'. She must be missing a man by now. Don't you want to—"

Anger surged, energizing Brian more effectively than caffeine ever could. "What kind of question is that? Of course I *want* to. I don't just take everything I want."

"For cripes' sake, Brian, I'm not suggesting you *rape* her." John fished more chips from the bowl and focused back on the Steelers, fourth down with seven yards to go.

Brian massaged his forehead. "I know." Maybe being tired made him hypersensitive. He rubbed his hand over his mouth, concealing a smile and thinking of a surefire way to end this line of conversation.

"If you're confused on what the Church teaches about sex, I'd be happy to give you a refresher." Mom had made sure the Perella kids never missed a parish youth group retreat—especially the one that covered dating and sex.

John gave him a side-eye. "Don't even."

Oh, he wouldn't get off *that* easy. "Isn't Brady in second grade this year? Getting ready to make his First Communion?" He took a long drink of Coke and reached for a few chips. The carbonated sweetness always made him crave something salty.

Eyes fixed on the game, John plunked one foot and then the other on the coffee table. "That's for me and Kate to worry about. Not your business."

Yeah . . . no. "Became my business when you asked me to be Brady's godfather."

No rebuttal came, only silence. Then, a change in subject.

"So, Melanie . . . you really like her? Like, *marry her* like her?"

The Steelers kicker nailed a field goal from fifty-five yards. *Yes!* John whooped and Brian clapped. A nervous thrill not related to the score zipped through his chest.

"Marry her? . . . Yeah. I think . . ." What did he think, really? He felt such peace with her, in her home. Time apart had become trying, boring, and lonely. He'd been tempering his feelings, taking it slow for her sake, knowing how tumultuous the last years had been for her life and her heart. But he couldn't deny how he felt about her. "I think I could live happily ever after with her."

John grinned, genuine happiness shining in his eyes. He raised his bottle for a toast. "Good deal. It's about time."

The giddy rush of happiness that came from saying it aloud to John couldn't be quashed. Brian tapped his aluminum can to John's bottle. "Yeah. It is." He swallowed the last of the Coke, finally sinking into the couch and relaxing.

The Bengals called a time out and the game went to a commercial.

"Be right back." John set his bottle on the table and strolled toward the bathroom.

A beer commercial came on, a bevy of women in Daisy

Dukes with flat, tan exposed bellies and ample cleavage crowding around a nerdy guy at the bar.

Create a clean heart in me, O God. He recited the rote verse more from habit than anything else.

Nothing. He felt nothing. Not a whit of temptation. If anything, a fleeting flash of pity struck him for the women in the ads, for everyone seduced by their objectification, for his past, and the broken world in which he lived. But no temptation. No recollection of other images, either his or his former co-worker Raymond Boyle's.

He sighed in relief and closed his eyes, a silent prayer of thanks on his lips.

Fingers jammed hard into his shoulder, forcing Brian's eyes open. "Huh? What's going on?" He blinked, trying to see through the mental fog.

John chuckled. "Uh, you slept through the game. There's two minutes left."

Brian rubbed his eyes and sat forward, squinting at the screen. "What's the score?"

"Steelers 43, Bengals 20."

"Good." He hadn't even realized he'd dosed off. Must've been while John was in the bathroom. Shoot. He never did that.

John tugged on the metal pull cord dangling from the light fixture and ceiling fan above them, and the light switched on. "You sick or something?" He stared, examining Brian's face.

"Huh?" Brian squinted in the bright light.

"You never fall asleep during a game, even when it goes long."

Pressing his hands against his knees, Brian stood to get his circulation going. "I don't know. The last few weeks, I'm just dead tired all the time. No matter how long I sleep at night, I can't shake it."

John's brow wrinkled. "You look clammy or sweaty or something."

He did? Brian swiped a hand across his forehead. He didn't feel warm, but he *was* a little sweaty.

"You should go to the doctor. You might be anemic or something."

Was a trip to the doctor necessary? He'd give it a few more days, see if he felt any better. If he had something contagious, he didn't want Melanie or her kids to catch it. He wanted to give them so many things—love, support, stability, his whole blessed life. But not whatever bug had depleted all his energy.

CHAPTER 16

Brian pulled his car into Melanie's driveway, shifted it into park, and gulped the last of an energy drink, his second today. Fat flurries drifted from the night sky, swirling in the breeze, their quiet descent so serene.

In the soft moonlight, the concrete steps leading to her door shimmered; the kids had decorated them with neon-colored chalk. Careful not to coat his soles in the dust, he climbed past a green alien with giant eyes and tentacles, an orange stick figure hanging from a noose, and random circular scribbles.

Brian reached for the doorknob but paused before turning it. Melanie had told him to come right in. It made him feel like one of the family. Is that how she thought of him? He hoped so.

He sighed and sent a grateful prayer heavenward, glancing up. At the empty porch light fixture. Oh yeah. He twisted his lips, irritated that he never remembered to ask her about it. Next week he'd bring a bulb along, screw it in, and see what happened.

Only two steps inside the door, warmth and the aroma of something chocolatey enveloped him. He pulled the door shut, careful to remain quiet, hung his coat on the rack, and slipped off his shoes.

Meandering through the dark living room toward the couch, the light coming from upstairs drew his gaze. He sank into the soft cushions, knowing he'd have to wait until Melanie completed the kids' bedtime routine.

The boys' manic voices interspersed with laughter and Melanie's shushing sounds filtered down the stairs, leading him to conclude Penny had already fallen asleep. After a few minutes, quiet descended. Probably saying prayers.

And then his heart stalled.

The strains of Melanie's soft soprano wafted down the stairs, lyrics about the stars, the moon, and a mother's love filled with tender affection. A few seconds of silence followed, and then the singing resumed.

Brian closed his eyes, for once not because sleep beckoned, but because the darkness allowed the sweetness of the moment to better penetrate his heart. Beauty existed, persisted even, despite the ugliness in the world and in his own heart. Some had reduced "blessed" to a hashtag, a superficial shortcut for one-upping your seemingly less-than-blessed neighbor, who suffered under the weight of any number of crippling crosses. But this, truly, was a blessed moment, one in which he surely glimpsed a glimmer of God's goodness.

Maternity had never ranked among the traits he found most attractive in a woman, but he discovered that with Melanie, it had rocketed to the top of his short list. Her devotion, even in the most difficult of circumstances, inspired him to be better, to be more. To be what and who God had called Brian Perella to be not only, he hoped, for Melanie and her children, but for its own sake.

"Hey." The whisper came soft and sultry in his ear as the warmth of her touch soaked through his shoulder.

Blinking, Brian opened his eyes.

Melanie sat beside him in the darkness, the light from upstairs now extinguished. "You're like a cat burglar, all stealthy. I didn't even know you were here." She kissed his cheek and then snuggled against him, propping his arm around her. In a long charcoal-colored scoop neck shirt and matching cotton pants, her body rested warm and soft against his.

"You told me to come in, so I did." He squeezed her shoulder, tugging her closer. "I heard you singing."

"Did I put you to sleep too?" She slung her arm around his waist and tucked her head beneath his chin.

"Not quite." He rubbed her arm, relishing her closeness. "It was beautiful." He shifted, forcing her upright so he could admire her in the dim light from the kitchen fixture. In the near darkness, her eyes appeared a deep, dark pine color and her skin a silky peaches-and-cream. With his free hand, he cupped her cheek and ran his thumb across her lips.

Heat flickered in her eyes before she closed them and pressed her lips to his in a kiss that left him aching for more—more of her, of them, of *life*.

Driven by the desire sweeping through him, he pulled her onto his lap and kissed her chin, her ear, and her neck.

A soft groan traveled from her supple lips to his ear, intensifying the deep yearning he had for her, one that tempted him to ignore everything he believed about love, sex, and integrity. With reluctance, he dragged his lips from her silky skin and settled her beside him, taking a moment to clear his mind.

His gaze flicked about the dark room, the too-quiet house. Maybe someday they'd add candlelight and soft music to this scenario, relishing the privacy borne of sleeping children. But not tonight. Not when he didn't share this home as her husband. And not before he'd told her he loved her—though that would happen soon.

Melanie pressed a closed fist to her lips, a bashful, almost apologetic look to her. "One thing leads to another pretty fast, huh?"

He laced his fingers through hers and squeezed her hand. "Yep." Good thing they were on the same page about that; not like it had been with his former girlfriend Abby.

She crossed her legs beneath her, keeping their joined hands on her lap. "So, I have a confession to make."

"Go ahead." Couldn't be too bad based on the flirty tone she used.

She met his gaze, head on. "You make me feel gooey inside."

Joy filled his heart, causing him to smile in what must've been a ridiculous grin. He hadn't forgotten her admission that her love for David, strong and real as it had been, lacked that spark, that sometimes-irrational euphoria that conjured fluttery butterflies in the belly, jellied knees, and dopey smiles like the one he was sporting right now.

"Yeah? You make me feel gooey inside too." Thank God John wasn't privy to this conversation. He'd never live it down. He raised her hand to his lips and let it linger there, realizing his heartbeat still well-outpaced the quiet ticking of the mantel clock.

She lowered their hands, her eyes wide and serious now. "I feel like I should confess something else too."

This confession wouldn't be as sweet. Of that, he was certain. "Okay."

She reached for the lamp on the end table and switched it on, bathing the room in pale light. Relaxing back into the couch, her hand went to her ring finger and then her wrist. An engagement ring already topped his shopping list, but he ought to buy the woman some more of those bangle-style bracelets she liked too.

She breathed deeply and blew it out, as if summoning courage. "When I didn't feel, y'know, that way about David, I did something stupid."

He nodded, waiting for her to continue.

"Not at first. A few years ago, I guess." She pushed off of the couch, rounded the coffee table, and paced in front of him, shoving aside a few stray plastic dinosaurs with her bare foot.

"I didn't mean to. I just sort of . . ." She shrugged. "Fell into it." She stooped to snatch another toy from the floor and tossed it into a bin alongside the couch. "Some other moms were talking about books that had, uh, livened up things in the bedroom." She faced him then, her hands twisted together, her cheeks flushed.

"Some of them were plain smut, and I knew that. I wouldn't read those. But I thought maybe a regular romance. One that had a pretty cover with flowers and a normal-looking couple." She sat beside him, her hands still, her eyes earnest. "But I learned quickly I'd have to be more discerning. I wanted the sweet romances that reminded me of how love could be. The kind that would remind me of how God put this attraction in our hearts." She tapped her chest. "It's such a gift, and I felt like I missed out. And I wanted that, maybe selfishly, with David."

The remorse in her voice pained him. "I don't think there's anything wrong with that, Melanie. It's like putting on a pretty dress or making a fancy meal or buying lingerie—"

"No." She shook her head. "It wasn't like that. You're right, if that was the kind of book I picked up. But it wasn't." She averted her gaze, staring off toward the mantel where pictures of her and David still stood. "I knew right away I'd gotten the wrong kind of book, even if it was by accident. But that didn't stop me from reading it. I didn't skip the bedroom scenes. I read them. And *re-read* them. And downloaded more of the same kinds of books and did the same thing."

She rubbed her forehead and bit her lips together, obviously troubled by her admission.

He scooped up her hand and pressed it between his, rubbing his thumb along hers. Thoughts swirled, stirring his conscience.

He'd resolved not to tell her about his struggle with pornography, reasoning that he hadn't had any setbacks. Not in years. The problem remained firmly in his past and posed no threat to their relationship. But he'd been tempted. Severely and recently, and she deserved to know. With sudden clarity, he knew that once she'd confessed, he needed to do the same.

"I didn't feel closer to David. I felt alienated." She gazed at him, begging, it seemed, for his understanding. "It made me secretive. I was ashamed, and I hid what I was doing. The books, the purchases. And when we were together . . ." She wiped a stray tear from her eye. "When we were intimate, I felt a spark, but it wasn't for him. I would never, *never* think of being with another man when I was with him. But somehow it seemed okay to think of imaginary people."

A tear rolled down her cheek, then another.

He brushed at them clumsily with his thumb, but she pulled away.

"I took what was supposed to bring us together and twisted it for my own pleasure." She gestured toward the upstairs. "We weren't renewing our vows in that bed. *I* wasn't anyhow. I was a voyeur, taking pleasure from . . . from fictional people."

They shared this temptation. Not the same. Not quite. But close. As a guy, he sought images. As a woman, she sought words. But they were both trying to quell their loneliness, both seeking their own pleasure. His pleasure came at the expense of women he didn't know; hers came at the expense of her own husband.

He let her words settle between them, gathering his own thoughts and mustering his courage. She'd humbled herself before him, baring her soul. His gut clenched. He owed her the same, difficult as it would be.

"So, even though the attraction thing isn't an issue here . . ." She motioned between them, a small smile brightening her expression. "I wanted to be honest. I stopped when I realized the damage it was causing. I got rid of the books. I refused to entertain the memories of those scenes anymore. When David was out of town, I dragged the kids to church early on a Saturday morning, and I went to confession."

He nodded, calm and reassuring, his heart swelling with admiration for her. And love. Deep, abiding love that claimed every part of his heart. He'd tell her, just as soon as he shared his struggles with her.

"Melanie, that you trust me with this means the world to me." He swallowed hard. He hadn't spoken of this with anyone in a long, long time. And never with a woman. *Come on, just spit it out.*

Despite the growing clamminess of his hand, he clutched hers. "I want you to know I don't think any of less of you. Just the opposite. I understand. I understand because—"

"Mo-ooommm!" Kevin wailed from upstairs. "Mom!"

Melanie darted from the couch. "Oh boy. Give me a minute." She jogged up the steps. "I hope he's not sick."

Maybe Kevin wasn't, but Brian was. He'd been on the verge of spilling his darkest secrets, unburdening himself of the guilt he still carried around, despite all reason. Though just an hour ago, he'd been convinced he should remain mum on the subject, he now felt an urgency to share it in all its ugliness, with Melanie. But he'd have to wait.

$\mathcal{A}$s Melanie turned the corner into the boys' bedroom, the nightlight revealed Kevin standing beside his bed, smeared with blood—his face, pajama sleeves, and probably his pillow. Bloody noses were a minor nuisance, but seeing one of her children looking like an extra in a slasher movie always unsettled her.

"My nose is bleeding." Kevin raised a hand to his nose in a futile attempt to wipe away the blood.

"Hang on." Melanie dashed to the bathroom, grabbing a washcloth and a box of tissues.

"Everything okay?" Brian called from downstairs, concern in his voice.

Oh, how good of him to ask! For once, she didn't feel like she was walking a tightrope without a net. Someone else stood ready to catch her because he cared—for her *and* her children. "Just a bloody nose," she called loud enough for him to hear, but not enough to wake the other kids. She hoped.

"Coach is here?" Kevin asked, the wad of tissues pinching his nose, making him sound nasally.

"Yep. Hold that tight." In a jiffy, she darted to the bathroom and returned with a fresh, damp cloth. Dabbing the blotches of blood from his face and hands, she surveyed his pajamas and bedding. A fresh top and a clean pillowcase should do the trick.

"What're you doin' with Coach?"

"Kissing and talking about my dalliance with bodice rippers" didn't seem like the most appropriate answer for a five-year-old. "Oh, I think we're gonna watch a movie."

"Oh." Seeming satisfied with that answer, he allowed Melanie to escort him to the bathroom, where she ensured the bleeding had stopped and got him cleaned and changed.

Back in the bedroom, she replaced the pillowcase and tucked Kevin into bed with a kiss and a blessing.

Making sure she hadn't gotten any blood on herself, Melanie descended the stairs with careful steps. She hoped tending to Kevin hadn't eaten up too much of their date time. But Brian had said, more than once, that he accepted all that went along with dating a mother of little ones. And bodily fluids leaking from various orifices at all times of the day and night were definitely part of the deal.

In the living room, picture-in-picture video played without sound in the corner of the screen, alongside a couple rows of movie titles. Brian reclined on the couch, head tilted back, lips parted, and sound asleep with the remote control in his hand

She smiled at the scene. He'd been such a sleepyhead lately. A twinge of guilt reminded her she was often the reason he kept late nights. But tonight was Saturday; he wouldn't have to get up early tomorrow.

She cleared her throat, hoping the sound would wake him, but it took a nudge to his shoulder too.

He jerked to attention. "Kevin all right?" His voice was rough with sleep.

"Fine. His nose bleeds from time to time. Messy, but not a big deal."

"Yeah. Used to happen to me when I was a kid too."

"So, did you find us something decent to watch?"

"I think so." He selected the movie at the top of the screen. "I think it meets all of our requirements: no gore, not too violent, no subtitles, not a chick flick."

"And no on-screen sex," she added, shooting him a mischievous grin.

"Yeah . . . Listen, Melanie, about before . . ." He laid the remote on the table.

"Did I make you uncomfortable?" Embarrassment kept her from looking him in the eye. "I'm sorry if I did. I've never told anyone about that. Not even David." Her tongue had a twitchy urge to ramble, so she clamped her lips shut.

"You didn't make me uncomfortable." He sat forward, rubbing his hands along his jeans. "I'm glad you told me. I, uh . . ." Despite what he said, his brow was pinched, his gaze unsteady, and his voice hesitant: the picture of discomfort.

"Maybe we should just watch the movie." *Oh!* She'd nearly forgotten. "I made cookies with the kids. Chocolate chip." She jumped off of the couch and bounced to the kitchen. "You want some? Something to drink?"

At the kitchen table, she stacked cookies on a dessert plate. Had he answered her and she'd totally missed it? She did that with the kids all the time, but seldom with adults. "Brian?"

"Uh, yeah. Whatever you want to drink is fine." Distance muffled his voice, but it sounded like he was moving, pacing the room. Why the anxiety?

"Is a glass of wine okay? I know it doesn't exactly go with cookies." But it did calm nerves, and after their conversation and the bloody nose incident, she could use it. It seemed like he could too. She grabbed a couple of glasses from the cupboard and a bottle of wine from its shelf. She hesitated, taking in the sheen of the olive-green bottle of Prosecco. Wine also tended to lower her inhibitions and put her in the mood for romance. She'd need to watch that.

Brian shuffled into the kitchen, his face brightening as he spotted the cookies. "Mmm. They look good." He snatched one, took a bite, and grabbed the plate, allowing her to pass with their wine.

Whatever had Brian on edge must've been forgotten. They enjoyed the movie, relaxed, and snuggled on the couch, munching cookies and sipping wine. The clock displayed 12:30 a.m. by the time the credits rolled.

Seeming stiff, Brian stood, stretched, and then rubbed his collar bone, his expression pinched. He rolled his shoulder a couple of times. "Man, it's like someone's stabbing a steak knife into my shoulder."

Nothing looked unusual about his shoulder or the way he was holding it. "Did you do something to it?"

He paused, eyes trained on the ceiling. "No . . . I don't think so." Again, he massaged the spot where it hurt.

"You want a couple of ibuprofen?" She stood, steadying herself with a hand to the couch arm, and then headed for the kitchen, anticipating his answer.

"Yeah. Thanks. And then I'd better go."

The floorboards in the foyer creaked as he walked to the coat rack. When she met him at the door, he'd already put on his coat, a knit cap, and a pair of gloves.

She handed him the pills and a glass of water. Cold air leaking in from around the door sent a chill through her, and she ran her hands over her arms, trying to warm herself. Pushing aside the curtain, she peeked out the window. Barren tree limbs created dark shadows on crumpled leaves littering the yard. No cars moved. No lights illuminated the neighbors' houses. "Feels like the temperature dropped."

He swallowed the pills and water and handed the glass back to her. "And it's not even winter yet."

She glanced outside again and then back to him. "I hate that you have to go out in the cold."

He stepped closer, placing a hand on each of her arms, drawing her nearer. "Me too. It's awfully cozy in here." The scruff of his beard scraped her skin as he kissed her cheek and then her lips. "Good night."

Cold air nipped at her nose and toes as Melanie shut the door behind him, disappointment causing her shoulders to sag. She walked through the living room, gathering stray cups, dishes, and random trash the kids had left behind in their slap-dash cleanup effort before bed.

Recalling the feel of Brian's beard stubble on her cheek and the faint scent of his sandalwood cologne, she smiled as she rinsed and stacked the dishes. She should be tired, but instead, a dreamy sort of elation left her wide awake.

A knock sounded on the front door, and she dried her hands on her pants as she shuffled to the foyer. She glanced around the living room. Had Brian forgotten something?

After peering through the window to confirm it was him, she opened the door, shivering.

Brian stood on the porch, rubbing his gloved hands together, little white puffs coming from his nose and mouth.

"What's wrong?"

"Car won't start. I think it's the battery." He stepped inside, closing the door behind him. "Do you have jumper cables?"

"Uh . . ." She ran a hand through her hair, trying to recall the last time she'd used them and where they might be. "They should be in the garage, but I don't know where. That was David's domain."

He started down the hall toward the basement door and access to the garage. "Mind if I look?"

"Of course not, but . . ." Her tummy tingled, and she blurted out, "Why don't you stay?"

Brian's shoe squeaked where he stopped short in the kitchen. "Stay?"

"Yeah." She gripped her wrist, searching for bracelets that

weren't there. "It's almost one, it's cold, you're gonna have to search the garage, and the light in there is horrible. And I . . ." Her gaze flicked to the door and back. "I worry about you driving when you're so tired. Especially because of, um, what happened to David."

He stared, his sympathetic gaze softening and growing warmer as he perused her, head to toe.

Her cheeks warmed. "I can make up a bed . . . on the couch."

Rubbing his chin, he seemed to consider it. "Are you sure it's not too much trouble?"

She shook her head, pushing aside the concerns that had suddenly surfaced. What about the kids? Would the neighbors notice Brian's car parked in the driveway all night? "Of course not. I'll go get some bedding."

She left Brian in the kitchen and jogged up the stairs. In a few minutes, she'd managed to cover the couch with a quilt, fluff a freshly-covered pillow, and drape a warm blanket over the back. "There." She stood, hands on her hips, admiring the crude bed.

"Thanks." Brian had hung up his coat again and slipped off his shoes. He rotated his shoulder again, and she hoped sleeping on the couch wouldn't make it hurt worse.

"Um, there are towels and stuff in the powder room to wash up, and there should be a couple of new toothbrushes in the drawer." She took a step backward, wanting to give him some space but reluctant to leave.

"Thanks." He stared, waiting, a slow grin spreading across his face. "Is there something else?"

She shuffled backwards to the stairs. "Just wrestling."

He wrinkled his nose and tilted his head. "Wrestling?"

"With my conscience." She scrubbed her bare foot back and forth across the floor. "It's just that I hate sleeping alone. Always have. You'd think after years of little ones in and out of my bed I'd be grateful for some uninterrupted sleep, but I hate that big, empty bed." She laughed, and it sounded hollow, even to her. "So, I'm standing here trying to talk myself out of inviting you to sleep upstairs. With me." She bit her lower lip, regretting the words as soon as they passed her lips. He'd misunderstand. She'd look foolish. "Just sleep, not . . . anything else." Suddenly feeling shy, she focused on her feet.

He ambled toward her, stopping only when his toes touched hers, and took her hands in his, rubbing his thumbs across her knuckles. "The couch is one thing, but, Melanie, as much as I love the idea of falling asleep together, I'm pretty sure that I can't lie in bed with you and just sleep. Tired as I am."

Her cheeks were aflame, but still she inched closer, closing the already tight space between them. Heart pounding and hand unsteady, she fiddled with the hair at his nape then caressed his neck, his cheek, and brushed her lips against his.

The heated look he gave her said she was getting to him, and part of her—not the better part—hoped he'd succumb.

Brian dug his hands deep into her hair and kissed her, the pressure as firm and resolute as the look he gave her once he'd released her. "Don't make me change my mind." He darted a glance at the stairs. "You've got kids up there." He turned and walked toward the couch.

She did. Three small people with impressionable minds. The reason she hadn't invited Brian to her bed already. Shame descended, its weight pressing on her shoulders like a heavy blanket. What had happened to her?

Beside the couch, Brian patted his pillow and adjusted the bedding, as if waiting for her to leave. "Good night." His tone remained affectionate as always, but she had no doubt she'd been dismissed.

Tears stinging her eyes, Melanie turned and trotted up the steps, admonishing herself to keep it together until she got to her bedroom.

"Melanie?"

She stopped, her foot on the top step. "Yeah?"

The warmth of his gaze travelled across the room, searing her heart. "All in good time, right?"

She nodded, her lips pressed together to hold the tears at bay, climbed the final step to the landing, and hurried to her room.

With the door ajar in case one of the children called for her, she sunk onto the mattress and buried her face in her hands, stifling a sob. When had she become so needy? Was she so bereft of a man's love that she'd become willing to compromise her beliefs?

Or had she always been this weak-willed and vulnerable? What if she had met Brian first, before David? When she'd lacked maturity, experience, and impressionable children? Maybe God sent her David first for her own sake. Or maybe grief and stress had snowballed into a moral backslide.

She breathed deeply and wiped the tears from her face.

With quiet steps, she slipped into the bathroom to wash her face and brush her teeth, never raising her head to the mirror.

onsciousness lingered on the fringe of a dream. Something was seriously, fatally, flat-out wrong with little hope of improvement and everything good had been lost. What that *something* was, Brian didn't know, but an uneasy melancholy roused him from a sound sleep.

He blinked.

"Holy—!" Big round eyes hovered less than six inches from his. A little boy's face . . . Kevin? Fortunately, Brian bit down on the word forming on his lips. He scrambled into an upright position, kicking off the blanket tangled around his legs.

In a second, he processed where he was—Melanie's couch—and why: dead car battery. What *didn't* make sense was why Kevin stood bright-eyed, deep into Brian's personal space.

"What're you doin' here still?" Kevin hopped onto the couch alongside him, his too short shark-print pajamas riding up mid-shin.

His stomach tightened. He'd hoped to be up and out first thing this morning, *before* the kids woke. He rolled his shoulders and tilted his head from side to side, stretching his neck muscles. Gosh, it didn't feel like he'd slept at all. "My car wouldn't start last night." He glanced at the window, trying to gauge the time based on the amount of light seeping around the closed drapes. Maybe he could still sneak out and get his car started before Matthew and Penny awoke. "Do you know what time it is?"

Kevin kicked his feet up and down. "I dunno. Can't tell time. But Matthew said it was time to get up so we could surprise Mom."

"Surprise her? What for?" Brian shoved off the blanket and shuffled to the window, pushing aside the drape. The sun was up, but just barely. It cast a dull, dusky haze over the front yard.

"We're makin' her pancakes."

Brian studied Kevin, wondering if that was something kids their age could do. Would Melanie be up soon? Maybe he should tell them to wait for her. "Do you usually make Sunday breakfast?" Cool air seeped in alongside the window, making him shiver. Yesterday's clothes stuck to him in spots, his skin damp with sweat.

"No." He slid off of the couch and skipped to the kitchen. "But today's her birthday."

Her *birthday*? Shoot! Why hadn't she said anything? There went his "Boyfriend of the Year" award.

Matthew galloped down the steps, fully dressed in navy blue pants and a pint-sized rugby shirt with maroon and yellow stripes. "Why are *you* here, Coach?"

His mid-section constricted again. *Caught.* Kids got right to the point, and Brian was doubly glad he'd slept on the couch and not upstairs, not that it had ever been a real option. "Your mom and I watched a movie last night—"

"His car broke." Kevin called from the kitchen, where metal bowls or pans clattered.

Yeah, and I should be outside fixing it by now. He'd search for the jumper cables once he made sure the boys weren't going to burn down the kitchen. And then come up with a last-minute birthday gift.

"Oh." Matthew breezed past him into the kitchen, the master chef ready to assume command.

Standing on a sturdy plastic stool, Kevin stared at a large recipe card smeared with who-knows-what. "I can't read."

"Gimme that." Matthew plucked the recipe from beneath his brother's face. "You get the eggs. I'll get the flour and the other stuff."

Kevin hopped off the stool, causing it to skitter across the floor. Brian imagined a dozen eggs splattered there, their yolks oozing between crushed shells.

"Hey, I'll grab the eggs." Brian squeezed between the boys to the refrigerator. "Kevin, how about you get out the griddle or whatever you make pancakes on?"

Brian set the eggs on the counter, alongside the metal bowls and a wooden spoon. "Why didn't you guys tell me it was your mom's birthday?" What could he get her at the last minute? Did regular department stores sell those bangle bracelets she liked?

Matthew shrugged. "She says she's not havin' any more birthdays 'cause she's old, but it's marked on the calendar." He pointed to the wall calendar, which had appointments, practices, and meetings scratched on nearly every square.

"Your mother is not old." Not by a long shot, but to little kids, everything over seventeen probably seemed ancient.

To Brian's surprise, the boys seemed to have the ingredients and the mixing well in hand. They'd obviously done this with Melanie many times. Maybe they could handle the rest on their own. He pulled a bottle of maple syrup from the refrigerator and set it on the counter to warm. Would Melanie be coming down soon? Should he go up and say goodbye? "So, does your mom drink coffee in the morning?"

"She likes Herb tea." Kevin lined three eggs on the counter.

They rolled every which way, and he scrambled to throw a hand in front of them before they dropped onto the floor.

"Herb tea?" Chuckling, Brian opened the cupboard, searching for tea bags. Despite the fact he'd wanted to be long gone, he treasured this camaraderie with the boys. "You mean, she's brewing some guy named Herb or she likes herbal tea, with a silent h?"

Matthew cracked the eggs over the metal bowl, tossing the goopy shells mostly into the trash. "It was Dad's joke. Herb, herbal." He shot a scornful look at Kevin. "Doofus doesn't know the difference."

Wielding a wooden spoon like a ninja weapon, Kevin kicked Matthew in the shin. "Yes, I do."

"Okay, guys." Brian fanned his shirt in front of him, uncomfortable even being around food preparation when he felt so sweaty and grungy. "How about I start the kettle boiling and then go wash my face. You wake up your mom. Then we'll cook the pancakes."

Brian grabbed the tea kettle from the stove and filled it at the sink. He didn't have anything to give Melanie, but maybe they could do something together today. Might as well accept the fact he'd missed his opportunity to sneak out. And truly, at this point, he didn't want to go. He'd take the family . . . somewhere.

"I wanna do butterfly-shaped pancakes." Kevin dragged the step stool across the kitchen, making an awful grinding sound as it slid over spilled sugar.

Butterflies. That sparked an idea! "Hey, your mom likes butterflies, right?"

Matthew turned from the mixing bowl and stared at the giant teal metal butterfly perched on the kitchen wall. "Uh, yeah."

"Do you think she'd like it if we took her to the butterfly house this afternoon? The one at the conservatory?" A workable plan. A birthday gift salvaged. Brian sighed in relief.

Kevin jumped up and down on the stool, shifting it this way and that. "Yeah!"

With a hand to his shoulder, Brian steadied Kevin. "Okay. We'll do that. Let me go clean up while you get your mom."

"You should get her." Matthew pointed a metal spatula at him. "It'll be more of a surprise."

Yeah, seeing him in her bedroom at dawn would be a surprise all right. "Okay. Give me a minute."

After using the bathroom, washing his face, and finger combing his hair, Brian climbed the stairs, nervous anticipation building in his belly. It was only pancakes, but the boys' excitement was contagious.

With a gentle touch, Brian pushed open Melanie's bedroom door. Dim light from the hall flooded the room. A red and pink stuffed monkey with Velcro hands lay in a heap atop her patchwork quilt, alongside a set of plastic handcuffs and a rubbery triceratops. Would an outsider consider she had young children or think she ran a kinky sex operation on the side? And would a normal person question that or only one with a history like Brian's?

He made out her shape beneath the quilt, where she lay facing away from him. And another, smaller shape, pressed tightly against her. Melanie hadn't slept alone last night after all.

Penny lay spread eagle atop the covers, her hand across Melanie's hair where it lay fanned on the pillow.

"Melanie." He touched her shoulder, hoping he could rouse her gently. "Melanie." He said it louder this time and shook her.

She grunted and rolled onto her back. Tousled brown hair fell into her eyes as she shoved Penny off of her and propped herself on her elbows. "Oh, uh, good morning." She rubbed at the corners of her eyes.

He smiled, imagining waking up to her face every morning. He had a hard enough time getting out of bed as it was. "I was gonna get up early, jump the car, and go, but the boys woke up first. They wanted me to wake you." He glanced at the door. "They've been hard at work in the kitchen making you a birthday surprise."

"They spilled my secret, huh?" She sat up, and the covers slid down, revealing a v-neck cotton sleep shirt with pink and blue stripes. Tucking the quilt against her, she yanked the sheets higher, causing Penny to moan and inch closer.

"Why didn't you tell me?" In truth, it hurt a little that she hadn't mentioned it, though he doubted that she'd intended that.

Her gaze dropped to her lap. "It's just another day. I don't need a big fuss."

"Why not?" He tilted her chin up. "It may be another day to you, but not to your boys." He included himself among her *"boys."* Melanie had been an unexpected, unadulterated dream come true. An answer to his prayers. Her life was worth celebrating.

Her eyes glistened in the dim light, and she nodded. "They do like birthdays."

"Well, I'm gonna start the griddle for them, so don't dawdle." He slipped out, closing the door behind him.

"Turn down the fire!" Matthew ordered from downstairs.

Brian, eyes wide, heart faltering, raced down the stairs for the kitchen. He hoped breakfast wouldn't end in him having to activate the fire extinguisher.

CHAPTER 19

In the driveway, below her bedroom window, Melanie spotted Brian's car. A thick layer of frost covered the front window where the morning sun hadn't reached. Would the neighbors have noticed it hadn't moved? What about sweet Mrs. Russell across the street? She always had a ready smile and a Bible verse to share.

With a hairbrush, Melanie smoothed her messy hair and then roused Penny. From the sounds of voices and clattering plates traveling up the stairs, the boys were serious about their pancake production.

Melanie stepped into the kitchen with Penny propped on her hip. Penny, clad in cupcake footie pajamas, fiddled with the tie on Melanie's robe. A buttery aroma accompanied by a soft sizzle filled the air. Open containers of flour, sugar, and baking soda sat on the countertop, and what she guessed was egg white splattered the floor below.

If she had a lilt in her step, despite the heft of a well-fed preschooler, her birthday was responsible. She'd told Brian she hadn't wanted a fuss, but she couldn't feign disappointment that her secret had been discovered.

Last year, she'd had little to celebrate beyond the survival of another day. This year had been considerably better. While she hadn't completely accepted the unwelcome changes to her life (Exhibit A: the cringe-worthy scene last night with Brian), she'd forged ahead, keeping her little family afloat in a storm-tossed sea. From her present vantage, the coming year looked like smooth sailing in comparison.

Matthew stood at the stove, carefully flipping a plate-sized pancake with a too-small spatula. Batter dripped from the stove top and along the counter between the griddle and the mixing bowl. Brian hovered behind him in yesterday's clothes, shifting his weight from one foot to the other, raising a hand and then lowering it in a dance so familiar to Melanie. It lacked steady rhythm but involved the persistent tug of wanting to take over and do things right, yet knowing you should allow the child to learn to do it himself . . . regardless of the mess involved and the less-than-perfect results.

Gazing on the scene, warmth filled her heart. They'd been careful not to let Brian become a surrogate dad when they weren't sure he'd ever assume that role. So despite the fact that they enjoyed spending time as a quasi-family and that the arrangement cost the adults sleep, they'd stuck with it. Oh, the kids knew she spent more and more time with "Coach Brian" while they slept and on date nights, but he remained a "friend" to them and not "Dad."

Still, at times like this, Melanie couldn't help but crave more of having Brian close, in their home, as if he belonged. He'd become much more than "coach" to her, filling her mind and heart with thoughts of him day and night. His interaction with the kids—not only when they were well-behaved, like now, but when they melted down—showed her what kind of dad he'd be. A good one. Involved, patient, kind.

Kevin ambled in from the dining room with a fistful of paper napkins. "Table's set." He spied Melanie, and a huge smile lit his face. He ran to her, arms wide. "Happy Birthday, Mom."

On impact, Melanie stepped back to steady herself and pulled Penny closer. "Thank you. What's going on down here? It smells delicious."

Matthew turned, proudly holding a pancake on his spatula. "We made pancakes for you." He stepped to the side, revealing a large stack of golden-brown pancakes on a platter. "We made a whole batch all by ourselves."

Brian turned toward her, his eyes tired but affectionate. "They did. I was the hands-off supervisor." He reached back and switched off the burner. "I did provide a short lesson in adjusting the flame on the burner though." Eyes wide, he gave her a tight grin.

She sent up a silent prayer of thanksgiving that there had been no accident. Once Brian had exited her bedroom, his footfalls down the steps had been fast, urgent, and, apparently, delivered him to the kitchen right on time.

Penny scrambled down, her hair sticking up in every direction, still clutching a tattered stuffed bunny in one hand. She crossed the room to Brian and hugged his legs.

"Hey, princess." He scooped her and her bunny up and away from the hot stove. "You're just as pretty as a picture this morning."

Penny giggled and tucked her head beneath Brian's chin, her legs kicking with glee.

Melanie just about melted like the butter puddling on the griddle. Imagine the fuss he'd make over a baby. His baby. *Their baby.*

"Sit down, so we can eat!" Kevin bustled around the room, pushing them all toward the dining table. In minutes, he and Matthew had managed to get breakfast to the table, complete with butter, syrup, orange juice, and only one minor spill.

Brian slid a steaming mug of tea in front of her. With a hand to her shoulder, he kissed her temple and whispered, "Happy Birthday, Melanie."

Her cheeks flushed warm. She laid a hand on his arm and whispered, "Thank you," hoping he grasped the depth behind those two words. Yes, he'd helped the boys avoid disaster this morning in preparing a surprise for her. But more than that, he'd single-handedly rescued her from months of loneliness steeped in grief not only for her husband but for the loss of a dream. And he'd done it in the most unassuming way imaginable by simply being there, seeing her, listening to her.

And loving her?

He hadn't said it. But neither had she. Yet.

They said grace, and Melanie lifted her fork to cut into her pancake.

"Look at the shape, Mom. See what it is?" Matthew bounced in his seat, eager for her answer.

Only she had no idea what it was. It resembled a fat hair bow, but she doubted that was intentional. "Oh. Um . . ." She glanced at Brian across the table, trying to communicate with her eyes a desperate plea for help.

"Butterfly," he mouthed, his hand blocking the view of his moving lips from the boys.

"A butterfly?" Yes, she could see it now. The wings weren't exactly symmetrical, but not too bad.

"Yeah." Kevin dragged a piece of pancake through syrup. "And Coach Brian is gonna take us to the butterfly house later."

Her eyebrows shot up. "Oh, he is?" She'd always wanted to visit but had been waiting for another adult to come along, not wanting to chase all three of them through the gardens alone.

"If that's okay." Brian sipped from a mug too, but it looked like he'd made coffee—strong and black. "After Mass."

"It sounds great." Her smile matched that of the kids, who seemed excited about the unexpected visit. This whole dead battery thing had really worked in her favor. "Did you get a chance to check on your car this morning?"

He shook his head and swallowed. "No. I'll try to start it when we're done here."

"What would've caused the battery to drain? Is it old?" Melanie was no expert on car troubles, but she'd had her share of dead batteries, broken starters, and failed alternators.

"No. Got it last year." He set his fork down, his lips and brow pinched tight. "An interior light was left on. I saw it as soon as I stepped out last night. I have no clue how it got on. I don't remember doing it."

Curious. "Maybe you bumped it."

"I don't think so." He poured more syrup on his pancakes and resumed eating. "I think jumping it will do the trick. I'll just need the cables, and I'll pull the van next to my car."

"Okay. You can do that while I help them get ready for church." He'd spent the entire evening with her, stayed the night, and now they shared breakfast with more plans for the afternoon, but she had to ask. "Do you want to come to Mass with us?"

He tapped his fork on the plate and glanced at each of the kids.

"Yeah, come with us!" Matthew sat alert, his eyes bright and eager.

"Sure." Brian forked another piece of pancake. "By the time I get home, I'll have missed it in my parish anyway."

"Good." The people at church would wonder who he was to her and the kids, but she didn't care. This birthday was shaping up as one of the best, and she wouldn't let her insecurities, petty gossip, or a dead car battery get in the way.

CHAPTER 20

Brian disengaged the jumper cables from the battery in Melanie's minivan and slammed the hood shut. Grateful that his car had started, he replaced the cables in the garage where he'd found them on a metal shelf next to a jar of used engine oil and a plastic jug of wiper fluid.

Relieved that a simple jump start had gotten his engine humming, he stood in front of the car, rubbing warmth into his cold hands. He'd swear that last night the lights had all been off and the car had been locked. But who would break into a car and flick on a light? Nothing in the car had been disturbed. Nothing was missing. Not that he kept anything of value in the car. Lately it had become a repository for empty energy drink bottles.

He entered the house through the garage and climbed the stairs to the first floor. Laying his jacket over the couch, he glanced at his shirt and pants. He'd managed not to get any dirt or grease on himself, thank goodness.

As he mounted the stairs for the second floor in search of Melanie, the kids marched down the steps in stocking feet but dressed for church. He high-fived each of them as they passed, his heart swelling at the sight of them. The boys' efforts to surprise Melanie with breakfast impressed him. And Penny, well, a smile from her tiny rosebud lips could set his heart aflutter.

Outside the open bathroom door, he tapped the wooden moulding, then leaned a shoulder against it, holding himself up. Despite the fact he'd only been awake for a couple of hours, he felt as if he could lie down and fall asleep in seconds. Especially since the shoulder pain had disappeared overnight.

Melanie stood in front of the bathroom mirror, wearing a teal green dress with a slim belt and pockets. The flared skirt hung to her knees. With her chin tilted up, exposing the soft, pale skin and delicate lines of her neck, she applied blush to her cheeks with her fingertips. "Did your car start?"

He redirected his thoughts from admiring her profile to his car, idling in the driveway. "Yeah. Jumping it worked. I'm letting it run for a while to charge the battery." He scratched the side of his head, still staring as she applied mascara with a little wand. "Y'know, I still can't figure out how I left that light on."

Could someone have broken into his car? Maybe mischievous teens? Or what would be a sorely-disappointed thief? The neighborhood seemed safe—well-lit; concerned neighbors; decent, hard-working people. Melanie hadn't mentioned any thefts or trouble—

"Brian?" Melanie's tone suggested she'd been talking while he'd been zoning out, thinking about his car.

"Yeah. Sorry. Can you repeat that?"

She returned her makeup to the drawer, closed it with her hip, and turned to him. "I said I could get used to this. You being here."

Had her cheeks grown pinker or was that the blush she'd applied? He could get used to it too. His heart still ached at how teary-eyed she'd looked before heading up to bed, after he'd as much as rejected her. She needed him. Needed his love. And he loved that she did. He wanted to give her everything she needed and deserved. "Me too."

He pushed off of the door frame as she stepped closer.

She placed a cool hand on either of his cheeks, the softness a contrast to the rough stubble. Despite the fresh splash of color on her lips, she kissed him, a sweet, soft, and short kiss that made him wish she had waited to apply the lipstick.

Her hands slid from his face, past his jaw, down his neck—and stopped. Her smile faded and a crease formed between her brows. "Are you feeling okay?

She pressed gently with her thumbs and forefingers. "Your glands . . . they seem a little swollen." Stepping back, she stared at his neck, tilting to look at one side and then the other. "Definitely swollen."

"Really?" He ran his hand along his neck but felt nothing unusual, although if he applied pressure, the spot did seem tender. "I feel good. Just tired."

"I can't find my shoe!" Penny called from downstairs.

Melanie sighed. "Every Sunday." She glanced at her wristwatch as she slipped behind him toward the hall. "We've gotta go."

"Okay." Brian moved to the sink. "I'm gonna wash my face and hands real quick." He wished he had time for a shower, even if he had to put on the same clothes afterward. The grungy feeling caused by sweating in his sleep made him itch for hot running water and a bar of soap. But, with no time left, he'd have to wait until after Mass.

A once-over with soap and cold water went a long way in making Brian feel human, if not presentable, and within twenty minutes they'd arrived at church.

Brian's heart swelled with pride seeing Melanie and her children trail into the pew ahead of him. Misplaced pride maybe since they weren't "his."

He genuflected and followed them, taking a seat alongside

Matthew. Brian pulled the kneeler down so that they could kneel and pray. A second later, the kneeler next to them fell with a thud as Kevin scrambled onto his knees.

Overwhelming gratitude marked Brian's prayers as they flowed formless from his heart to the heavens. He could easily enumerate a lengthy list of things in his life for which he was grateful, starting with Melanie.

The lector, a stooped elderly man with gray hair and dark-framed glasses, strode to the ambo and read from a sheet of announcements.

Striving to maintain his concentration, Brian covered his face with his hands. Penny whisper-whined somewhere to his left, but he blocked the sound of her voice too.

In silence, he repeated the rote prayer he'd uttered countless times on his knees before Mass: *"Lord, if it's Your will, lead me to the woman who will be my wife."* He didn't give thought to the words, his mind racing ahead to prayers of thanksgiving and petition, including the healing of whatever infection left him tired and sweaty, now with swollen glands.

Unbidden and unmistakable, he heard in his heart: *"She's here with you today."*

His eyes flashed open, but his surroundings remained unchanged. The lector descended the steps, his announcements finished. Matthew knelt beside him, his face behind his hands, mimicking Brian's posture. Kevin flipped through an upside-down missal, and Penny played with the fringe of Melanie's black wrap as Melanie dug through her purse for something.

Emotion clogged Brian's throat as he took in the ordinary scene. These children and this woman were his life, his future. Unlike any petition Brian had ever made—and there had been many—this was the first God had confirmed in his heart. It rang true, reverberating in the core of his being.

The remainder of Mass passed in a distracted blur. The priest spoke about waiting, its purpose, and the need for waiting with patience. Kevin dropped the missal on the pew in front of them at least twice. The line for Communion moved at a snail's pace.

Once the recessional hymn concluded, Melanie sat and gathered their things. She shoved a couple of kids' bulletins, a pen, a baggie filled with crayons, and two crumpled tissues into her purse.

"Did we distract you?" she asked, busily handing the kids their coats. "They get fidgety, and—"

Seeing Penny struggle, he held open her coat. "Stop worrying. They were fine." He waited until Melanie met his gaze. "Really."

She nodded, seeming grateful for his reassurance.

The boys had already moved halfway up the aisle toward the back of the church. Penny struggled to keep up. The threesome stopped when they reached the line forming to greet the priest.

Eventually, Brian and Melanie reached them. Only a young woman with an elderly lady stood in front of them now, speaking to the priest in low tones.

Penny and Kevin inched forward, nearly bumping the women, eager for Father to acknowledge them. When their turn came, they hugged the priest's vestments as Matthew shook his hand. The priest, a slim middle-aged man with salt-and-pepper hair and an easy smile, asked them about school.

Kevin wheedled between his siblings, grabbed Brian's hand and pulled him forward. "Father Bob, this is Coach Brian." Kevin's eager voice and obvious pleasure gratified Brian. "He slept over at our house last night."

Brian's throat went dry. *What?* Of all things to say, why did Kevin choose that? *Exactly* what Brian had wanted to avoid by slipping out of the house early this morning.

Melanie's eyes grew wide with horror even as she grabbed Penny's hand to keep her from drifting into the sea of people leaving the church.

His voice suddenly choked, Brian managed a few words. "On the couch."

Father Bob smiled wider and nodded, amused it seemed.

Relief coursing through him, Brian's throat and tongue loosened and he elaborated. "I wanted Melanie to jump me, but it was late, so she suggested we go to bed."

Melanie hid her eyes behind her hand.

His necked warmed and his underarms grew sweaty. Oh . . . *no!* That didn't come out right.

Father Bob chuckled and then, shaking Melanie's free hand, leaned forward and kissed her cheek. "So, how's it going, Melanie?" He darted a glance at Brian. Not too discreet, this priest, but thankfully he seemed affable enough and likely hadn't misunderstood.

Melanie laughed too, looking relieved. "It's going well, Father."

Once they reached their vehicles, the kids piled into the minivan. Melanie set her purse on the front seat. "So, butterfly garden?" Her eyes twinkled with expectation.

"Yes. The butterfly birthday expedition." He slid his hands into his pockets and shifted his weight onto his heels.

She smiled, biting her lower lip, a combination that Brian found an appealing mixture of sweet and sexy. "After Penny's nap, around two?"

Ah, sleep! Penny wouldn't be the only one napping. "Two sounds perfect."

After dropping them off at home, Brian pulled his car alongside his apartment and spotted Mrs. Hosler, his seventy-something neighbor, peeping out her window. No doubt the nosy lady knew every one of his comings and goings. His absence last night must've thrown her for a loop.

Feeling cheeky, he smiled and waved as he emerged from the car.

Nose in the air, she turned, the curtain flapping down in her absence.

Brian stepped inside, tossed his keys on the end table, and headed straight for his bedroom, where he stripped off his clothes. He lifted his shirt to his nose, inhaling. *Sweaty.*

Eager for a shower, he balled his clothes and threw them in the hamper. He savored the warm water coursing over his head and shoulders longer than usual. Pressing his fingers to the sides of his neck, he felt for swollen glands.

Using the towel hanging on the back of the bathroom door, he dried himself and then pulled on an undershirt and sleep pants. His bed beckoned him, much more comfortable than Melanie's couch.

Lying on top of the bedspread with only a light blanket covering him, Brian closed his eyes and thought back over the morning. Melanie had seemed to enjoy the pancake breakfast, which had turned out better than expected.

He regretted that he didn't have more to give her for her birthday, aside from the trip to the butterfly house. No card, no cake. Oh well. He'd be buying her a better gift soon anyway—a diamond ring.

In seconds, his thinking became fuzzy and sleep descended.

CHAPTER 21

$\mathcal{M}$elanie peered through the living room window into the afternoon sun, scanning the street for Brian's car. A blue pickup truck rumbled past, followed by a banana-yellow Volkswagen beetle. Across the street, Mrs. Russell carried two sacks of groceries from her car toward her house, her black Dachshund Bentley nipping at her heels.

Behind her, the couch cushions squeaked in time with Penny's and Kevin's giggling.

"Stop jumping on the furniture!" she snapped, weary of their misbehavior.

"Is Coach here yet?" Matthew asked, coming alongside her.

She'd answered that question eight times in the past hour. And now, number nine. "No, he's not here yet."

Breathing deeply, she reprimanded herself for her short answers and even shorter temper. The kids were just excited about her birthday and the trip to the butterfly garden.

Her watch said Brian should've been here twenty minutes ago. While *she* sometimes showed up at appointments that late, hurried and harried, Brian always arrived on time.

157

She grabbed the phone from the end table and tapped out his number.

One ring . . . two . . . Had something happened to him after Mass?

"Hello?" His voice sounded husky. Groggy.

"Hey, it's me." She motioned to Kevin to stop launching himself from the furniture. Again. "We were expecting you about twenty minutes ago, and the kids are getting antsy. Is everything okay?"

He cursed, something he didn't do often, and never around the kids. "I'm sorry. I took a nap and overslept. I'll be there in . . . uh, fifteen minutes."

She glanced at her watch again. At this rate, by the time they got through the butterfly garden, the kids would be starving. "Okay." She tried to infuse her voice with something other than disappointment. "We'll see you soon."

The moment Brian pulled into the driveway, the kids barreled down the steps and propelled themselves into the van. Their excitement only grew as, twenty minutes later, they reached their destination.

Melanie scanned the families and patrons filling the conservatory lobby. Apparently, they'd unwittingly timed their visit with the grand opening of a pollinator garden. People milled about in every direction. She gripped Kevin's hand and double-checked to be sure Brian had hold of Penny.

Penny sat comfortably, held tight in Brian's arms, her eyes wide and alert as she took in the bright colors, floral scents, and the chatter of dozens of conversations.

"Stay close." Melanie held the gazes of Matthew and Kevin. "You two are to stick together and stay within my line of sight. Or Coach Brian's. Got it?"

They nodded, but their attention flitted about the room and toward the butterfly house.

Maybe she should've brought the stroller for Penny, but

Penny wasn't one to be pushed around. She wanted to stretch her legs and be free. Besides, it would be nearly impossible to push a stroller through the lobby crowd or along the narrow garden paths.

In turn, they proceeded through a set of double doors to a garden filled with tall, flowering plants. The warm, humid air brought out an earthy, loamy fragrance. According to the signage, these plants provided nectar for butterflies and foliage on which they laid their eggs. People shuffled across the room, admiring flowers on either side. Matthew and Kevin batted at blooms hanging over the walk.

Penny cooed with pleasure as Brian lowered her to sniff a long, pink blossom. She grasped at it, but Brian turned her around and deposited her on the ground

Melanie's heart pattered faster, watching him with her little girl. Each of her children needed a father, but she marveled at the different reasons why. The boys primarily needed a firm hand and a solid male role model. Penny, however, seemed to need affection, as if the loving attention of a father fostered her independence, making her more self-assured. This morning, before Mass, she'd twisted this way and that, showing off her plaid jumper and hair bow, her whole countenance blossoming with Brian's attention.

They passed through a screened doorway into a small ante-room. Once their party was wholly inside and the door closed behind them, they proceeded through another screened door into the butterfly house. By using a double set of entries and exits, no butterflies could escape.

Penny squealed with delight at the dozens of colorful winged creatures flitting from flower to flower. More butter-flies rested on the walls, plants, and even the walkway.

Melanie touched Kevin's shoulder. "Watch where you step. They're on the ground too."

Penny walked on tiptoes while the boys moved purposely

from plant to plant. Brian held out the laminated guide they'd been given. "Look, this one's a Red-spotted Purple. Isn't it pretty?"

Together they traversed the intricate path several times, spotting previously unseen butterflies on a small plate of citrus fruit, dangling from the netting high above them, and, occasionally, on themselves.

"Mom, look!" Matthew called. He pointed to a zebra-striped butterfly on Kevin's shoulder.

Kevin turned in circles, trying to see it, his whirring motion finally driving the poor bug away.

They reached the exit, laughing at Kevin's dizzy, stumbling movement toward the doors.

Penny squatted, examining a brown and orange butterfly with spots resembling eyes. Its wings were ragged and torn, and it sat motionless.

"C'mon, boys." Brian opened the door, ushering Kevin and Matthew into another anteroom while Melanie and Penny remained behind.

Inside, several mirrors lined the walls, and an attendant encouraged patrons to examine themselves and each other carefully to be certain no butterflies clung to them.

Brian brushed a black and blue-spotted butterfly from Matthew's shin. "Don't want this little guy hitching a ride."

Apparently convinced he was butterfly-free, Kevin opened the second screened door, his eyes on the exit to the common area. Matthew, free of the freeloading butterfly, moved to follow, but without warning, Penny stood and darted ahead of Melanie, toward the anteroom. Penny pulled at the door, opening it enough to slip through, joining Matthew and Brian.

Melanie followed.

"Wait!" Brian directed Matthew to stop, although Kevin had already stepped out.

"Geez, Penny." Exasperation dripped from Matthew's words,

and he stomped his foot. "You can't do that. The butterflies will get out. Now we gotta wait for you."

The complexities of the butterfly safety system lay well beyond Penny's comprehension. She stared at the mirror, ignoring Matthew.

Kevin stood six or seven yards away on the other side of the screen door as people flowed around him in the concourse.

"Wait right there." Melanie made her instruction firm, hoping Kevin would obey. Why couldn't it have been Matthew on the other side?

Matthew stood holding the door handle, Melanie behind him. "I'm gonna open—"

"Wait a sec." Using his index finger, Brian ruffled the hem of Penny's dress, causing a perfectly-camouflaged butterfly to flutter toward the screen wall.

Melanie glanced at Kevin, wanting to be sure he hadn't roamed. People passed between them, partially obstructing her view, but Kevin remained in the same spot. She blinked, and as a bulky double stroller rolled by, she spotted a stocky man in a black hoodie next to Kevin.

The man crouched at Kevin's level, his arm around his shoulder.

Melanie's heart clenched, fear rippling through her. She smacked Brian's arm repeatedly, trying to convey her urgency. "We've got to go. Now!"

Brian brushed Penny's dress a last time and turned in the direction Melanie now pushed him. "What's the—?"

"Call me paranoid, call me overprotective. I don't care." She shoved everyone forward. "I need to get out there."

Matthew stood with his hand still to the door, his gaze following the butterfly that had flown from Penny's dress.

"Go, Matthew!" Melanie's voice pitched higher as her apprehension increased.

With a start, Matthew glanced at his mom and then opened the door.

Brian, holding Penny's hand, and then Melanie, tumbled out behind him.

In her peripheral vision, Melanie caught sight of the attendant bustling behind them, batting at a butterfly. *Too bad. Children trump butterflies every time.*

"C'mon, c'mon," Brian murmured as he weaved through the crowd ahead of her.

The man stood erect, facing away from them, and then blended into the crowd, a swarm of people obscuring him.

Pushing ahead of Brian, whose progress was hampered by Penny, Melanie squatted in front of Kevin, a hand on each of his shoulders. "Who was that? Are you okay?"

"I'm okay." Kevin gave her a bewildered look, completely unconcerned.

"Do you know that man?"

Kevin twisted his lips and then shook his head. "No."

Brian came up beside her, boosting Penny onto his hip. "What did he want, Kevin?"

"He asked me if I liked the butterflies." His troubled gaze bounced from Brian to Melanie.

Melanie's heart rate slowed, returning to a normal pace. Kevin was unharmed. It had probably been an innocent encounter. A bystander making small talk. "You're not in trouble." She rubbed his shoulders, kissed his forehead, and released him, taking the opportunity to re-iterate the importance of using caution around strangers.

Brian peered over the crowd, scanning the people in the direction the man had moved. "I don't see him."

With a deep breath, Melanie steadied her nerves. "Stay with us, okay?" She gave Kevin a pointed glance.

He nodded and then turned his attention to Matthew, who rambled about the butterfly that had been on Penny's dress.

Still unsettled, Melanie felt as if she should do *something*, but what? The man hadn't harmed Kevin in any way. She grabbed Kevin's hand and they headed to the final portion of the exhibit, a display of caterpillars and pinned chrysalides.

They spent a few minutes admiring the colors and variations, wow'd by the whole metamorphosis. Melanie particularly admired the gold of the Monarch chrysalis, though her thoughts remained scattered and uneasy.

She rubbed Brian's back as he held Penny aloft so that she could see. "I think we're ready to go."

He nodded. "Okay. . . . Everything all right?" The concern in his eyes eased the lingering tension in her chest and shoulders.

This had been her birthday present after all, and he wanted them to enjoy themselves, especially her. She smiled. "It's fine. I just think . . ." She glanced at the people milling around. "As much as we've loved it, it's enough for today."

"Sure. I thought we'd pick up some pizza and a cake on the way home."

Birthday cake! She'd completely forgotten. The kids would want cake for sure. "That sounds perfect."

Truly, the afternoon had been enjoyable and memorable, despite their late start and the minor incident with Kevin. She dropped her hand to his arm, squeezing it. "This was wonderful. Thank you." He couldn't have known how she loved butterflies as a girl, collecting them and identifying them as they visited her family's sprawling, wild backyard. And yet, he'd chosen it.

Her heart stirred. She couldn't pinpoint when it had happened—while fixing the kitchen drain, during quiet conversations on her living room couch, or over a plate of misshapen butterfly pancakes—but she'd fallen in love with Brian Perella.

*B*rian stood and snatched the small stack of paper plates from Melanie's hand. "Uh-uh. I'll clean up. You sit." Clearing the table was the least he could do in trying to make her day near perfect, especially since she'd made his *life* near perfect.

With an appreciative smile, she dropped back into the kitchen chair. "Thank you." Obviously unable to just sit, she pushed crumpled napkins and dirty forks in his direction.

A giant yawn overtook him, and he covered his wide-open mouth and turned away, a bit embarrassed. "Sorry. Don't know why I'm still tired."

The kids, their bellies full of cheese pizza and chocolate cake, had retired to the living room, where a cartoon played. Following the afternoon at the butterfly garden and Melanie's birthday dinner, he hoped they'd settle quickly for Melanie and go right to sleep.

With any luck, he'd be asleep within the hour himself. That afternoon nap hadn't cut it. And it should have. He'd waited a few days, and things hadn't improved. If anything, he was getting worse, not better. Bone-tired, all the time. He'd call the doctor first thing in the morning.

Melanie stopped him with a hand to his arm as he dumped the plates into the trash. "I'm worried about you." She stroked his cheek and caressed his neck, lingering over the swollen glands. "Believe me, I *get* being tired all the time. But this isn't normal tired."

He lifted her hand and brought it to his lips. "I'll be fine." No need for her to worry. He'd get checked out and be his old self in a few days.

"Go home and rest." She angled him away from the trash can toward the center of the room. "I had a great time today . . . this morning . . . last night." Facing him now, she slid her arms around his neck. "Thank you so much for making the day special. We loved the butterfly garden."

He warmed to her touch, squeezing her closer. "I'm glad. Your birthday should be special because—"

"Ow!" Kevin yelled from the living room. "Ow! Ow! Ow!"

Brian peered over Melanie's head at Kevin hopping on one foot while gripping the other. Matthew's gaze remained glued to the TV. Penny lay on the floor, arranging doll furniture.

"Stubbed toe, I think." No first aid intervention necessary, at least by his estimation.

Her gaze hadn't drifted from his face. She stretched toward him, her lips almost touching his.

With his hands to her waist, he resisted. "What if I'm contagious? I don't want you to—"

"I'll take my chances," she whispered and pressed her lips to his.

In an instant, any notion of being tired fled, leaving in its wake her cherry blossom scent and the sweet, sweet taste of her lips, redolent of birthday cake and even sweeter affection. His heart hammered a steady rhythm against his ribs until he thought it might explode.

He needed to tell her how he felt about her, to release a smidgen of this pressure in his chest. His hands, tingling, tightened on her waist.

In response, she drew him closer, causing his head to dip lower.

He broke the kiss, pulling in a lungful of air. "Melanie," he rasped, trying to steady his racing heart. "I—"

A small, warm body crashed into their legs, setting them off balance.

Leaning back, he loosened his hold on Melanie and she on him.

Penny hugged their legs and rubbed her face against her mother's pants.

Tired, he guessed.

"Mama, Mama, Mama. I wanna go to bed."

Bingo.

Mood killed.

Moment gone.

Chest pressure, still corked.

Melanie sighed, giving him a disappointed glance. "You started to say something?"

He shook his head, his eagerness deflated. If he was going to say "I love you" to Melanie for the first time, he'd like to get it all out in one sentence.

Yet, how could he be irritated with Penny? Especially when he, too, wanted little more than to go to bed. He'd only wanted to say those three words first.

He squatted, putting himself on Penny's level. "You be good for your mama, okay?"

She nodded, rubbing her eyes with her fist.

"Sleep tight, sweet pea."

He bid them each goodnight, lingering in the entryway with Melanie, wishing her a happy birthday and enjoying a last kiss.

To his relief, his car started right up. He sat for a minute, letting it idle and warm.

Their day together felt incomplete. He'd *so* wanted to tell her he loved her. For months he'd known, but he hadn't wanted to rush her. Today, her birthday, would've been the perfect time.

He grabbed his cell phone from its holder between the seats and called her. Telling her he loved her for the first time shouldn't be done by phone, but he could still tell her how much he cared and how rich she'd made his life.

The phone rang several times before it jumped to voicemail. He sighed, disappointed, and considered what to do. She must've already taken Penny up to bed. The recording played, and he cleared his throat, gathering his thoughts. He'd leave a message, and she'd get it before bed.

There would be another opportunity soon. He wouldn't *wait* for an opportunity: he'd *make* an opportunity. The next time they were together, she would know how he loved her—now and forever.

CHAPTER 23

The alarm sounded, jarring Brian from sleep. Morning already? He smacked the snooze button, intent on grabbing another eight minutes of sleep. Unfortunately, the alarm had done its job, waking him enough for his brain to start ticking through the day's agenda. He shifted and flung back the sweat-drenched sheets clinging to his bare chest and back. *Gross.*

Dull morning light cast an ashen hue over his bed. The rumble of a diesel engine came from the street, reminding him that the neighborhood had already sprung to life. Kids with overstuffed backpacks and colorful lunch boxes waited at the corner, cars bumped out of driveways into the street, and dog walkers followed their furry charges armed with orange poop-scooping bags.

Steeling himself for the day ahead, he left the sheets to air dry while he shuffled to the bathroom. He grabbed a hand towel from under the sink and dried the sweat from his body, his mind scrolling through his "to-do" list and his eyelids heavy. Nine hours of uninterrupted sleep and still tired. Ignoring the obvious had become impossible. He had some kind of infection. No fever, but too many symptoms to brush off.

After forcing down an English muffin and large cup of coffee, he shaved, showered, and scheduled an appointment with his family doctor for the end of the day.

Once he'd reached the office, Brian's day slipped by amidst several cups of coffee, a department meeting that dragged well beyond its scheduled time allotment, and troubleshooting a network installation at a satellite office thirty miles east.

"Hey, tech." Steve, a lanky middle-aged man with a booming voice and horn-rimmed bifocals, tapped on Brian's desk. "One of the sales laptops has a virus or malware or something. You take a look?"

Brian glanced at the wall clock. Forty minutes before his scheduled doctor's appointment, exactly ten minutes before five o'clock. A slow burn started in Brian's chest then inched upward, heating his neck and ears. Always, *always*, at the end of the day. Why couldn't people ever come to him earlier?

He bit his lips together and tapped a stack of papers on the desktop, lining them up evenly. Steve didn't deserve the irritated snap tickling Brian's lips. "I'll get on it first thing in the morning. I have an appointment I need—"

"We've got a training call at 7:45, and Bryce needs to get a half-dozen door swings in tomorrow. He needs the laptop running *now*." Steve shrugged uncomfortably, as if irritated by his starched shirt. "That's your job, right? Making this stuff run?" He tapped a foot against the cube wall.

The tap-tap-tap only increased Brian's annoyance. "Yes, it's my job. Any other day, I'd stay, but not today."

Steve sighed, the irritation evident as he shifted his weight onto one hip and propped a hand there.

How could he solve this guy's problem *and* get to the doctor's office on time? Brian swiveled his chair and pushed off the floor, rolling into the walkway. "Jason?"

Jason Marston had worked under Brian all of about six days. Could he diagnose the laptop's problem? Guess they'd find out.

"Yeah?" Jason emerged from his cubicle and sauntered up to Steve, standing a good eight inches shorter. Jason's baby face and stocky build accentuated their differences.

Brian stood and grabbed his jacket from the back of his chair. "Steve, I've gotta run, but Jason'll take a look for you." He patted Jason's back, nudging him toward Steve as he slipped behind him.

"I will? What's, uh, what's the problem?" Jason's voice nearly cracked.

Glancing back, Brian glimpsed Steve gesturing in explanation while Jason nodded dumbly. Brian sighed. Well, at least he'd bought himself a reprieve until morning.

In only twenty minutes—quicker than he'd expected—Brian arrived at the doctor's office. The family practice had moved to a brand-new plaza sometime during the last year. As he pulled into the parking lot, he took in the businesses alongside the medical offices: a nail salon, a fancy-looking pet groomer, a sushi restaurant, and a jeweler.

In the jeweler's window, a full-color advertisement showed a man's hand sliding a ridiculously large diamond solitaire onto a woman's slim, perfectly-manicured hand. Brian's breath caught as he imagined the feel of Melanie's hand in his, the indescribable joy of starting a life together written on her face and in his heart. Ten minutes would be just enough time for him to peruse the jeweler's cases, ask a few questions, and get out without being roped into an impulsive purchase.

Electronic bells jangled overhead as Brian entered the jewelry store. Long glass cases sparkled beneath the overhead lights. An older gentleman in a pale blue suit stood behind the far case hunched over a spreadsheet, pen in hand and calculator in front of him.

Brian's gaze bounced about the room, taking in watches,

earrings, and long strands of pearls before landing on the ring case. He took a few steps in its direction, blue suit meeting him on the opposite side of the counter.

"Wedding bells in your future?" Blue suit's toothy grin made Brian's skin crawl, and suddenly he felt fifteen again, embarrassed that John had caught him doodling Stacey Quentin's name in his algebra notebook.

In fewer than ten seconds, Brian had decided he wasn't buying here, based on blue suit's vibe alone.

"I only have a minute, and I really don't know what I'm looking at. Do you have a guide or anything I could take with me?" Brian kept his distance, careful not to look too eager.

His shoulders sagging, blue suit reached behind him and grabbed a brochure from atop a wooden credenza and slid it across the glass case toward Brian. "This has everything you need to know. Let's set up a time for you—"

Brian backpedaled to the door, waving the brochure. "Thank you. I'll read this, but I have to get to my appointment."

Back outside, Brian exhaled, relieved to have made his escape. He unlocked his car, tossed the brochure onto the passenger seat, and trotted to the doctor's office. As he opened the door, a woman with a baby in a car carrier made her way out. He held the door, smiling at the tiny infant buried beneath a blanket and sporting a green knit cap. He'd wondered whether men had anything akin to a biological clock. Because, lately, the sight of little babies twisted him all up inside.

In the office, he provided the receptionist with his insurance card and identification. Despite the half-dozen people in the room, he waited only ten minutes.

"Brian?" A gravelly-voiced nurse stared at papers in her hand and held the door to the medical suites open with a sensible white shoe.

He followed the heavyset nurse in aquamarine scrubs to a

patient room where she measured his height, weight, pulse, blood pressure, and body temperature.

"What brings you in today?" she croaked, hands poised over a small laptop keyboard.

Brian shifted on the exam table, the paper crinkling beneath him. "I've been extremely tired, round the clock, for at least a few weeks now. Even a nap doesn't help. My appetite's off, sometimes I sweat in bed at night, and, uh, my glands are swollen, I think." He rubbed his fingers along his neck. "And a little sore."

Hearing himself say his symptoms aloud, he wondered if he had mononucleosis. He'd hate for Melanie or her kids to catch that from him. Maybe it was a bacterial infection, and the doctor could prescribe an antibiotic that would do the trick.

The nurse tapped away at the keyboard, making him wonder what notes she'd added beyond what he'd told her. "Patient is a wuss. He winced when I tightened the blood pressure cuff. Can't sit still. The exam table paper is a wrinkled mess. When is my cigarette break?"

She clicked the laptop closed and stooped to grab a cotton gown from the drawer beneath the sink. "You can leave your underwear on. Gown open in the back. The doctor will be in shortly."

Yeah, right. Brian accepted the gown and waited until she'd pulled the privacy curtain and left the room before undressing.

His feet grew cold as he padded barefoot across the room to the magazine rack on the wall. *People, Reader's Digest, Motor Trend, Brides.* A bride. His heart swelled at the thought of meeting Melanie at the altar. He could picture Penny in a frilly white dress with ribbons in her hair carrying a basket of, uh, whatever they put in there. Flowers?

But he was getting ahead of himself. He needed to tell Melanie he loved her. See how that went over. After all, she hadn't said it to him yet either. What if she didn't feel the same way? She had to. Maybe he would propose to her at Christmas. A wave of nervousness rolled over him. Could he just ask? Or did he have to make it some kind of YouTube event? Did you need a photographer? What did women expect these days? Pretty sure John had just dropped to one knee in the living room when he asked Kate.

A knock drew his attention to the door, and he scuttled back to the exam table, trying to close the back of his gown and flatten the paper before sitting again. "Uh, come in."

"Brian, I haven't seen you in a long time." Dr. Howard, smiling, squeezed a dollop of hand sanitizer from the wall dispenser and rubbed his hands together. "How are you?"

Dr. Howard's hair had become more salt and less pepper since the last time Brian had seen him. He leaned against the counter, his posture reflecting the easygoing manner Brian remembered.

"I'm okay. Tired, mainly. Really, really tired." Brian shifted and the sound of ripping paper creased the air.

"Tell me about that." Dr. Howard removed his glasses and maintained steady eye contact with Brian as he repeated his symptoms.

Finally, the doctor replaced his glasses and pushed off of the counter. "Let's take a look." He examined Brian's heart and lungs and then palpated the glands in his neck. "Hmm."

The faint smell of the doctor's spicy aftershave tickled Brian's nose as he continued to press gently on either side of Brian's neck. After examining his underarms, abdomen, and groin, he patted Brian's back and returned to his station along the counter.

Brian struggled with the paper where it hung over the exam table in two ripped, twisted segments. Sitting, he adjusted the waistband of his briefs, relieved the groin exam was over.

"You probably have a virus, but I'd like to rule out something more serious, so I'm going to order some blood work." He turned and opened the laptop that up to this point, he'd ignored. "I think we should also do an x-ray and take a sample of tissue from one of those lymph nodes." Stylus in hand, he gestured toward Brian's neck.

Brian's chest tightened. An x-ray? A tissue sample? That didn't sound like standard procedure for a virus. "What do you want to rule out?"

Dr. Howard glanced up from the laptop and removed his glasses again. "Your symptoms are consistent with Hodgkin's lymphoma. And, you're in the age range it commonly presents. So, we want to be sure we're not missing anything."

Alarm bells sounded in Brian's head, and his throat tightened. "So, when you say 'take a sample of tissue,' you mean you're going to do a biopsy?"

"Yes." Dr. Howard remained silent, meeting Brian's gaze with confidence. "Do you have any other questions?"

Did he? He should. He should have a dozen, at least, but at the word "lymphoma" his entire thought process had scrambled. "I'm drawing a blank. I guess we need to wait and see what these tests show."

"Precisely." He tapped on the laptop and shut it. "I'll have the nurse come in and draw blood, and a prescription for the x-ray will print out at the desk. You can have that done here, in the adjoining suite. As far as the biopsy, I'd like to get you in for that in the morning."

"What all's involved in that?"

"I'll give you a local anesthetic, and it's a simple needle biopsy. The whole appointment won't take more than a half hour. Then we'll have some cells to look at. And a diagnosis by the end of the day."

Brian nodded, trying to process all the information. He hadn't expected this at all, and the possibilities scared him.

Dr. Howard, who'd probably had hundreds of similar conversations with patients over the years, must've sensed his apprehension. "It's a lot to take in, and, I'm sure, not what you hoped to hear, but we need to rule it out." He placed the laptop under his arm and smiled. "Most likely, you've got a virus, so let's not worry until we're sure there's something to worry about."

Dr. Howard's confidence and kindness helped ease Brian's concern. "Okay. So, blood work now, I go down the hall for the x-ray, and biopsy in the morning."

"Yes. They'll schedule you on the way out." Hand on the door, Dr. Howard turned back. "Try to get some good rest, and I'll see you in the morning."

"Thank you." The door clicked shut, but Brian didn't move. He stared at the floor, wanting to focus on the fact he probably had a virus, but the word "lymphoma" rattled around his brain.

Lymphoma.

Lymphoma.

Cancer.

He might have cancer.

He yanked on the ties at the back of the gown, slipped it off, rolled it into a ball, and left it on top of the ripped exam table paper.

A half-hour later, blood drawn and x-ray taken, he drove home, barely conscious of the route he took. He pulled a container of chicken and stuffing from the freezer and popped it into the microwave, not because he was hungry but because it was time to eat.

The microwave hummed as the glass bowl turned in circles, showcasing the bland meat. Would chemotherapy affect how things tasted? He'd heard that could happen.

He plodded to the couch, unbuttoning his shirt and loosening his belt as he went. Would treatment mean he'd have to take disability leave from work?

Enough! He flicked on the table lamp, and the light cast a yellow glow over the dark room. It was too soon to worry about the implications of a diagnosis. He'd wait for the test results.

He reached for his phone on the end table and stopped short. His heart ached to talk to Melanie, but he didn't want to worry her. Dr. Howard said it was most likely a virus. Once that was confirmed, he'd tell her. Better that he didn't speak to her tonight.

Tapping quickly, he sent off a quick text message.

Late appointment. Exhausted and going to bed early. I'll talk to you tomorrow.

Though his heart whispered "what-ifs," stealing the light-hearted joy he typically felt when texting her, he added a little kissy-face emoji and hit send.

Instead of waiting for a reply, he ate his dinner at the counter then showered and climbed into bed. This time of year, darkness came early, so going to bed didn't seem wholly unnatural.

As he lay in bed, he reminded himself that whatever happened, he wouldn't have to endure it alone. God was with him. Always.

Only he didn't feel God's presence. Just a gaping nothingness that left him hollow and half-sick.

He mentally recited the series of rote prayers he usually said before falling asleep and then lay there, trying to formulate a prayer from his heart, which basically consisted of begging God to let this be a virus.

CHAPTER 24

A blaring horn throbbed through Brian's head, and his eyes flickered open. The red figures on the bedside alarm clock may as well have flashed LATE. Freeing his hand from the sheets—not quite so sweaty this morning—he smacked the snooze button and then fumbled with turning the alarm off as he sat up.

He stumbled to the bathroom, calculating what part of his morning routine he'd have to skip in order to make it to the doctor's office on time. He'd stick with the essentials: shave, brush his teeth, and dress. If he got hungry, he'd grab a wrap and a coffee at a drive-through after his appointment.

As much as morning traffic allowed, he exceeded the speed limit, arriving for his biopsy only minutes late. With sweaty palms and pounding heart, he endured the mercifully quick and fairly painless procedure.

He arrived at work, a tuna salad bagel sandwich and extra-large coffee in tow, and spent hours hand-holding Jason.

"You wiped the laptop?" Brian drilled Jason, looking from him to the laptop screen in front of them. He struggled to shift gears from anxious patient to patient supervisor.

A blank look on his face, Jason shifted his stance. Poor newbie Jason was so green he could've been called Kermit. His protruding belly bumped the back of Brian's chair. "Yeah. I ran the diagnostic—"

"You backed everything up first, right?" Working with Computers 101. That's what this was.

Jason nodded. "Yeah, it's—"

"Yo, tech." Steve sidled up beside Jason, a hard stare fixed on Brian. "Bryce has an eleven o'clock, and he needs a working laptop for his preso."

Preso? Brian fiddled with the computer mouse, clicked through a series of questions, and willed the computer to complete the sequence faster. Ah, preso. Sales lingo for presentation. "Gimme, uh, ten minutes. Should be ready." Assuming Jason had done his job properly.

Steve glanced at his wristwatch. "Ten. Got it." He headed for the sales end of the office, already on a phone call.

Brian held his breath, waiting for the computer to reboot.

With a bored expression, Jason stood, one hand in his pocket, the other scrolling through something on his phone.

Frustration burned in Brian's chest. From what he'd seen, the kid wasn't stupid, but he lacked the ability to communicate with anything that didn't run on battery power.

"Did you give Bryce or Steve an update on this? Last night? This morning?"

"Uh . . ." Jason stared at the phone, scrolling, and then tapping with his thumb. "Texting a reminder about my dad."

Tempted to whap the device from his hands, Brian gritted his teeth.

The laptop screen brightened as a beach scene wallpaper materialized and icons appeared, dotting the digital workspace, one by one.

Brian breathed deeply, quelling his frustration. "Well, looks like everything is okay now. Return it to Bryce and tell him not to open anymore attachments from unknown senders."

Jason pocketed his phone, finally, and slunk off, laptop under his arm.

Time seemed to slow after lunch. Brian glanced alternately at the time on his computer, his wristwatch, and the wall clock.

2:15 p.m.: Melanie texted him back a kissy-face emoji. He replied with a dancing Snoopy gif. He couldn't wait to hold her in his arms.

2:47 p.m.: Steve dropped off a couple of local brewpub tchotchkes for him and Jason as thanks. Nice of him.

3:28 p.m. Heather from Human Resources brought around a sympathy card for their co-worker Richard, whose wife died yesterday. *Cancer.* A tension headache threatened.

4:07 p.m. Brian propped his head on his hand, struggling to stay awake during a training webinar. His fingers brushed the bandage on his neck. His muscles tensed, anxious.

4:35 p.m. His phone buzzed and shimmied, the medical office's number lighting the screen.

His throat suddenly tight and his mouth dry, Brian asked the caller on the other end to hold for a minute as he filled a paper cup with water at the cooler on his way to the conference room. He closed the door behind him, grateful the space wasn't in use and that it would offer him the privacy he needed.

With fingers poised above the touch screen, he paused and closed his eyes. *Lord, Your will not mine, but, please, let it be a virus.*

Eyes open, he tapped the icon to unmute the call and sunk into a padded leather chair.

The gravelly voice of yesterday afternoon's nurse came over the line. "Dr. Howard will be with you in a minute."

4:37 p.m. Prepare for doom.

Only seconds passed before Dr. Howard's familiar, confident voice greeted him. "Brian, how are you feeling today?"

Brian swiveled the chair this way and that, his gaze on the

shiny tabletop unfocused. "About the same. Tired. And anxious for the test results."

A two-second pause. Couldn't have been more. But it was enough to signal to Brian that the results were not good.

"I wish I had better news for you. You have Hodgkin's lymphoma. The biopsy is consistent with what the x-ray and the blood work show."

Brian squeezed his eyes shut. *No, no, no.* It couldn't be. He'd been tired and all the rest, but seriously ill? Nah.

Shoving the chair back, he stood, phone in hand, and paced the perimeter of the room. He'd always been blessed with good health. His sick days went unused year after year. This had to be a mistake.

Dr. Howard still spoke in his calm, fatherly tone, but Brian couldn't make sense of it. Something about a stage and a letter designation.

"I'm referring you to an oncologist who will see you later this week. She'll sit down with you, answer all your questions, and recommend a course of treatment. Probably chemotherapy and radiation."

Dread pitted in his stomach. Chemotherapy and radiation. He'd spend weeks, months, sick and weak before he got better. *If* he got better.

"Between now and then, I'd advise you not to go crazy surfing the internet. Stick with a reliable site like the Mayo Clinic for the basics. Then leave the rest to the doctor. I've known her for twenty years, and she's an excellent physician. She'll give you a more accurate prognosis than I'm qualified to give, but your chances of going into remission and living a long, normal life are excellent."

Brian sat numbly, dumbly. Maybe they'd screwed up the tests or gotten the results mixed up. Whatever the doctor said was probably important, but he'd be surprised if he remembered anything Dr. Howard told him even ten minutes from now.

"I'd also recommend you make a list of questions for the oncologist. The nurse will get back on when we're done here and give you all the particulars about the appointment."

Brian nodded, only half aware Dr. Howard couldn't see him. The oncologist could give him a second opinion, straighten out whatever Dr. Howard's office had screwed up.

Silence crossed the line, and then Dr. Howard spoke, his voice soft and sympathetic. "Brian, I'm very sorry. Please don't let the diagnosis discourage you." Another pause. "Do you have any questions for me?"

Brian's mouth had gone dry again. He cleared his throat and swallowed. "Uh, I'm not sure. I don't know."

"That's understandable. Take your time with it. And I'd advise against making any major decisions. Get the appointment scheduled and then do a little research, have some questions ready. And I'll be monitoring your progress as well. If you have any concerns, feel free to call me at any time tonight or tomorrow and throughout the treatment. The oncologist is going to be better able to answer your questions as they directly pertain to the lymphoma though."

Brian nodded. "Okay. Thank you, Dr. Howard."

"Best of luck to you, Brian. Hang in there."

His dry throat tightened and tears stung his eyes. He was kidding himself; there was no mistake. He'd had an exam and three separate tests that all pointed to the same diagnosis. *Cancer.*

A pre-recorded message about the local medical center's paid studies droned in his ear as he waited for the nurse.

The gravelly-voiced nurse, speaking with more compassion than he'd heard in her tone before, provided him with the oncologist's name, her office location, and an appointment time for the end of the week. Her instructions dissolved into a coughing fit, and she ended the call with an abrupt, "Have a good day."

Yeah.. The best.

He ended the call and shoved the phone toward the center of the conference table. Swallowing the emotion clogging his throat, Brian pressed his fingertips to his closed eyes, pushing it all back. The fear, the grief, the tears.

He'd spent a grand total of five seconds processing his diagnosis when a knock sounded on the door.

Brian cleared his throat and blinked away any tears. "Yeah?"

Jason poked his head in. "There you are. Been looking everywhere for you. Even checked the men's room."

"Well, you found me. What's up?" How could he concentrate on work when he'd just been delivered a cancer diagnosis, maybe a death sentence?

"The, uh, hot mom at the support desk . . ." He gave a creepy grin that looked part snaggle-toothed snarl.

"Carol?" To be fair, Carol was extremely attractive and she had five kids, but reducing her to "hot mom" seemed to fall somewhere between disrespectful and unprofessional.

"Yeah, Carol. She's getting an error message. I can't figure it out. You wanna take a look?" Jason's phone dinged in his hand and he glanced at it, smiling.

Could he? He should. That was his job. Steve had even said so. But he'd be distracted and useless for the remainder of the day. He glanced at his watch. Ten minutes to 5:00.

It never failed. It didn't matter that he'd received the worst news of his life. That his entire world had just been upended. That the future he'd imagined with Melanie, Matthew, Kevin, and Penny—

Brian's stomach churned and bile rose in his throat. "Sorry. I've gotta go."

He snagged his phone and nearly ran from the conference room, ignoring Jason's protests, and headed for his desk. Jacket, iPad, car keys . . . He grabbed the essentials and took the fastest route through the cube farm to the exit.

In his peripheral vision, he recognized Carol and vaguely heard her address him. Jason's voice trailed him too, further in the distance. The double glass doors closed behind him, and he ignored the sound of his name, intent on getting to his car.

Fire me. I couldn't care less.

He yanked opened the car door and slid into the driver's seat, plopping his belongings onto the passenger seat and crushing a glossy brochure. He yanked it out from under his stuff, and his gaze ran over the crumpled paper: "The Four C's: Color, Cut, Clarity, and Carat."

An ache started in his chest, and his stomach rolled again. He gritted his teeth, forcing back the tears pooling in his eyes. Skimming the text, his gaze caught on explanations of oval, princess, and pear shape diamonds; prong, bezel, and channel settings; and more things he'd never heard of or cared about before. Before Melanie.

His fist squeezed around the brochure, wrinkling it. Useless information now. He tossed it on the seat and slammed the iPad on top of it.

Finally, he let his thoughts go where they'd been wont to go for the last twenty-four hours.

Melanie.

He'd finally met the woman who was, quite literally, an answer to years of prayers. Hadn't God confirmed as much in his heart?

To ask "Why me?" seemed arrogant. Why *not* him? Brian Perella was no better than anybody else. He didn't deserve an exemption from suffering.

The question he couldn't answer, the one that had already begun to fester deep in his soul, echoed in his mind.

Why now?

CHAPTER 25

Brian turned the key in the ignition and insipid pop-country music blared from the car speakers. The singer crooned, ". . . and I got down on one knee and asked you to marry me." He winced and punched at a button, turning the system off. The *last* thing he wanted to hear was a love song.

He eased onto the highway, foot on the pedal to keep up with traffic. A little green Hyundai plastered with heart-shaped stickers zipped by. Glancing to the opposite side, he glimpsed a sign advertising a local bridal show, and a fleeting pang of grief stabbed his heart. Brian slipped into the passing lane and sped around a pokey Oldsmobile, intent on getting home. Oh, look, a giant billboard for hospice care. It seemed as if the entire universe conspired against him, mocking the foolishness of his dreams, the deepest desires of his heart.

Thunder cracked overhead, and sheets of rain beat against the windshield. Brian flicked on his windshield wipers and then his headlights, which should've been on already, but he'd been too distracted to realize.

The gray skies, heavy with precipitation, matched his mood —dull, dark, burdened. Wind blew, forcing the rain sideways and rocking his car slightly. A damp chill ran through him and he shivered. At least it wasn't freezing rain, which would make the evening commute downright dangerous. Melanie's husband skidding on black ice, careening to his death, flashed in his mind. Ah, what did it all matter? He may not have one foot in the grave yet, but with today's diagnosis he was at least dipping his toe in the proverbial pool.

With his hands and eyes occupied by the road, he unleashed all the pent-up questions that had been swirling just beneath the surface. Hodgkins lymphoma. Would this be the thing that killed him? Would he suffer, alone and miserable? If he *did* live, would he be ruined—his health, his finances, his life? Self-pitying, despairing thoughts ran through his mind, unguarded and untamed.

He rolled through a deep puddle, water spraying the sides of his car, as he pulled up to his apartment. Morbid thoughts having occupied his mind, he had little memory of the ride, but somehow, despite the poor conditions, he'd made it home. Inertia pressed on him, making him want to sit in his car, the rain rolling over the windows as he wallowed in misery.

Gritting his teeth, he scooped up the stuff on the passenger's seat, stuffed it into his vinyl work bag, and shoved open the car door.

Inside his apartment, he dumped his belongings on an end table, tossed his jacket over a chair, and plodded to the kitchen. Shoving aside the clutter atop his refrigerator, he opened the small, high cabinet where he kept the nearly-untouched liquor. He rooted through the bottles he'd recovered from his parents' house after his dad's death and closed his hand around the neck of a dusty whiskey bottle.

He plunked the bottle on the kitchen table, its amber liquid sloshing against the glass. A thin layer of oily-grime coated his fingers, and he wiped them on his pants.

In a lower cupboard, he shoved aside plastic cups and

ceramic mugs, searching for a rocks glass or tumbler. The closest thing he found had Shrek's fat green face on it.

He sighed and took the glass to the table, where he filled it halfway with straight liquor, turning the whites of Shrek's eyes to caramel. Bone weary, Brian hooked his foot around a chair leg and pulled, causing the chair to scrape across the tile floor. He dropped into the seat and curled his fingers around the glass, tilting it and swirling the liquid.

Brian recalled the one time in his life he'd been drunk. At a frat party on his first visit to John in college. His stomach turned just to think of that night, which remained a haze of strangers' faces, loud rap music, and vomiting in the boxwood bushes outside the frat house. He'd vowed *never again*.

That's why this would be his first and last drink this evening. He didn't intend to lose his faculties, only to ease the fear and anxiety clawing at him, dragging him down into a pit of despair. For a minute, he sat, spinning the glass between his hands. Then he took a long draught.

He puckered his lips and his throat burned, creating a trail of fire down his chest. Almost instantly, he relaxed. And then every filter dissolved, every wall he'd erected crumbled, and his heart broke open.

Melanie.

Her face appeared before him. Soft, loose brown waves framed her cheeks. Her eyes, sharp and green, twinkled with life. Love shone there. At least he thought it did. If not love, certainly affection.

What would his diagnosis mean to her? She'd buried her husband not too long ago. Would she have to bury him too?

He closed his eyes, recalling the night she'd told him about David's death. With her head pressed against his shoulder, she'd cried, soaking his shirt. She couldn't go through that again. Wouldn't. Hadn't she said as much to him? That she couldn't bear to put her children through that again?

Even if his prognosis was good, his health would only return after months and months of treatment. Treatment that would probably make him sicker than the disease.

Melanie already seemed pushed to her limits, as evidenced by the perpetual circles under her eyes. She took care of three young children, a house, and herself. Well, marginally took care of herself. It didn't seem like she had a lot of time, energy, or money left for self-care. He'd wanted to do something about that. To lighten her burden, pamper her a bit.

He spun the Shrek glass, turning the ogre's ugly, smiling mug away from him. And recently, she'd begun talking about finding work. He guessed insurance money only went so far. He'd wanted to offer her another possibility . . . The glass slipped from his grip, banging on the table but, fortunately, not spilling anything. Heartache doubled him over until his head rested on his hand. Marriage. Maybe they could've made it work on his income, if that's what she wanted.

But this, this *cancer* . . . He squeezed his hands into fists. She'd feel compelled to nurse him, upending her already chaotic life. And for what? The possibility of watching him die a slow death?

He lifted the glass to his lips, taking another long drink, relishing that burn.

Swirling the remaining drops in the glass, he chose his course of action. Now. Tonight. Before he weakened or lost his nerve, he would end things with Melanie. He would not subject her to his drama. He wouldn't cause her to grieve again. He didn't want that for her. Or for Matthew, Kevin, and Penny.

No doubt she'd find someone else. A man who would be a good husband and father. One who could provide for her family, not suck the life from it.

Tightening his grip on the glass, he downed the last drops of whiskey. Then he stood, a little unsteady, and marched to the living room to retrieve his cell phone.

His hand tingled as he held the device, trying to strengthen his resolve. It had to be now, before he caved.

The phone vibrated in his hand, playing the Super Mario Brothers ringtone Matthew had chosen. His heart lurched, and he nearly dropped the phone. *You've put her off long enough. Answer it.*

He swallowed down the lump in his throat, tapped the phone, and held it to his ear. "Hey, there."

"Hey there yourself. What's going on? All I've gotten are a couple of lousy texts. When can I see you?"

The eagerness in her voice just about cracked his heart in two.

"Uh . . ." *Do it tonight. Get it over with.* "How about tonight? The usual time."

"Perfect." Perky, but marred with a twinge of worry. "Is something wrong, Brian?"

He paced the length of the room, feeling steadier now despite the mild burn lingering in his chest. "I'm okay. Just a lot on my mind." At least the last part was true.

"Well, you tell me about it tonight, okay?" She paused, and Penny yelped in the background. Then, "I want to hear everything."

"Yeah, okay." His voice sounded lifeless compared to her warm, affectionate tone. "I'll see you later."

He ended the call and sunk onto the couch, burying his face in his hands. An ache started in his neck, and he massaged it. Dread pitted in his stomach at the thought of what he had to do. The hope and pleasure in her voice? He'd quash it. Still, better that he end things now, sooner rather than later.

He'd broken off more relationships than he could recall. More than most guys. It should be easy; same as all the rest.

But this was different. She was different. And it would not be easy.

CHAPTER 26

The rain stopped and the steel gray skies darkened to an inky black. Brian's headlights created a glare on the wet roadway as he rolled toward what might as well be his execution, based on the sickening dread pitting in his stomach.

A hint of whiskey lingered on his lips. Did the alcohol have any lingering effects? A dull ache throbbed in his neck. No way could he be under the influence and have this soreness in his neck, his collarbone . . . He shifted his weight, gripping the steering wheel tighter. Even his groin. The pain in his neck . . . this had happened before, after the wine with Melanie—

The lymphoma. That had to be it. The doctor hadn't said anything about the effects of alcohol, but that had to be it. The stupid disease set off something in his lymph nodes when he drank.

He massaged the soreness in his neck. Good thing he'd stopped at one drink.

The car bumped over the curb in her driveway, and he pulled behind her minivan. All windows on the second floor were dark, but a dim light shone through the living room window. *Good. No kids awake.*

Brian rolled his neck and shoulders, trying to ease this discomfort. He pocketed his keys and climbed the stairs to her door, his feet leaden.

On the porch, the gooseneck gourds, bumpy and rotting in spots, lay twisted together in a macabre embrace. One side of the pumpkin had caved in, rotten.

Brian clenched his fist and swallowed then gave a light knock. Stepping back to avoid being smacked by the opening door, he glanced up at the hollow socket where the porch light should be.

Tears gathered in his eyes. Why hadn't he fixed that for her? She needed that light for safety and protection. Why couldn't he have done that? An ache in his chest joined the one in his neck.

The door swung open, and Melanie waved him in. "You're finally here!" Her eyes shone bright with excitement and she bounced on her toes.

"Yeah." His heart leapt into his throat. How could he do this? Brian squared his shoulders and cleared his throat. "The rain slowed down the commute and—"

She launched herself at him, throwing her arms around his neck and pulling him into a warm, delicious, affectionate kiss.

Brian stiffened and tried not to respond, as if participating in the kiss would weaken his resolve.

She slid her hand from behind his head, grazing his aching neck. He willed himself not to flinch. The ache intensified, a good reminder of why he was here.

She pulled away, her hands drifting down his arms until she grasped his fingers. "Now I *know* something is wrong," she said, pressing the door closed with her backside. Pulling gently, she led him toward the living room. "Sit and talk to me. But not about poop or superheroes, because I've already exceeded the maximum daily allowance on both counts."

He couldn't help the smile he let slip, imagining the questions she'd been subjected to today.

As if encouraged by his smile, she leaned closer to him as they neared the couch.

Hoping to put some distance between them in order to keep his head clear, he tossed a throw pillow, two puzzle pieces, and three random Cootie parts onto the floor and sat at the end of the couch.

Deep breath. *Just another breakup. Same as all the others, Brian.*

"You went to the doctor yesterday, right?" Melanie sat in the middle of the couch, a mere eight inches from him, crossing her legs beneath her and pulling her long skirt over them. "Did you find out anything?" She tilted her head from side to side. "Your glands still seem swollen."

He rubbed the back of his neck. "Yeah, uh, they referred me to another doctor." Not the whole truth, but true nonetheless. He didn't want to dwell on his health and invite more questions.

He angled himself toward her, careful not to move closer. "Melanie, do you remember when we first started spending time together, and you asked me—more than once—if I was up for it?"

She nodded. "You said yes." Melanie smiled, happily oblivious to the anvil about to drop.

He dismissed the growing queasiness in his stomach and fisted his hands, needing something to do with the tension coiling in his veins. "And I told you . . . I told you that if I changed my mind, you'd be the first to know."

The shadow of understanding crept across her features, her eyes dimming, her smile sagging. *How he wished he didn't have to do this! Why, God?* But the pain of their breakup would be nothing compared to the loss he'd be sparing her.

"I'm not, uh, I'm not up for this anymore." Not able to meet her eyes, he stared just above her brow. "Y'know, I'm used to being a single guy, doing my own thing. I just don't . . . I don't think I want to be tied down with kids yet."

Her cheeks and chin dropped, and her eyes widened. If

pressed to describe her expression, he'd use one word: shell-shocked.

She pulled a throw pillow to her and squeezed it against her chest. Seconds passed, the only sound the low hum of the refrigerator in the kitchen.

"Wow." She uncrossed her legs and stood, holding the pillow and shaking her head. "I didn't see that coming."

He stood, his arms itching to reach out and pull her to him. Instead, he forced his hands into his pockets.

She paced the room in an erratic pattern. "I guess when you've been out of the dating world a decade or so you lose touch. I—" Melanie glanced at the stairs and lowered her voice. "I—you . . . you seemed to enjoy the kids."

"Your kids are great. Smart, kind, well-behaved."

She snorted a sort of humorless laugh and kept pacing.

"No, really. They're polite and friendly and . . ." He shouldn't oversell it, but finally, something he could be honest about. "It's really me." He shrugged and bit his lips together, knowing that she deserved a better explanation. Too bad he didn't have any he wanted to share. "I guess I still have some growing up to do."

Her gaze snapped to his, anger flashing in her eyes. "So that's it?" She threw the pillow onto the couch and it bounced and tumbled to the floor. "After last weekend when you spent the night, and Sunday, my birthday . . ." Her voice cracked ever so slightly. "We had, well, I thought everything was good. Great, in fact. And that's it? We're done?"

He didn't want to hurt her any more than was necessary to convince her. "I'm sorry, Melanie." He stepped closer and pressed a hand to his chest. "I am. None of this is what I hoped for. But I think you'll see it's for the best."

Torn between giving her a fair opportunity to vent and wanting desperately to leave, he counted out a minute in his head. Fifteen seconds in, she sunk onto the couch and he remained standing, eyes shut in prayer. Thirty seconds in, she buried her head in her hands and he bit the inside of his cheek to keep from crying. At forty-five seconds, she uncovered her face and stared at him, her expression confused and lost.

At one minute, he leaned down and kissed her cheek, ignoring the way she flinched when his lips touched her skin. Then he slunk to the door and let himself out.

Two things kept him from looking back: his fear that he wouldn't find her watching and the tears rolling down his cheeks.

CHAPTER 27

Melanie sat on the couch in the exact place Brian had left her a half hour ago. She ran a hand over the cushion, pulling a few pilled fibers from the upholstery. How many nights had she and Brian sat here, feet propped on the coffee table, watching movies? They'd start by sitting upright, popping chips or some other snack into their mouths and end with her dozing against his warm, solid chest, his arm draped around her shoulder.

Thank God the children were in bed. She couldn't possibly deal with them now. Their silliness, pleas for food, or incessant questions. Even their sweet smiles. None of it.

Threads of thoughts passed through her mind, but she couldn't connect them. In their place, a single-word question formed: Why?

She imagined the scene Sunday morning as Brian had described it. He'd been sprawled face down here, sound asleep, only to wake to Kevin about three inches from his face, dressed and ready to flip pancakes. And then he'd guided both boys, helping them make her birthday special (and free from any accidental conflagrations).

Only a fool would believe Brian's story about wanting to be free of the responsibilities of children. Hadn't he told her the opposite? That his deepest desire was to marry and have children? Maybe it wasn't *the idea* of a wife and children that was the problem. Maybe it was *her* and *her* children. How had she read everything so wrong?

Her chest burned with embarrassment at her obvious stupidity. Did she really believe a good-looking single guy, who'd admitted he'd dated *a lot*, would go for her, a thirtysomething woman with three kids and the stretch marks to prove it? Not when he'd been with taut little twenty-somethings with interesting careers and clothes free of mystery substances smeared by tiny hands. And she'd been so needy, so starved for adult companionship and male attention that she'd let herself imagine an attachment that didn't exist. At least not on Brian's end.

Her eyes filled with tears. Melanie thought she'd exhausted her supply of tears long ago, but apparently not. She hugged the throw pillow, overcome by a sweeping sense of melancholy and déjà vu. Only the last time she sat here, alone and muffling her cries, it had been for David. But David hadn't left her willingly. That pain cut deep, but this one . . . this cut wasn't clean. Its edges, jagged and twisted, brought fresh pain with every memory, every unrealized dream. She let the tears come, knowing even her wracking sobs wouldn't wake the kids upstairs.

Tears finally spent, she dragged herself to her bed, doubting she'd sleep but with mere hours to pull it together before assuming the burdens of another day.

* * *

Brian stumbled through the door to his apartment and slammed it behind him. He'd driven home through a haze of tears, intent on putting as much distance—physical and emotional—between him and Melanie as possible.

The only light shone from the ever-vigilant electronics: a blue glow from the microwave, a red glow from the digital video recorder, and an orange glow from the power strip connected to his computer.

He plopped onto the couch, his mind and his emotions both numb. He wanted one thing: to escape.

Physically, he had nowhere or no one to go to. He'd confined himself to his own personal hell. But a temporary escape, one to take his mind off his mounting troubles—*that* he could manage.

He massaged his still-sore neck. Drinking to get drunk wasn't his thing, and even if it were, the pain from that single glass of whiskey would've cured him of that notion.

Indulging in a carton of ice cream wouldn't be too damaging but he didn't have an appetite.

He snatched the remote control from the end table and flicked on the TV. With his thumb on the control, he clicked by dozens of entertainment options, skimming over sports programming, family dramas, and religious channels. He hadn't let the thought develop, but in his heart, he knew where he was headed. Adult content.

Conscious of his past, he'd blocked access to everything he could when he'd first set up his home entertainment system. But settings could be adjusted. Nothing sketchy showed on his palette of movie channels, but he knew of a back door. He could add a private channel.

Gritting his teeth, he punched the off button and tossed the remote onto a chair.

No! He'd promised himself he wouldn't go down that path again.

He glanced around the dark room, desperate for something to latch onto. He switched on a lamp and it flooded the room with dull yellow light.

He couldn't corral his thoughts or emotions to do anything that required concentration, and his listless body couldn't muster the energy for anything that required physical effort. That didn't leave a lot of options.

Sleep.

He'd done a lot of that lately. Didn't seem to do any good anyway. And though tired, he didn't think the passive power of sleep could overcome his soul-deep unrest.

Pray.

Where did that thought come from? No, not now. Call him childish, but he did *not* feel like talking to God right now. He would—soon. He'd beg for mercy, pray for healing, and seek His comfort. But not tonight. Angry, hurt, and still in shock, he searched for a quick, easy fix. Something to temporarily dull this pain.

He imagined how it could've gone, how things might've been had he gone to Melanie's to share with her what he faced. He closed his eyes and pictured the tender look in her eyes, the warmth of her arms encircling him, the sound of her words soothing and consoling him. They'd sit side by side on her couch, the homey fragrance and soft light from a candle filling the room. They'd hold each other, and beneath the mantle of her love—did she love him?—he'd be safe and at peace. Maybe then they'd kiss, and he'd be reminded of all he had to live for and all he'd dreamed of but had yet to realize.

His eyes shot open, his heart pounding. He'd been robbed. That dream was dead. He'd killed it because in spite of the comfort it might bring him, it could eventually destroy her.

Dejected, he ambled to the desk where his laptop lay open. He punched it on and waited as it trilled and beeped through its startup sequence. In about three minutes, he'd uninstalled his accountability filter, opened a private browser and had ready links to "high-class porn." And look at that!—these sites were free.

His hand cupped the computer mouse, his index finger itching to double-click and satisfy his curiosity and a laundry list of other needs waiting to be satiated. He could move his hand a fraction of an inch and still shut down the software. He could, but he wouldn't. Because tomorrow's regret couldn't compete with tonight's impulse.

CHAPTER 28

*M*elanie started the engine and glanced at the dashboard clock. Running late, again. And they had to pick up Matthew's friend Mason and be at the scout meeting in ten minutes. Well into fall, darkness already blanketed the neighborhood by mid-evening, bringing with it a crisp coolness.

The boys wrangled with their seat belts in the back row.

"Let's go, boys. Get buckled in *now!*" She tapped her fingers on the wheel, her foot poised over the gas pedal.

Two clicks told her the belts had been secured, and she backed out of the driveway, bumping over the curb and murmuring a hasty prayer both for their safety and her aching heart.

Slowing to a stop at the deserted intersection, Melanie fished the phone from her purse. A black sports car approached from behind, waited less than two seconds, then honked its horn and passed her, gliding through the intersection without ever stopping.

"Matthew," she called, glancing in the mirror. "Call Mason and tell him we're on our way. Just find his great-grandma's name, June, in the contacts and hit the little phone icon." She tossed the phone, hoping it reached Matthew's lap and didn't lodge itself beneath a seat instead. She'd pay for that toss later, when one of them used it to justify whipping something from the rear of the car.

A few seconds later, Matthew relayed the message to Mason's great-grandma then sat scrolling through something on the phone.

"Mission accomplished, Matthew. Turn the phone off now. The button on the top." Electronic devices: they had a magnetic pull on kids. Adults too, she guessed. One whiff of momentary boredom, and they sat ready to fill it with mind-numbing content.

"Okay. But I think you have messages on here. There's a little two by the phone thingy." He reached around the seat in front of him and set the phone down, luckily out of the reach of Penny in her harness-style booster seat.

Melanie wrinkled her brow. The phone hadn't rung. Or maybe . . . she'd probably forgotten to turn the ringer up after Mass on Sunday. And since she'd received only one short text from Brian, other than the brief conversation she'd initiated yesterday afternoon, she hadn't noticed.

"Thanks, bud. I'll check 'em when we stop to get Mason."

They pulled up in front of Mason's great-grandma's place, a red-brick duplex that had seen better days. The mortar crumbled around the porch pillars, and the gutter hung low on one side. A bare metal glider sat on the otherwise empty porch and the mailbox lid sat open next to the door. In the corner, a leather baseball glove lay on the concrete floor amidst dirt and dead leaves.

"Go ahead and get him, Matthew."

Matthew leaped from the van before the door slid shut, a move he'd been perfecting due to the faulty closing mechanism.

Getting that door fixed should've been a priority. One of these days it would squash a kid.

Kevin chattered with Penny, grabbing at her raised hands from his seat in the back.

Melanie retrieved the phone Matthew left lying on the seat behind her and tapped the phone app. The voicemails popped up, Brian's name attached to the first message. The date stamp said he must've called right after leaving her house on Sunday. Her index finger hovered over the play button, her heart tripping. She closed her eyes, breathed deeply, and hit play.

"Hey, there. I just wanted to tell you how much I enjoyed this weekend."

Her heart clenched at the sound of his voice, sincere and intimate. But his words? She rolled her eyes. Yeah, right. Enjoyed it so much he decided to break up with her

"You, well . . . Y'know how in the beginning of The Wizard of Oz, *Kansas is all black and white?*—then softer, as if he were talking to himself—*"Or maybe it's sepia tone."*

She glanced at the house. The door swung open and Mason stood, shoulders back and chin jutted, backlit by the blue glow of a screen. He turned, addressing someone behind him.

"And then Dorothy's house lands in Oz, and suddenly everything is in Technicolor. The yellow brick road, the ruby slippers, the Emerald City."

Matthew and Mason walked toward the van. Mason, with his dirty winter jacket wide open, revealing jeans and a t-shirt, not the uniform the boys were instructed to wear.

"That's what happened to my life when I met you. I went from sepia to Technicolor, and the whole world is a better, more beautiful place." A couple seconds of silence ticked by. *"I want to build a life with you, and with Penny, Kevin, and Matthew. Happy birthday, hon."* Another second. *"Good night."*

Melanie clamped a hand over her mouth, choking on the emotion in her throat. Tears welled in her eyes, but she pushed them back, conscious of Penny's whines and the escalating irritation in Kevin's voice behind her.

What happened between her birthday and last night that resulted in a complete turnaround? She hadn't seen or spoken to Brian during that time, so what could she possibly have done to provoke that kind of reaction?

The other phone message, one from the boys' school, awaited, and she played it back.

"Mrs. Lombardi, this is Mrs. O'Connor, principal at St. Michael's. Something unusual happened at recess today with Kevin. It's not an emergency, but please call me at your earliest convenience. Thank you."

Matthew yanked open the van door, and he and Mason scrambled in.

"Hi, Mason." She cleared her throat, dislodging some of the raw emotion. "Sorry we're late." How late were they now? Was it even worth going?

"Hi, Mrs. Lombardi." Mason fist-bumped a giggling Penny on the way back.

Melanie made a mental note to call Mrs. O'Connor in the morning, unsure what could've happened. Kevin hadn't mentioned anything out of the ordinary.

While the boys sorted out who would sit where, she replayed the message from Brian, pinching her eyes closed with her fingers to restrain the sobs mounting in her chest.

"Let's go, Mom," Matthew called.

She brushed a stray tear from her eye, confident the children didn't notice, and saved the phone message. Brian hadn't given her the whole story. A story she deserved to hear.

She'd begun to hope for a future with Brian for herself and for her children, same as he had. Didn't she have a right to the truth?

* * *

AN HOUR LATER, the van door slid closed, nearly clipping Mason on the heel.

The den meeting had proven an effective distraction, getting her out of her own head and interacting with other people. Using a fingernail, Melanie scraped at the Elmer's glue on the leg of her jeans. At least she'd managed not to get any paint on her. The boys, on the other hand, would need a good scrubbing. Maybe if she'd been able to supervise their den project better tonight it would've been different, but instead she'd spent the evening chasing Penny between the long rows of tables, all the while struggling to understand what had spurred Brian to dump her.

Ten minutes and two fits of laughter from the back later, they pulled up to Mason's house.

"Y'see that car?" Mason pointed to a rusted-out green muscle car on blocks in his great-grandma's driveway. Weeds and grass grew around it, hiding the rear wheel wells. "That's my dad's. His sentence is up next month, and I'm gonna go live with him."

"You are?" Whether that meant good news or bad for Mason, Melanie didn't know, but her decision to not allow Matthew to play at Mason's seemed more prudent all the time.

"Yep. Thanks for the ride, Mrs. L. See ya', Matthew." He hopped out of the van and jogged to the house.

Mason's great-grandma let him in and waved to Melanie. The poor woman, stooped and frail, didn't seem to be in the best of health. And now she'd have to deal with her grandson re-entering their lives, for better or for worse.

With a glazed look, Penny stared out the window as they pulled away, oblivious to the boys talking in the back about a videogame.

Melanie's thoughts returned to her own problems. Like Mason's great-grandma, she'd been left to pick up the pieces following someone's untimely departure.

What had changed Brian's mind? Trying to concentrate on anything else was futile until she knew. They reached the first intersection, and Melanie hesitated. Going left took them home by the quickest route, but going right would take them on a scenic detour past Brian's apartment.

Predictability meant manageability. Isn't that how she'd lived her life? How she'd chosen David? And since his death, established routines had kept her sane and the kids flourishing. Spontaneous, unexpected actions blew the status quo to smithereens.

Like accepting Brian's invitation to a picnic almost six months ago.

Her heart pounded in her chest, and she gripped the wheel tighter then flicked on the turn signal. She pressed on the gas and the van lurched right.

CHAPTER 29

Melanie wiped the sweat from her palm on her jeans while steering the van down Brian's street. Clouds obscured any starlight, leaving only the odd streetlamp to light the residential street. By the time his apartment came into view, the knot in the pit of her stomach had coiled tight.

Six months ago, she thought she'd put her emotional exhaustion behind her. They'd survived the school year as a single-parent family. The seasons had changed, changed, and changed again. They'd adopted a new normal. And now, hurt, anger, and fear swirled in her belly. This was where her silly infatuation had gotten her. Feeling *gooey* about a man left her stuck, paralyzed by a new kind of grief, toting three kids on Operation Heartbreak when she should be helping them get ready for bed.

In plain sight of Brian's door, she parked the van, cracked the front windows, and turned off the engine.

A barrage of questions came from the back seat.

"Where are we?"

"Why did we stop here?"

And the timeless, "Can I have something to eat?"

Melanie swiveled in her seat, drawing the kids' attention. "I need to see Coach Brian for ten minutes. I'll be right there on his porch the whole time." She pointed to Brian's small, dimly lit porch. An American flag hung, motionless in the still air, and a dead, potted chrysanthemum sat atop a metal plant stand.

The Victorian-style house with white clapboard siding had been divided into four apartments: two upstairs, two downstairs. The entrance to Brian's first-floor home sat on the far end of the wrap-around porch. Venetian blinds hid any lights, making it impossible to see inside.

"Can we come with you?" Kevin pleaded.

"Not this time."

"But, Mom!" Kevin unbuckled and squeezed between the seats, inching toward the door.

"I said no, Kevin." Her voice betrayed her frustration. *Ugh.* The kids weren't at fault. Just tired and ready to go home.

"There's a party in the car, a party in the car," Matthew chanted, bouncing in his seat.

"I have to speak to him alone, Kevin. This is very important, and I need you—all of you—to behave until I come back. If there is some kind of emergency—and only if there is an emergency—Matthew may honk the horn and I'll come right over. An emergency means someone is sick or bleeding. Understand?" *Please, Lord, help them understand.*

Three heads bobbed up and down. Huh. She'd anticipated more resistance, but maybe on some level they understood that this was a big deal. Though she'd tried to disguise her emotions today, they'd likely picked up on her sadness.

And then Kevin flicked Matthew's ear, earning a shove.

"I'll be sure to make a special report to Santa about who was naughty and who was nice while Mama was out of the car." *That should ensure compliance.*

Tossing a frantic prayer heavenward, both for herself and her kids, she exited the van, locked the doors and tramped to

Brian's door. All the while, she willed her racing heart to just slow down already.

She opened the screen door and rapped three times on the old wooden door. Waiting, she glanced at her watch. She'd told the kids ten minutes. Any longer than that and they'd get squirrely in the van. Besides, it gave her a quick out if the conversation proved fruitless, or worse, painful. Maybe this was a mistake, but she had to know—

A lock turned and then the door opened. Brian stood in the shadowy entrance in black sleep pants and a faded t-shirt. Sleeping? At this hour? His hair stuck out here and there, and stubble dotted his typically clean-shaven cheeks.

"I thought maybe it was the Jehovah's Witnesses again." If he'd meant to lighten the mood, he'd failed, mostly because of the dim light in his eyes and his miserable expression.

She peered behind him at the blue glow from an open laptop.

He followed her gaze and then stepped onto the porch, pulling the door closed behind him.

"You'll have to get your copy of *The Watchtower* elsewhere." Her humorless tone rivaled his. "We're on our way home from scouts. The kids are in the van." She pointed to the curb where the kids waited. "I can't stay more than . . ." She glanced at her watch. "Eight minutes. And I won't try to change your mind. Can you just hear me out?"

She grew self-conscious under his stare. Any makeup she'd applied had long since faded. Surely bags hung under her red-rimmed eyes with all the crying she'd done. And then the glue from the scout meeting. . .

A brisk breeze sent a chill down her spine, and she tightened her coat.

She gave him a once-over, unruly hair to bare feet, with what looked like sleep clothes in between. "Don't you want to get a jacket or some shoes?"

He crossed his arms over his chest and shrugged. "Not sure it matters at this point."

She didn't get his meaning, but her minutes were ticking down. "Okay, then." She slipped her hands into her jacket pockets for warmth and looked at him, though his gaze bounced all over, landing at various points near his feet, as if he couldn't bring himself to face her. "When you say you don't want to be tied down with kids, I don't believe you. I've seen you with my kids. I've seen you with your nephews. I've seen you with a team full of boys, a few of whom are unruly, undisciplined brats. You love kids. So, I'm not buying your lame excuse, and I think you owe me the truth. Why did you dump me?"

He winced as if her words caused him physical pain, but he didn't speak.

She couldn't have more than five minutes left. He'd better get to it.

He stared then sighed, his shoulders sagging. "I'm sorry it happened like this, but I couldn't see another way."

Not much of an apology and even less of an explanation. Tick-tock, tick-tock. *I'll wait him out. I'll just stand here until he explains.*

His hands fell to his sides, a look of utter despair twisting his features.

Melanie's heart clenched even before he spoke, and then his words came as if from a horrible dream. If only she could press her hands to her ears and make them stop.

"I've been diagnosed with Hodgkin's lymphoma. I'll be starting chemo and radiation, and I . . . I need to focus on getting better."

Sucker punched by his words, she hugged her arms around her belly.

"I won't put you and your kids through all that. Not after what you've been through already." He shook his head, his eyes finally meeting hers. "No way."

She hated the news of this serious illness, but she hated even more that he'd hidden it from her instead of sharing his burden. He didn't trust her. And now she couldn't trust him. "You lied to me. You could've confided in me, but you chose to get rid of me instead."

He hid behind his hands, his fingertips buried in his hair. "Like I said, I didn't want to put you through all of this."

"So you decided it'd be better to dump me."

He turned away, pacing the length of the side porch. "Why do you keep saying that? I didn't *dump* you."

For a quarter of a second, she considered holding back the sarcasm. "Oh no. You let me down easy, right? Me and my kids, we're just great. Peachy."

"You are, Melanie. I didn't—"

"Since when do you decide what I want?" She yelled, not caring a whit if his neighbors heard. "If I want to break things off because you're sick, I will."

By the blank look he wore, she'd finally shouted him into submission.

"What do you think this teaches my kids? Because I'm not going to tell them that little charade you made up about not wanting kids. It would break their hearts. How can I tell them you're sick—very sick—but we won't see you anymore? Don't you think it's about time we started thinking about somebody else for a change instead of ourselves? That maybe it would be a blessing for my kids and I to help you through this?" She paused, catching a glimpse of the elderly neighbor lady in her window. "Never crossed your mind, did it?"

The wind kicked up again, whistling and sending a few dead leaves skittering around them.

Brian's gaze dropped to his feet.

"You know what their little impressionable minds are going to take away from this? It's fine to love somebody when everything is good and easy and they're healthy, but when the going gets tough? You're outta there."

Oops.

His gaze darted up to hers.

She'd said it. Out loud.

And he'd heard her.

Melanie loved him.

She'd been determined to keep from crying, but this lymphoma, this cancer, caught her off guard. That and her stupid admission. Using the back of her hand, she wiped tears from her cheeks. A futile effort seeing as how more replaced them in an instant.

After a few seconds, it became obvious Brian wouldn't acknowledge her slip. He couldn't even look at her. He paced the length of the porch, stopping at the end nearest his door, and braced his hands against the balustrade. With his eyes squeezed shut, he faced the nosy neighbor's direction.

Melanie blinked hard, squared her shoulders and squelched her tears.

"I'm sorry," he croaked. The brokenness sounded in his voice, yet he didn't recant. He wanted to stay broken up . . . or maybe just broken.

She shivered again and her tear-soaked cheeks burned in the cold air. How could Brian stand it without a jacket? "If I didn't have three kids to bathe and put to bed, two loads of laundry to do, and lunches to pack, I'd come in and . . ." She threw up her hands. "I don't know. Be some comfort to you? As it is, my time is up."

As if on cue, a yelp emanated from the minivan. Somehow her three small children, weighing in at 125 pounds combined, managed to rock the vehicle.

She turned to Brian, exasperated. With him, with her kids, with life.

He'd moved away from the rail and stood, arms crossed over

his chest, an immovable wall. How could his body look so strong and healthy yet be so diseased? The only softness lay in his eyes, which betrayed his fear and loneliness.

"Can you please come over tonight so we can talk? This is no way to end whatever it is I thought we had." Her arms ached to hold and soothe him. "Just give me ten minutes. Then I'll leave you be."

Not bothering to wait for a response, she wiped a stray tear and stomped off of the porch, her shoes slapping against the concrete walk.

Matthew bellowed something indiscernible from the small slit in the driver's side window.

She yanked opened the door, slid into the driver's seat, and started the engine.

"I'm really hungry," Matthew said, buckling his belt.

Penny rubbed her eyes and kicked her legs. "Kevin hit me."

"I did not," Kevin protested. "She's just sayin' that 'cuz she's a dumb girl."

Melanie massaged her forehead, wishing she could make it —them—stop. She glanced in the mirror and took in their faces. Hungry and tired, yes, but these precious faces meant everything to her. These were the faces that got her out of bed when she wanted to pull up the covers and hide. These faces made her laugh on the darkest, longest days. Their little hands clung to her waist and her neck, loving her in spite of everything.

They kept her mind and her body busy, never allowing her to wallow for long. They brought enough joy and hope to lighten the responsibility that, in her weakest moments, seemed insurmountable. The four of them would ride this storm out too.

"What's the matter, Mom?" Matthew's question brought her out of her reverie, his thoughtful glance causing her to tear up again. She could tell him the truth—would have to, soon—but she feared now it would tumble out too fast in an avalanche of words and tears. Tomorrow. She'd tell them then.

"I'm fine. Everything is going to be okay. We'll talk about it tomorrow, but the first order of business is getting you home and into bed." She pushed her cell phone into its dock, thumbed through playlists until she found some kid music, and let it play loud enough to drown out any possibility of conversation. Then she resolved not to think of Brian, his illness, or their breakup until she put the kids to bed.

Home, baths, bed. One thing at a time.

Maybe Brian wouldn't show up at her house. And maybe that would be for the best.

CHAPTER 30

With no moon to light his path to Melanie's door, nor, of course, any light on the front porch, Brian peered through the late evening darkness. His feet grew heavier with every step, but he trudged forward, determined to see this thing through by answering Melanie's questions and affirming their relationship's end. Done. Severed. Cut off at the knees.

He'd unwittingly made his job easier the night of their breakup when, without a mite of resistance, he gave in to the devil's persistent harrassment. Ah, maybe the devil didn't have as much to do with it as Brian would like to think. Maybe his own weakness, his own sin led him back to his favorite vice like a dog to his vomit.

He'd have guessed that faced with a life-threatening illness he'd be more conscious of the state of his soul, eager to rack up as many graces as he could, offer every bit of his suffering for the salvation of his soul, and renounce every sin he'd ever committed.

But nope. Instead, having hit rock bottom, his gut urged him to go deeper, to wallow in the death, disorder, and disappointment that pulled him with a gravitational force stronger than any he'd experienced.

He rapped on the front door, dreading another confrontation. Doggone it, he *loved* this woman. Breaking her heart, making her cry, and disrupting her life ranked dead last among things he wanted to do.

Steeped in self-loathing, he saw his decision to let Melanie go as the only righteous thing he'd ever done. She deserved a faithful lover. Her kids sure as heck deserved a better role model.

A click-click-click sounded from the other side of the door. Didn't she realize the socket had no light bulb?

He rubbed his forehead, trying to force down the self-disgust and irritation clawing at him.

Melanie opened the door and glanced at the empty light socket, sighing. She'd changed her clothes since she'd been at his house an hour ago. Gone were the dirty jeans and top, replaced with Capri-length lounge pants and an oversized sweatshirt.

"Come in," she said, a cool distance in her voice. "Sorry I'm not dressed. We had an, uh, incident necessitating a change."

He cocked an eyebrow. Should he ask? Did it matter? The kids' escapades weren't really his business anymore. He'd miss that. This house teemed with life in all its messy glory. By comparison, his apartment was a mausoleum.

He glanced around her living room. It looked the same—family photos on the wall, toys scattered here and there—yet completely foreign.

A post-mortem examination, that's what this was. Maybe there'd be another in the near future.

"Please, sit down," Melanie said, as if welcoming a stranger.

He glanced at the couch, where he'd slept just days ago, and opted for a straight-back chair instead. He could almost conjure the feel of the lumpy pillow beneath his cheek and the aroma of pancakes frying in butter.

Wrapping her hair in a messy bun at the back of her head, Melanie sat on the chair opposite him. "So, if you don't mind me asking, what happened with the doctor and the diagnosis?"

He crossed his feet at the ankles and leaned back. "You know how tired I was, like, all the time, and my glands swelling." He ran a finger along the bandage on his neck. "I'd also been having night sweats off and on for a while. The doctor said it was probably an infection."

"Only that's not what they found."

He shook his head. "He did an exam and took an x-ray, a blood test, and a biopsy of a lymph node."

Her gaze drifted to that bandage on his neck, and he shifted, angling that side away from her.

"Hodgkins is really treatable though, right?" She probably meant to sound detached and somewhat disinterested, but the anguish seeped in around the edges. "What kind of prognosis did they give you?"

He folded his hands in front of him, grateful this conversation seemed to be all about facts and not about feelings. He could do facts. "I don't see the oncologist until Friday morning, but, in general, survival rates are pretty good with treatment. Something like 80 percent after five years."

Melanie nodded. "So, those are pretty good odds." Too bad she couldn't hide the way her eyes welled with tears as she said it. See? He didn't even have a treatment plan yet, and it was ripping her up.

"You said you'll have chemo?"

"Yep. Radiation, too, probably." Clamping his jaw shut, he found a point on the wall above her and fixed his gaze on it, desperate to finish this conversation.

"Who's going to take you?"

"Huh?" Take him where?

"You know, to go to treatments or bring you home. That

kind of thing." She'd apparently slipped into mom mode, worried about details that were no longer her concern.

He shrugged. "I'll go myself. Or John. He can go." Although he'd yet to even inform John or any of his siblings about his condition.

She stared, not betraying her feelings on that topic.

After a minute, he stood and ran his palms down his pants. "Are we about done here? Because I didn't sleep well and . . ." She'd think the disease left him tired, not that he spent a solid hour perusing porn when he should've been asleep.

Melanie stood and moved toward him. "Uh, yeah. I guess we are." Her eyes softened with her voice. "Are we?"

Clear as day, she'd given him an opportunity to take it all back. He could apologize and beg her forgiveness. He could ask her to stand by him and support him, and he'd bet every dollar he had in the bank that she would. Because she didn't know him. She loved an impostor, an upstanding guy who respected her and could fix a leaky drain. Not the moral backslider, the black-hearted liar he saw in the mirror this morning.

He ambled to the door, hoping she'd follow.

Relieved to hear her footsteps behind him, he turned the handle and pulled the door open. She stopped too close, way into his personal space, setting off a burning sensation in his chest. Not the burn of attraction he usually felt when she got close, but a deep discomfort that allowed a seed of doubt to niggle its way in.

Cold air seeped in from outside, and she shuffled closer, her arms lost in that giant sweatshirt as she hugged her chest.

"We'll pray for you." She'd been composed back in the living room, but now that he'd rejected her for what, the third time? Now, she wore her emotions on her face plain as day.

Tears trickled from both eyes, but she didn't bother wiping them away. One trailed down her cheek, past the corner of her lips and then dripped from her jaw.

He sucked in a breath, willing himself to hold it together and revisiting the mantras he'd repeated all night long. *She's better off without you. You'll only hurt her.*

"If you could update us once in a while, I'm sure the kids will want to know how you're doing." She sniffed and blinked, but the tears kept coming.

He shouldn't have come. What good had this conversation done for either of them?

A bed creaked upstairs, but no footsteps followed. A glance at the stairs confirmed the kids slept on, oblivious to their mother's pain. Pain he'd caused.

How was it possible that mere days ago he'd stood here trying to tell Melanie he loved her? Sometimes she acted is if she didn't deserve his attention or a life outside of her kids. He'd vowed that when he saw her again, she would know how much he loved her and he'd erase every crazy, unworthy notion she had with a kiss that brooked no doubt.

His lips tingled in anticipation. Why shouldn't he have that kiss? Why shouldn't she know how precious she was to him—and that she would be to any man with an ounce of sense?

His conscience said not to do it, that it'd be a mistake that would hurt her even more. But he'd successfully dulled his conscience last night, not even regretting his sins, if he were honest with himself.

One last kiss. One that said what he hadn't. One to remember in the long months ahead.

Teary green eyes stared up at him, lost, maybe lonely.

Brian hooked an arm around her waist and pulled her to him.

She shivered, but how could she be cold under that big fleece thing? Her bloodshot eyes ripped another hole in his heart.

With his free hand, he cupped her face and dropped his lips to hers. He poured every mixed-up, raw, ragged emotion tearing at his heart into that kiss. All the hopes and dreams he had for their future dissolved somewhere between his mouth and hers.

He'd miscalculated or misread his own feelings because her lips moving beneath his and her hands at the back of his neck didn't feel like goodbye. It felt like home. Like acceptance. And for a moment, the idea of staying, of begging her to stand by him, to take care of him, tempted him.

Funny how he resisted *that* temptation.

He pulled away and traced a tear's trail down her face.

Her eyes drifted closed, but she took hold of his shirtsleeves and leaned into him.

He stepped back, forcing her to drop her hands and open her eyes. Were his life a movie, this would be the point where the love interest slapped the hero. But Melanie didn't slap him. She stood there, a numb, bewildered look on her face.

He hit the porch, raced down the steps, and reached his car at a near jog. Did she wait at the door or had she closed it already? Ignoring the urge to look, he slid into the driver's seat and started the car.

A gray sedan pulled out from in front of the neighbor's house, and a chill ran down his spine. In his rearview mirror, he saw it make a U-turn in the middle of the street, its taillights growing smaller as it headed toward the main road.

The blast of warm air from the car's heater unnerved him, and he quickly dialed the temperature controls back. Gripping the steering wheel, he let his forehead fall on the cold vinyl. His heart pounded with such force he thought it might explode.

Lifting his head again, he reached for his cell phone from the console between the front seats. His thumb and fingers hovered over the keypad for a few seconds.

He pressed his lips together and scrolled down his contacts until he found Melanie's number. Then he tapped out his message and hit send. Breathing deeply, he re-read his words.

I know my timing is bad, but I love you.

He shifted the car into drive and glanced up at her living room window.

Melanie stood at the window's edge, the curtain draped around her shoulder. She looked down at the phone in her hand, its soft glow illuminating her face in the dim room.

Brian swallowed, unsure of how she'd react. Maybe she'd fling open the door and run down here, urging him to reconsider.

Instead, she raised her arm above her head and hurled the phone across the room. It grazed the lamp shade, and he imagined the clatter as it skittered across her hardwood floor. She reached up and yanked the curtain shut.

CHAPTER 31

$\mathscr{A}$ sheen of sweat coated Brian's chest and back as he wrangled with the damp bed sheets. Breaking an arm free, he batted at the alarm clock, turning it in his direction. Did it go off? He hadn't heard it. The red numbers threw off more light than what seeped in around the windows. For eight o'clock in the morning, it sure seemed dark.

The fog cleared from his brain and despite a full night's sleep, it took an act of sheer will to get out of bed. The weight of a new day, compounded by all his cares, settled on his shoulders, leaving him dejected before he'd even offered a morning prayer.

He padded to the bathroom and blotted the sweat with a hand towel then peeked between the window blinds. Another dark and dreary November day with voluminous gray clouds smothering every patch of blue.

On his way to the kitchen, he passed his open laptop on the end table and slammed it shut, repulsed by memories of last night.

He'd left Melanie's house utterly bereft. If someone had wrenched his heart through his rib cage with a bare fist, he doubted it could hurt more. He'd driven home, pedal to the floor, half wishing he'd strike a tree or oncoming traffic and end his pathetic existence.

But after he'd gotten home, gulped a tall glass of water and cowered on the couch, numb, for a good twenty minutes, life seemed a smidgen less bleak.

He may be terminally ill. He may have destroyed the best relationship he'd ever had. But there sat his old friend, waiting. Always available. Never challenging. Never judging. A one-stop remedy for stress, boredom, loneliness, and unmet physical needs and desires. Price of admission: a valid credit card. *And a little piece of his soul.*

While he waited for a cup of coffee to brew, Brian checked his phone. Three work-related messages, but nothing that couldn't wait. When he'd gotten the diagnosis and fled the office a couple of days ago, he didn't care if they fired him. He'd since changed his mind, cognizant that the only thing now standing between him and financial ruin was his employer-provided health insurance.

He'd done his best to put in a full day's work from home yesterday, thanks to an understanding boss. Today he'd called in a personal day. He'd use the morning to visit his brother. This afternoon, he'd see the oncologist, who got him in a day early due to a cancellation.

With a mug of hot coffee in hand, he meandered through the living room, pulling open the drapes. The gray light streamed in, casting shadows on the disarray. He tossed the throw pillows into their place, toed a pile of magazines into a semblance of order, and flipped open the lid of the laptop he'd just shut.

How long could he go on like this? Two nights now he'd knowingly, willingly indulged in porn. He could continue down this path, revert to his old habits. Or he could stop here and now.

Bringing the mug to his lips, he prayed the dark roast's rich aroma and taste would soothe his frayed nerves. People raved about coffee, the miraculous cure-all in an eight-ounce mug. *Not feelin' it.*

He set the coffee on the kitchen table then glimpsed the paperwork for this afternoon's appointment. Brian gripped the chair back with both hands, his knuckles whitening.

He lifted the chair, slammed it, then flung it to the side.

The legs knocked the edge of a cast iron baker's rack, rattling a couple of mason jars filled with junk—pens, paper-clips, a pair of scissors.

With the back of his arm, he swiped them onto the floor. The contents spilled onto the rug. He could knock over every useless piece of crap in the place and it wouldn't relieve his frustration.

A growl grew in the base of his throat. "Why now?" he yelled at no one. "I don't wanna suffer. I don't wanna break Melanie's heart!"

He'd been running scared since he'd received the diagnosis, shoving aside his values, giving in without so much as a whimper. Only he couldn't outrun the morass of guilt and shame ensnarling him.

He slammed the laptop shut again. The little Sacred Heart of Jesus decal he'd affixed to the lid stared him in the face. Meant as an obstacle to temptation, it hadn't done the job lately. As he gazed at the gentle face of Jesus, nausea swirled in his gut, followed by a rush of something indescribable that pinched his chest and brought tears to his eye. Peace? Mercy? The decal's efficacy seemed restored today.

* * *

MELANIE SAT cross-legged on the couch, Bible open in her lap. Penny snuggled beside her, eyes glued to the dancing Claymation sheep on the TV.

Dishes remained piled in the sink, the hampers overflowed, and the dust bunnies in the corner appeared to be assembling for a *Night of the Lepus* remake. But she'd tried to be gentle with herself today. Experience told her that grieving was real work, needing time and patience. So at eight o'clock, after she'd kissed the boys goodbye and put them on the school bus, she'd crawled back into bed with Penny. While her sweet daughter snoozed, pink lips parted and dark lashes twitching, Melanie had prayed and prayed. She'd prayed both for herself and for Brian.

Her anger at him had dissolved pretty quickly after she'd cracked the screen on her cell phone. *What a stupid move!* Now she felt sorry for him. Not so much because of the lymphoma, horrible as it was, but because she sensed the sickness in his soul ran far deeper than the sickness in his body.

Melanie flipped a page and scanned the words, perusing her long-neglected Bible for a verse or psalm. Something that spoke to her, that could help her make sense of her turbulent life.

From across the room, her phone chimed. That's right!— she'd set a reminder to call the school principal back.

She shifted Penny's weight from her side and retrieved the phone. The blasted crack obscured the words on the screen. Phone to her ear, she walked to the kitchen and sat at the table, waiting to be connected to the principal's extension.

"Mrs. Lombardi, thanks for returning my call." The older woman sounded every bit the professional but also communicated concern through her tone. "I hope my message didn't alarm you. It seems such a minor thing, but I wanted to make you aware of it."

"Uh, no. I am curious though." More so now that she'd called. With everything going on with Brian, she hadn't given much thought to the reason for the principal's call.

"One of Kevin's classmates alerted the teacher on recess duty that a man had approached the fence near Kevin on the far side of the parking lot where the children play. He remained on the other side of the fence, a few feet back, and at no time was Kevin in any danger. The teacher approached and he turned and left. The whole thing lasted less than a minute."

"I'm surprised he got away so quickly. Kevin loves to talk." She let out a nervous laugh, but the silence on the other end of the line said the principal didn't find it humorous. "Did you ask Kevin what happened?"

"Yes, the teacher, Mrs. Ruppert, asked him if he knew the man. He said that he didn't, but the man had called him by name."

A chill ran up Melanie's spine. "He knew his name?"

"Yes, according to Kevin. He asked him if he liked to watched movies and then if he wanted to be in one."

Melanie switched the phone to her other ear. "What? A movie?"

"Yes. And that's all that happened. Did Kevin mention it to you?"

Melanie's heart sank. Had he? Did she not hear him because she'd been mired in her own drama? She didn't think so. Kevin knew how to get through to her when he wanted her attention. "No. Not a word."

"Well, it's probably nothing, but as I said, I thought you should know. I've asked the teachers to be vigilant about anyone approaching the children from the neighboring property, particularly during Kevin's recess period."

"Thank you. I appreciate it." Melanie ended the call with a sense of unease bordering on foreboding heavy on her heart. Had this been another example of Kevin's tendency to stray, to engage strangers in conversation or test his limits? Or was it something more sinister?

* * *

BIRDS CHIRPED HAPPILY in the trees as Brian crossed his brother's driveway and rubbed a fist over the garage door window. He threw a scowl at a pair of cardinals as they fluttered by. The filth on the window distorted his vision, but inside sat John's blue Ford. Kate's little silver SUV was gone. That meant she'd left for work and the boys were at school. He and John could talk alone.

Dread and anxiety shadowed him as he walked around back, climbed the steps to the deck, and rapped on the door. John was probably in the kitchen, finishing his coffee or making some phone calls before he left for appointments.

John pushed open the door while adjusting his necktie with the other hand. "Hey, what's up? Why aren't you at work?" He let the door close behind Brian and glanced at the wall clock. "You take a day off?"

"Yeah." Brian squeezed by him, eyeing John's steaming mug. His first cup hadn't fixed his problems and this one wouldn't either, but it might make the conversation more bearable.

John must've followed his gaze to the java. "You want a cup?"

"I'd love one. Thanks." The chair squawked as Brian dragged it away from the kitchen table and sat. He tapped his fingers on the table, glancing about the room. On the counter sat a small pile of mail next to a gargantuan box of frosted-wheat squares. Beyond the window above the sink, another cardinal flew by. *This place must be bird central.*

John set a mug on the table in front of Brian, sipping from his own cup. "Sick? Or are you playin' hooky with Melanie today?" He grinned, obviously having something totally different in mind for Brian's day than meeting with a cancer specialist.

Brian shook his head. "Nah. No plans with Melanie." He stared at the steam swirling above the mug. It whirled, smooth and orderly, and then just—poof!—dissipated into nothing.

"What's wrong?" John crossed his arms over his chest, looking intent on learning why Brian had shown up unannounced with no plans for the day.

He shoved the coffee away and ran a hand through his hair. "So, I saw the doctor on Monday about being so tired. And other stuff."

"Other stuff? Like what?"

"I've been sweating a lot at night, and Melanie noticed the glands in my neck were swollen." He ran his finger over the spot where he'd replaced the bandage last night. "And, uh . . ." There was no good way to deliver bad news. "He examined me and did some tests, and . . ."

"And?" John grabbed his laptop from the table and slid it into his bag along with an iPad.

"I have Hodgkin's lymphoma."

John's mouth fell open, his gaze laser-focused on Brian. "Cancer?" He set aside the work bag and sunk into his chair, head resting in his hands.

"Yep." Without anything to add and afraid of breaking down, Brian remained silent, waiting for John's response.

For a half a minute, Brian twiddled his thumbs and stared at the table, not sure how to soften the blow.

"Is the doctor sure?" John asked.

Brian sighed, wishing he had doubts, but he felt this diagnosis to his bones. "Yes, he's sure. They did a biopsy and everything." He grabbed his mug, stood, and ambled to the living room. As usual, action figures and LEGOs cluttered the end tables. On the couch, a bed pillow and a rumpled blanket lay piled in the corner.

John came up behind him and cleared his throat, ignoring the fact Brian knew either he or Kate had slept on the couch last night.

None of your business, Brian. You have your own problems.

John put a hand to Brian's shoulder and squeezed. He may have been the younger brother, but he was a fixer. Without a doubt, the cogs and wheels in his brain were turning already as he tried to solve Brian's problem. It had been simpler when they were teenagers and Brian's biggest dilemma was how to hide the dent he put in the fender of the family car.

"Hodgkin's is curable, right?" John's voice sounded uncharacteristically husky.

Brian turned, and John's hand fell away. "I'm gonna see the oncologist this afternoon, but from what I understand, most people go into remission and get better. Most, not all."

"You're young, you're healthy. You'll beat this." He smiled as if the outlook were rosy. Trying to convince himself or Brian?

Brian smiled, the muscles in his face unused to the movement. "It's pretty serious, John, but, yeah, I hope I can beat it."

"You will, man. You will." Then for the first time in what seemed like forever but had probably been a decade, John pulled Brian into a half hug. He gave Brian a manly pat on the back then shoved him away.

"Well, thank God you've got Melanie." He ambled back to the table and picked up his bag, sifting through its contents. "She'll get you through this. And so will we." He glanced up, catching Brian's gaze. "Whatever you need, Kate and I are here."

Brian held John's gaze and bit his bottom lip so hard he nearly broke the skin.

John's eyes widened. "What? What'd I say?"

Brian grabbed his cooling coffee from the table and forced down a gulp of the lukewarm liquid. "Melanie's out of the picture."

John let his bag topple over on the table with a thud. "Excuse me? What?"

"You heard me. I broke up with her." John didn't hear that little crack in his voice, did he? Brian didn't want to demonstrate either how much he hurt or how ludicrous his decision sounded.

John muttered a couple oaths and smacked his palms on the table, his voice pitching higher. "Why on God's green earth would you break up with her? And why *now* of all times, when you need her?"

Add John to the growing list of loved ones he'd managed to anger. It wasn't like he'd been given a handbook on how to handle this stuff. Maybe he should write one: "Dealing with Your Diagnosis: How to Piss Off Friends and Family in 3 Simple Steps."

"To spare her, that's why." He let his head fall into his hands and raked his fingers through his hair. "Geez, John, she already buried her husband! I can't put her through that again. I won't be responsible for that."

John zipped his bag and went to the kitchen and mopped a cloth over the countertop. He flung it down, scattering crumbs. "Are you insane? You *need* her. And she's gonna *want* to help you. Let her." He planted his hands on his hips. "You need to go over there and beg her to take you back. Tell her you weren't thinking straight. You made a rash decision. Whatever. Go now."

Brian smacked his fist against the table and one of the boys' bouncy balls rolled from the center onto the floor. "No. We're done. She needs to take care of herself and her kids. Not me too."

John shook his head, his gaze on the floor. "You're supposed to be the smart one, but I don't see it. This makes absolutely no sense."

Brian stood rubbing his temple where a twinge of pain signaled a headache coming on. "It makes perfect sense," he mumbled.

John grabbed his bag and slipped the strap over his shoulder. "Not to me. If it were me, I'd want Kate with me every step of the way. No way I could do it without her."

Well, lucky for you, you're not me.

"She's your *wife*." Brian shoved in his chair, assuming by the way John shuffled toward the basement door that he had to go.

John stopped, his hand on the door. "She's the woman I love." He met Brian's gaze again and his voice softened. "You can't tell me you don't love Melanie."

How could he deny it? He loved her more than anyone in the world.

With a ragged sigh, John pushed open the door. "You're stubborn. I know you won't change your mind." He glanced at the clock. "I've got an appointment."

"I figured." Brian slunk past John and down the basement steps. Enough dim light shone from top and bottom to illuminate the steps. The piney scent of laundry detergent drifted toward him from the laundry room.

"Hey, come over later, okay? Have dinner with us." John shut the kitchen door behind him and pounded down the steps. "I'll be home around 4:30. Just give me time to tell Kate and the boys first. Y'know, about the, uh, diagnosis."

Brian nodded as he entered the garage. "Sure." Not like he had any other plans. A long, lonely night loomed ahead of him and a few images from last night's swim in the digital cesspool crossed his mind. Better to limit his time home alone.

"We can talk about your appointment and treatment and all that stuff." John stopped in front of his car and opened the back door. "You should have someone go with you, y'know." He muttered something about Melanie and tossed his bag in the backseat.

"Not necessary," Brian said as he opened the garage door, blinking against the gray light.

"Next time," John called as he slid into his car. "Just give me some notice."

The sun peeked through a patch of thin gray clouds, the light glinting off the windshield of Brian's car. Now that he'd told John, the load on his shoulders had lightened a bit. Next up: getting through the doctor's appointment. He needed to get it together—get over the anger, quit the porn before it got out of hand, and find a glimmer of hope to hang onto.

He reached for the car door handle and stopped. In the center of the window, a giant splotch of wet bird poop dribbled downward. A whistle sounded from the tree next to the driveway, ending in a trill. Hope had never been so hard to come by.

CHAPTER 32

Having fully adopted the "be kind to yourself" adage, Melanie served the kids microwave meals for dinner. She shoved down the guilt of presenting high-sodium, highly-processed rubbery food to meet her growing children's nutritional needs. It wasn't like they ate it every night. And Melanie needed to conserve her energy until after dinner, when she'd sit the kids down and tell them about Brian. She swallowed, pushing down the rising dread.

"Mama, this is the best meal ever," Kevin said, stuffing a dinosaur-shaped chicken nugget into his mouth.

"Yeah, I give it . . . fourteen stars!" Matthew sucked milk through a straw, smiling.

When had the kids eaten with such gusto? Who knew TV dinners were the key to winning the suppertime sweepstakes?

Melanie averted her eyes from the feeding frenzy, focusing on the Greek salad she'd made herself, paired with a glass of Sauvignon blanc. She ordered her thoughts, preparing to address the worrisome recess incident with her middle child first.

"So, Kevin, I talked to Mrs. O'Connor." Melanie stabbed an

olive with her fork. "She said that during recess last week, one of your friends saw you talking to a man on the other side of the fence." Would he brush it off? Did he even remember the incident?

"Mmph, yeah. Fb-at gri." He chewed, cow-like, mouth wide open.

"Chew your food and then answer." If only she had a dollar for every time she'd uttered those words.

Kevin swallowed and wiped crumbs from his mouth with a fist. "Yeah. That guy."

"Yeah, uh, that guy." Melanie set her fork down. "Did he know you?"

Kevin shrugged. "Just asked me if I liked movies. So I told him about *Monsters University*, when Mike Wazowski—"

"Yep. I know." They'd watched it a million times. "He say anything else?"

"Huh-uh." Using his fingers, Kevin scooped corn onto his spoon. "Oh, something about bein' in movies or somethin'."

Obviously the exchange hadn't been memorable.

"Do you remember what he looked like?" She slid a forkful of feta cheese into her mouth.

Kevin shrugged. "Like a guy." He tilted his head, deep in thought. "Old but not as old as Paps. And fat." He puffed out his cheeks then giggled.

Melanie sighed. Not much to go on. "Just steer clear of strangers like that, okay? And if he comes back, tell the teacher on recess duty, got it?"

"Okay. Do you know who the worstest kid in my class is?"

"You!" Matthew shouted.

Melanie scowled at him.

Matthew giggled.

She bit her lips together but couldn't hide her grin.

And then the conversation turned to the circle time shenanigans of the worstest kid, Landon.

Once they'd cleared the dinner dishes, which took all of fifteen seconds since everything but the flatware could be thrown away, Melanie gathered her courage and ushered them to the living room.

A lump grew in her throat, and she prayed to the Holy Spirit to get her through this discussion. She'd put off telling them about Brian for long enough. Maybe part of her subconsciously hoped she wouldn't have to, that he'd change his mind and decide he needed her after all. Even then, she'd still have to tell them about the cancer.

"Pile on the couch there, guys." She moved the throw pillows onto the floor, giving them ample room, then sat cross-legged on the floor in front of them.

Penny climbed onto the couch, elbowing for position between her brothers.

"C'mon, Penny," Matthew whined. "That's my spot."

"I want to tell you what Coach Brian and I talked about the other night when we stopped at his place." She squeezed her ring finger, still missing that wedding band. Maybe she should buy some costume jewelry to replace it.

Penny hid her eyes, trying to engage her in a game of peek-a-boo.

Melanie shook her head, dismissing Penny's unspoken request. "Brian went to the doctor on Monday because he hasn't been feeling well for a while." How long had it been? Maybe she should've encouraged him to go sooner. Would it have made a difference?

"Stop it, Penny!" Kevin moved as far from Penny as he could, a deep frown making grooves in his forehead.

"And the doctor told him he has a disease called Hodgkin's lymphoma. It's a kind of cancer that starts in the lymph nodes, which are—"

"Didn't Grandpap have cancer?" Matthew leaned forward, his eyes wide and worried.

Only Matthew had a few vague memories of her dad, who had died almost five years ago. "Yes, but he had stomach cancer. This is a different—"

"Is Coach Brian gonna die?" Now that Matthew had made the connection, Kevin understood the seriousness of that ominous word: cancer.

Penny's gaze focused on her, oblivious to the word "cancer" but probably possessing a semblance of the seriousness of dying.

"Most people with this kind of cancer don't die from it . . ." Tears burned behind her eyes. In seconds, they'd hit on her greatest fear. *Please, Lord, heal him.* "But the treatments that'll make him better, well, they're gonna make him pretty sick too."

Matthew scrunched his nose. "Like bad-tasting medicine?"

"Sort of, but—"

"Is he gonna be in the hospital?" Kevin scooted closer. "Can we catch it from him?"

If they'd just let her finish! Penny tugged on her sock, paying little attention, but the boys' concern cracked her heart a tiny bit more. "No and no. But we're not going to be seeing him much anymore."

She stretched her legs out in front of her then brought her knees up to her chest. "He wants to work on getting better and, uh . . ." She'd had days to come up with an explanation, and words still failed her. "Well, he'd rather do that alone. He doesn't want to be a bother to us, and—"

"Huh? He doesn't bother us, Mom. We love it when he comes over." Dear, sweet Matthew. God bless him, but if he said one more thing, she'd cry.

"I know, hon. This isn't what I wanted. When we get sick, we take care of each other, right?"

Kevin nodded.

Penny slid from the couch, grabbed her little kitty toys from the floor, and started lining them up.

"Is his hair gonna fall out?" Matthew asked. "Because Gina and Ashley got their hair cut and donated it to people that have cancer."

Melanie flexed her fingers, imagining the feel of Brian's hair between them, thick and silky at the nape of his neck. That last kiss, in this very room, flashed in her mind. Oh, she hoped he wouldn't lose his hair! "I don't know. It probably depends on what kind of treatments they do and, I'm not sure. Just let me finish, okay?"

The boys sat closer together now, silent. Penny glanced up, a couple of kitties clutched in her hands.

"We're not—I'm not—going to be seeing Brian, but we should pray for him, and I did ask him to update us once in a while on how he's doing." Would the kids respect the distance he wanted or would they be clamoring to see him?

They wrapped up the conversation, and she told them to play a board game while she straightened the kitchen and prepped their lunches for tomorrow.

In the kitchen, she grabbed her wine glass and finished off the remaining mouthful, the last time she and Brian had been together suddenly fresh in her mind. She'd answered all of the boys' questions, but she had one of her own that she couldn't answer. What kind of a man breaks up with a woman and then kisses her with such . . . *ardor*? The warmth from the wine spread through her chest while a tingle shot up her spine. And what was she supposed to make of that final *I-love-you* text? He'd said, *"I know my timing is bad."* Understatement of the century.

No mind. She could muster the discipline the kids lacked. Brian wanted to go it alone? He'd go it alone.

CHAPTER 33

Brian took the literature the oncologist had given him and fanned the stack out on his kitchen table. A print-out from his appointment, some photocopied pages explaining treatments and side effects, and a couple of brochures. He should read it. All of it. He'd had two days and hadn't gotten past the first paragraph. Like wading in a stagnant pool, this limbo between diagnosis and treatment had become toxic. Something had to give.

He smoothed a page, read two sentences, and set it aside, unable to focus. He'd hoped that once he'd seen the doctor, he'd have a better sense of understanding and purpose. He did, to a degree. But he couldn't quell the disquietude in his heart and soul. His feelings fluctuated, always some combination of bitterness, anger, agitation, and fear—with a side of heartbreak. But that had been his own doing.

His gaze drifted to the closed laptop. Indulging in his vices hadn't brought him any solace. Not that he'd ever thought it would. It killed his soul with a speed and precision cancer couldn't match.

His gaze drifted to the cross hanging on the wall and then the clock opposite it. Maybe he did have someplace to go.

* * *

HIS NERVES ALL AJITTER, Brian withdrew a gloved hand from his jacket pocket and yanked open the heavy metal door. He blinked as his eyes adjusted to the dim light, a contrast to the bright afternoon sunshine. With his jacket unzipped, the warm, indoor air seeped through his thin shirt.

As he entered the main church, he blessed himself with holy water from the font affixed to the wall. He used to keep a little bottle of it on hand at home for when the lure of lascivious images got too strong. Why had he let that practice go by the wayside?

Only the sanctuary lamp lit the altar. Natural light, tinged varying shades of blues and reds as it streamed through stained glass windows, brightened the aisles. The only sound came from a periodic clicking that emanated from the ancient radiators on the perimeter of the church.

His feet, heavy from equal measures of fatigue and guilt, propelled him midway up the aisle where he stopped, genuflected, and slid into the wooden pew.

The boards creaked as he sat, elbows on his knees, head bowed.

He waited for a prayer to form in his heart. A fire engine siren sounded outside, rising to a shrill crescendo. A minute or so passed. Then another. The kneeler creaked as he shifted his weight. Nothing. He had no words for God, but to be in His presence felt like enough. For now, anyway.

He stared alternately at the larger-than-life crucifix suspended above the altar and the scuffs on his boots where they rested on the floor. Occasionally, a lemony-clean scent drifted his way. His gaze slid at last to the red sanctuary lamp suspended from the ceiling and, beneath it, the tabernacle. The burnished gold box with ornate trim sat cold and unassuming.

Compelled by an unseen force to move from the pew, Brian shifted uncomfortably. No longer able to relax, he twisted in his seat and glanced around the empty church. No one beyond the glass doors in the back. Choir loft, vacant. Altar, bare.

Brian slid out of the pew and strode toward the front of the church, his boots clapping against the floor. When he reached the point where the pews ended, he got down on one knee, then the other. With a last glance to make sure he was alone, he lay face down on the floor. His heart stirred and awareness swelled in his chest. It seemed as if a protective hand hovered above him, heightening his sense of being loved and secure.

The cold marble floor sent a shiver along his body, chest to toes. If he could've gone lower than the floor, he would have. For the first time this week, the broken pieces of his life fell into place. The ability to reassemble them escaped him, but somehow that didn't matter. He could entrust each ragged-edged piece to the One who'd made them, confident that somehow they fit. His illness, his unchastity, and his fractured relationship with Melanie. While it had seemed to him that his life had spun wildly out of control, an order and a purpose existed, even if he couldn't discern them.

Perfectly humbled, he lay there until the click-clack of heels broke his concentration and forced his eyes open. Immediately, his tentative connection to God withered and anxiety crept in.

What would someone—a woman, by the sounds of those shoes—think, seeing him prostrated in the aisle? Maybe the click-clacking came from a side aisle and she wouldn't see him. Or maybe she'd think he'd collapsed.

The clapping heels sounded closer together, their approach rapid.

Brian pushed up onto his knees, sat back, and made the sign of the cross.

Four-inch high black heels came into view alongside him and a hand pressed on his back. "Are you okay? Do you need help?"

Heat crept up Brian's cheeks, his embarrassment rising as he took in his would-be rescuer. Instead of a dowdy, blue-haired widow more commonly seen in darkened churches, a young woman with jet black hair to match her shoes crouched beside him. Flawless ivory skin, professionally-applied makeup, and finely manicured fingernails—stunning.

"Um, I'm fine." He stood, shrugging off her attempt at assistance. He wasn't an invalid yet. "I was just . . ." He gestured toward the floor in front of the altar where he'd lay sprawled. "Just praying."

"Oh." She stepped back, a curious look on her face. "I'm sorry. You're good then?"

"Yep. I'm good." He nodded and tried for a smile to demonstrate his well-being. "Thanks for checking though."

She nodded and proceeded up the aisle then around the corner toward the sacristy.

Heaving a sigh, he returned to his pew and knelt, this time ready to lay it all out for God—all his confusion and fears, his shame and regret, his hopes.

As the sunlight brightened on the western side of the church, more people began to filter in for confessions and then the evening Mass. An old man pushed a walker and an oxygen tank slowly up the aisle. A pimply teenager slid into a pew and knelt, his backside resting on the bench and his head hanging toward his arms outstretched on the seat in front of him. An elderly woman trailed a preteen boy, and a middle-aged couple escorted seven stair-step blond children whose serial genuflections reminded Brian of a crowd creating a wave at the ballpark.

Brian hadn't planned on confession or Mass, but now that he was here . . .

The confession line moved at a snail's pace, the father of

those perfect-looking blond kids taking a good ten minutes in the box. As the person in front of Brian held open the confessional door for him, his heart lurched. His love/hate relationship with the Sacrament of Reconciliation swung wildly to hate. He dreaded having to hear his sins out loud—which was probably why the Church, in Her wisdom, required it. So many times he'd recited the same sexual sins, trying to sandwich them between less humiliating ones like gossiping or being envious of others. *So clever.*

Eyes closed, he rattled off the most serious sins, thankful for the screen preserving his anonymity with the priest.

The priest offered some advice, all of which Brian, well-versed in ways to combat lust, porn, and "impurity with himself," as he called it in the confessional, had heard before. The priest offered the words of absolution, and Brian's love/hate meter swung dramatically in the opposite direction. He left the confessional walking on air.

Despite the outpouring of grace he'd received, Brian's attention, as usual, flitted in all directions during Mass. What would he have for dinner? Did he remember to make his car payment? What were Melanie and the kids doing this weekend? He merely went through the motions, sitting, kneeling, and standing, according to the rubrics. And then he homed in on the priest's words:

"Deliver us, Lord, we pray, from every evil, graciously grant peace in our days, that, by the help of your mercy, we may be always free from sin and safe from all distress, as we await the blessed hope and the coming of our Savior, Jesus Christ."

Another weight lifted from his shoulders. Like clouds dissipating after the rain, every care faded in the knowledge that God maintained control.

Unlike Keith, the quiver-full guy at work, Brian had committed few Bible verses to memory, but one came to him: "I can do all things through Christ who strengthens me."

After Mass, Brian knelt again, grateful and with a fresh perspective. He concentrated his prayers on two petitions. If they aligned with God's will—and he didn't see why they wouldn't—he prayed that God would hear his prayers and accept his sacrifices. Because he had a feeling he'd be given countless opportunities to offer up his suffering in the coming months.

Brian strode out of the church with a sense of peace he hadn't felt since he'd received the doctor's fateful phone call. By his own doing, he'd face this cancer mostly alone. Mostly, but not all.

CHAPTER 34

A wadded ball of red and gold wrapping paper whizzed by Melanie's head, landing on the floor amid more wrapping paper, toy packaging, and Styrofoam peanuts. Smiling, she grabbed her brand-new "Savage Mom" mug filled with hot cocoa from the end table and ambled to the living room picture window, dodging a pair of binoculars, an art set, and a pink princess gown puddled on the floor.

Behind her, Matthew and Kevin created incessant popping sounds with their new Trouble board game. Penny hummed from inside a giant cardboard box, where she played with her set of Strawberry Shortcake dolls. Morning sun shone, casting a beam on the Christmas tree. A clump of silver tinsel glimmered, drawing her eye to a sparkly lighthouse ornament she and David had bought on a weekend getaway to Lake Erie as newlyweds. Such happy, carefree days!

Steam from Melanie's hot chocolate rose, its rich, minty aroma tickling her nose and making her belly growl. She sighed and leaned against the window sill. In a minute, she'd start making the gingerbread waffles she'd promised the kids for Christmas morning.

She gazed out at the empty street, the neighborhood silent. Frost dotted the lawns and Christmas decorations in areas still shaded from the morning sun. A single red bird flew by, alighting on the bare limb of her neighbor's cottonwood tree. Her gaze trailed through the yard and along the driveway. A steady puff of exhaust caught her attention. The gray car, again.

Her shoulders tensed. The car didn't belong to her neighbor; she'd asked. Old Mr. Siddle, practically a recluse, barely drove his blue Oldsmobile, which remained tucked away in his garage.

"Hey, Matthew?" She turned, sipping her drink. "Can I borrow those binoculars Santa brought you?"

Matthew yelled at something that had happened in the game and rolled backward, his space pajama-clad legs in the air.

She repeated her request, her gaze darting back to the car idling outside.

"Sure, Mom." He handed her the small black case. "Don't break 'em."

Melanie grinned. "I'll be careful."

While peering at the car with her bare eyes, she removed the binoculars from their case. Then she lifted them to her eyes and tried to find the car through the eye piece. Pale blue sky, brown tree—there! A figure sat behind the wheel. She adjusted the focus but still couldn't make out features. It appeared by size and build to be a man. A dark knit hat covered his head. His skin seemed light brown, not Caucasian, but not very dark either.

Her cell phone rang from the end table. With reluctance, she returned the binoculars to Matthew and crossed the room. She smiled, seeing her brother's name on the screen, then swiped her finger across the phone and held it to her ear.

"Merry Christmas, Scottie."

A squeal of delight and loud kid voices sounded. "Back atcha'. Was Santa good to everyone?"

She nudged aside a discarded package of brand-new boys'

socks and sat on the couch. The wreckage around her said that Santa had been very good. At least to her kids. The contents of her own stocking had been rather meager. Filling her own stocking to preserve Santa's mystique left her sad and disappointed. Would it always be this way? If Brian hadn't—

"Hey, you still there?" More celebratory squeals came from the background. What had those kids gotten?

"Yeah. Sorry. Santa is always good. The boys have new baseball gear for when the weather breaks, and Penny is awash in a sea of pink things—dolls, clothes, jewelry."

"Awesome. How about you? Treasures from the kids? Diamond ring from Brian?"

Melanie's heart faltered. Scott didn't know. They'd never had a particularly close relationship, but unlike her two other brothers, Scott made an effort to call her at least once a month since David died, despite how busy his family of six kids kept him. November's call had obviously been *before* the breakup with Brian.

She cleared her throat and steeled her nerves. Missing Brian already had her on the verge of self-pitying tears today. She'd hoped to celebrate with him—Mass together, assembling toys into the wee hours, a delicious turkey dinner, and maybe a drive around the neighborhood to peep at the Christmas lights. "I got a lovely mug from Matthew, a pair of knit gloves from Kevin, and, um . . ." She lowered her voice. "I got a dog toy from Penny."

Scott laughed. "A dog toy? Do you know how many jokes that invites?"

She rolled her eyes. Yes, the baby sister knew all about jokes at her expense. "It's a plush candy cane. I think she picked it up at Santa's secret shop thinking it was a stuffed toy, but it's a squeaky toy. For canines."

"Oh, that's hilarious. And what about from Brian?" A door clicked and the background noise subsided.

Melanie swallowed, gathering her composure. "We broke up. Before Thanksgiving, actually."

"I'm sorry, Mel," he said softly. "I didn't know. Last time we talked, it sounded serious. I thought I'd be digging my tux out of the closet soon."

Yeah, me, too.

"Do I need to beat the snot out of him?"

She stood, tightened her bathrobe, and wandered to the window. "Tempting, but no. Life's gonna do that all on its own. He could actually use your prayers."

The gray car had vanished and a sense of relief washed over Melanie.

She explained to Scott about Brian's cancer diagnosis and his convoluted reasons for breaking up with her.

"Huh. Well that sucks. Part of me thinks he's an idiot and *does* want to beat the snot out of him, but I gotta give him props for wanting to protect you."

Melanie turned from the window, dodging the debris on the floor, and drifted to the kitchen, rolling her eyes. Was this some kind of macho thing? "Protect me? Seriously? Yeah, I'm much better off slogging through the day like a zombie and crying myself to sleep every night."

Silence came from Scott's end. Had her confession been too much?

"Okay, yeah. Now I wanna kill him." There might've been a hint of a smile on his words. Hard to tell. "Come visit us. We'd love to have you. Stay through New Year's. I finished the basement, so there's plenty of room. It'll get your mind off of—"

The offer tempted her. A family visit, a distraction from Brian. Then she calculated the airfare to South Carolina. Nope. No can do. "Thanks, but we don't want to intrude—"

"You're family. You're not intruding."

Melanie grabbed the cookbook with the gingerbread waffle recipe on the counter and pulled a stainless steel mixing bowl from the cupboard. "I, uh, I also have a job interview next week."

She hadn't confirmed it yet, but the digital media company had given her several possible dates, including one next week. Flipping the cookbook pages, she paused a moment at the recipe for the jelly-filled cookies David loved so much, a pang striking her chest. From beneath the sink, she retrieved the waffle iron. As always, her gaze darted to the trap Brian had fixed. Still no leak. He'd done a good job.

"You're going back to work?"

Her heart ached at the thought, but she'd gone through the budget with a fine-toothed comb. David's life insurance only went so far. She needed income. "Yep. The kids are established in their school year routine, and we could use the extra money."

He sighed, probably wondering how big a check to write her. It wouldn't be the first, but she wouldn't accept this one. She needed to stand on her own two feet. "Dad!" someone called from the background.

"Hey, I'm gonna have to go." Conversation started up behind him.

"I didn't even get to ask you about *your* Christmas or the kids." She'd been right when she'd told Brian that helping him through his illness would be good for her family. They were too wrapped up in their own problems. They needed to think about others more often, move outside of their insular little bubble.

"Everything's good here, but I'll call you later in the week, okay?"

She ended the call and proceeded to assemble the waffle ingredients: flour, sugar, eggs, butter . . . This second Christmas without David proved harder than the first. All the memories of Christmas mornings past flooded her, every ornament a reminder of another time or place. The mistletoe they'd bought their first Christmas as a married couple. The hokey, stop-motion Christmas specials he loved. Even his grumbled complaints about the commercialization of Christmas. The big Scrooge! And to compound the deep sadness the holidays brought, the loss of Brian and all she'd anticipated this Christmas loomed over the house.

What plans did Brian have for Christmas? Surely, he wasn't alone, was he? He had a married sister in California and another in college in the South. And, of course, John and Kate and his nephews.

As she stirred the waffle batter with a wooden spoon, she imagined Brian huddled on the floor with Patrick and Brady, showing them how to operate a new toy, a Santa hat perched on his head and a strand of silver garland around his neck.

Emotion swelled in her chest, and she wiped tears from her eyes. Brian would be fine. Maybe his choice to concentrate on his treatment was for the best. He could make his health a priority without worrying about her little clan. He'd be surrounded by a loving family, enjoying a great Christmas feast.

* * *

BRIAN LAY ON HIS COUCH, his gaze affixed to the TV screen, where *It's a Wonderful Life* played. George Bailey's touring car slammed into a tree. *Poor guy.* He'd never been so sympathetic to George's plight.

Since that first week after his diagnosis, Brian's dejection had lifted, but he still couldn't call his outlook optimistic. He'd accepted that the Hodgkin's, timing and all, was God's will for him, but he couldn't say he'd embraced the illness or had mustered the will to fight it.

His phone sounded once . . . twice. Probably more texts from Kate, sending him pictures of Patrick and Brady on Christmas morning. For the past two days, she'd been trying to coax him to come over for Christmas. Initially, he thought he'd make it, but for some reason, this round of chemotherapy hit harder than previous weeks'.

He'd managed the nausea. Mostly. But the fatigue! He considered it a heroic act just to get his butt off the couch to go to the bathroom and back. His eyes drifted closed.

The phone sounded again.

He silenced it and shoved it across the coffee table, out of reach.

Brian yanked his grandmother's afghan higher, tucking it under his chin. Even though he'd bumped the thermostat up a couple of degrees, the cold still teased his nose and toes. With the drapes drawn, he couldn't tell whether the clouds had cleared this morning. Other than the TV, the only light came from the tree Kate and John had foisted on him.

The four-foot artificial tree sat in the corner, its fiber optic tips glowing in a sequence of colors: red, gold, blue, green. His stomach turned watching it. Brian stood staunchly in the "real tree" camp. He'd tried ignoring the offensive little decoration, but every time Kate stopped over, she turned the tree on. He'd felt bad when she'd had to remove the jacket he'd thrown atop it. He hadn't intended to hurt her feelings; she'd meant well.

No presents sat under the little tree. He'd had two bags of toys. One went to Patrick and Brady. The other, intended for Matthew, Kevin, and Penny, ended up in a Toys for Tots collection box, along with a piece of his heart.

What were they doing this morning? He imagined the ruckus as they ripped open gifts, their faces gleeful as they pulled little treasures from their stockings and sucked on candy canes.

His heart aching, he flung an arm across his face and tried to stem the tears building in his eyes. He'd thought by now the sadness would have lifted, that it would get better. But each morning dawned more pointless than the one before, its gaping maw mocking him. The joy had been sucked out of his life from the minute he'd left Melanie. Would he ever know the comfort of her presence again?

According to the calendar, December held the shortest days, but to Brian, they'd become the longest, eclipsed only by the nights. Staring blankly as George Bailey called helplessly to his unhearing wife, a question formed. Which would kill him faster? The cancer or his broken heart?

CHAPTER 35

$\mathcal{U}$sing her hip, Melanie shoved open her front door and boosted a sleeping Penny higher on her shoulder. *Note to self: put a light bulb in that porch fixture, pronto!* How long until this day—this week!—ended?

Inside, the house sat quiet and dark—as it should for almost ten o'clock on a Tuesday night. A brisk blast of February wind followed her, trailed by Matthew and Kevin, who hugged his bandaged hand to his chest.

"Grab the keys from the door, please, Matthew. Just set them at my place in the kitchen." She let her purse slide from her arm onto the floor in the foyer and switched Penny to her other arm. The muscles in her thighs burning, she carted the little girl up to her bed, removed her shoes, and tucked her under the covers, fully clothed in a lavender pantsuit covered in rainbow-colored ponies.

Melanie sighed and shook out her aching arms, kissed and blessed her sweet girl, and then trotted downstairs to corral the boys into bed. Matthew lay face down on the couch, one foot on the floor. Kevin sat next to him, his hand still pulled tight to his chest.

She ran a hand over Kevin's silky hair. "Still hurt?" She stretched a hand toward his.

He twisted away from her. "A little."

"You were very brave." True enough, at least in so far as the urgent care office was concerned. At home here? After he'd sliced open his hand on the jagged edge of a soup can lid? Minor hysteria.

The boys needed to get to bed, but she craved a minute to get her bearings. She flopped onto the chair and lifted one foot onto the ottoman.

The phone rang from the kitchen. The landline? No one called the landline except for telemarketers, but they didn't call this late at night.

Worry spreading in her chest, she strode to the kitchen dimly lit by the microwave's soft glow and grabbed the phone from its base. Her heart thumped in her chest. "Hello?"

"Good evening, ma'am." The last syllable in each word was clipped short, giving the voice a robotic quality. "Time for bed?"

Her brow wrinkled in concentration as she tried to identify the somehow familiar voice. "Who is this?" She pulled the phone from her ear and glanced at the caller ID. It read, "anonymous call."

A couple beats of silence followed before the call disconnected.

Creepy. Even though the voice wasn't natural, it reminded her of someone. A celebrity or actor maybe? She returned the phone to its cradle and headed back to the living room, resigned to half-hauling, half-dragging the boys' sleepy bodies up the stairs.

The phone rang again, sending a frisson up her spine, and she spun back, examining the caller ID. This time it read, "Perella, John."

Her heart beat double-time. Why would John call her—let alone this late?

Brian.

What had happened?

"Hello?" She put a hand to her throat, which had suddenly gone dry. "John?"

Tension gripped her as a memory transported her to the day she'd taken the call from David's manager. The call that changed everything, that shattered—

"Yeah, uh, Melanie, it's Brian's brother." His weary voice ground out the words.

Oh God, please no! Please, let Brian be okay.

"Uh, hey, sorry to call so late. I figured I'd wait until the kids were in bed."

Her gaze darted through the doorway to the living room. Now both boys lay draped on the couch, their heads touching in the middle. Asleep, but not in bed.

"They're asleep. What's up?" Her voice came out high and strained, and she held her breath, bracing for the worst.

"It's about Brian." As if finally realizing she'd assumed the worst, he rushed ahead. "He's okay. I mean, no emergency or anything like that."

She let out the breath she'd been holding, relief coursing through her. *Thank you, Jesus!* "I haven't spoken to Brian since a few days after he was diagnosed. So, I'm completely out of the loop."

"Yeah, I know. I think that's the problem."

Melanie meandered toward the sink and gazed through the window into the darkened yard. A patch of dead wildflowers and ornamental grasses bent in the breeze. "I don't understand." What if the cancer treatments weren't working? Maybe she should've insisted on sticking by him, regardless of what he said he wanted. Maybe she'd capitulated too soon.

"I talked to Brain's oncologist today. She's a little surprised he's not responding better to treatment. I mean, it's working, I guess, but aside from this, he's a healthy, young guy. He should be kickin' this thing's butt."

Emotion tightened her chest. "But he's not?"

"Sounds like things should be working faster and better. The doctor thought maybe, I don't know, his attitude or his state of mind could be the problem. She asked if anything personal was going on, and I thought . . ."

"You thought of me." Melanie paced the room, one hand tucked around her waist. This was *not* how things were supposed to be. She should've been with Brian, going to appointments, checking in . . .

"Yeah. He's been depressed, an' I kinda chalked it up to bein' sick. But maybe it's more about things with you than the lymphoma."

A spark of irritation grew in her chest. "Y'know, John, breaking up wasn't *my* idea. I wanted to be there for Brian. He didn't want me. He made it very clear." Had he though? In words, yes, but in actions, not so much. That kiss . . . that last text message.

"I know. Believe me. He got an earful from me about that." He sighed, and she got an inkling of the toll his brother's illness had taken on him too. "He's stubborn. And I have no right to come to you—"

She stopped in front of a wall calendar covered with appointments, events, and other time-sensitive notes. "I'm not sure what you're asking, but I'm gonna level with you, John. I'd do anything I could for Brian, despite how it ended. But I've got a lot on my plate right now." She replayed tonight's crazy dash to the urgent care, Kevin's bleeding hand wrapped in a rag, Penny with remnants of lunch smeared down her dress, Matthew toting his homework along for the ride. "I'm a single mother to three little kids, and I'm working full time now." Not to mention that in her nearly nonexistent spare time she'd decided to redo her bedroom.

"I wouldn't ask, but I don't know what else to do. Kate and I are beatin' our heads against the wall here. Would you consider a visit? Just stop in, see how he's doin'?" A feminine voice, probably Kate's, sounded in the background. "Maybe take him dinner?"

Melanie closed her eyes. *What do you want me to do, Lord?* She didn't wait for a response. Her heart wouldn't allow her to refuse. "I can take him a meal a couple nights a week. Make sure he's eating right."

"Thank you." John's relief was palpable. "I'll give him a heads up. And Melanie, I really appreciate this."

"It's okay. I want to help. I, um . . ." Seldom had she been so forthright, but three hours at urgent care had worn her defenses thin. "I don't want to see anything bad happen to him. I still love him too much to pretend I don't care."

"He's crazy, you know? What he did was stupid."

Why did she want to defend Brian? Yes, she agreed his decision was counterproductive, at best. And her heart still ached every time she thought of him, which felt like every waking minute almost three months later. But he'd meant well, right? He'd been willing to sacrifice his own happiness and security for the sake of sparing her more suffering.

"John, you know you have everything Brian wants, don't you? A wife and kids."

He snorted. "Well, if that were true, you'd think he'd make an effort to . . . never mind."

"You remind him of what he's missing. Especially Patrick and Brady. But a solid marriage too."

John scoffed. At which part of her statement, she wasn't sure. "That's crazy."

But true.

"Mama . . ." Matthew whined from where he'd tumbled onto the living room floor.

"I gotta go, John. I'll take Brian dinner, um . . ." She slid a finger over the calendar. "Thursday. Around six." Assuming Hannah could watch the kids for a bit. "Say a prayer he opens the door for me, huh?"

CHAPTER 36

A shrill ring sounded from the stainless steel kitchen timer on the coffee table, jarring Brian awake. He untangled his arm from beneath the blanket where he lay on the couch and glanced at his watch. His heart skipped. Melanie would be here in about ten minutes. Or thereabouts. She typically ran late, but maybe without her kids along, she had a shot at punctuality. That first date, when they'd all climbed pell-mell out of the van at the park . . . He smiled.

A yawn crept up his throat, but he stifled it. He'd made it through the workday—barely—and had been asleep since about five seconds after walking through his door. If John hadn't told him Melanie would be by, he'd have slept straight through to bedtime. Or maybe morning.

He shifted, resigned to the fact he couldn't lie on the couch any longer. The fatigue took the edge off his nervousness about seeing Melanie again. Even so, he scanned the room, hoping she'd overlook the mess. He hadn't had the energy to do much—okay, any—housecleaning. Mail lay piled on the end table, several pairs of shoes sat haphazardly by the door, and dishes lined the counter by the sink.

He sat up and finger-combed his hair, relieved that he hadn't lost any. At least not yet. The treatment affected his appearance in other ways though. He noticed every time he caught a glimpse of himself in a mirror. A look of perpetual fatigue, complete with huge bags under his eyes. Sallow cheeks. Dull eyes.

Time to motivate himself to get up. *Okay . . . standing up . . . any minute now.*

As the fog of sleep lifted, his nerves began to jangle. Would Melanie be angry with him? The last time he'd seen her, she'd chucked her cell phone across a room in irritation.

Yet according to John, she'd agreed to bring him dinner.

He sighed and scrubbed a hand over his face. After witnessing her tears and how upset he'd made her, he hadn't gone farther than a block from her home before he realized the truth. He hadn't spared her one iota of pain. He'd only compounded it, forcing her to come to terms not only with his illness but his rejection of her too.

A knock sounded on the door. He sucked in a breath and finally forced himself to stand. Conscious of how wrinkled and disheveled he must be, he pulled the tails of his work shirt out of his pants and loosened his button-down collar. Reaching for the doorknob, his hand quivered. With an unspoken prayer, he twisted the knob and opened the door.

Melanie—even prettier than the vision he so often pulled from his memory—stood holding two casserole pans covered in aluminum foil, one on top of the other. As she breathed, little puffs of white escaped, dissipating in the wintry air. The sky behind her remained gray as it'd been all day, a layer of thick clouds blocking any evening sunshine.

Hope flickered in his chest, and despite the uncertainty about her feelings for him, his heart felt immeasurably lighter than it had in months. He smiled. "Hey, uh, come in."

She smiled back, but it seemed more a courtesy than an

expression of happiness. "Thank you." Melanie brushed passed him and stood in the center of the room, waiting.

She wore jeans and an oversized college sweatshirt with her hair pulled into a short ponytail. With pink cheeks and bright eyes, she looked the picture of a healthy mother.

He stood, tongue-tied, realizing how difficult being *around* her but not being *with* her would be. "Can I take those?" He nodded toward the dishes.

"They're frozen. Just tell me where to put them." Her gaze wandered over him—his hair, his face, the way his shirt hung loosely on his frame.

He inhaled, trying to inflate his chest, maybe fake the virile man he wanted to be. Not this weak, needy impostor.

"It's frozen lasagna and chicken tetrazzini," she added, lifting her burden higher. "They're divided into portions that you can heat up whenever you're hungry."

Which means almost never. "Thank you. I'm sure they're delicious." He took the pans from her, surprised at how heavy they seemed and the ease with which she'd carted them around. "I'll just put them in the freezer."

He returned from the kitchen, and she stood, hands folded, thumbs twiddling as she gazed at his mess of mail and other papers on the end table.

"Uh, do you have to get home? If you'd like to stay for a little bit . . ." His insides twisted. He longed for company but lacked the energy to entertain. Before, he'd never thought of Melanie as a guest he had to amuse, but now this distance yawned between them. *Distance I put there.* He rubbed at the knot of guilt in his chest.

"Hannah's with the kids. I have a little time." She glanced from him to the pile of debris again.

"You want to sit?" He gestured to the armchair.

She could stand, but he sunk into the couch, propping a pillow behind him.

"What can I do for you?" She shifted from foot to foot, seeming eager to do *something*. "Clean your bathroom or run the sweeper or mop the floor?"

His heart sunk. What had she said to him that time, about pitying her and earning his do-gooder badge by being her handyman? The tables had turned. "I don't expect maid service from you, Melanie."

"Good. That's not what you're getting." She finally made a break for that end table that seemed to be bothering her so much. "This is what friends do, though. They help."

She considered them friends? Okay. Maybe the damage to their relationship wasn't irreparable.

Melanie lifted the magazines and papers in small stacks, tapping them against the table to even the edges. A few items slid to the floor: a cardstock mailer, a thin newspaper, and a glossy brochure. She stooped to retrieve them, and her hand stilled on the brochure.

Brian's breath snagged, and he covered his eyes with his hand, massaging his brow. The engagement ring guide. Of all the things for her to find!

She stared at it for a second or two and then stuffed it between the other papers and returned it to the pile. "So, uh, can I—"

"The bathroom, I guess. The bathroom's a wreck." He'd said it without thinking. The entire place needed a good cleaning, but in his haste to take her focus off the ring guide, he'd blurted out the most personal, most degrading job he could assign. Though in truth, he couldn't tolerate the bathroom cleaner chemicals anymore. Their pungent odor turned his stomach.

"Bathroom it is." She stood, her fake smile failing to hide the pain in her eyes.

"The cleaning stuff . . ." He motioned down the hall to the bathroom. "It's under the sink."

"Great!" She bounced down the hall as if scrubbing his commode were some kind of reward.

While she cleaned, Brian sat on the couch, elbows on his knees, mulling over what to say to Melanie when she finished. Beg her to come back soon? Tell her to keep a safe distance for both their hearts' sakes? Offer to pay her for her work? Or say what really weighed on his heart?

"All done!" Her perky voice snapped him to attention.

While before he'd noticed her healthy complexion and her vibrant eyes, now he recognized the tiredness around the edges, the world-weary tilt of her head. He'd had a hand in that.

"Can you sit with me for a minute?" He sat straighter, making plenty of room for her on the couch. He had to see her eyes when he said what he needed to. If only he could find the right words.

She hesitated a moment and then sat. "I can't stay too long. Hannah has something this evening."

"I'll be quick." He swallowed and mustered his courage. "I'm so, so sorry. I thought I was sparing you pain when I broke up with you, but I knew right away that I was wrong." He reached for her hand then pulled back, changing his mind. "I should never have lied to you or made a decision for you."

Melanie stared at him, solemn, and slid a hand up her arm, reminding Brian of the bangle bracelets he'd bought her for Christmas but hadn't given her.

"And then pride and stubbornness kept me from doing anything to fix it. Plus, I . . . you wouldn't have wanted to be around me. I struggled a lot at first." His explanation was cagey, but he wasn't ready to tell her about the porn yet. Not on the first time they'd been together in almost three months. "I kinda felt like I deserved to suffer alone. Maybe I do. But if you're willing to come by now and then—at least that's what John said —I'd be grateful."

A tear rolled down her cheek and she bit her lips together.

"Don't spend another minute being sorry. All your energy should go toward getting better."

A warm sensation grew in his chest, spreading to his limbs and bringing tears to his eyes. Just like that, she'd freed him from his crippling regret.

They chatted about her kids for a few minutes and then she repeated the bit about Hannah's plans for the evening. Melanie left seeming spent, as if their conversation had depleted all her energy.

Brian grabbed a container of yogurt from the fridge, more because it was time to eat than because he was hungry. At the kitchen table, he committed the image of Melanie to memory. His feelings for her had somehow grown in her absence. He allowed his mind to wander, daydreaming that she'd somehow coaxed Hannah into caring for the kids tonight so she could be with him. He craved her closeness, realizing the only people who had touched him in months were medical personnel. He couldn't imagine a prettier antidote to the chronic loneliness he felt.

But this wasn't the optimal time to court a woman. Pitching woo was fundamentally incompatible with round-the-clock fatigue and persistent nausea. He'd content himself with her friendship. For now. But she'd delivered more than a couple of casseroles and a sparkly-clean bathroom tonight. Melanie had brought hope.

CHAPTER 37

Melanie tightened her fingers around the steering wheel and then released them. With a sigh, she turned off the car and stared at Brian's apartment. Visit number two. After exactly five days of replaying the awkward, emotional reunion of visit number one.

Bits of ice and snow clung to her windshield in the corners, obstructing her view. Not much to see anyhow. Gray evening skies. Bare porch. Window blinds closed.

Someone had cleared Brian's walk. Someone other than him, she hoped. Did his neighbors know he was ill? The nosy lady next door was the only one she'd ever seen.

You can do this, Melanie. Corporal work of mercy: visit the sick. Ooh—and feed the hungry. Two for one! She adjusted the foil covering the pan on the passenger seat. She'd spent Sunday afternoon in the kitchen, preparing enough to feed her family and Brian and to restock the freezer. She'd been labeling the portions this evening when Hannah arrived to babysit for a couple of hours. If Brian wanted her to clean something or do some other chores, she'd be ready. If he wanted to talk . . . well, she was there to offer practical assistance, not a listening ear. John and Kate would have to handle that.

Stepping carefully across remnants of yesterday's wintry mix, as the weather forecasters called it, ice and frozen slush crunched beneath her snow boots. Her left foot slid, and she tilted the casserole, trying to right herself. Her heart pattered harder in her chest as she envisioned Brian's meals scattered across the snow-covered lawn. *Just a few more yards . . .*

She rapped twice on the storm door and waited, stomping her boots and scraping them on the mat. A thump, a click, and a man's voice sounded on the other side of the door, spurring her heartbeat faster. *You can do this, Melanie. With God's help. You're already broken up. He can't hurt you anymore.*

The door swung open, and Brian greeted her with a smile. He held his cell phone in one hand and mouthed, "John."

She slid past him, dragging ice and slush across his floor. Not wanting to create a mess, she searched for a place to set the casserole while she removed her boots.

"What the heck's wrong with you?" John's voice came through the phone, mildly irritated.

Brian shut the door and turned to her, taking the casserole from her and rolling his eyes. "Uh, I've got cancer?"

She bit her lips together, not wanting to laugh out loud and give away her presence.

Brian set the phone on the counter and opened the freezer. He shoved things aside then forced the pan in, closing the door twice until it shut.

Melanie tugged off a boot and set it behind the door, then hopped on one foot as she wrenched off the other, taking a sock with it. She pulled the damp sock back on and turned, hugging her arms to her chest in the cold entryway.

John complained about something she couldn't make out from this distance—other than the word "idiotic."

Brian braced himself against the counter, head down,

listening to John she presumed, allowing her to stare, unobserved. He'd gotten thin. Too thin. His wan cheeks seemed sunken. But he hadn't lost any hair—something she'd tried to mentally prepare herself for before both visits. He didn't need her showing up at his door all agog at how sickly he looked.

Finally, Brian tapped the phone and held it to his ear. "Just apologize to her, man. Ask her to forgive you." He shifted his weight, eyes downcast. "Yeah, well, maybe you need some time alone." His shoulders sagged. "I know. Hey, tell Kate Monday at ten o'clock." He glanced up and made a circle with his hand, silently urging John to wrap up the conversation. "Yeah, bye."

He shoved the phone away and caught her gaze, his chest sinking on a sigh. "Hey. Thanks for . . ." He jutted his thumb toward the freezer, covered in crayon-scrawled artwork. One drawing she recognized as Penny's handiwork. The others she presumed came from Patrick and Brady. "The sustenance."

"Oh, it's a cheesy potato thing." She shrugged. "The kids love it. And I craved it when I was nauseated and pregnant with Kevin. I thought maybe it'd go down okay."

"That'd be great. Don't have an appetite for much lately." He tugged up his sweatpants, which sagged around the waist.

Self-conscious about staring at his emaciated physique, her gaze bounced around the apartment. Funny how little time they'd spent here together. With her kids and late-night dates, hanging at her place made more sense. Things appeared more orderly this week, but the place gave off a sad, dreary vibe. A houseplant or a pet would liven the place up.

"How are the kids?" He shuffled to his favorite spot on the couch and shoved aside a rumpled blanket.

"Good." A few moments of silence ticked by while Brian waited for her to her elaborate. Keeping this a simple sick call might be more difficult than she imagined. "They pray for you. Every night. A decade of the Rosary. So, you know how *that* goes." Last night Penny had spent the entire time rolling herself in the throw rug, her big, wooden beads pressed against her chest. The boys did better. Marginally. She smoothed her hands down her jeans, not sure if she should sit. "I'm glad I can give them an update now."

"Well, I'm my own worst enemy, according to John. Sabotaging my own recovery by being 'glum.'" He made quotes with his fingers and ran a hand through his hair. Then he glanced at his hands as if checking that no hair had been lost by the motion.

An anxious mixture of regret and pity swirled in Melanie's belly. "So, I have a little time if you need me to clean something or run to the drugstore or the supermarket or whatever."

The expression in his eyes, shimmery and sad, said her aloofness hurt him. God knew she didn't want that, but this was about self-preservation. What a cross these twice-a-week visits would be, for both of them. Did they do more harm than good?

She'd never seen someone in such desperate need of a hug or some kind of human connection, and yet she'd shut down his personal question. Maybe she hadn't forgiven him as completely as she'd thought. Or maybe her reluctance to watch the man she loved waste away in body and spirit proved too much for her selfish nature.

In either case, the rift created by his illness, his lies, and his dumping her—she couldn't seem to let go of that phrase—made for two lonely, distant people. Just last night, in the quiet darkness after her children had succumbed to sleep, she'd been tempted to download a new book—the kind she'd sworn off—for the first time in ages. Though intimacy with David had lacked that elusive spark, she missed the closeness, the feeling that they were stronger being part of an indivisible whole. She missed being touched, lovingly and unselfishly. She missed the pleasure. She missed the security. That emotional, spiritual place that despite the spark, she and Brian had never quite reached.

Last night she'd had the resolve to dismiss the temptation in an instant, but experience told her that wouldn't put an end to it. She faced an interminable number of lonely nights in which she'd have to choose virtue over indulgence. Where would the will to fight *that* battle come from?

Brian coughed and cleared his throat, drawing her attention. He hadn't caught something, had he? The treatments probably compromised his immune system.

"I don't need you to run any errands, Melanie." He yanked at the blanket, arranging it over his legs.

His phone sounded from the counter, and she glanced at it and then Brian. Should she answer it?

He waved a hand. "Let it go. I get junk calls all day long. If it's a real call, they'll leave a message."

She returned to the living area, ready to make an excuse and say goodbye. She'd have time to run an errand of her own and get the poster board Matthew needed for his Social Studies project. "I'm gonna—"

The phone sounded again, indicating a message.

Brian's forehead wrinkled. "Huh. You can play it back. On speaker."

Melanie retrieved the phone, set it on the coffee table in front of him, and played back the voicemail.

"Cancer kills," a robotic voice said.

Melanie's breath froze. It was the same voice she'd heard last week.

The background music grew louder. John Lennon's "Instant Karma," with the dead Beatle warbling, "Pretty soon you're gonna be dead."

The voice message ended, and Melanie snatched the phone from the table. She tapped this and that, trying to maneuver through an app different from her own. "It just says, 'anonymous call.'"

Brian's face blanched. "That's the second time I've gotten that."

"The voice," Melanie said, her own voice nearly failing. "It sounds like it's going through a voice changer or something. I've gotten that too. But not the song." She'd nearly forgotten about that call, coming right before John's call like it did. But now, with Brian getting something sort of similar . . . were the calls connected?

"It's a prank call. I looked it up on YouTube. People do that, it's—"

"You think that's a coincidence?" She lifted a hand, disbelieving. "You have cancer and you get that call twice now?"

He shrugged. "It's not like I broadcasted being sick. The only people that know are you, my family, and some of my co-workers, the ones that need to know." A little color returned to his cheeks. "I can't imagine any of those people doing this. Just forget about it."

No way could she forget that hurtful call. And she'd bet he couldn't either, but he obviously didn't want to deal with it. Not now at least.

"Well, if either of us gets another call, I think we should call the police."

"The police? What are they gonna do about it? There's nothing to go on. And the calls are just an annoyance." He grabbed the TV remote control from the back of the couch. "You're free to go home. The kids probably need you. I'm good here." He stared at the screen as it sprung to life.

Melanie sighed, resigning herself to the cool distance growing between them. That's what she wanted, wasn't it? An arm's length friendship. She could pat herself on the back for being a concerned friend, the lone engine on the meal train, while guarding her fragile, slow-healing heart. So why did his indifference make her throat tighten and bring unwelcome tears to her eyes?

CHAPTER 38

$\mathcal{M}$elanie ran a glass pan, the last of the dinner dishes, under hot water, rinsed the suds from the outside, and set it in the drying rack. Happy laughter came from the living room—the kids' giggling and their grandparents' chuckles.

She smiled, enjoying both the sounds and the momentary peace, even if it came while she did dishes. Her feet ached from traipsing all over the zoo all day, and she longed to prop them up, lean back, and close her eyes. Maybe David's parents would want to tuck the kids into bed. To them, it'd be a novelty; to Melanie, on nights like this, when she longed to climb into her own bed, it was drudgery.

It had been too long since her in-laws' last visit. Since David died, their visits had, understandably, been less frequent, but she wanted them to maintain a relationship with Matthew, Kevin, and Penny. When they'd called and said they'd like to spend the weekend, she'd been happy to accommodate them.

Their presence also kept her from fixating on Brian, wondering whether he'd eaten or how he felt. She'd visited him six times now over the past several weeks, each time more painful than the last. If their interactions were cool and distant, she mourned the warmth and closeness they used to share. If they joked and chitchatted, she craved more of what would never be. The whole thing had been a losing situation as far as her heart went, but, remarkably, Brian had gained a few pounds and generally seemed more positive and hopeful than when she'd first visited.

With a snap, she removed her dishwashing gloves and laid them on the sink's edge. What next? She yanked the plastic bag from the garbage can, using her foot to dislodge the plastic container and break the suction holding the bag in place.

The landline phone, forever the bearer of bad news and annoying—lately creepy—calls, rang. At the third ring from "wireless caller," Melanie called to the other room. "Hey, Matthew, can you get that?" She finally wrestled the bag from the can, tied the plastic handles, and plopped it in the corner to be taken out.

Obviously Matthew hadn't heard her. She darted across the room and pulled the phone from its cradle. "Hello?" she said, her breathing ragged.

"Melanie. It's Kate."

Her heart lurched as it had when John called last month. "Hi, Kate. Is Brian okay?" She'd barely said a handful of words to Kate during baseball season. What did she think of Melanie? Was she grateful she'd stepped in to help, or did she think Melanie a fool for inserting herself in Brian's life when he'd— she couldn't get around the words—he'd dumped her?

"He's been super sick since yesterday, after his treatment. I stayed with him last night. John's over there now, but we have tickets to take the boys to a hockey game tonight, and we don't want to disappoint them." A couple shouts came from the background, the soundtrack of Melanie's life. "I hate to ask you this 'cause I know you were over there a couple days ago, but is there any way you could stay with Brian a few hours tonight? I'd be glad to pay for a sitter for your kids, and I'll be back around ten o'clock." She sounded tired, her voice tinged with desperation.

"Uh . . ." Melanie glanced at the clock. She could make this work. "My in-laws are visiting, so I can do it without needing a sitter—not that I'd let you pay me anyway." She glanced around the kitchen, making sure everything had been set to rights. "What time do you need me?"

"In a half hour?" Audible relief sounded in Kate's voice.

Melanie absently pressed more paper napkins into the holder on the kitchen table. "I'll be there. Does he need anything?"

"I don't think so, but God knows John would be oblivious if he did. You'd think a grown man could—never mind." She paused, maybe quelling her irritation? "If you can get some calories in him, that'd be good. Heck, water would be good."

He hadn't been eating or drinking? She sighed, worry weighing heavy on her heart. "I'll try."

She ended the call wondering how to explain the situation to David's parents. Mike and Brenda didn't know she'd been dating Brian in the summer and fall. Any woman's dream in-laws, they'd been wonderfully supportive during her marriage and after David's death, but how would they react to her dating another man?

Since she and Brian were no longer romantically involved, she didn't *have* to give them all the details, did she? She had no obligation to tell them she was in love. Pathetically, hopelessly in love with a seriously-ill man who hadn't wanted her around but now . . . now, what? Now regretted his decision and tolerated her awkward presence?

Melanie slipped on her tennis shoes, switched off the kitchen light and joined everyone in the living room. "Hey, kids, I need a minute with Granny and Paps."

The kids ignored her, but Brenda and Mike sat back on the couch and turned their attention to Melanie.

How to say it . . . "I have a . . . a friend who's battling Hodgkin's lymphoma. He's doing chemo now, and his sister-in-law just called and asked if I could sit with him tonight. Apparently, he's feeling really bad, and—"

Brenda waved a hand at her. "Go. Go, help your friend. We'll keep an eye on these munchkins." She grinned as Penny climbed onto her lap dragging a makeshift cape.

"Sure," Mike said, seeming grateful for the opportunity. "We can hold down the fort here."

Ten minutes later, on a whim, Melanie pulled through the McDonald's drive-thru with Shamrock Shakes for her and Brian. Loaded with calories and able to be sucked through a straw. She hoped it would go down easily.

As she stepped onto Brian's dimly-lit porch holding the shakes in a cardboard carrier, John emerged and closed the storm door behind him. He pulled on a light jacket, all that was needed for the evening's mild temperatures.

"Melanie. Thanks a million," he said, sinking his hands into his jacket pockets. "The boys have been looking forward to this game. I told Kate not to buy the tickets, but she doesn't listen to me much." He shook his head, his features twisted with irritation.

"No problem." Melanie faked a happy smile. "It worked out fine with my in-laws being in town."

His features relaxed. "I'm glad. We've been kinda stressed lately, y'know? Work, the kids . . ." He nodded toward Brian's door. "Him."

"I understand." All was not well in John's world, and she suspected his troubles ran deeper than the current stressors. He and Kate gave off some bad vibes about each other. "How's he doing?"

He shrugged. "Feels like—feels like crap. No energy. Won't

eat or drink." He patted her on the shoulder on his way to the car. "Good luck."

Okay then. She clutched the rosary ring in her jacket pocket. *Lord, please let Brian feel better. And help me to help him.* Melanie was no nurse, not beyond tending to her kids' needs. What was she walking into?

CHAPTER 39

Melanie rapped lightly on the storm door, grateful she could help Brian—and John and Kate—but wishing it was morning already. And that she could enjoy a night of sound sleep and the uncomplicated, simple joy of a Sunday morning.

A moment later, hearing nothing from the other side of the door, Melanie twisted the knob and stepped into Brian's apartment. Inky darkness obscured the room, and she blinked, hoping her eyes would adjust. She slid her hand up the cold plaster wall alongside the door jamb until she hit a switch and flicked it on.

Pale light flooded the entryway. Careful to keep the milkshakes upright, she backed into the door until it clicked shut. The mild temperatures outside had made it warm inside, and the air smelled stale.

Brian lay on one end of his couch, perfectly still, his feet propped on an ottoman.

She tiptoed to the kitchen and set the shakes on the counter. A clock ticked somewhere in the room, and a faint electrical buzz came from the TV and entertainment system. Sipping her shake, she rounded the couch, not sure where to sit and not wanting to wake Brian.

Baggy green sweatpants hung loosely on his legs, his hands lay folded on his flat belly, and his head tilted back, striking her more as stiff than relaxed.

She shifted the books, magazines, and devices on the coffee table and set down her shake. Her gaze snagged on a Bible and a set of rugged black rosary beads. Something about them, about Brian's vulnerability and his need for God moved her, warming the tender place in her heart reserved for Brian alone.

With quiet steps, she strode to the window, reached behind the blinds, and unlocked the clasp. Gripping the old window, she tried jerking it open, but it wouldn't budge. She tried again, using more muscle power and grunting for good measure. The pane squeaked and lifted, letting in a stream of fresh air.

"How'd you get drafted into service tonight?" Brian's groggy voice came from his vantage on the couch.

Surprised, she spun in his direction. "Just my lucky day, I guess." She grabbed her shake from the table. "Sorry. I didn't mean to wake you."

"Wasn't sleeping." Yet his eyes remained closed.

"Not feeling so great, huh?" She sipped the shake and then set it in the kitchen, next to his.

"I've never been so sick for so long." He rotated his ankles and crossed one over the other. "Whatever the doctor prescribed isn't working. At all."

A sense of helplessness dampened her already-sagging spirits. Melanie hated seeing him sick. She caught sight of a shallow plastic pan at the foot of the couch. A familiar sight in a house with young children, but not here. "Are you throwing up?"

"No. Just constant, severe nausea." He rolled his head toward her, his eyes finally open. "Apparently John and Kate think I need a babysitter for that."

She stood in the space between the kitchen and living room and held up his shake. "Think you could drink this?"

He grimaced, rolled his head back, and closed his eyes. "No."

"Maybe later." She finished off her shake, tossed the cup in the nearly-empty trashcan, and slipped his into the freezer. "John and Kate probably don't want you to be alone and miserable."

"Never seemed to bother them before." Did he just crack a smile?

"Well, they're probably worried about you getting weak and dehydrated." Ice cubes, freezer pops, and a bagged frozen meal sat on the lone freezer shelf. Had he been eating the meals she brought? "You need to eat or drink something."

She knew from experience that nausea and conversation didn't go well together, so she fluffed a cushion and sat on the opposite end of the couch, resolved to let him rest. What would she do now? She should've brought a book to read.

"Sorry," Brian mumbled, "that you had to come tonight."

"It's okay." She shifted sideways and leaned her head against the cushion. At least she'd get some rest here.

Eventually, he breathed more heavily, his chest rising and falling in a steady rhythm. She gazed at him, lingering on the spot between his stubbly chin and his shoulder—the place where her head belonged. That sweet spot where his heartbeat thumped strong and steady in her ear. Where his strong arm curled lazily around her back. Where his breath tickled her forehead when he spoke.

Pretending to be a disinterested nursemaid was useless. When it came to Brian Perella, Melanie Lombardi was anything but disinterested. She scooted closer, careful not to jostle him. Ever so softly, she brushed her fingertips over the hair at his temple, down along his sideburn and feathered them across the light bristle on his cheek.

He lay so still. And yet a battle raged inside him. Physically, mentally, emotionally. And spiritually. Baking casseroles and lounging on the couch beside him seemed insufficient. Was there nothing more she could do?

Her gaze caught the black beads on the table again. She missed praying with the kids tonight. Nightly prayers with them tested her, but she persisted. Not because the lot of them —Melanie included—were particularly devout. But because they cared more about Brian than their own boredom or distraction. Good things would come of this illness. She'd known it, but Brian hadn't seen it until too late.

She dozed for a while, then woke with a start and glanced at her watch. *Bedtime.* She texted Brenda and confirmed that the evening had gone well and the children all slept peacefully. Then she texted Kate and told her not to bother coming back. She'd spend the night on the couch.

As she set her phone on the table, Brian shifted, and his eyes flicked open. His gaze landed on her sitting much closer than when he'd fallen asleep. He gave her a half smile. "Isn't your shift up?"

"Nope. I'm pulling a double." She slid the rosary beads through her fingers, thinking that she'd pray and then try to get some sleep herself.

"Thank you," he mumbled, drifting off again.

Melanie grabbed a throw pillow, fluffed it, and stuffed it behind her head. As she fingered the beads in her hand, she realized she'd forgotten how tired she'd been before Kate had called. Apparently, a quiet evening on the couch provided the rest she needed.

* * *

Gripping the sides of the porcelain sink, Brian stared into the bathroom mirror. Death warmed over was a new look for him but it beat flat-out death, no? For all the misery they caused, these treatments had better darn-well be working.

He grabbed a bottle of mouthwash from the cabinet beneath the sink, swished the minty liquid around his mouth, and spit. With a wooden brush, he tamed his hair. He even slapped his cheeks, hoping to restore a little color beneath two days' growth of beard.

Outside, a dog barked in the distance. He lifted the bathroom window shade and stared into the pre-dawn darkness. No reason to move to the bedroom at this point.

He flipped off the light and shuffled to the living room, feeling almost human. He peered into the darkness, making sure he hadn't woken Melanie. Despite what he'd said about not needing a babysitter, he'd been grateful to see her. Even more so when she'd apparently volunteered to stay the night. Ordinarily, she couldn't get away from the kids for very long. Who was with them now?

For the first time in days, the thought of food didn't repulse him. Knowing he should take advantage of that feeling to nourish himself, he changed course and retrieved the shake Melanie had brought from the freezer.

A pang of hunger hit him, and he sucked greedily at the straw. Sadly, the shake had frozen solid and all he got was air.

Back in the living room, he set the shake on the coffee table to thaw.

In his absence, Melanie had unconsciously slumped into his spot on the couch. She lay on her side with her head flat on the cushion, her arms folded beneath her, and her knees drawn up. If he had the strength, or the right, he'd scoop her onto his lap and let her sleep there.

Instead, he nudged her shoulder. "Hey, Mel, can you skooch over?"

"Hmm?" She rubbed her eyes and pushed herself into a sitting position. "You okay? Do you need anything?"

Brian sat in the space she'd vacated and reached for the milkshake. *Still frozen.* "I'm fine. Go back to sleep."

Instead of finding a new sleep position, she straightened in her seat. "You've got the milkshake. You're feeling better?"

He grinned, happy he could please her with so simple an action. "Yeah. I, uh, threw up. And I feel about a hundred times better. The shake sounds good now."

"I'm sorry. You should've woken me. I could've—"

"I'm fine, really." He'd been relieved he didn't have an audience.

They sat in silence a few moments, Brian struggling to suck some melted shake through the straw.

"It has meaning you know," Melanie whispered. "Your suffering."

He nodded. "How did you say it that time? I know more with my head than with my heart."

He glanced at her, her eyes wide now, expression stoic. He'd have thought years of middle-of-the-night kid emergencies would have taught her to move in and out of sleep easily, but her posture said she was alert.

"Not going back to sleep?"

She shook her head. "I don't think so."

How many times had he caught himself fantasizing about her spending the night? More than a few. But never like this.

"We're even," she said.

Did he miss something? "How so?"

"This couch. It can't be any more comfortable than mine."

He chuckled, remembering the night he spent on her couch, sweaty and dead to the world, only to wake with Kevin's face in his.

The nighttime silence wrapped around him, peaceful now, swinging his mood to contemplative. Three little kids at home with no real support system. A full-time job. Melanie had plenty of excuses not to be here. So, why was she? Did she still feel the same way about him? Did she, despite the pain he'd caused her, still love him after all this time? What had he given *her*, other than heartache? He hadn't even given her the full truth. His heart stirred, prompting him to speak. "There's something about me you don't know. That I failed to tell you."

She uncrossed her arms and laid them in her lap. "You don't owe me anything."

"It's not that. I-I *want* to tell you." She deserved the truth whether they resumed their relationship or not.

She raised her face to his. "Go ahead."

He angled himself toward her, readjusting the loose bulk of his clothing. "Nothing fits anymore." Frustrated, he pulled his shirt down, letting the fabric puddle at his waist.

"I wish I could donate a few pounds to you." She ran a hand down her middle.

His gaze trailed her hand then moved slowly back up until he met her eyes. "I like all of your pounds exactly where they're at."

Her gaze dropped, and without more light, he couldn't see the color of her cheeks, but he'd bet she blushed.

Focus, man.

"I'm a contradiction. Ask anyone from high school or college or whenever. They'll tell you I was a good kid. Never in trouble. Yeah, I dated a lot, but nothing serious, never disrespected a girl. I was the proverbial 'nice guy.'"

Finally, the shake seemed somewhat defrosted. He sucked through the straw, enjoying the cold, sweet, minty flavor. "Went to youth group, Mass every Sunday, served on the altar."

Melanie smiled sweetly, probably creating a mental image of the upstanding young man he was. The one that fooled everyone.

"I bought everything I was taught about relationships and marriage. And more often than not, I was the one trying to avoid after-prom parties, empty dorm rooms, and backseats, defending why I wanted to wait." More often, but not always.

"And Abby, my only real girlfriend, I think I mentioned her. We absolutely took things too far. More than once." He averted his eyes, sorry still that he and Abby hadn't shown more restraint. "But I never crossed that one line. And so, everyone thought I was someone I'm not."

Melanie's brow wrinkled. "We all make mistakes, Brian. I don't know what you mean about people thinking you're some-thing you're not."

Of course she didn't. It was dark o'clock, and he was being cryptic. He needed to say what he should've told her months and months ago.

The green milkshake curdled in his stomach, and he swal-lowed the rising bile in his throat. He squinted in the dark, determined to make eye contact with her so she'd know the gravity of what he was about to say.

"I have a problem with pornography."

CHAPTER 40

Outside Brian's apartment, a car door slammed and a diesel engine rumbled to life. Inside, the heat clicked on and a warm blast of dry air blew down from the ceiling. At the edge of the window, the faintest glimmer of light crept in and partially illuminated Melanie's face, allowing Brian to better gauge her reaction.

I have a problem with pornography. Understatement of the year! I have a decades-long, deep-seated, recurrent proclivity for viewing unadulterated filth that would make my sainted mother vomit, God rest her soul. And, yeah, I'm technically still a virgin.

Since only a couple of trusted college friends—his accountability partners, who struggled with the same addiction—knew of Brian's problem, he had no experience with sharing his shameful actions. He hadn't opened up to John about it, let alone a woman. A woman he loved. One with three impressionable young children.

He had no expectations for Melanie's reaction, but with every second that ticked by, he grew more anxious. If her blank stare was any indication, he'd dumbfounded her.

"It started when John and I found our dad's stash. I told you about that, right?" He'd keep rambling, give her some time to think.

She nodded. "Yes. I was worried about Matthew visiting Mason."

"Yeah. And you were right to worry. Those images . . . they stick, and they take root. At first I was disgusted by them. Then, when I was older and came across some magazines . . ." He shrugged. "Not as much. I was older. And curious."

He sipped the milkshake, recollecting how it had steam-rolled, the twisted urges spreading and multiplying. "Then high school. Hormones, boredom, unrestricted internet access, and a few lowlife friends were not a good combination. Then loneli-ness when I started college . . . that's when it really got its hooks in me. It became the focal point of my day. I'd even skip classes to watch more. It was this relentless compulsion. It'd just nag at me." He fisted his hand, as if he were gripping something, hard. That's how it felt—like a vice. "I couldn't silence that voice that wanted to be fed. Again and again, no matter how bad it made me feel or how much I loathed confessing the same sins over and over and over again . . ."

He buried his hands in his face, humiliated at sharing his disgraceful habits. Once the sun came up, Melanie would run from this place if she had even a half-ounce of sense.

And yet, when he raised his eyes to hers, biting the inside of his cheek to check his emotions, he saw only compassion.

Her features had softened, giving him the will to continue.

"That's when I knew I had to do something. Something to stop the cycle. I knew a couple of my housemates were pretty heavy into it, and they wanted out too. So, we made each other accountable. I started seeing a priest for regular confession. That helped." He shrugged. "We just white-knuckled it, the three of us."

"And that worked?" She'd finally spoken, her question hesitant but without a hint of judgment.

"Yeah. I mean, we had setbacks. Lots of them. But over time, yeah, it worked." One by one the chain links snapped, freeing them little by little. "By the time we graduated, watching porn wasn't even a thing for any of us anymore. I felt freer than I had in my whole life. It had no hold on me."

"But it does now." She said it rather than asked it, knowing, of course, that hadn't been the end of the story.

"Not like it did, no. But I fell last fall, for the first time in years and years."

"When?" She knew when. He didn't know how, but she did. It was written on her face.

"The day I got the diagnosis." He lowered his voice. "The night I broke things off with you."

She nodded, solemn. "But not while we were dating. And not after that day you broke things off."

"No, not while we were dating. And only a few times after that awful day. But it was more than the cancer and the breakup. I'd been tempted for months. Ever since they busted that guy for porn at work. And I had to testify. But since those few times, I've been clean. And I've not been tempted lately at all. Could be just 'cuz I'm sick though. I don't know."

His heart pattered faster. He'd just laid it all out there. Melanie now knew more about him than anyone ever had. He swallowed hard.

She inched closer until they were almost side by side and extended her arm between them, palm up. Her gaze bounced between her hand and him.

He'd half expected condemnation, but what he'd gotten was an invitation. An overwhelming sense of gratitude flooded him as he slid his palm into hers.

Her hand was smooth and warm, her palm smaller than his

but strong. Her fingers closed over his and she squeezed. If he weren't half dehydrated, he might've cried.

She sat silently, absorbing the implications of his story, he guessed.

What should he say? He wasn't her boyfriend anymore, but he'd never felt this close to any girl or woman. Something still bound them, otherwise she wouldn't be at his proverbial sick bed when she had people depending on her at home.

His heart burned with the assurance he'd felt in church long ago. The feeling that God willed them to be together, that she was the woman he'd waited for all these long, lonely years. She'd fallen into his lap. She was the one. He may have screwed things up, derailed their relationship, but God hadn't told him otherwise.

"My wife will be the first and only woman I give myself to." He turned their hands over and stroked her thumb with his. "But my innocence was lost a long, long time ago."

Her eyes glistened, even in the dim light.

He wouldn't worry about whether this conversation made her rethink their relationship and what course it might take. This conversation was long overdue. And like he did when he left the confessional, he felt lighter and freer having spoken his sins aloud.

They sat in silence for five, ten minutes.

She wriggled her hand free of his and turned toward him. "I've been struggling lately too." Her expression was open and honest, her gaze sincere.

"I told you . . . about the books. Since we've been, uh, apart, it's lonely after the kids go to bed. I'm lonely." She slid a hand up and down her wrist, making a twisting motion. "I haven't downloaded anything, but every night I consider it. Just a 99-cent book." She gave him a sad smile.

"What stops you from doing it?" He had an insatiable desire to know Melanie. To understand her. And this subject, he got.

She sighed. "I guess what comes after. That empty, guilty feeling. Knowing that I'll have to confess it. Knowing I've cut myself off from God. Deliberately. For my own selfish satisfaction."

She got it. She got him and this, this scourge he lived with. Was it a sacrilege that the first words that popped into his head were a Bible verse? "This one, at last, is bone of my bones and flesh of my flesh."

"And then of course, there's my pint-sized purity patrol," she said, smiling.

He shot her a questioning look.

"If I don't go to Communion, they're all over that. Why are we sitting in the pew, Mama? And I do not want to have to explain that."

He laughed. "No, you do not." He'd skipped Communion a lot of Sunday mornings, fearing that he was in mortal sin, but at least he hadn't had a passel of curious kids to answer to. Feeling that they'd exhausted the topic, at least for now, he hoisted himself from the couch and shuffled to the kitchen. He flicked on a light and started the single-cup coffee machine.

Melanie excused herself to go to the bathroom. When she returned, she folded the blanket and draped it over the back of the couch. "Do I smell coffee?"

"I made some for you." Too bad he couldn't stomach some himself. But that shake, he'd finish that off. Maybe fry an egg or two.

"I thought the smell of it made you sick." She leaned across the counter, inhaling the aroma.

He shrugged. "I thought you'd like a cup to go." He glanced at the wall clock. "You have to get the kids ready for Mass, right?"

"Yup. Somehow between last Sunday and this Sunday, all their dress shoes will have disappeared. Oh! And it's Palm Sunday. Maybe we can get there on time—for once." She slung her purse over her arm and accepted the travel mug he handed her. "You're okay, right?"

"Fine. Go home already." He followed her to the door.

She pulled it open and turned to him. "Eat something besides the shake, okay?"

He gave her a mock salute. "Yes, ma'am."

Awkwardness filled the momentary vacuum, worse than the end of a first date. He felt closer to Melanie than he had to anyone in months—maybe years—yet kissing was off-limits and a hug was insufficient. On impulse, he touched her elbow, angling her closer, and kissed her forehead. "Thank you."

She nodded, her eyes teary, and then turned and hustled toward her car.

He fell against the closed door, bereft, yet grateful. For one, he felt good—or at least not horrible. But even better, his unexpected conversation with Melanie had stolen the power from his sins, giving him hope.

He shuffled to the kitchen, considering whether he could stomach some cheese with his eggs. From inside the refrigerator, he grabbed a couple eggs from the carton.

His phone rang, derailing his breakfast mission. His sisters had apparently made a pact to see that one of them checked in with him every day, but he doubted either of them would call so early.

"Anonymous call" showed on the screen, stealing his paltry appetite. He set down the eggs, accepted the call, and then scrambled to keep them from skittering off the counter and plopping onto the floor.

"What's the matter, Brian?" The robotic voice, same as last time! "Did your nurse leave?"

Brian's gut tightened. Whoever this freak was, he'd seen Melanie leave.

Tires squealed outside, and a fraction of a second later, over the phone.

Moving faster than he had in weeks, Brian darted to the window, shoving aside the drapes.

Outside, a gray car peeled away, head and taillights off despite the murky dawn. He squinted, but making out the model or plate numbers was impossible. Thankfully, the car hadn't headed in the same direction as Melanie. Brian cursed and returned to the kitchen. From the junk drawer, he grabbed a pen and notepad and jotted down the time, the location of the car, and the caller's exact words. Melanie had been right: these calls were about both of them—they were connected.

CHAPTER 41

Maybe it was the lack of sleep. Or maybe it was the heart-to-heart with Brian in the wee hours of the morning. Could've been the taxing conversation with the kids about why they had to go to Mass when Granny and Paps were still in their pajamas sipping coffee. Or it could've been the missing shoes. The infernal missing shoes. Whatever the reason, Melanie was off her Palm Sunday game. Sure, she'd reminded the kids the palms they'd dutifully taken from the table at the rear of church were blessed objects, not swords. But she'd failed to remind them they were also not light sabers, ticklers, or fans. And they should not be peeled into a hundred swirly pieces and strewn all over the pew.

"Is it o-o-over?" Penny lay on her back, knees bent and shoes on the pew. A red blotch near her brow marked how close Kevin had come to jabbing the pointed end of his palm into her eye.

"Feet down, Penny." Melanie swatted her legs from the pew. "Yes, Mass is over."

"Yay!" She rolled onto the kneeler, dragging her dirty stuffed lamb with her.

Melanie gazed longingly at the altar. If only she could have a few minutes of peace to pray. She hadn't had time to process what Brian had told her. She'd rushed home from Brian's, herded the kids into the car, and barreled into church a couple of minutes after Mass began. Then she spent the next hour policing the palms in the pew.

She glanced at the cry room, the room at the rear of the church with giant glass windows, where a woman toted an infant carrier toward the exit. If Melanie could just contain the kids safely for a few minutes . . .

"Hey, Matthew, would you take Kevin and Penny into the cry room? You guys can play in there for a little bit. I just need a few minutes of quiet."

"Sure, Mom." He turned to his siblings, motioning them out of the pew like a crossing guard. "C'mon, guys."

They'd only be a few pews behind her in a safe, enclosed area. Why hadn't she thought of this before? And could she install a similar soundproof room at home?

She slid onto her knees, not sure where to begin. *Help a gal out, huh, Lord?* Based on the feelings she and Brian still shared, she fully expected that once the lymphoma went into remission, he'd want to pick up where they left off. In her heart, she wanted the same thing. Despite his dumb decision to dump her and what he'd confessed to her, she loved him.

Still, a mother of three young children couldn't afford to bring the wrong man into their lives. Would it be prudent to commit herself to a man who admitted he'd been addicted to pornography? What kind of damage did that do? What things couldn't he un-see? Things he'd bring to their marriage bed. And what if he repeated the cycle started by his father? If he lapsed into viewing porn again and her kids found it . . . No, she shouldn't risk it.

She fixed her gaze on the large crucifix suspended above the altar. But what about redemption and second chances? Brian had owned up to his problem and changed. And with the exception of a few days last year, he'd successfully avoided porn for a very, very long time. Should she hold his past sins against him?

Wouldn't refusing to date him make her a hypocrite? After all, wasn't her dalliance with raunchy books essentially the same sin? It varied by degree, sure, and by medium, but at its root, it was the same. Both were sins against chastity. Was sharing the same weakness a good or bad thing? Of course it was a bad thing. How could it be otherwise? She would be a friend to Brian and continue to help him in his time of need, but then she would fade out of his life, move on, find someone new.

Would she find someone else? What were the odds of a thirty-something widowed mother of three finding another man who not only cared for her but made her feel the way Brian did? Her heart pattered faster just thinking of him.

Brian wasn't perfect, but neither was any other man. And he possessed so many good qualities. The pornography notwithstanding, Brian was about as upstanding a man as she'd find. He practiced his faith, he was loyal, hardworking, great with her kids, and didn't get drunk or angry.

And she loved him. Her heart fluttered, refusing to slow and settle.

Her gaze drifted to the side altar and the statues of Saint Joseph and the Blessed Mother.

She'd been satisfied with her marriage to David. Her very rationally-chosen decision to commit to him and raise a family. A decision driven by intellect. Now, which should she follow—her head or her heart? The brain was the more reliable of the two organs, not running off full tilt without permission. Did they have to be in opposition to one another? Couldn't they be in sync?

Behind her, someone pounded on the glass wall of the cry room.

Penny ran a large plastic car over the window, ramming it into the wooden trim.

Time's up!

Okay. So, nothing solved, but at least she'd laid it all out there. *What now, God? I love Brian, but I want to do what's best for my children. I want to marry again and give the kids a dad, but I don't want to make a bad decision.*

* * *

BRIAN SHUFFLED BACK to the couch. Breakfast didn't sit well in his stomach, but he still felt much better than he had yesterday. Or the day before that.

He grabbed a book from the coffee table, read one paragraph, and set it aside. His gaze bounced around the room, seeking something to do.

The laptop.

He bit the inside of his cheek, staring. No. No way.

Get behind me, Satan.

Think, Brian. What's going on here? You're bored, that's all.

A change of scenery would help, but he wasn't up to it. Exercise usually worked, but that was a no-go too. He walked to the laptop and ran his hand over the Sacred Heart of Jesus decal.

His phone shimmied across the end table, buzzing with a text message from John.

How you feel?

He tapped his reply. *Much better.*

Want company?

He'd already taken too much of his brother and sister-in-law's time. *Nah. Stay with your family.*

I'll be over after the kids go to bed.

Brian tossed the phone on the table and sighed. He'd be grateful for the company, truly. Especially now that temptation had cropped up again. But this wasn't about him. This was about John avoiding Kate. And using Brian's health as an excuse.

John hadn't confided in him yet, and knowing John, he wouldn't. But anyone with eyes could see the signs—the stilted conversations, the brush-offs, the lack of physical contact.

Brian wanted better for his own marriage someday. To be a good husband and a father, if those were the plans God had for him. And God willing, Brian would be well and self-sufficient again soon. One more week of chemotherapy, ending, fittingly enough, on Good Friday. One week until Easter. A new beginning.

He scooped his rosary beads from the end table. He'd carted them all over the apartment the last few days, wanting to pray but feeling too sick to concentrate. Now would be a good time to put them to use, seeing that John wouldn't arrive for a while. He sat and bowed his head, determined to get through at least a decade of prayers for his health and his two special intentions.

CHAPTER 42

Sunny yellow daffodils waved in the breeze, their cheery heads bobbing as Brian bounded up the steps to John and Kate's front door. Morning sun shone bright in a cloudless blue sky, warming his neck and bare arms. Birds chirped in the trees then several fluttered to the ground. On their stoop, he closed his eyes, tilted his head back and soaked in the warmth, grateful to God for so many things. He breathed deeply of the crisp air, transferred his carton of breakfast goodies from one hand to the other, and rapped a knuckle on the storm door.

Through the storm door, he saw his nephews lying on the living room floor and poked his head in. "Anybody home?"

"Uncle Brian!" Patrick and Brady bounded toward him. As he stepped inside, they hugged his legs.

Happier than he'd been in a long time, Brian staggered through the entryway, laughing. He hadn't seen enough of these boys the past few months. Kate and Melanie both worried about their kids carrying germs that could sicken Brian. But, oh, how he'd missed them!

Brian set the carton on the kitchen table and unloaded

gourmet bagels, cream cheeses, fresh-squeezed orange juice, and piping hot coffee. "Where's your mom and dad?"

"In bed," Patrick said, standing on a kitchen chair and peering into the carton.

Brian glanced at the wall clock. "They're not up yet?" The various trains, Hot Wheels, and LEGOs strewn around the living room seemed to confirm the boys had been on their own this morning.

"They're up," Brady said. "They told us to watch cartoons, and then they locked the bedroom door and said to knock only if there's an emergency."

"Oh. I think I understand." Brian bit down a smile. Maybe John and Kate had finally resolved their issues and made up. "They'll come out when they're ready. Let's eat."

"Hey, I want the chocolate chip one," Patrick said, grabbing a bagel.

He and Brady smeared their bagels with cream cheese and toted them to the living room, where they stood watching some kind of ninja-warrior cartoon.

Brian sipped a coffee, unable to concentrate on anything but the good news ricocheting around his brain, ready to burst his seams if he didn't tell someone soon.

A raised voice seeped through the wall, John's. Then a softer one, Kate's. A thud sounded, like a drawer slamming shut then more raised voices.

So maybe Brian had the wrong idea about what had been going on behind that closed door. Way wrong.

Kate stomped down the hall in sweatpants and a long-sleeved t-shirt, nearly jumping as she spotted Brian at the table. "Brian! This is a surprise."

John followed a few steps behind, also in sweats and a t-shirt. Like twinsies! He nodded toward the boys devouring their bagels, cream cheese smeared on their cheeks. "What's the occasion?"

Brian sat straighter, relieved to share his news. "My oncologist called last night." His gaze moved between John and Kate. "Tests all came back good. Lymphoma's in remission."

Kate squealed and flew at him, throwing her arms around his neck and nearly toppling him out of his chair but also filling his heart with sheer joy. "I'm so happy for you."

John waited for Kate to disentangle herself and then slapped Brian on the back, muttering his congratulations.

Kate got the boys' attention by blocking the TV screen and translated the happy news for them. Brian grinned from ear to ear as he endured their messy cheese-stained, crumb-filled hugs. Within seconds, they reverted to the TV, leaving the grown-ups to eat and talk.

"So, that's it? Any follow-up?" John asked, munching a bagel from his seat at the table.

At the counter, Kate stirred creamer into her coffee and shot him a scowl, chewing her own food, mouth closed.

Brian ignored her look, trying to preserve his bliss. "They'll keep an eye on me, but unless something changes, no more chemo. I can go back to life as usual."

Surprisingly, the idea didn't leave him overjoyed. What *was* life as usual? Life before he met Melanie? Lonely and boring with an unending series of bad dates? Or could he and Melanie pick up where they left off, on her porch, when he'd kissed her—

"Brian!" John's tone as he dug in the cream cheese said Brian had zoned out for a second.

"Yeah. Sorry." He sipped more coffee, refocusing on John. Maybe he should've bought food for Melanie's clan too. To go along with the other thing.

"Have you told Melanie yet?" John poured orange juice from the carafe.

"Nope. Headed there now." He imagined Melanie's reaction, and a wave of happy nervousness crashed over him.

* * *

TEN MINUTES LATER, Brian stood atop a rickety lawn chair on Melanie's porch, screwing in a new light bulb. The scent of blooming lilacs tickled his nose. Kids cackled as they ran through the yard across the street, sending an empty tire swing sailing through the air.

The front door creaked open, and Melanie stepped out wearing worn jeans and a soft burgundy knit top. Her bare feet curled on the cold concrete and she squinted up at the porch ceiling. The better he felt, the more ravishing she looked. "Brian? What are you doing?"

He gave the bulb a final twist, then careful to balance himself with a hand to the back of the chair, stepped down. "Something I should've done a long time ago—replacing this bulb." He pointed to the light fixture.

She smiled and helped steady the chair. "That thing hasn't worked since Matthew was a baby."

Brian reached inside the door and flicked the switch. "It does now." He switched it off and on a few times for good measure.

"Thank you." She dusted off her hands and opened the door to him. "You didn't come over just for that, did you?"

He stepped inside, and the smell of buttery pancakes and syrup made the whole place seem even cozier than usual. "Actually, I have something I want to tell you. In person."

"What's that?" She pressed the door shut behind them and turned toward him, a curious look on her face.

He breathed deeply, in and out, trying to calm his racing nerves. "The cancer's in remission."

A smile spread across her face, her eyes crinkling in the corners. She pulled him into a hug, squeezing tight. "Oh, Brian, that's wonderful news!"

He soaked in every bit of her warmth for the fleeting seconds she held him.

She released him, elation lighting her entire face, and her lips passed dangerously close to his. Her signature scent—cherry blossoms—filled his senses, creating a heady sensation.

He held her arms, keeping her from escaping his reach. He stared at her mouth, his own burning to kiss hers. Their gazes locked for a second before she wriggled from his grasp, her smile looking a shade less genuine than before.

He should've expected this. After all, last time they'd been together he'd unloaded his sordid past on her. Of course she had reservations about him. What woman wouldn't? Heck, he had reservations about himself half the time, but day by day since he'd confessed to her, he'd been growing in confidence that with God's help, he could keep temptation at bay again—indefinitely.

"Do you want to tell the kids? They've been praying for you every night." Despite how she'd just evaded him, affection sparkled in her eyes.

"Can I?" He peered around her, wondering why the kids and their busybody radar hadn't already found him.

They came stumbling down the stairs in capes and crowns, picking up speed as they spotted him in the entry way. He could stay here with these kids and their mom forever. And he prayed that despite his sinful past, God would make a way for him to do just that.

CHAPTER 43

Using her knee, Melanie nudged an uncharacteristically lethargic Penny forward across the threshold of Brian's brother and sister-in-law's house. The boys trailed somewhere behind her—she hoped. She'd had to prod Matthew every step of the way.

While Kate always looked about thirty times more put-together than Melanie felt, their small ranch house appeared firmly average. A minor boost to Melanie's lingering insecurity, but a boost to an increasingly stressed-out mom, nonetheless.

Inside, a giant bouquet of spring blooms—tulips, daffodils, and hyacinths—drew her gaze to the mantel. Any floral fragrance had been overpowered by the savory aroma of pizza. A large-screen TV, tuned to a pop music channel, hung on the adjoining wall. Snippets of scantily clad dancers slithered across the screen. She hoped the boys would soon be otherwise occupied and not notice. The living room, accented by cherry wood molding and a Persian rug, had a lived-in but cared-for look. John and Kate either had a separate space for the boys' excess toys and clutter or they hid it well behind doors and drawers.

Kevin squeezed around her and raced toward Patrick and

Brady, who knelt on the floor assembling an orange Hot Wheels track.

"C'mon in," John said, taking her jacket and Penny's and plucking Kevin's from the floor where he'd dropped it. He gave a cursory smile, not the warm welcome she expected. "Food's in the kitchen. Brian too."

"Thank you." The invitation to the little celebration of Brian's clean bill of health had surprised but pleased her. Something as monumental as the lymphoma's remission should be marked by something, if only a small pizza party.

Melanie twisted around, searching for Matthew, who skulked behind her. Ever since he'd gotten home from a scout service project early this afternoon, he'd been quiet and withdrawn. "Hey, the boys have Hot Wheels out."

He glanced in the direction of the boys and moped toward them, his eyes downcast.

Melanie sighed, weary of trying to discover what had dampened his mood. He'd left the house this morning, excited and happy about a park cleanup project, and *something* had robbed him of his joy.

Kate's congenial voice travelled from the opposite side of the living room, and Melanie trailed John in that direction, Penny clinging to her leg.

Brian stood pressed to the wall like a tween at his first boy-girl dance, hands in his jeans' pockets, his attention on Kate as she plopped three pizza boxes on the countertop.

"Melanie, you're here!" Kate circled the counter and came toward her, arms outstretched.

Melanie hadn't thought of them as hugging friends, but being welcomed and included eased her tension. Interaction with Brian was bound to be uncomfortable given the phone conversation they'd had last night.

With the kids tucked into bed, Melanie had sat at the kitchen table with a lined notepad and pen, asking Brian horribly awkward, but what she felt were necessary, questions meant to satisfy her qualms about what exactly Brian's pornography "problem" entailed. She'd never dreamed of asking such questions of David before they'd married, but given Brian's admission and how her feelings for him refused to wane, she forced herself through the list.

She'd fallen into bed emotionally spent but satisfied that he'd demonstrated the ability to overcome his addiction, if that's what it was, and maintain a healthy relationship. Just one issue remained, an obstacle to her taking up again with Brian.

A burst of laughter from the other room caught Penny's attention, and she loosened her grip on Melanie and tottered back to the living room.

"Hey." Brian pushed off of the wall and approached Melanie, hands still tucked in his pockets, looking more abashed than triumphant.

She smiled brightly, hoping to infuse some excitement into the evening. She hadn't meant to bring him down last night, only to get at the truth. And only because she cared so much about him.

"Thanks for coming." He hesitated, reaching and then pulling back before squeezing her in a sort of side hug. "How was your day?"

Penny had complained off and on that her tummy felt "weird," Kevin had broken the drawer in the bathroom vanity by using it to support his entire body weight, and Matthew had come home mute or close to it. "Fine."

John plopped paper plates on the counter and spoke to Kate in an irritated tone.

The smell of tomatoes and oregano filled the room as Kate responded, shoving aside her husband with her shoulder.

John tossed a pile of napkins on the plates and stomped out of the room, leaving awkward silence in his wake.

Brian gave Melanie a commiserating look and leaned around her. "Time for pizza, guys," he called with his hand to his mouth.

Five kids barreled into the room, with Matthew bringing up the silent rear. Brian and Kate plopped greasy slices of pizza onto their plates while Melanie poured them drinks from a couple of plastic two-liter bottles.

Melanie squatted alongside Penny's seat and, feeling a little self-conscious, led her kids in a quiet prayer while the Perella boys gobbled their slices. After they said "amen," Penny took two bites and abandoned her pizza, but Kevin ate with gusto.

Brian came up beside Melanie, sipping from a can of ginger ale. "Something wrong with Matthew?"

John and Kate's boys sat with Kevin at the end of the table. Matthew sat two seats apart from the other boys, eating in silence.

"Yes, but I can't get out of him what." She grabbed a slice of pepperoni pizza and a few napkins for herself and slid into the open seat next to Matthew.

"Pizza good?" she asked.

Matthew nodded but kept his gaze fixed on his plate.

"Y'know, in my experience, it's better if you talk about it. Whatever it is." Even the painful, shameful things she and Brian had been discussing, like regrets and sins. She took a bite of pizza and wiped her chin where the sauce dribbled.

Matthew finally looked at her, his lips pinched together and his eyes teary. "I saw something on Mason's phone."

Possibilities ran through Melanie's mind. Something scary? Evil? Obscene? She worked to keep her voice neutral. "What was it?"

He pushed away his half-eaten slice of pizza. "Somethin' his dad posted. . . . His dad's outta jail now."

"I heard." Now she knew the source but not the content. "What was it? A picture or something he wrote or—"

Matthew pushed away from the table, the chair legs screeching over the floor. "I'm gonna go play."

Brian sat in the chair Matthew vacated and scooted forward. "So, did you make any headway?"

"A little. He saw something on his friend Mason's phone. Something Mason's dad posted somewhere." She took another bite of pizza and scanned the counter for beverages.

Brian placed his hand on her arm. "Can I try talking to him? If it's, well, if it's what I think it was, he might be more comfortable talking to me about it than you."

Melanie's gaze darted to Brian. "But I'm his mother. You really think he'd rather talk to you?" *And, oh, could we just not do this?* Yes, she knew they lived in a porn-saturated culture, but she didn't need to be reminded of it day in and day out.

Brian shrugged a shoulder. "Maybe. It's nothing against you. He may be more comfortable talking to a man is all."

She nodded and her heart clenched, thinking of the kinds of things Matthew could've seen that would make him uncomfortable speaking to her. "Okay. Give it a shot."

Brian excused himself and meandered into the living room, presumably to find Matthew. Meanwhile, John returned, said something that made the boys at the table laugh, then grabbed himself some pizza and a beer. Kate went about her own business, combining pizza slices into fewer boxes.

After finishing her pizza, Melanie sauntered to the living room and leaned against the entryway wall. At the far end of the couch, facing away from her, Matthew spoke in hushed tones to Brian, the boy's arms raising and falling as he gestured.

Brian sat with his elbows on his knees, nodding his head, listening. A minute later, he patted Matthew on the back and stood.

Matthew smiled—smiled!—and dashed past her to the kitchen, where the other boys still ate.

Brian caught Melanie's gaze, his eyes serious.

Ignoring the knot in her belly, she joined him in the living room. The kids' laughter carried from the kitchen, occasionally intermixed with John's or Kate's voice.

Brian moved closer so that they stood toe to toe. "He's okay. It's what I suspected. He saw something explicit."

"Oh, my gosh. Mason's a nice boy, but this is exactly what I feared." Melanie gritted her teeth, angry at herself for allowing Matthew to be in situation where this could happen.

"It would've happened sooner or later, Melanie. I'm not saying you've been lax, just that it's impossible nowadays to prevent it indefinitely. If it wasn't now, it'd be next month, or next year. Some other friend or a pop-up ad while he's searching for something innocent. An innocuous-looking website that turns out to be something else."

He was right, but it still rankled. Parenthood seemed to require hypervigilance about a million different harms—real or imagined, and yet Melanie couldn't help but think something about that hypervigilance itself could be detrimental.

"What exactly did he see?" She wrestled with whether she wanted to know or not.

Brian shook his head. "Not much more than he'd see during primetime TV. It was a gif of a man and woman in bed together."

She breathed a little easier. Could've been a lot worse.

"He was afraid you'd be upset with him for looking at it, but it sounds like he didn't know what it was until too late. One of those, 'look at this' kind of things."

Melanie nodded, wishing she had a magic wand to wave over all of them, clearing all the trash from their minds and their hearts. Not just the images, but the shame and the sadness that came after. They were supposed to be celebrating Brian's clean bill of health tonight, not discussing serious matters by themselves. She'd had quite enough of that already.

"Thank you." Melanie patted his chest, careful not to linger.

"Thanks for talking to him. I'll have a talk with him tomorrow too."

Brian inched closer, his head bowed so that it hung right above hers. "You're welcome." His voice, soft, smooth, and oh-so-close, warmed her.

"We're supposed to be celebrating," she said. "Let's—"

Penny slumped against her leg. "Mama, Mama, Mama, I don't feel good. My belly feels yucky."

Melanie smoothed the little girl's hair away from her face. Pale cheeks, glassy eyes. Ate only two bites of pizza. Yep. Penny was going down fast.

The boys all sat at the kitchen table, engrossed in a game of Jenga.

"Sorry, kids," Melanie said. "We need to go." She swooped through the kitchen, hyper-focused on gathering her kids and making explanations and apologies to John and Kate, hoping beyond all hope they could get home before Penny got any sicker.

"Aw, Mom, can't we stay?" Kevin begged. "Me and Matthew aren't sick."

Melanie stopped, silently correcting his grammar and wondering how they could make this work. Matthew had finally joined in the fun, and the four boys really did get on well together.

"You go," Brian said. "I'll bring the boys home."

"Would you do that?" A sense of relief washed over her. "I hate to make them leave when they're having such a good time."

She scooped Penny onto her hip. "Thanks, Brian."

He smiled. "No problem. I think I owe you."

A little thrill passed through her, driving an impulse. "Would you come over next Saturday? I'll get Hannah to babysit."

He turned his head, giving her a side eye. "Are you asking me on a date?"

A little laugh burst from her lips. "Yes. Yes, I guess I am.

After you dumped me. I must be crazy."

He shook his head, smiling. "I did *not* dump you. And no, you're not crazy. I'll be there."

Penny's head fell against Melanie's shoulder and she moaned.

"Gotta go." She stepped towards the door when two phones chimed—one, then another. Wait, was one *her* phone, buried in her purse?

Brian reached in his back pocket, his brow pinched. His phone had chimed too. He stared at the screen. "We need to talk about this again too." He held up the screen and a blank message from an anonymous caller. Worry lines creased his brow.

She nodded, lugging Penny to the door. Brian had told her last night on the phone about the gray car. Yes, they needed to talk. Who had both of their numbers? And her home number? Knew where they lived. When they came and went. And why? Why stalk them? Was it *stalking*? A chill shot up her spine despite Penny's warm body pressed to hers.

Brian had shared every odd call he'd gotten and every time he'd glimpsed the gray car, going back to their first date in the park. He'd started keeping a log, and strongly urged that Melanie do the same, so that they could take their case to the police—a reversal of the dismissive attitude he'd had about the calls before. She'd make that list tonight—no, it would be a long night with Penny. Tomorrow.

Melanie feared one day she'd buckle under it all. Each day brought with it new challenges and little relief. Thank God her kids kept her grounded in the moment with the demands of caring for their little bodies. Otherwise, she feared the worries —the ones just beginning with Matthew—would overwhelm her. And this prank caller, the guy in the gray car maybe, made her feel like life—despite the bright spots—was hurtling toward a giant showdown. She glanced at Penny, pasty and warm on her shoulder. Or maybe a giant meltdown.

rian drummed his fingers on the desk, the bright sunshine from outside the office window taunting him. Weekends were for system maintenance. Or warriors, or waffles, or whatever.

Beside him, Jason leaned back on his swivel office chair, aiming number two pencils at the dropped ceiling. Bags sagged under Jason's bleary eyes. Together with his extra-pasty skin, the portly kid looked liked he'd pulled another all-nighter with his Xbox and a six-pack of cheap beer. He'd been distracted all morning, wandering the office aimlessly, checking his phone, and nosing around Brian's personal stuff. Five minutes ago, Brian had caught him with his stubby fingers in his desk drawer as if anything in there was his business. Who hired the kid? Competence wasn't beyond his ability, but his work ethic and his attitude . . . The kindest thing Brian could call them was subpar.

The little hand on the stupid wall clock neared twelve. Brian's leg jiggled, and he stilled it with his palm. Stupid clock: "I don't stop when I'm tired." *Yeah, well, I stop when I'm bored out of my gourd and have someplace better to be.*

"Jason, you got this." He stood and pushed in his chair.

Jason's chair back snapped into an upright position, and he glared at Brian.

"I've been here three hours." Brian pointed down the hall toward the server room. "All you gotta do is babysit our two-terabyte little lady back there. Should only be another forty-five minutes or so. You can straighten things up back there too." The Snickers wrappers, busted pencils, and sports sections of the local newspaper hadn't escaped Brian's notice.

With a grudging harrumph, Jason ambled toward the server room, his girth—or maybe it was just his lackadaisical attitude—slowing his pace.

The seconds crawled by until Brian reached Melanie's neighborhood. The afternoon sun shone brightly, lending vivid color to the spring blossoms in every yard on her street. Brian drank it all in as he pulled into the driveway. The lush green grass, the yellow-green leaves, the brilliant pink azaleas, and sunny yellow forsythia. A perfect spring day. A great day to be alive. This afternoon, life was perfect—or nearly so.

Brian bounded up the steps to Melanie's porch. He glanced at the light fixture and smiled. He needed to come back at night just to see it in action. Was the wattage sufficient? Did it attract too many bugs?

He pressed the doorbell, then turned and scanned the street and the neighbors' driveways. No sign of a gray car today. That, too, boded well for the afternoon. He sucked in a lungful of fragrant air, sweetened by multitudes of tree blossoms.

The door clicked behind him and he spun around, a tingle of anticipation rippling through him.

Melanie, in beige Capri pants and a plum t-shirt, slipped out the door, a finger pressed to her lips. She'd clipped her hair back, keeping stray hairs from falling into her face. Her cheeks glowed, healthy and vibrant with just a touch of makeup on her lashes and lips—good enough to kiss! With slow, silent movements, she pulled the door shut.

"Hurry! Let's go," she whispered, pulling Brian by the arm.

Brian kept pace, chuckling as they jogged down the steps and onto the sidewalk. "Are you sneaking out?"

Melanie slowed her pace. "Not exactly. Hannah's there. The boys are entertained by some dollar store puzzles. But Penny is roaming the house with her 'Mama, Mama, Mama,' wanting me to read her *Little Llama, Go Home* for the thousandth time today."

After Melanie had left John and Kate's, she'd spent the night awake with a very sick Penny and the next day tending to Kevin and Matthew. Patrick and Brady had it, too, the day after that, but Brian and the other adults had been spared. "Has everyone recovered and the disease been neutralized?"

"Oh, yes. Everyone is back to normal, eating umpteen meals a day." Her arm swung between them, brushing his.

His hand itched to grab hers. She'd called today a date. Would it be okay to hold her hand?

"I feel bad that Penny was the carrier that gave it to your nephews though. I should've known something was off with her."

Her hand grazed his. Unable to stop himself, he snatched her hand and held it tight.

She glanced at him, a smile playing on her lips. "The boys have been doing this new move nonstop. The super chop, I think they call it. I don't know where they got it."

"I do." Brian grinned, remembering the scene. "They came up with that move at John and Kate's. I suspect Patrick and Brady are still at it too." The boys accompanied a signature karate chop move with a one-two kick and a loud "hi-ya!"

Melanie shook her head. "I guess they'll tire of it eventually. They've already knocked poor Penny on her little heinie about five times." Her gaze toggled between the neighbors' blooming trees and Brian. "I thought it'd be fun to walk to the park and hang out."

"Sounds perfect." The sun warmed his shoulders. Neither the weather nor the company could get any better than this. Gosh, it felt good to be alive and well! He hoped Hannah had blocked off the afternoon.

A gray coupe—not the dreaded gray sedan—rolled by, reminding Brian that they needed to discuss the prank calls. Not that he needed reminding since lately the menace remained on the edge of his thoughts 24/7.

Melanie's gaze followed the car too. Probably thinking the same thing as him.

"So, did you write down all the times and dates on those prank calls and what was said?" he asked. When looking together in hindsight, he realized that there had been more incidents than either of them had recognized.

"I did." Melanie's hand stiffened in his. "Best I could remember. Maybe we can call the police together later, if I can keep the kids from interrupting us."

"Okay." The sooner the better. Brian had been on edge, waiting for the next call, but that didn't worry him nearly as much as wondering when the creep would contact Melanie again. Or what he might do. People like this escalated, right? Calls and lurking in a darkened car might give way to—he didn't want to think of it. Melanie assured him she locked doors and windows and took every precaution, but he still worried.

In a few minutes, they arrived at the neighborhood park. The grassy area with mature oak and maple trees covered only a few acres but offered a convenient place for play and picnics. On a knoll at the far end, a couple of kids attempted to get a kite in the air. Closer, young moms pushed babies on swings while a few older children ran helter-skelter around the playground equipment, screeching and laughing.

Still holding Brian's hand, Melanie steered them to a quiet

ridge set apart from the play area. On the steepest part of the hillside below the ridge, Melanie dropped to the grass dotted with clusters of violets, bringing him with her.

Her shoulders raised and fell on a deep sigh. "Thanks for coming with me. I needed some time to breathe." She lay back in the grass, her knees bent and her hair splaying over the little wildflowers.

Brian mimicked her position, not sure what Melanie had in mind for the afternoon. Since he'd been diagnosed, their sole interactions revolved around his health needs. The prospect of an afternoon date with Melanie had sent his hopes soaring. At any second, he could blurt out how much he loved her and how he wanted to see her again—like, all the time. But he would make a concentrated effort to let her lead. He'd taken away her choice when he'd unilaterally decided to suffer alone, and he wouldn't make the same mistake twice.

Melanie folded her hands across her belly and stared into the sky. Cumulous clouds, bright white and super puffy, moved at a slow but steady clip from west to east. The air thickened, becoming noticeably more humid than when they'd left the house a short while ago.

Comfortable silence grew between them, and Brian closed his eyes, soaking in every sensation—the thick air, warm sun, earthy fragrance, and birdsong.

"What hurt the most is that you didn't trust me." Her words came sure, certain, and out of the blue. Though he guessed they'd been on her heart and mind for months. He'd wounded her deeply and while she'd forgiven him, she'd obviously not forgotten.

She rolled her head toward him, her eyes clear and confident.

He got the sense this wasn't about the hurt he'd inflicted. Not really.

"You didn't trust us. And you didn't trust God." She held his gaze, her expression tender.

He understood. *And now you don't trust me.*

"You have to trust me with the bad stuff, Brian. There'll be more of it. Sickness, money trouble, lost jobs. The kids will absolutely drive us insane. That's a given."

His heart beat faster. The future. She was talking about their future. Together. "I can do that." He rolled onto his side to face her, grabbed her hand, and squeezed it between both of his. He could do that and so much more. "Starting now."

Her brow wrinkled, and she faced him. "There's more bad stuff already?"

His palms, still encasing her hand, began to sweat. Brian nodded. "Maybe."

CHAPTER 45

Jagged grass prickled the back of Melanie's legs, and she flicked a little black ant from her wrist. A cloud shifted, and sunlight burned her eyes. Using her hand as a visor, she squinted to see Brian's face. How else could she gauge the seriousness of his remark—more "bad stuff" on the horizon?

He'd gotten a clean bill of health. The cancer had gone into remission. They'd talked the pornography issue to death. Yes, the gray car prank caller was still unresolved, but there would be no news to report on that. *Can we catch a break here, God? How many obstacles to this relationship are too many?*

"This isn't something new. Not exactly. I mean, I wasn't keeping it from you. It wasn't relevant information until now. Until you started hinting that we have a future together." He squeezed her hand, his gaze intent but still warm, compassionate, and sincere. "I want that future. Very much. But you need to know, well, that might not be . . . everything I'd always hoped for."

She freed her hand from his and pushed into a sitting position. A cloud blocked the sun, and the world dimmed. Dread gathered and pitted in her stomach. Hadn't life taught her to take nothing for granted? That Melanie Lombardi was not in the driver's seat? She sat comfortably in the way back where loose change and empty to-go cups littered the seats and floor, fully at the mercy of the driver for temperate air, music selection, and bathroom breaks.

Her fear must've been plain on her face, because Brian's expression softened as he sat across from her. "It'll be okay. The thing is, chemo has side effects. And one of those is infertility." His eyes grew watery, and he bit his lips together. "Melanie, I may not be able to give you any more children."

With a pang, Melanie's heart registered the potential loss of those sweet babies she'd imagined. The one with Brian's blue eyes. A tiny newborn asleep on his chest, its little bum high in the air. The toddler seated on his shoulders, clinging to his neck and head. Fuzzy-headed living, breathing proof of the love that they shared.

"May not?" Already her heart searched for a glimmer of a hope. "So, it's not definite one way or the other?"

Brian nodded and his Adam's apple bobbed as he swallowed. "I talked about it with the oncologist, and she chose drugs less likely to cause infertility, but we won't know for sure until we try. It's not an issue now because I'm single, but they don't advise me, uh, getting anyone pregnant at the moment. Not for a good six months or more."

Not wanting to compound the worry and grief Brian surely felt, she resolved to stifle her disappointment and be one-hundred-percent positive about this challenge. She banished the baby images and set her chin. "Well, then we'll just follow the doctor's advice and leave the rest in God's hands."

"I'm sorry, Melanie. You know I love kids. I mean, I couldn't even pull off that lie—that I didn't want to be tied down by them. If there was anything I could do—"

She waved him off. The treatment had worked, and they

were grateful. They'd deal with the rest as it came. *God, give me the grace to accept it.*

CRACK!

Thunder clapped, and a low rumble rolled, reverberating in the ground beneath them.

Melanie jumped to her feet, Brian beside her. They'd enjoyed gazing at the puffy clouds and blue skies, but once they'd looked away, dark clouds, nearly black, had rolled in behind them. A gust blew leaves from the trees. Sand whirled over the volleyball court across the way, and the sweet, pungent smell of ozone tickled her nostrils.

"Think we can beat it home?" Brian grabbed her hand, poised to sprint.

Melanie glanced at the sky where clouds the color of an angry bruise churned. "We can try."

Thunder cracked again as they dashed down the ridge and across the park. As they set foot on the sidewalk, the sky let loose. Fat raindrops dotted the sidewalk, darkening the pavement in seconds. Rain stung Melanie's bare arms and cooled her back as she ran toward home. The last time she'd run this fast she'd been chasing one of the kids through a parking lot.

Beside her, Brian breathed heavily, his steps lagging behind hers. His wet hand slipped from her grip.

Melanie stopped, the soles of her shoes skidding on the pavement.

Brian stood a yard behind her, catching his breath. "Go ahead," he yelled over the downpour and another rumble of thunder. Wet hair hung over his brow, and he swiped it away. "I can't keep up."

A flash of lightning lit their surroundings as a wave of compassion struck Melanie. Another side effect of the chemo, reminding her that life wouldn't go back to normal for Brian for a while, despite his prognosis. The possibility of infertility was only one way his body had changed.

Sheets of rain blew at them, soaking Melanie to the bone. "Why keep running? We can't get any wetter." She stretched her arms out and tilted her head back, letting the cool water run over her face and neck.

Brian laughed. "True."

He held out his hand.

She grasped it and resumed the trek home at a more leisurely pace, stomping in puddles and ignoring the rivulets of water coursing down her chest and back. If it weren't for the thunder and lightning, she'd bring her kids out to play.

How often did she chide them to stay out of puddles and get inside? Had they ever experienced the simple joy of letting the rain soak them without a care for wet clothes or shoes or the fuss their mom would make when they inevitably traipsed into the house? She promised herself they would soon.

"So, I guess we should've checked the weather, huh?" Rain soaked Brian's too-big t-shirt, the bunched fabric clinging to his skin in places.

In ten minutes of walking through the deluge, they arrived at Melanie's house, drenched. They entered around the back, slipping into the mudroom to kick off their sopping shoes, laughing and giddy.

Melanie shivered in the air conditioning and grabbed a couple of old towels from the rag bin. Water trickled down her nose and from her hair. It dripped down her back and puddled on the vinyl floor.

"This should help." She tossed a towel to Brian then wrung the water from her hair. Using a second towel, she patted it dry.

Brian ran the towel over his arms and legs, his gaze catching on her for a moment, eyeing her from wet head to soaked socks.

Was he checking her out? Her cool cheeks grew warmer. "That shower not cold enough for you, Brian?"

He sauntered toward her, grinning. "Not nearly enough.

How about I give Hannah another five dollars to keep the kids upstairs for a while?"

"Five dollars?" She wrinkled her nose. "Is that all it's worth to you? Hannah doesn't come cheap." It was so good to play with him. She got enough of pretending with her kids—letting them act like dogs, putting on a show, or playing they were sea creatures in the bath tub. But to be playful with a man she cared for, to just let go and walk through the rain, to flirt and tease, refreshed her like no nap or bottomless cup of coffee ever could. It rejuvenated her spirit.

"Hardly." His smile dimmed, leaving a more earnest look in its place. He pulled her into his arms, his gaze at her hairline, then her eyes, her cheeks, her lips.

The awareness of being wanted and cherished sent another shiver through her. Her heart rate quickened, and her knees quivered. She crossed her wrists behind his neck as he tugged her closer, his wet shirt pressing to hers.

"I thought it was just a saying," she whispered. "Weak in the knees. I never dreamed that at my age I'd feel it for the first time."

Brian leaned closer, his warm breath on her neck as he nuzzled her ear. "I make you weak in the knees?"

She shut her eyes, reveling in the soft touch of his lips as they skimmed her jaw. He hadn't kissed her since that night so many months ago. He'd ended their relationship, then contradicted his words with a kiss so soulful, so filled with passion that the memory of it stirred something inside her. Her skin tingled as his cheek brushed hers.

"I love you, Melanie. More than before. So much more." His lips brushed the edge of her mouth.

She turned her head the slightest bit so that her mouth aligned with his.

His hands, strong and solid, pressed the damp shirt to her

back, and he kissed her carefully and deliberately, giving credence to his profession. He took her face in his hands as his lips caressed hers, pressing forward.

Melanie's heart skittered faster, and her awareness of anything but the two of them slipped away. Her stocking foot edged backward, seeking to steady herself. One foot, the other, and then—

A heavy duty bucket tipped behind her, rattling against something. A basket of shoes and boots? Umbrellas? Who knew? Who cared?

A little giggle escaped her lips, and she felt Brian's smile.

He didn't relent, his kisses moving along the other side of her neck.

A burst of light came from the door to the kitchen, and Melanie's attention snapped to the doorway.

Hannah stood, framed by the light, in denim shorts, a baggy top, and a messy bun, her eyes wide as saucers. "Oh!" She slammed the door shut.

"Brian," Melanie breathed, patting his shoulder.

In a second, the door creaked open. "Sorry!" Hannah called, her hand awkwardly over her glasses, blocking her eyes. The door clicked shut again.

That teased a chuckle from Brian, and he stepped back, giving them room to breathe.

"I'm so embarrassed." Melanie steadied her breaths. "Poor Hannah and her virgin eyes."

Brian scoffed. "Hannah's what, twenty? We were only kissing. I'm sure Hannah's seen worse." He extended a hand and guided Melanie away from the bucket and a container of garden tools, which she'd apparently jostled. "And how come you're not concerned about my virgin eyes?"

She grinned and smacked his chest. "Your eyes were closed." And they'd seen so, so much more than a few impassioned kisses. And yet, at that moment, she couldn't muster an ounce of worry about it. She and Brian belonged together. She was certain of it.

CHAPTER 46

With a goofy smile plastered to his face, Brian's head grazed the ceiling in Melanie's minivan, and he fumbled with the levers at his side. The seat lowered, allowing him to sit straight. He tugged his seatbelt into place and adjusted the mirrors. The whole vehicle smelled vaguely of overripe banana. Probably best that he didn't ask why.

Behind him, Melanie tossed a drawstring bag packed with pajamas onto the empty seat. Across from her, Penny kicked her sandaled feet with excitement. And in the back row, Kevin and Matthew super chopped each other, giving a quick one-two chop with the hand and a jab with the elbow, straining against their belts into the empty space between them.

A buzz of excitement and a feeling of connectedness—like he was part of this little family—made him feel a little light-headed. Or was that still from the chemo? They all deserved a fun night out. Brian had even considered capping the evening with a marriage proposal, but he couldn't find that darn ring guide. In fact, he hadn't seen it for months, not since he and Melanie had pretended it didn't exist when it had fallen to the floor of his apartment. He also needed to know from Melanie where her kids stood on her remarrying. Would they welcome Brian as their dad? He thought they would.

"Is everyone ready for Laurel Woods?" He glanced at the mirror giving him a full view of the backseat shenanigans.

"Yes!" the kids screamed.

Melanie slid into the passenger seat and closed the door. She smiled, snugged her ponytail, and sighed. "I kinda like this idea —an evening at the park. Not a day-long marathon that ends in sore feet, overtired kids, and empty pockets."

"It's how my parents used to do it. Feed everyone at home and then go when the rates drop for a few hours of fun." Brian, John, and their sisters shared many happy memories of carefree summer nights in the park. He wanted to create some for Melanie's kids too.

A half hour later, they bounded for the entrance gates. Penny clutched both Brian's and Melanie's hands, urging them to swing her through the air. The boys ran ahead, Kevin in the lead.

"Wait up, Kevin!" Melanie called, frowning at the overeager boy.

Late afternoon sun singed Brian's bare arms and the back of his neck while it drove the temperatures higher, making it hot even for an early summer day. Flowerbeds teemed with colorful, blooming annuals, but only the hardiest flowers didn't droop in the heat.

Inside the gate, families and couples ambled in every direction, pushing strollers and hoisting tired children onto their shoulders. Sweaty kids darted ahead of their parents in a last-ditch effort to ride everything in the park. Teens wove in between the families, some holding hands, others in small groups. Blue cars on a silver steel roller coaster whizzed by, the roar failing to drown out screams as it made a corkscrew. Pop music sounded from speakers and a game vendor chattered into a microphone, trying to attract players to pound a target with an oversized mallet and win a giant stuffed bear.

Releasing Penny's hand, Brian jogged ahead and snatched Kevin's hand before he got lost amidst the chaos. "What do you wanna ride, buddy?"

Kevin stared slack-jawed beyond the kiddie rides at the higher, faster, wilder rides—roller coasters, drop towers, and thrill rides. He and Matthew had already groused at the prospect of riding with and waiting on Penny and the tame rides suited to her age.

"I'm too big for baby rides," Kevin said. The whine in his voice intensified as he tugged Brian's hand, trying to get him to move toward the Wild Mouse.

"The carousel and the train are for everyone," Melanie said. Sweat glistened at her temple and her cheeks shone, rosy and full. "And then we can get ice cream cones."

A rush of affection for her burned in Brian's chest, and he grabbed her free hand and pressed a kiss to the back of it.

She shot him a what-was-that-for look.

He leaned toward her and whispered in her ear. "I love you."

Her cheeks couldn't possibly get redder, but her shy smile and brilliant eyes said Cupid's arrow had hit its mark.

One ride each on the merry-go-round and the steam train, and they sat on a concrete wall devouring waffle cones. Penny's dripped ice cream down the sides, over her hand, and onto the ground. Matthew licked his meticulously before biting into the cone. And Kevin devoured his in messy mouthfuls, leaving bits of chocolate on his cheeks, lips, and hands.

Brian sat next to Melanie, their arms and legs brushing. "I was thinking, why don't you take Penny on some more kiddie rides while I take the boys on a roller coaster? Everyone's happy."

"Good idea." She hung on his gaze, her eyes dancing, teasing.

"What?" Did she have something in mind? His chest

warmed. Maybe he'd propose tonight anyway. He didn't *have* to have a ring. They could pick one out later. She'd know what she liked, and he hadn't a clue what to buy anyway.

About forty paper napkins and three baby wipes later, Brian ushered the boys into line for the Ghoster Coaster. The sign above the entrance to the corral marked it as a thirty-minute wait. From their spot in line, they probably had twenty minutes to kill. Brian peppered them with questions about what they wanted to ride next as they inched toward the front of the line. Finally, the boys became engrossed in their own conversation, allowing Brian's mind to wander, creating an imaginary scenario for the remainder of the evening.

Clad in their pajamas, the kids would nod off in the car on the way home. He'd help carry them upstairs to bed, and then he and Melanie would have privacy. If the mosquitoes weren't bad, they could sit in the backyard.

They'd talk and laugh about the day. And then he'd tell her again how much he loved her. And her kids. He'd talk about the future he imagined for them. Did the kids think of him—

"Ow!" Matthew cried, clutching his middle and stumbling backwards. He bumped a surly, pimply teen with more hardware on his face than Brian had in his toolbox.

"Sorry." Brian nodded an apology to the teen. "Boys, no super chops in line."

Finally at the front of the line, they piled into the roller coaster cars, Matthew in front and Kevin and Brian behind him.

Kevin gripped the safety bar so hard his knuckles whitened.

"Loosen your grip, buddy. It'll be fun, right Matthew?" Brian nudged Kevin, trying to distract him from what looked like full-on fear mode. All this paternal encouragement kinda made Brian feel like a real dad, and his chest swelled with pride.

The car drifted forward and Matthew turned, yelling, "Here we go!"

The cars jolted out of the station and began a quick, steep

descent then climbed a moderate-sized hill. Down, up, around. Chains ground and wooden beams creaked, transporting Brian to his own childhood. Rickety-sounding wooden coasters had always been his favorite. At the highest summit, Matthew flung his arms in the air, and Brian yelped while Kevin's eyes grew wider and whiter. They plummeted at a solid fifty miles per hour or so, took two hard curves, and coasted into the station.

They disembarked, and Matthew backpedaled down the ramp, chattering excitedly. "That was awesome!"

Brian followed on Kevin's heels. "What'd you think, Kevin?"

"Wicked." His face lit, incredulous but happy.

Brian laughed. "Wouldn't have known it from the look on your face."

Matthew prattled on about the ride and its awesomeness.

Gliding his hand along the painted wooden railing, Kevin slid alongside Brian, eventually surging forward and ahead of the people in front of them.

"Kevin, wait up," Brian called.

Not hearing or not caring, Kevin drifted along, undeterred by people, big and small, thin and fat, as he squeezed behind them.

With a tug to Matthew's t-shirt, Brian kept him at his side and leaned outward over the rail trying to spot Kevin. "Kevin, stop!" he yelled.

The exit path took a quick turn, and as Brian and Matthew rounded the bend, Brian lost sight of Kevin. His heart jumped into his throat as he scanned the bodies crammed in front of him ambling into the heart of the park.

"Kevin!" Brian called, his heart pounding. "Kevin!"

Matthew, realizing Kevin had wandered ahead, called too. "Kevin!" He and Brian pushed ahead, making apologies and excuses as they squeezed between sweaty bodies.

After what seemed like minutes but was probably seconds,

they cleared the last cluster of people exiting the ride and jogged down the path toward the main thoroughfare.

Brian's lungs constricted as his eyes darted left and right, scanning the throng of people. He'd lost Kevin.

Lost him.

He gripped Matthew's hand, determined not to lose another.

In which direction should he look? Where would Kevin have gone? The longer he stood there deciding, the farther away Kevin got. He turned in a slow circle, scanning the crowd. "Kevin! Kevin Lombardi!"

Compressors from nearby rides sounded, another roller coaster whooshed, and the park loudspeakers boomed with bass-heavy music. Who could hear him anyway? And where was a security guard when you needed one?

Fear gripped Brian. The scene at the butterfly garden flashed in his mind. Kevin had gotten ahead of the family there too, and a man in a black hoodie had stopped him. Brian hadn't connected that incident—hadn't even thought of it. But the similarity . . .

Please, Lord, keep him safe and help me find him. Guardian angel, protect him.

A kid's raised voice caught his attention. Was the kid calling his name? For a second, the noise level dipped during a break in the music.

"Listen," he ordered Matthew. "Do you hear him?"

Brian stood still, searching and praying, his heart banging against his ribs and his throat thickening.

There it was!

Just a syllable before a roller coaster zoomed by, but he'd heard it. Faint but urgent. "Bri—!"

Taking Matthew with him, Brian whirled in the direction of the voice.

About fifteen yards ahead of them, Kevin stumbled backwards over a gravel path toward a catering pavilion. A stocky figure in jeans and a black long-sleeve t-shirt—in this heat?—dragged Kevin by the wrist.

Brian's breath caught, and his muscles tensed, ready for action.

From a distance, Brian couldn't make out tears, but Kevin's face shone red and the look on his face—pure terror.

CHAPTER 47

With his eyes trained steadily on Kevin—Brian would *not* let him out of his sight—Brian gripped Matthew's arm.

Matthew whimpered, probably scared. Nothing to be done about that now.

Hoping to communicate urgency by glaring into Matthew's eyes, Brian rushed his words. "Go to the Whirly Cups and tell the operator someone has taken your brother and to call security. Have security call your mom. Then you wait *right* here for her. Do *not* leave this spot."

He released Matthew and sprinted toward Kevin, hoping Matthew obeyed and the ride operator cooperated.

Further ahead, maybe a half-football field away now, Kevin dragged his feet, slowing his captor.

Brian raced, gasping for air like he had in the thunderstorm. Is this what it felt like to be asthmatic? Like you couldn't pull in enough air? Curse the Hodgkins and chemo!

Being half-dragged through the picnic pavilion, Kevin hooked his foot around a bench leg. As the man tried to dislodge him, Brian glimpsed pale skin, no beard or heavy facial hair. Short, probably on the young side.

With agitated moves, the kidnapper knocked Kevin down, freed his leg, then yanked him to his feet.

Kevin yelped and twisted away, his body weight stalling but not stopping his captor.

Keep it up, Kevin. Let me catch up to you.

The ground dipped where a narrow brook ran behind the pavilion and beneath the Ghoster Coaster and the Timber Falls, a water ride in which log-shaped cars cruised through chutes and down cascading waterfalls. He couldn't lose sight of them! Brian pumped his legs faster, forcing himself to take deep, measured breaths.

Sweat gathered on Brian's forehead and behind his neck, and a stitch in his side left him squeezing the pain below his ribs. He pumped his legs harder, splashing through the brook, determined to close the gap between him and Kevin.

About twenty-five yards ahead, the stocky man forced Kevin onto a narrow green service ladder.

The wooden coaster zipped by overhead, the track rattling and the passengers laughing and shouting. A light breeze blew, carrying with it the stringent odor of chlorinated water mixed with the sweet aroma of kettle corn.

Brian's graze trailed the ladder. It climbed to a walkway along the uppermost part of the Timber Falls. Beyond it, the sky dimmed as the sun sank fast, obscured by a smattering of pink and gray clouds.

Below, heavy foliage and the looming rides obscured the little remaining natural light. While large overhead lamps kept the park well lit, the empty pavilion area remained dark.

The man urged Kevin upward, pushing his buttocks and lifting his legs by the ankles when Kevin didn't move fast enough.

By the time Brian reached the bottom of the ladder, Kevin had scooted onto the walkway, the man directly behind him.

"Let him go!" Brian called. They couldn't be more than thirty, forty feet away now.

With a lurch, the man twisted and peered over the rail at Brian. Hadn't he known he'd been followed?

Kevin sobbed, and the sound tore at Brian's gut.

Brian's wet tennis shoes squeaked as he clambered up the metal ladder. Sweat stung his eyes, and he rubbed at them, trying to clear his vision. Who had Kevin?

The would-be kidnapper's face came into focus for a split second before he jerked away from the rail.

A flicker of recognition and then . . . utter confusion. Brian gripped the metal rails as he climbed, his breathing hard but the stitch in his side gone. His wet, rubber soles slipped on the slick rungs, causing him to lose his footing. Between concentrating on his feet and devising a way to get Kevin back, Brian's mind tried to connect the dots of how and why. It didn't make sense. Again, his sole slid from a wet rung.

Nearing the top of the ladder, Brian glimpsed Kevin's leg, scraped and bloodied, as he reached the crest of Timber Falls. An empty log car glided by, sloshing water over the side of the chute, spraying Kevin and his captor. Yards behind it, another empty car followed—had security stopped the passengers?— dipping low then dousing Brian.

Cool water soaked his hair and ran down his face, back, and arms, blinding him for a moment. Brian blinked away the water and hoisted himself onto the narrow walkway as the first log car plunged down the chute.

Ahead, the captor had Kevin around the neck, held to his ample belly along the rail. He yanked his forearm, nearly choking Kevin.

Kevin clawed at the man's arm, gasping and bawling.

The man shuffled his feet in a quick, agitated fashion, scowling at Kevin and his attempts to break free.

Brian, seething and overcome by a fear unlike anything he'd known, stared into the vapid eyes of his co-worker Jason Marston. In a second, a surge of anger and protectiveness drowned the fear. "You!" he sputtered. "Let go of him."

Jason squeezed tighter, stepping backward, his gaze darting wildly in every direction.

Brian froze. He wouldn't do something crazy like leap over the edge, would he? With Kevin?

Kevin's choked scream died in his throat as a steel roller coaster whooshed in the distance.

Moving slowly and steadily toward Jason and Kevin only a half-dozen yards away, Brian glanced to the side, measuring the drop and what lay below them. Best guess: thirty feet stood between them and a dirt- and weed-covered slope dotted with rocks. Overhead, a light affixed to the top of the ride flicked on, illuminating the walkway.

Jason's foot skidded as he pedaled backward, and his grip loosened.

"Coach!" Kevin yelled, his eyes wide and hands pawing at Jason's arm around his neck.

Jason glanced toward the chutes.

No log cars floated through now. Only water sloshed by.

Brian stopped ten feet from them, afraid to press forward for fear of what Jason might do trapped at the ride's peak. But his heart raced, his chest pounded, and a mixture of fear and anger swirled in his head and his gut. What should he do? And where was park security?

Kevin wriggled beneath Jason's grasp.

An idea floated to the forefront, eclipsing Brian's questions. Would it work?

"Kevin!" He stared intently into Kevin's eyes, willing the boy to focus and understand. "Super chop!"

Kevin stilled for a moment before understanding sharpened his gaze.

Then he thrashed against Jason, freeing his arm.

Jason batted at Kevin, a futile attempt to regain control.

Kevin's little chest swelled, his chin lifted, and then his arm swung as he delivered a super chop—hard and fast.

A well-placed chop to his brother had gotten Matthew in the stomach. A chop against a man, even a stocky one, landed in a more sensitive spot.

A string of curse words came from Jason's mouth as he curled forward, releasing his grip on Kevin and cupping his hands to his groin.

Hope surged in Brain's chest, and he beckoned Kevin forward. "C'mon. Come to me." The wet walkway glistened under the light. "Careful!"

Wet and filthy, blood trickling down his shin, Kevin lunged toward Brian, but then his foot slipped and his arms flew out.

Brian's heart stopped, and he reached out as if he could somehow help. If Kevin fell to the right, the drippy chute would prevent a free fall. But to the left, only a tree branch stood between him and solid ground.

Kevin grabbed the rail just in time, steadying himself—to Brian's relief. Then he surged forward.

Beyond Kevin, Jason had one knee up, grunting as he balanced himself with a hand to the floor.

Below, a garbled voice rang through a megaphone, the message undecipherable. Three security guards, identifiable by their brown-and-white uniforms and caps, jogged toward them, the beams from their flashlights darting back and forth over the ground and swinging upward. The tallest man wielded a billy club.

Where's your gun, man? That stick ain't gonna do jack from down there.

A siren wailed in the distance.

Kevin slipped again, fell onto his hip, and slid until his feet and legs dangled over the edge of the catwalk.

Brian lurched forward, reaching again, though still a few yards away. *No, Lord, no. Please!*

He dropped to his knees and scrambled ahead, desperate to close the distance between them without either of them plummeting to the ground.

Kevin grabbed a support rail and hung tight, wrapping himself around it and scooching his legs and feet back onto the walk.

Movement caught Brian's eye, Jason staggering toward Kevin. Anger dripped from his snarled lips.

Kevin lay closer to Brian than Jason, but only about four yards lay between Kevin and that vile menace.

Brian clambered to his feet. "Watch out, Kevin!"

Heavy boots thudded and clanked against metal rungs behind Brian, and more lights swung their way from below. Beyond Jason, a guard appeared at the peak of the Timber Trails, probably coming from another ladder on the other side. Hope surged. In a half minute, tops, that guard would be on top of Jason.

Jason advanced, seeming oblivious to the guard and impervious to the slippery surfaces that had sent Kevin skidding. He couldn't be more than a dozen—no, ten feet from Kevin.

Hiccupping and eyes wide with panic, Kevin pulled himself to his feet.

Another slosh of water poured from the chutes, coating the walkway.

Before he gained his balance, Kevin's front foot slid on the slick walkway. He toppled backwards, arms flailing, landing on his backside. Too close to the edge. But his body didn't stop when he landed. It skidded on the wet walkway.

Panic spiking, Brian lunged for him, reaching, reaching . . .

Kevin slid on his backside, arms up, hands groping for the rail, grasping only air as his body careened over the edge.

Every movement unfolding with morbid clarity, Brian's hand brushed Kevin's arm, but it slipped past him. His arm, his wrist, his fingertips . . . In an instant, he had nothing left to grab of Melanie's little boy.

A series of sharp, horror-filled screams punctuated the atmosphere as Kevin fell, his body twisting in midair.

Brian lay face down on the catwalk, sick in every way from pounding head to aching chest and churning stomach. "Kevin!" he wailed, his entire world disintegrating around him.

CHAPTER 48

Returning Penny's look of pure elation, Melanie hoisted her from the Buzy Buzzers onto her hip. "Was it fun, sweetie?"

Penny clapped and grinned then stretched her sticky limbs around Melanie's chest.

A toddler in the next car screamed as a man extracted him from the belted seat. "No, buddy, three rides is it. We're gonna try something else."

Melanie smiled, sympathetic but relieved their evening so far had been uneventful. Penny had been happy and compliant while the boys were off having an adventure with Brian. How grateful she was for Brian's presence in her life and that he cared for her boys and they for him.

She bounced Penny on her hip and glanced at the time on her wristwatch. "Time to meet up with your brothers." Melanie stopped outside the ride's gate and glanced in either direction, trying to orient herself. A wooden, arrow-shaped sign directed her toward the Ghoster Coaster.

Melanie wove through the crowd, the delicious aroma of

smoked turkey legs drifting toward her, making her hungry. The ice cream had been delicious, but some real food would be satisfying. Maybe they could find an empty picnic table and share a bucket of French fries or some chicken strips.

Colored lights flicked on, illuminating the roller coaster tracks and main thoroughfare. A musical quartet in red-and-white-striped uniforms marched through the concourse, the tuba booming.

Penny covered her ears. "Too loud, Mama."

Melanie agreed. Once they got home, she wanted to sit in the silence with Brian, holding his hand, resting her head against him, feet propped up.

The crowd parted, and Matthew stood ahead of them at their designated stop near the Ghoster Coaster exit. A female security guard stood with him, one hand on each of Matthew's shoulders, speaking intently to him. Where were Brian and Kevin?

A pang of worry pricked Melanie. Something was wrong. Very wrong. Her bones ached with dread as she raced toward Matthew and the guard, Penny bouncing on her hip.

"Matthew, where are Kevin and Coach Brian?"

Matthew turned to her, his eyes wide with recognition and something else—alarm? "Mama, someone stole Kevin, and Coach Brian went after him." He stood on tiptoe, pointing across the way, toward the picnic shelter.

Stole Kevin? "What? What do you mean, 'stole' him?" She let Penny slide down her hip and clutched her hand, probably too hard, but fear coursed through her veins as she struggled to understand the situation.

"Ma'am?" The security officer, a twenty-something woman whose brown hair was pulled back in a severe ponytail, touched Melanie's arm.

Matthew plowed into Melanie, hugging her legs.

She absently rubbed his back. "Where's my other son, Kevin? He's small, five years old, brown hair. He's wearing . . ." Oh gosh, what had he worn today?

"Ma'am, Matthew informed a ride attendant that someone had taken his brother. Your husband followed them, he said. We know where they are, and five guards are there now. Police are on the way."

Her husband? "Husband" was synonymous with David, but he was gone. Melanie's mind spun. Where were they? What had happened? Oh no—did this have to do with their stalker? There hadn't been an incident in weeks. She'd been afraid to voice it, but she'd secretly hoped the annoyance had passed.

"Can you take us to them?" She squeezed the kids against her sides, tears stinging her eyes. *God, protect him . . . them. Help us!*

The two-way radio on the security guard's belt crackled. Through a patch of static, someone called, "We need an EMT here."

A click and a response. "Copy that. What kind of injury?"

The guard pulled the device from her belt and stared at the screen. Seconds passed, the only sounds the noise of the compressor on the bouncy frog ride behind them and the conversations of passersby.

Melanie's chest tightened, her breathing quickened. They needed to go—now!—to wherever Kevin was. Would the person on the other end of that device ever answer? A lightheaded sensation caused her to stumble, and she pressed a hand to her forehead to quell it. She'd never passed out in her life, but she thought she might.

A response rippled through the airwaves. "Uh, uncertain. Juvenile male fell thirty feet. He's nonresponsive."

Melanie clasped a hand over her mouth. *My God! No, not Kevin. Not my baby boy.*

She willed herself to hold it together, if only for her children's sake. "Take me to him!" she demanded, her voice shrill, sounding hysterical even to her own ears.

* * *

Brian winced at the thud made by Kevin's small body hitting the ground. His feet had grazed a tree limb, slowing his fall, but was it enough? Was he dead? Injured? Had he hit any rocks? A flashlight beam found his body, illuminating his grass green t-shirt, denim shorts, and motionless—maybe lifeless—body, face down on the weedy ground.

Security rushed toward him, and the distant siren grew louder, accompanied by another.

A growl rumbled behind Brian, and he rolled onto his back in time for Jason's boot to smash into his side.

Pain radiated through Brian's ribs as he twisted and grabbed Jason's ankle.

Jason kicked again, but Brian held fast, anger rising, fueling him with a sorely-needed burst of energy. He tugged hard, and the booted foot slid over the slick metal.

Jason toppled and landed on his side with a yelp and another string of curse words.

Brian propped himself on his knees then pulled back a fist. He hadn't punched anyone since the eighth grade. Never thought he'd do it again, but he had to immobilize Jason until the guards reached them—not long, judging by the clomp of boots on metal.

Using all the force he could muster, Brian slammed his fist into Jason's jaw. He pulled back his hand and shook out the ache.

Jason's head fell back against the catwalk, his eyes unfocused. With a fist, he swiped at the blood dripping from his lip.

"I don't understand." Brian sat back on his heels, panting.

A guard approached, clanking down the catwalk, billy club drawn, for what it was worth.

"Why me? Why . . . why an innocent boy?" Brian flung his arm in the direction Kevin had plunged from the catwalk, the memory causing a fresh ache in his chest.

"You took everything from my family," Jason spat.

"Your family?" Brian had never met Jason's family. Their sole interaction had been work-related, contained to the office.

"My stepdad. Raymond Boyle. The sole support of my mother and his other family. 'Member him? Because of *you* he lost his job, his wife, his whole life!" Jason wiped the smeared blood on his shirt. "When my dad left, we had nothin'. We stayed in shelters with meth heads, my mom cleanin' rich people's houses. My stepdad gave us a home off the streets. He treated me like I was *someone*."

Brian struggled to connect the dots. Jason was Raymond's stepson? How . . . ? "I didn't take anything from Raymond Boyle. I did my job. He lost everything because of his sick perversion." The long columns of explicit images and videos on Boyle's computer sprang to mind.

Was Boyle's perversion so different from mine?

Brian blinked, sickened at the realization. How different were they, truly?

Jason raised himself onto his elbows, his eyes wide, their expression wild. "Your job? Your job was to do your nerd magic with the computers. The rest was none of your business!"

A shout drew Brian's attention to the ground. Security and medical staff hovered around Kevin. Red and blue lights flashed at the nearest service entrance. A horn beeped, and a golf cart with a red first-aid symbol affixed to the top trundled toward the catering pavilion.

Brian stared, mumbling rote prayers for the little boy he loved like his own. And for Melanie. Had anyone found her? Told her what had happened? Had Matthew—

Jason lunged at him.

A half-second before impact, Brian dodged, leaning to the side.

Boyle's thick frame smacked then slid across the catwalk, the weight of his lower body pulling him over the edge. His fingertips scraped across the metal, and he clung to the edge, his legs dangling. His knuckles whitened where he gripped the ledge.

Giving him a once over, Brian doubted Jason had the upper arm strength to hang on, let alone pull himself up.

Behind and in front of them, security skidded to a stop, seemingly afraid to move lest Jason fall.

Brian flopped onto his belly, pain from his side making him wince. He stretched out his hand to Jason. "Take it!"

Jason cackled. "I hoped you'd die. From the cancer. You should've, you know."

"Take my hand, Jason!" Brian doubted his own strength, but he'd try. He reached for Jason's wrist—

Jason let loose a torrent of vile, filthy slurs about Brian and then Melanie.

His chest burning with rage, but unwilling to let a man die—no matter how despicable—Brian latched onto a wrist. "Take my hand!"

Despair and death loomed in Jason's eyes. His words scraped out, dark and rough. "I'd rather die."

Palms splayed, Jason plunged backwards, freefalling.

Around him, the security guards called to the officers and EMTs below. Phones and two-way radios clicked to life.

Brian squeezed his eyes shut, but it didn't stop the sickening thud from sounding in his ears. His stomach turned, and he rested his head on the catwalk, willing himself not to vomit.

A cacophony of noises rang in Brian's ears: sirens, horns, voices, a crying child. Even with his eyes closed, dizziness overcame him.

A hand to his back brought him around.

"Sir, are you okay?" The quavering voice must've come from one of the security guards.

Brian took stock. His head spun, his stomach roiled, and he hurt—his hand, his ribs, his head, his heart. His heart might never recover. "I don't know."

CHAPTER 49

Melanie's throat ached and her eyes burned as she trailed the park security guard, Matthew and Penny clutched in either hand. If she could hold back the tears, she had a shot of keeping her kids in check too. She couldn't afford to be distracted from whatever lay ahead.

Hand on her two-way radio and ponytail bobbing, the guard, whose nametag read Ana, strode toward the catering pavilion. That's where Kevin and Brian were, she'd said. Ana hadn't said anything about Kevin's condition, but Melanie couldn't unhear the call of an EMT for a juvenile male. *Kevin.*

Our Father, who art in heaven—Please, God, please! If ever there'd been a time to pray, this was it, yet Melanie couldn't finish a single prayer. But God knew what she needed, right?

On the opposite side of the pavilion, roving beams of lights and flashing emergency signals lit the dark area. Since the sun had set, this area, set apart from the rides, lay hidden in darkness. She could make out a little brook and a dark slope dotted with a few saplings, several mature trees, and weeds. Flashlights lit the drippy chutes of the Timber Falls and the ladders and catwalk that provided maintenance access for the ride.

"Mama, Mama, Mama," Penny whined, her little legs struggling to keep up. "I'm tired."

"Shut up, Penny!" Matthew snapped. "No one cares if you're tired. Kevin's missing."

Melanie gripped their hands tighter and quickened her steps. Under normal circumstances, Melanie would've addressed the whining and the rude remark. But not tonight.

The dusky sky served as a backdrop to three silhouettes near the top of the water ride. Two appeared to be security guards, with their baseball-style caps and bulky radios. The other, between them, hunched over his legs. Then he stood, and one of the guards held his arm, steadying him. Thin with those khaki shorts with the big pockets—*Brian!*

Melanie's chest heaved in relief. If he could stand on his own, he was relatively okay.

Ana rounded the park golf cart blocking the path, where police milled about and EMTs gathered, working on someone, she guessed. Kevin? Her chest tightened.

Peering between bystanders' shoulders, Melanie glimpsed a person on the ground. A black-sleeved arm and a thick waist . . . enough to confirm this was an adult, not Kevin. Exasperated tears threatened, and she blinked hard, pushing them back.

Ana spoke into her radio, disregarding Melanie and her kids completely. Where was Kevin? Melanie wanted to scream it! Her child was missing, maybe injured, maybe—no, not dead. He couldn't be dead.

Her brow pinched and her stomach swirling as if she'd been riding the teacups, Melanie skimmed the crowd. Another cluster of EMTs lifted a stretcher into an ambulance. Kevin?

She jogged toward the ambulance, dragging Matthew and Penny and ignoring their complaints, if that's what they were.

Only a few more yards . . . There! Kevin's green t-shirt. That's what he'd worn. Why couldn't she remember earlier?

"Kevin!" she called, running toward him.

"Ma'am." One of the EMTs turned and held up a hand. "We're taking him to the hospital."

"That's my son. My baby! What happened to him?" The tears fell now, uncontrolled.

Kevin lay on his back, eyes closed, deathly—*deathly*—still.

Matthew pressed into her belly, sobs wracking him while Penny yanked on her hand, oblivious.

"He's unconscious, ma'am. Fell from up there. Grazed a couple of tree limbs." He pointed toward where Brian and the guards had been standing, though they'd nearly descended the ladder now.

Melanie's hand flew to her throat. "Oh, God! Is he gonna be okay?" That catwalk was so high up. Where had he landed? How? On what? He could have broken bones. Or worse! What if he'd hit his head? Broken his neck?

"Ma'am." The EMT touched her arm, trying to gain her attention. "Do you have a ride to the hospital?"

Did she? They'd all come in her van. She couldn't drive. Not now. She didn't even know which hospital they were taking him to.

"I'll take you." Ana appeared at her side.

Melanie breathed a sigh of relief. "Thank you."

Ana stepped back, making room in their circle. Room for —Brian!

Melanie's first instinct was to fly into his arms, to hold him, to feel his warmth and his strength. One glance told her he didn't possess much of either.

Despite the still-warm night, someone had draped a blanket over him. Beneath it, his clothes appeared wet, the front of his shirt and shorts streaked with dirt. Blood crusted on his hand, around his knuckles. His hair hung, damp, on his forehead, and his skin shone pale in the dim light. He looked worse even than he had during chemo.

She searched his half-hooded eyes. "Are you okay?"

He nodded. "I will be." He opened his arms, and she fell into them.

Matthew grabbed onto his leg, while Penny remained glued to her mom's side.

"How's Kevin?" He spoke against her ear, his voice rough with emotion.

Melanie pulled back. "I don't know. They're taking him to the hospital. He's unconscious."

Careful to avoid touching any scrapes, she caressed his face. "What happened?"

Behind them, doors slammed and radios chattered.

His cheeks blanched, and his eyes filled with tears. "He got ahead of us, and Jason grabbed him. I chased them up there." He turned and pointed to the Timber Trails ride. "I caught up with them. It was wet. Kevin fell. Then Jason . . . let go."

Melanie took it all in, trying to comprehend what had happened. "Who's Jason?"

Brian rubbed a hand over his eyes.

How had he cut his hand? Had he hit something?

"He's been behind all of it, I think. The calls. He was the guy in the hoodie with the gray car." He shook his head, and his eyes widened in disbelief. "I work with him."

"Why?" This made no sense. The man had been practically terrorizing them for months. "Why would he do this to us? To Kevin?"

"Revenge, apparently." Brian tugged the blanket tighter around himself. "He said I took everything from his stepdad, Raymond Boyle. The guy I testified against."

"You? But he was the one with kiddie porn—"

"I can take you now," Ana interjected before Melanie could wrap her mind around any of this.

The ambulance engine rumbled behind them. Kevin, unconscious, inside. The kid who an hour ago had bobbed up and down on the carousel, eaten ice cream, and balked at the kiddie rides.

Melanie's head spun. She needed to be with Kevin, but Brian—was he okay? And who would care for Matthew and Penny?

As if reading her turmoil, Brian drew the kids closer to himself. "Go ahead." He straightened, looking stronger. He didn't look well, but he had a determined air about him now. Capable. Ready to take care of her and her family.

Her heart swelled with emotion. "Are you sure? You need—"

"I'll let them check me out, but I'm okay." He swung Penny up into his arms as if trying to prove his competence. "I'll need to talk to the police, but then I'll take Matthew and Penny home and stay with them."

She nodded. Scared, grateful, confused, and probably twenty more emotional states she couldn't put a name to. "Here." She pulled the house keys from her pocket and handed them to Brian. "I'll call when I know something."

"Okay." He smoothed a hand over Penny's head where it lay against his shoulder.

"Pray for him," Melanie said, her chin quivering.

Brian met her gaze. "Haven't stopped."

* * *

It had required all the persuasive skills Brian could muster, but he'd been cleared to go home. No hospital observation. He'd made his report to the police, and now he needed to get Melanie's kids to bed.

He flexed his wrapped hand, and pain shot through it. He had to be able to move it though, at least a little. The park staff would assist him in getting Matthew and Penny, who both lay asleep atop picnic tables, to the minivan. The rest was on him.

At Melanie's house, he parked in the garage and carried Penny upstairs first, his back protesting the entire way. He laid her on top of her pink princess quilt, slipped off her shoes, and covered her with a white crocheted blanket. Her hair, silky gold and wavy, reminded him of Melanie's. Her long, dark lashes stood out against her fair skin like a delicate china doll. He prayed she wouldn't wet the bed. He had no idea when she'd last been to the potty.

He returned to the garage and carried Matthew to his room, thighs burning and lungs screaming by the time he reached the top of the steps. Any niggling doubts he'd had about treating Melanie's kids as his own had been demolished today. He'd do anything—*sacrifice anything*—for them. He loved them.

He repeated the bed process with Matthew, more confident that this kid, snoring lightly and already tangled in his blanket, would keep the mattress dry.

Every muscle in Brian's body ached, along with some joints. Even his hair hurt. A hot shower might help.

He stepped into the bathroom, and his hand went automatically to the light switches. Would the fan wake the kids? Nah. He flipped everything on and fished a towel from the bottom of the vanity.

He stripped off his clothes, twisted a plastic bag around his hand, and stepped under the water. Immediately his mind returned to the cold dousing he'd had on the ladder. Then the sight of Kevin falling . . . That memory would haunt him for as long as he lived. His stomach lurched with a hint of the sick dread he'd felt when it happened.

Water sluiced over Brian's shoulders and down his back. The night had gone horribly, sickeningly wrong. He'd envisioned lounging in the backyard, holding hands with Melanie, kissing her, talking about their future. Instead, they'd stepped into a nightmare.

Wrapped in a towel, Brian plodded to the basement and threw his wet, filthy clothes into the washer. He wished Melanie would call. Surely she knew *something* by now, right?

In the kitchen, his phone rang, and using the last ounce of energy he possessed, he hustled up the steps to grab it.

He glanced at the phone. *Melanie!*

His finger unsteady, he punched at the speakerphone. "How's Kevin?"

"He woke, only for a few minutes, but he knew me. He's gonna be okay. Scraped up, six stitches along his temple, wrist is broken in two places. But it could've been so much worse. If he had landed a different way . . ."

She didn't need to say it.

Brian knew. Kevin could be dead. But he wasn't, and some of the tension in Brian's body eased, knowing the boy would recover. *Thank you, God!*

"How are Matthew and Penny?" She sounded tired. More than tired. Weary.

"Asleep."

"Good. Thanks for taking them home."

"Of course. That's the least I could do." Logically, he knew he wasn't to blame. Jason was. But the only reason Jason had targeted Melanie and her family was because of their connection to Brian.

"The least you could do? The way I heard it, you saved Kevin's life. If you hadn't gone after them, who knows what would've become of Kevin! I don't want to think about—"

"Then don't." God knew Brian didn't want to think of it either. He hoped his tone hadn't been too sharp. The stress of the night, both bodily and emotional, had caught up to him.

"Are *you* okay, Brian? Did the EMTs check you out?"

"Yes. Thoroughly." He'd had to clue them in on the Hodgkin's and the chemo. They'd prodded, poked, and checked all over.

"What about your hand?"

"Oh, yeah, they wrapped that." He stared at the white

bandage, which he'd managed to keep mostly dry. "I hit Jason. Probably hurt me as much as it did him."

"If something had happened to you . . ." Her voice cracked.

He squeezed his eyes shut, trying to keep his emotions in check.

They were both on the brink of emotional meltdowns. He wished they could be together tonight, but she was where she needed to be, for her own sake and for Kevin's. "After all you've been through." A couple sniffles. "I can never repay you."

Repay him? "You don't need to repay me for anything. Ever."

She sniffed. "I have a million questions for you, but I'm exhausted, and my phone's about to die."

"I'll come by in the morning." He hoped between now and then he could sleep. Maybe John and Kate could help with the kids.

"We're in Room 342."

He grabbed a pencil and pack of sticky notes and jotted it down.

"I love you." The call cut off. Her phone battery had probably died.

Her words soothed him more than the hot shower. He trudged upstairs and sat on the edge of Melanie's bed. In a half hour, he'd need to run back to the basement and move his clothes to the dryer.

He breathed deeply, and his exhale caught on a sob. Another sob followed. And another. And before he knew what hit him, he sat weeping into his hands.

CHAPTER 50

The hospital room door swished open, rousing Melanie from an uneasy sleep where disturbing dreams filled in the missing details from last night. The morning shift nurse breezed into the room along with the aroma of breakfast being served elsewhere in the hospital. Sausage and hash browns?

The nurse held Kevin's limp wrist, gazing at her wristwatch.

Melanie straightened in her chair and adjusted the window blinds, allowing the morning sun to creep in. Would it be as warm as yesterday? Inside, the room remained a comfortable temperature round the clock.

Reclining in the bed, Kevin slept soundly in a rigid position uncharacteristic of his usual starfish sleep style. A small bandage covered the stitches on his temple, where his head had collided with a rock. Scrapes on his cheek proved it hadn't been a clean fall. Though it pained Melanie to imagine his skin skimming jagged branches, the tree limbs had probably spared him further injury.

His wrist, hidden by a plaster cast, lay over the white

hospital blanket. For the next six weeks, he'd have to make do with the use of his right hand only.

The nurse, whose exotic beauty reminded Melanie of a fuller-figured Miss Universe winner, lifted her gaze from Kevin and offered Melanie a smile. "Still asleep, huh?" she said with a slight accent Melanie couldn't quite place. She planted her hands on her hips, her long, dark braid falling behind her shoulder.

Melanie returned the smile from her seat next to the window. The boxy, uncomfortable one in which she'd spent the night. She rubbed her neck where a crick had developed from her twisted sleep position.

"It was pretty late when he finally dozed off." Melanie's eyes pricked at the memory.

"Mama, my head hurts," Kevin had said, his squeaky voice scraping out. Tears streamed down his pale cheeks.

Her heart ached for him. How frightened he'd been. How confused. How hurt. She'd have taken his place in a heartbeat if she could. She'd stroked his hair, held his hand, and prayed aloud with him, all without shedding a single tear . . . at least not until his breathing had settled and his eyes had closed again. Then she'd wept too. Part sadness, part relief, part emotional train wreck.

The nurse fussed with something on the wheeled metal cart. "Breakfast will be here in a little while." She smiled and padded out of the room in her sensible on-her-feet-all-the-living-day shoes.

Within a half hour, Kevin's food arrived. He half woke, whimpered a bit, then twisted in the sheets, trying to sit upright.

Using the controller affixed to the bed, Melanie elevated the upper mattress and arranged the tray in front of him. At first, he'd been reluctant to try anything.

"How about just some toast with jelly?" Melanie asked, smearing butter substitute and grape jelly across half a slice.

He proceeded to eat not only the toast but a hard-boiled egg as well. Once he'd filled his belly, he grew more alert. "How long do I have to wear the cast?" "When can I go home?" "Will the bad man find me here?"

Melanie answered his questions as best she could—the last one ripping at her heart. Before long, he dozed off.

Melanie's stomach rumbled. She could almost imagine the savory aroma of that turkey leg at the park last night. Probably not on the hospital cafeteria menu. Maybe she could sneak out for a few minutes and grab something once Brian arrived.

What would she have done without him last night? Who would've taken care of the other kids? How grateful she was that she didn't have to go it alone anymore.

She paced the room trying to keep her mind off of food and stared out the window at cars moving in and out of the parking lot. With some effort, she dragged the boxy chair to the foot of the bed for a change in perspective.

A light knock sounded on the door, and a moment later, Brian stuck his head in.

Her heart stirred at the sight of him.

"Hey." Wearing a cleaner version of yesterday's clothes, unshaven, and with circles under his eyes, Brian entered with a brown paper bag in one hand and a small rust-colored duffle bag—her bag—in the other. When she'd last seen him, he'd looked more like a beleaguered refugee than a suburban dad-type treating the fam to an evening at the amusement park.

The aroma of something heavenly wafted from the brown bag, making her react like Pavlov's pup. Something savory . . . onions? Garlic?

He crossed the room in six steps, set the bags on the floor, bent to her level, and pulled her into a hug.

Emotion swelled in Melanie's chest and tears filled her eyes. She relaxed in the security of his warm, soft embrace. Oh, what a blessing this man was to her, for all his faults—and her faults.

He'd attempted to rescue her son, taken care of her other children, and now he'd brought her breakfast. And the support and companionship she needed.

She stroked the soft hair at the back of his neck and buried her head in his polo shirt, which carried the breezy fragrance of her fabric softener. "I am so glad to see you." She slid back, letting her eyes roam his face, wanting to be sure he was truly okay.

Gently, she examined his bandaged hand. It seemed an odd time for her thoughts to jump to David, but seeing Brian and knowing he'd risked his own safety to save Kevin . . . well, he'd proven without a doubt his selfless love for her children and for her. David wouldn't object to Brian being a father to his children. A strange nervousness shot through her at the thought.

"I told you, I'm fine." He turned toward Kevin. "How's he doing?"

"Good. He woke up, ate breakfast, and went back to sleep. We're expecting a visit from the police and the doctor, and then hopefully he's discharged." She picked up the brown bag and peeked inside. Bagels!

"Good news." Brian sighed. "I feel like we need to debrief each other, but first things first. Looks like you're hungry."

She grinned sheepishly. "Starved. I'll take one of these everything bagels with cream cheese." The wonderful fragrance intensified as Melanie reached inside the crinkly bag, and her mouth watered. "Do you want one too? Or . . . blueberry?"

"Blueberry's good. And this bag . . ." He held up the duffel. "Kate suggested I bring you some fresh clothes and your toothbrush and stuff."

"Oh, God bless her. I'm guessing Matthew and Penny are with her and John?" She smeared cream cheese on the bagel with a plastic knife. Could she pray silently and dig in or did she have to wait for him? She couldn't wait.

"Uh, with Kate. She brought Patrick and Brady over to your

place. I hope that's okay. Penny wet the bed—I was afraid of that —and, anyway, Kate was a big help. John is, well, he's missing in action."

Melanie froze, bagel to her lips. "What do you mean?"

Brian tore apart his bagel and took the cream cheese. "They had an argument last night, and he left. I'm sure it's not forever. Just, I don't know, checked into a hotel. He wouldn't answer her calls or mine. He's at the Holiday Inn Express a half mile from his house."

"So he finally called you?" she asked around a mouthful of bagel.

"Uh, no." He patted the phone in his rear pocket. "Find My iPhone app."

Oh boy. "Have they been having trouble? At your remission party they seemed kind of cold with each other." Iceberg proportions cold.

"Yeah. This has been going on since, gosh, I've been noticing little things since before I got sick." His concern for his brother and sister-in-law showed in the worry around his eyes.

Melanie didn't know what to say. Their marriage was their business. But every marriage had ups and downs. Husbands and wives drifted apart then came back together. So long as they shared the same goals, the same commitment, it worked out. Did John and Kate have that kind of stability? The kind that allowed you to pull through the rough spots without crumbling?

Kevin slept through their meal, and once they finished, Brian pulled a chair close to Melanie and they rehashed last night's events from both of their perspectives, connecting all of the incidents leading up to it—Jason's calls, his being parked outside her house, his encounters with Kevin.

"Why Kevin?" Melanie asked. "I mean, I don't even get why *you* or *us* because any sane person knows what happened to

Jason's stepdad was his own fault, but why not come after one of us, and why Kevin over Matthew or Penny?"

Brian rubbed his temples as if fighting a headache. "Raymond Boyle was really the only father Jason knew. So, even when Boyle divorced his mother and remarried a woman with two kids of her own, I think Jason stayed tight with his stepdad. He talked about him like he was a buddy. I just had no idea it was Boyle."

He sat back in the chair, his gaze settling on Kevin's sleeping form. "Why a kid? If Jason thought I took away his stepdad, maybe he thought he'd keep someone else from having a stepdad?" He shook his head. "I really don't know. But I wouldn't be surprised if he and Boyle shared a twisted interest in children. I guess we'll know when the police complete the investigation, but maybe his hard drives are loaded with child porn too. He's got a lot to answer for once he recovers from his spine fracture and all his internal injuries."

Brian turned his attention back to Melanie. "And Kevin? Don't take this the wrong way." He searched her eyes for something. Understanding? "He's a regular boy, but he's a little more, uh, adventurous than Penny or Matthew."

Melanie laughed. "He's a reckless daredevil. Just say it." She recalled Kevin hitting Brian in the crotch with the baseball bat. Falling into the creek. Climbing the fence at the ball field, yapping at Brian.

If he wasn't the impulsive kind of kid who did that, would she and Brian have ever spoken? Maybe he wasn't so much reckless as courageous. And courage was a virtue. One Brian had demonstrated beyond all expectations. One she could stand to foster in her own life. With her own heart.

Brian grinned and gazed at Kevin, who shifted in the bed. "Nah, not reckless. He's full of life is all. That spirit's gonna take him places."

Spoken like a parent of said spirited boy.

Melanie gathered their breakfast debris, stuffed it into the bag and threw it in the trash. She took her seat next to Brian, a mixture of emotions swirling inside her. "Thank you. For everything." She held his face in her hands. "I like doing life with you. When you let me." She giggled, teasing him.

He smiled and glanced away from her, then met her gaze again. "One horrible decision that you'll never let me forget, huh? I want you to do life with me from here on out, got it? Good and bad, ups and downs. How's that?"

"Works for me," Melanie breathed against his lips.

He wrapped his arms around her, pulling her as close as the boxy chairs would allow.

She savored the security of his embrace. Only God had control. They knew that better than most. But when life spiraled out of control, they didn't need to bear it alone. God remained present forever and always, of course, but God had given them each other too. And kids. And siblings. Weren't people meant for communion with both God and one another? Some days, some seasons, the "communion" in Melanie's life suffocated her, and some days it dripped with an empty loneliness regardless of the number of people with whom she shared her days. And her bathroom.

Today, with Brian, a spark of something flooded her heart. A feeling of being loved, cherished, protected. Of being held in the palm of God's hand.

Brian's kiss made her think he felt it too.

She was not alone.

They were not alone.

The metal supports of the hospital bed creaked and sheets rustled.

"Eww." Kevin's childish distaste for romance broke through her thoughts.

Yep, not alone.

rian tugged the pink princess quilt up to Penny's chin. Last week, he'd only needed to place her unconscious body on the bed and cover her. This week, he had to pull off some kind of magic that would result in her going to sleep. According to Melanie, it involved a combination of prayers, stories, and songs.

Penny gave him a big, toothy smile, her eyes squinted nearly shut.

The sun hadn't yet set, but the room-darkening shades could easily fool a body into thinking it was time for rest. Or so he hoped. He hadn't a lot of experience in putting kids to bed, but Melanie's trust in him and his love for these kids in particular convinced him he was up to the task.

Melanie would be home with Kevin in a half hour or so, after their first visit to the counselor and a promised dessert.

In the corner, a flower-shaped nightlight threw off a dull glow guaranteed to chase monsters away. On the floor beneath it sat a half-dozen stuffed animals—a panda bear, Scooby Doo, and a creepy wide-eyed, dirty Sock Monkey, among others. "You want a buddy to sleep with?"

Penny sat up, ruining all Brian's tucking. "I want Peanut." She bounced on the bed, all smiles.

Peanut? That would be . . . His gaze roamed over the plush menagerie. "This one?" He held up a rainbow teddy bear.

"No." She giggled. "That's not Peanut."

"This one?" Brian held up a . . . a praying mantis?

More giggling. "No. That's Minty. Peanut is my doggie."

Her doggie? Must be the pancake-flat, well-loved thing with floppy ears and only one eye. "This one?"

"Peanut!" She stretched out her arms, bouncing again.

He delivered Peanut to the bed, tucking it next to Penny. "Okay. A story." He grabbed the hardcover picture book Penny had selected from the shelf and read the title. "*A Nightlight for Bunny.*"

Three pages in, he felt Penny's gaze on him. "Are you listening to the story, Penny?"

"I was wonderin'." She pulled her arms out from beneath the covers, exposing the top of her frilly purple nightgown with dancing hedgehogs. "Why don't we call you 'Daddy'?"

Brian's breath froze. "Daddy?" This little doll with her damp strawberry-smelling tresses, sparkly blue eyes, and a voice sweeter than cotton candy might melt him into puddle. "Well, I'm not your daddy, honey." *But, I want to be.*

"But you're like a daddy. 'Cept you don't sleep here." She clutched Peanut closer. "You could sleep with us."

Brian grinned. "Thank you, but I don't think I'd fit." He knew Melanie squeezed in on occasion. Couldn't be very comfortable.

Penny bolted upright, eyes wide. "I know! Mama's bed is huge. You could sleep there."

Yeah, not touching that comment. "I have to marry your mama first."

"Oh." She flopped backward onto the pillow. "Whatevs."

Whatevs? Brian chuckled at the remark she'd probably picked up from Matthew. "Let's finish the story so we can pray and you can go to sleep."

Ten minutes later, after Matthew had joined them for prayers, Brian switched off the light. He left Penny's bedroom door open, praying she'd fall asleep quickly.

Then he walked Matthew, clad in his Hulk pajamas, toward his room.

"I heard you talking to Penny," Matthew said. "About bein' our dad."

So, had this been on the kids' minds? Penny seemed okay with the idea. But she had no memories of her father. Matthew did. Would he feel the same way?

"How would you feel about that? Me marrying your mom." Brian usually felt as if he were on firm footing when it came to kids, but waiting for Matthew's answer, tension knotted in his stomach.

"Mama asked me that, like, a year ago." He climbed into his bed, arranging the sheet and blanket on his lap.

And? Matthew's comprehension of time was better than Kevin's or Penny's, but "a year ago" might mean a few months ago or last year, before Brian was sick. He didn't know which. Did it matter?

Brian waited, clenching and releasing a fist. Ouch! Still hurt where he'd walloped Jason.

"I said it was okay with me. And now Penny keeps askin' why we don't have a daddy." He fiddled with the hem of the blanket, not meeting Brian's gaze.

Brian sat at the foot of the bed, his heart pattering harder with each beat.

"Kevin ain't like he used to be." Matthew raised his eyes. In them Brian saw a smidgen of the fear that now tinged Kevin's eyes.

"Isn't, not ain't." Grammar issues—easy to solve compared to actual problems. But Matthew's assessment of Kevin was correct. He'd been quiet, withdrawn, and clingy the past week. Understandably so, but contrary to his normal exuberance.

"He feels safe when you're here." He worried his bottom lip, thoughtful. "I do too."

Emotion clogged Brian's throat. He cleared it and counted to three. "I want very much to marry your mother. But married or not, I will do whatever I can to keep you safe. Understand?"

Matthew nodded then lay down, turning so that he faced the wall.

Brian stood and straightened the navy quilt. He patted Matthew's back. "Good night."

"Good night," Matthew said, his voice slightly muffled by the pillow.

Brian strode toward the door, the sound of Matthew's voice stopping him on the threshold.

"I love you."

Joy flooded Brian's heart, unexpected but oh, so welcome. He smiled in the darkness. "Love you too, bud."

Wearing a silly smile, Brian galloped down the stairs. This was a different kind of love, but he felt an emotional rush almost identical to what he'd experienced the first time Melanie had said she loved him.

Brian kicked off his tennis shoes by the front door and sat on the couch. An orange-pink glow poured through the window from the setting sun. He sat, basking not so much in the sun's warmth as in the warmth generated by Matthew. And Penny.

He glanced around the room at the family photos, the stray toys, the pile of books and worn furniture. Nothing about this home would be Instagram-worthy. Not unless you were really careful with the angle and zoomed WAY in. And yet he hadn't felt such contentment anywhere but his childhood home.

The question wasn't whether he'd ask Melanie to marry him,

but when. He'd been on the verge, and then last week at the amusement park, well, that had dashed his plans.

Would it be better if he waited until things settled? Until Kevin recovered somewhat from his trauma? Or did recent events make his asking more urgent? The kids seemed to want Brian here with them. Matthew and Penny had said as much. And Kevin had been his shadow this past week whenever they'd been together.

Melanie hadn't said anything about the kids' questions about a dad. But she wouldn't, would she? It might seem like she was pressuring him. And that wasn't her style.

He'd have to be blind not to see how much his presence meant to her last weekend though. Especially at the hospital.

In the months since Brian had been diagnosed with lymphoma, he'd gained perspective on his readiness to be a husband. He knew that at some point he'd likely be tempted by pornography again, married or not. But he also recognized how he'd overcome the problem for years, backsliding only during a brief time of tremendous stress. In hindsight, he saw what he could've done better and knew how to prevent it from happening again. Plus, Melanie would be a great accountability partner.

Guidance. That's what Brian needed. Some wisdom from on high. *Hear that, God? You can chime in any time here. I'm all ears.*

The sunlight faded, and Brian flicked on the table lamp. Getting dark . . . Melanie should be home with Kevin soon.

He slid his phone from his pocket and opened a Bible app. Nah. In this case, he needed a *real* Bible. One with pages.

He shuffled through the books and papers on the end table then looked at the shelf beneath. Melanie kept her Bible around here somewhere.

There! He pulled the softcover book onto his lap. Time for a little Bible roulette.

He closed his eyes and flipped the pages back to front, front to back. Then he stopped mid-flip, opened his eyes, and stabbed at the page with his finger. He studied the verse, Isaiah 36:12.

"But the commander replied, 'Was it to your lord and to you that my lord sent me to speak these words? Was it not rather to those sitting on the wall, who, with you, will have to eat their own excrement and drink their own urine?'"

Alrighty. Best of three, maybe? Oh—and a reminder he should've had Penny use the potty one more time before bed. Drat!

Brian repeated the process, eyes closed. Another verse. What book was he in? Sirach. Chapter four, verse ten.

"Be like a father to orphans, and take the place of a husband to widows.

Then God will call you his child,

And he will be merciful to you and deliver you from the pit."

Whoa.

I guess that settles it.

CHAPTER 52

The melody of evening birdsong couldn't match the raucous laughter of Matthew and Kevin accompanied by Penny's giggles. Dim, gray light surrounded the green vinyl tent erected in the backyard. It should signal that the time for shenanigans had past, but after eating s'mores around the fire pit, the kids had grown wild and giggly. For the past ten minutes, they'd been rolling back and forth on the air mattress that would be Melanie's bed for the night. Assuming they hadn't punctured it already.

"All right. That's enough. Time to sleep!" Melanie ordered then zipped the kids inside.

Oof!—a thud—and then Penny's whiny cries.

Melanie glanced at Brian, who sat in a lawn chair next to the fire pit. Its orange coals glimmered. The evening had cooled and their warmth would be welcome if only she could get these kids to quiet down and go to sleep.

Brian shrugged, obviously out of fresh ideas for taming her little crazies.

Penny's fake-sounding sobs ebbed, and Melanie dared to cross the yard to Brian. With a new navy button-down shirt and belted beige shorts, he looked sporty and handsome kicked back next to the fire.

And here Melanie was in plaid sleep shorts and a white t-shirt. She slapped at a mosquito on her shin. Getting closer to the fire should reduce the number of blood-sucking creatures eager to attack her.

Three steps from Brian, her bare foot caught on the electrical cord running from the house to outside the tent, where she'd inflated and then refilled the air mattress. She stumbled forward, landing with her hands pressed to Brian's chest, half hanging from his lap.

Brian closed his arms around her, pulling her closer. "You okay?" He chuckled.

She straightened and wrapped her arms around his shoulders. Relishing the feel of being held by Brain, she realized there might be an upside to being clumsy. "Yeah. That's one way to get onto your lap."

He smiled, staring into her eyes with a bemused look. "Do you remember the first time you fell onto my lap?"

With her thumb and forefinger rubbing her chin, she gazed across the yard in thought. A single lightning bug flashed along the property line. The first she'd seen this year. "Hmm. I make so many graceless landings, it's hard to recall."

"I'll help you." He rubbed circles on her back.

The kids' conversation drifted from the tent, ending as Melanie opened her mouth to reprimand them.

"Not long before we met, I swore off dating. I told John that if God had someone for me, He'd have to drop her into my lap. And a couple months later, at that baseball game, you were taking the kids out to the restrooms or something, and you fell right into my lap."

Melanie cringed and covered her eyes with her hand, chuckling. "I remember that. I was so embarrassed, but you didn't make a big deal about it. Thank you for that." She flattened the collar of his shirt where it wrinkled.

"I didn't connect the dots at first, but soon I realized God had possibly answered my years of prayers. With you." His eyes held a tender look, and he caressed her cheek.

She closed her eyes, loving the sensation of his fingers on her cheek and recalling their afternoon at the ballpark.

"He's answered many of my prayers where you're concerned."

Melanie opened her eyes. "Like what?"

Sighing, he dropped his hand and laid his arm over her lap. "When I hit rock bottom after I'd been diagnosed and"—he flashed a grin—"dumped you"—he winked—"I . . . how to say it? I guess I humbled myself before God and resolved to lay it all on Him, just fully give it all over to Him."

A breeze blew, carrying with it the scent of the neighbor's rose bush along with the odor of campfire.

"I knew a boatload of suffering was headed my way, so I offered it all to Jesus to make something good come of it. I had two intentions, and one was for you and your kids."

Her love for Brian burned in her chest. Did he know how much it meant to her that he'd prayed and sacrificed for them, even then?

"I knew I'd made a royal mess of things with you. That I'd thrown our relationship away when God meant for us to be together. I prayed that He'd send someone to comfort and care for you and the kids, even if that meant I wasn't the guy. Which, let me tell you, about killed me."

She smiled, his bittersweet admission tugging at her heartstrings.

"Everything that came my way, I offered up. The big stuff like the depression, my broken heart, the chemo, and the constant nausea. And the little stuff, like the fact that peanut butter didn't taste good anymore, or my pants were saggy in the butt or later, when you'd leave my apartment and I couldn't tell you that I loved you."

Tears filled Melanie's eyes, and she glanced away. Thankfully, it seemed all was quiet in the tent, and the kids had finally gone to sleep.

"So, when I got better and we started dating again, I felt like my prayers were answered." He cleared his throat and visibly swallowed. "I've thought about it, and I've prayed about it, and I believe God wants me to care for you and your kids. I want that too."

She had an inkling now of where this conversation was headed. It wasn't wholly unexpected but surprised her all the same.

He grabbed her hand and intertwined his fingers with hers. "Melanie, will you marry me?"

A tingling sensation shot from her chest straight out through her limbs, and her breathing quickened. Oh, Brian was surely the answer to countless prayers Melanie had sent heavenward over the past years. "Yes," she whispered through tears. "Yes, I'll marry you."

The look of joy on his face matched how she felt. "I'd like to make it legal with Matthew, Kevin, and Penny too and adopt them when you think the time is right."

She nodded, smiling through more tears.

Time was a funny thing. Sometimes it zipped by in a happy blur. Sometimes it moved interminably slow. And that speed could turn on a dime, especially when tragedy or danger struck. Sometimes, like the moment she now shared with Brian, reality seemed to transcend time, making them part of something greater than themselves. Something that bespoke eternal things —like love. And that was always worth waiting for.

EPILOGUE

*B*rian stabbed at the tiny buttons on the phone, his eyes darting between the device and the road. Three times now he'd backed up the audiobook and replayed it. The closer he got to home, the more his mind wandered, reaching his destination long before the car would get him there.

Outside, the barren landscape did nothing to entice or distract. Barren trees, gray skies, clumps of dirt-spattered, icy snow on the roadside. A dingy white film, residue from whatever road crews used to melt ice, coated the asphalt disappearing beneath the front of his car.

No wonder people went overboard with St. Valentine's Day decorations this time of year. Who could stand more of this gray, gray, gray?

A green exit sign whizzed by. Only about thirty miles to go! By then the sun would be almost set, and he'd be half-starved, but he'd be home. The thought of it sent a rush of warmth through him.

Ordinarily, ten days in Burlington, Vermont, would be a welcome change in scenery, but Brian didn't want to be any place Melanie and her kids weren't.

Mandatory job training put him ten hours from home, but his new job meant more income and better benefits, which were more important now than ever. Not to mention he didn't have to think of Jason or Raymond Boyle every time he set foot in the workplace.

A half hour later, he pulled into the driveway, his entire body relaxing after the long drive and hours of anticipation. He jotted his mileage on the back of a fast food receipt. He'd grab the snack wrappers and his luggage later. But for now, he grabbed the gift bag.

In his peripheral vision, Kevin scuttled from the porch and down the steps. No jacket, no shoes, despite below-freezing temperatures.

A smile grew on Brian's face as he exited the car, shook out his stiff legs, and rounded the front of the car. In his chest, a warm feeling spread, growing stronger the closer Kevin got.

The wiry boy launched himself at Brian. "You're home!"

Brian stumbled backward, grabbing hold of Kevin and laughing. "Yep. I missed you, Kev. Have you been good for Mom?"

Kevin ignored the question, instead clinging to Brian's neck and shimmying up to wrap his legs around Brian's waist.

Matthew, half-lugging, half-dragging Penny—also sans coats or shoes—came barreling down the steps toward them, and the warmth in Brian's chest spread and grew. Penny latched onto his leg while Matthew started chattering about his latest video game boss showdown as if it were the most important thing to happen over the past ten days.

Kevin slid to the ground and grabbed Brian's hand. He tried to sneak a peek in Brian's bag, but Brian tugged it closer to his side. Kevin would have to wait like everyone else.

With his free hand, Brian scooped Penny off the ground and pressed kisses to her silky hair.

A door slam sounded over the kids' excited chatter, and Brian's gaze lifted to the porch. The light shone brightly in the dim early evening, creating a halo effect above Melanie's head. His beautiful bride.

His heart leapt into his throat, and a shiver of anticipation shot through him. How he loved being married to her! It wouldn't always be like this, he knew, but the past two months had been the best of his life.

With Penny in his arms, Kevin latched onto his side, and Matthew backpedaling in front of him, Brian staggered up the stairs and to the porch.

Melanie stood with her arms folded in front of her, her burgundy sweater bunched and her long skirt flapping in the cold breeze. Ugly brown wool socks covered her feet, which were scrunched on the cold concrete. "Welcome home, stranger."

Her exuberant smile and dancing eyes messed with Brian's heart.

"Thank you." He glanced at the kids, still half-clinging to him. "Can't say I've ever gotten this kind of welcome." A guy could get used to this real quick. It made traveling worthwhile.

Melanie opened the door, and he set Penny inside the threshold and motioned the boys in after her.

Not ready to go inside yet, Brian shut the door behind them, let the gift bag slide to the concrete floor, and pulled Melanie into a hug.

Her fingertips emerged from the end of her long, thick sleeves as she wrapped her arms around his neck.

With his hands at her waist, he pulled her close, feeling her soft hair against his cheek and her warmth against his body. "I missed you."

She smelled like something savory with a hint of . . . cinnamon? Whatever it was, she smelled good enough to eat, and it had been a long time since lunch.

"We missed you too. More than expected, I think." She pulled back. "I had to mark up a special calendar for the kids so that they could see how many sleeps until you came home."

The breeze picked up, catching her skirt and chilling Brian's neck and ears. "Let's get inside."

"Timer's going off!" Matthew called from the kitchen.

Melanie bustled ahead of him. "Dinner will be ready in twenty minutes," she said over her shoulder.

Inside, the delicious aroma clinging to Melanie hung heavily in the air. Roast beef maybe? And, the cinnamon . . . he guessed some kind of apple dessert. His mouth watered. Ten days of hotel food and restaurant fare proved about nine days too many.

Brian closed the door behind him and, bag in hand, settled on the couch. He untied his shoes and kicked them off beneath the coffee table then dug into his bag. "Let's see . . ."

At the rustle of brown paper, all three kids materialized. Penny kneeled next to Brian on the couch and the boys at his feet.

He withdrew a soft package wrapped in white tissue paper from the bag. "For you, Matthew," he said, handing it to him. A medium-sized, handled bag went to Kevin and one the same size to Penny.

Paper crinkled as the kids unwrapped their gifts.

"Cool!" Matthew said as he unfolded a long-sleeve green t-shirt depicting a dinosaur with flippers.

"That's Champ." Brian flattened the shirt on his lap. "He's like the Loch Ness Monster but in Lake Champlain."

Kevin and Penny made quick work of wrestling open their gifts, a stuffed moose for Kevin and a Vermont Teddy Bear in a lacy white gown for Penny.

Matthew fished a small, square gift box from the bottom of the bag. "Who's this for?"

Brian snatched it from his hands. "Your mom." He set it on the end table, out of the kids' reach.

Melanie emerged from the kitchen, her cheeks rosy and her hair now swept in a knot atop her head. "Dinner's almost ready. You kids go upstairs and wash your hands." She planted her hands on her hips. "Matthew, help Penny. And Kevin, there *will* be a sniff test, so do it right." Her gaze followed the kids as they trudged upstairs grumbling.

She turned to Brian. "Can you come in the kitchen, please?" The corner of her lips twitched as she spun on her heel and returned to the kitchen.

"Uh, sure." He stuffed the paper and smaller bags into the bigger one then followed her.

Melanie leaned toward the center of the table and lit two taper candles. Since when did they have candlelit dinners with the kids? She'd gone all out for this welcome home meal.

"What do you need?" He leaned against the door jamb, inhaling the aromas and savoring the homey ambience.

She returned the lighter to the cupboard and turned her back to the countertop. "I need you to tell me how much you missed me." She dipped her chin, a coy look on her face.

Brian's pulse kicked up a notch. Oh, he'd missed her all right. "This much," he said, crossing the room in three steps. He slid his hands through her hair, pulling her face to his. Ten days may as well have been ten months. He kissed her like a sailor who'd spent the past year at sea. Too much? Maybe, but he'd leave no doubt as to how much he'd missed her.

Breathless, she pressed the back of her hand to her mouth. "Is that all?"

He swatted her behind. "More later," he said grinning, his voice low and smooth. "I'm all in favor of the kids going to bed a little early tonight." A bright bouquet on the countertop caught his attention. "Where'd that come from?"

A large arrangement of orange and yellow zinnias sat in an ornate ceramic vase decorated with hand-painted vines. A plastic stick held a card, which he plucked from its tines.

"Oh, that came today. John and Kate sent it. For your new job." She busied herself at the sink, transferring gravy from a saucepan to a gravy boat.

"Huh. That was nice of them." The small card confirmed what Melanie had told him. Brian surveyed the stove and countertop—steaming pot, timer ticking down, pie cooling. "Do I have a couple minutes to call John?"

She glanced at the timer. "Yep. We've got five, ten minutes yet."

Overhead, stomping akin to a herd of young elephants rattled the light fixture. *Washing their hands for dinner. Right.*

Brian dialed John and sat at the table. He'd only talked to his brother a few times since the wedding. And that made him feel a little guilty. In truth, he'd been avoiding John and Kate, not wanting their marital drama to impinge on his newlywed bliss.

"Hello." John sounded almost cheery, a tone Brian hadn't heard from him in ages.

"Hey. I just got home. The flowers you guys sent are here." Based on the size, they'd cost a pretty penny.

"Yeah? Good. Congratulations on the new job." The positive energy flowed through the phone, causing Brian to double check the number. John, a wrong number, or a pod person masquerading as John?

"Thanks. And for the flowers too." Had anyone ever sent him flowers before? Brian didn't think so.

Melanie slid them to the side as she set a steaming serving bowl filled with mashed potatoes in the vase's place.

"You're welcome. Training go okay?"

"Yeah. Boring and lonely, but it was okay. I'm excited to start something new."

The conversation petered out. Well, dinner would be ready soon anyway, so—

"Hey, last weekend Kate and I got away together. Went on a marriage retreat. For couples having trouble."

Interesting. Brian had mentioned the very thing to John months ago after saying he and Kate could probably use some time alone. He doubted John would follow up on it. "Was it helpful?"

"Got us thinkin', that's for sure. Like, look at you and all the stuff you've been through the last year or so. You got lymphoma, you broke up with Melanie, and the whole thing with Kevin. And you and Melanie got through it stronger than you were goin' in." Patrick's and Brady's voices sounded in the background. "After your wedding, I guess Kate and I had to wonder what all that would've done to us. I mean, everything's been smooth here—our jobs, the kids—and we've barely been keepin' it together."

That had been Brian's assessment too. A divorce announcement wouldn't have surprised him. Saddened him but not surprised him.

"So, we decided to make some changes. Maybe based a little on what you've got goin'."

"Yeah?" Which was . . . ?

"We're, uh, well . . ." The way he stumbled, the words must've been difficult. "We're gonna go to church. Starting Sunday. With the boys."

A lightness grew in Brian's chest, and tears stung the backs of his eyes. His godsons were going to know God. At last. "That's great! I think that's a good decision. I don't know what would've happened to me, or to me and Melanie, if we didn't have our faith and our church. And the kids . . . it's real important to them."

"Yeah. I maybe couldn't—or didn't want to—see that." He chuckled. "You win, brother."

No, *you* win. We all win.

Feet pounded down the steps and shouts followed as the kids burst into the kitchen. Kevin stuffed his hands into Brian's face for a sniff. The timer buzzed, and plates clattered as Melanie set them on the table in front of him.

"Listen, man, I've got to go. Dinner's ready."

"Enjoy." More ruckus on his end of the line. "Talk to ya' later."

Brian ended the call, nodded to Kevin that his hands passed muster, then lowered his head into his hands and let John's words sink in.

Melanie touched his back. "Everything okay?"

The kids lapped the table once then chased one another into the living room.

"Better than okay." He raised his head to meet her gaze.

The sweet look of concern in her eyes touched him.

"I don't know how much of it you've seen, but John's always had a way of cutting me like no one else could. He knew exactly what buttons to push, and his favorite was my faith, especially if it related to sex. Or the fact I wasn't partaking in it." Had John known the depth of Brian's pornography problem, would it have been any different? Or would he have laughed it off as not a problem at all—just Catholic guilt?

"Siblings are good at that. Pushing buttons," Melanie said, sitting alongside him.

"John's an ace at it. Anyway, he stopped going to church regularly as soon as he was out from under our parents' roof, and I don't think Kate was raised with any kind of religion."

Melanie nodded, her eyes flicking to the stovetop for a second.

"I told you there were two things I prayed for when I was sick." He took her hand in his and rubbed his thumb over hers.

"One had to do with you. But the other had to do with John and his family. I didn't ask for much. Just that his heart would soften, I guess. I'm the boys' godfather, and it's bugged me that they aren't taking them to church. Patrick should've made his First Communion this year.

"God answered my prayers concerning you. Above and beyond anything I could've dreamed. But John . . . I figured His answer there was no. For whatever reason—God's timing, John's free will—I don't know. I didn't think anything would happen. Not now."

Melanie smiled and hooked her thumb around his. "God surprised you."

"I'm just amazed by how good God is, which is pretty stupid, I guess. Of course He's good. I can't get over how He's blessed me."

Melanie's almost bubbly smile seemed a little brighter than he'd expect for the news he'd shared. Almost as if she had some other blessing in mind. She stood, poked her head into the living room, and called the kids to dinner.

Once they'd finished the meal and filled each other in on what they'd missed over the past week and a half, including a fair amount of tattling, Brian and Melanie began clearing dishes.

"I'll get the kids ready for bed," Brian offered, "and I'll set you up with a nice, hot bath, candlelight, and a glass of wine."

Melanie grinned at him. "Sounds heavenly, minus the wine." She dumped a fistful of silverware into the sink with a clatter.

Minus the—?

"What about the gift for Mama?" Matthew asked. "Did you give it to her yet?"

Brian slid a platter into the sink. "I almost forgot about that. Let's go in the living room and let her open it."

Melanie narrowed her eyes. "What are you holding out on?"

"Just a little something." He guided her into the living room with a hand to her lower back.

Apparently, Brian hadn't put the box out of the kids' reach because Matthew was handing her the small gift box the second she walked into the room.

She sat and carefully lifted off the sparkly navy lid. Inside rested a small jewelry box.

"So," Brian said, "I took a side trip yesterday to a little island on Lake Champlain called Isle La Motte. There's a shrine to Saint Anne on the island. I had a nice talk with the priest there, who's going to pray for us, by the way. And I got you a little something."

Melanie lifted the second lid, revealing a silver pendant of Saint Anne cradling her child, Mary. "Oh, it's beautiful. Thank you."

The kids peered over her shoulder, trying to glimpse the medal.

"It's pretty," Penny said. "Can I have it, Mama?"

"Sorry, sweetie. This is a present for *me*." She kissed Penny's head. "*You* got a new bear."

Penny hopped off the couch and retrieved her bear where it had been discarded on the floor. Forgotten already.

"Saint Anne's the patroness of mothers," Brian said. Then, his voice softer, "And also fertility."

"Would you put it on me?" Melanie turned her back to Brian and smoothed up a few stray hairs.

"I realize the fertility is my issue, not yours, but—"

"Apparently Saint Anne's prayers work fast," Melanie said, turning back to Brian.

Whoa. Wait. "What do you mean they work fast?"

"Guess." Her eyes lit with mischief, her smile broad.

Brian's heart pounded in his chest. *Please, God.* "Penny's not going to be the baby much longer?"

Melanie shook her head, a little laugh bursting from her lips. "Two positive tests, yesterday morning."

Brian's heart was a champagne popper, and the string had been pulled, releasing a riotous symphony of color, joy, and endless possibilities.

The boxes slid to the floor as Brian engulfed Melanie in a hug, squeezing her to himself and pressing kisses to her temple, her cheek, her lips.

The kids, as usual, took their display of affection as an invitation to insert themselves between them in any way possible. Penny's head rammed into his side, Kevin's arms snaked between Brian's and Melanie's bodies, and Matthew stretched his arms around them all, best he could. Did they even know what they were celebrating?

Sometimes life's surprises slowed you down. Like every ten-minutes-of-five disaster Brian had endured. And sometimes they stopped you in your tracks. Like the lymphoma.

But *sometimes* . . . sometimes they exceeded your deepest hopes and wildest dreams.

ACKNOWLEDGMENTS

Thank you to Theresa Linden, whose friendship provides encouragement in this writing life and whose skill makes everything I write so much better. Thanks also to Patrice Fagnant-MacArthur for her careful eye. Sarah Hansen, the cover you created is gorgeous!

For all my writer friends at Catholic Teen Books and the Catholic Writers Guild: your friendship and support are invaluable. To everyone who has so generously shared my book news with others or sent me an encouraging word—it means more than you know.

And finally, to Pope Saint John Paul II, whose life, writings, and creative spirit have enriched my life in countless ways.

RESOURCES

Bloom for Catholic Women

Our mission at Bloom for Catholic Women is to provide healing for women that have been impacted by their husband's pornography use and/or addiction.

* * *

Covenant Eyes

Covenant Eyes is designed to help you and those you love live free from pornography.

* * *

Fight the New Drug

Fight the New Drug is a non-religious and non-legislative organization that exists to provide individuals the opportunity to make an informed decision regarding pornography by raising awareness of its harmful effects using only science, facts, and personal accounts.

* * *

Integrity Restored

Our mission at Integrity Restored is to help restore the integrity of individuals, spouses, and families that have been affected by pornography and pornography addiction.

* * *

National Center for Sexual Exploitation

Exposing the connections between all forms of sexual exploitation.

* * *

Project Young Minds

Kids CAN learn to reject pornography.

* * *

STRIVE 21-Day Detox from Porn with Matt Fradd

Thousands of men are breaking free from porn with STRIVE.

* * *

Talitha Ministries

Empowering women struggling with lust, porn addiction, masturbation and sexual sin, to live a life of purity, authenticity and healing.

ABOUT THE AUTHOR

Carolyn Astfalk resides with her husband and four children in Hershey, Pennsylvania, where it smells like either chocolate or manure, depending on wind direction. She is the author of the contemporary Catholic romances *Stay With Me, Ornamental Graces, All in Good Time,* and the coming-of-age story *Rightfully Ours.* She has contributed short stories to the anthologies *Secrets: Visible & Invisible* and *Gifts: Visible & Invisible.*

Carolyn is a member of the Catholic Writers Guild, Catholic Teen Books, Pennwriters, and is a CatholicMom.com and *Today's Catholic Teacher* contributor.

True to her Pittsburgh roots, she still says "pop" instead of "soda," although her beverage of choice is tea.

Visit Carolyn's blog, My Scribbler's Heart, and sign up for her author newsletter at www.carolynastfalk.com.

www.ingramcontent.com/pod-product-compliance
Lightning Source LLC
Chambersburg PA
CBHW031930110726
47902CB00001B/119